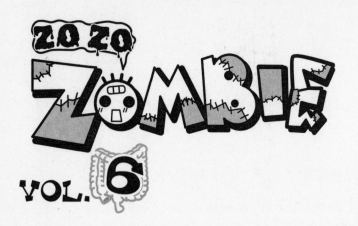

ZO ZO ZOMBIE

VOL. 6

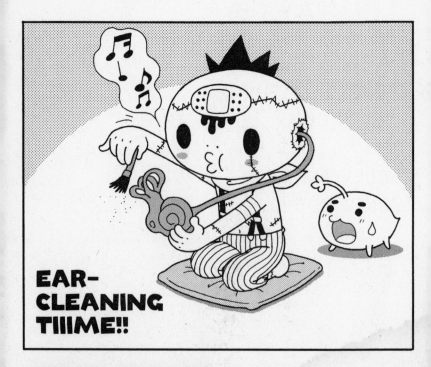

EAR-
CLEANING
TIIIME!!

YASUNARI NAGATOSHI

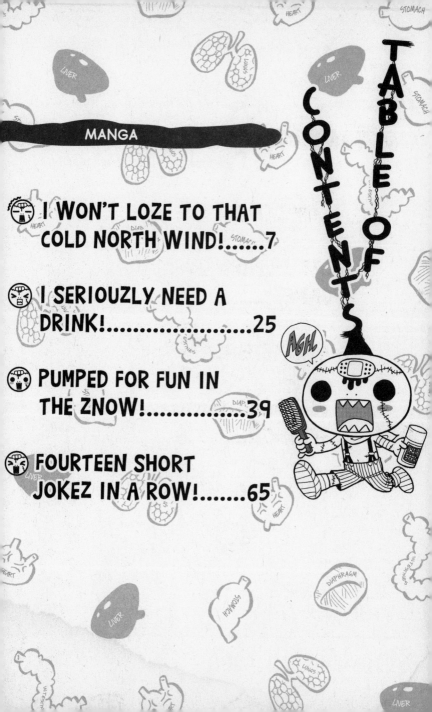

TABLE OF CONTENTS

MANGA

AGH

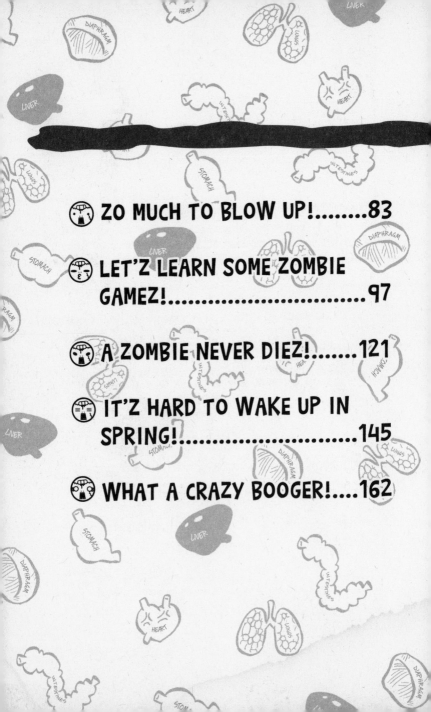

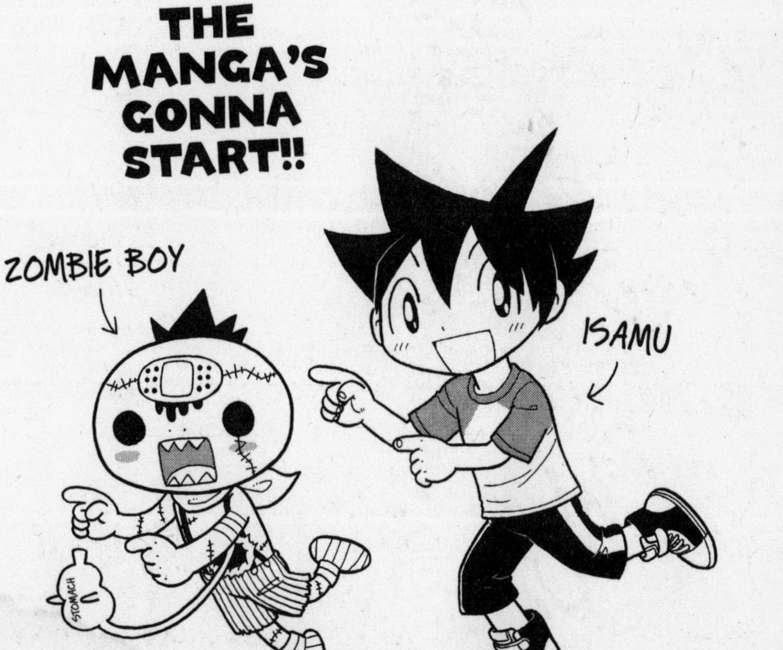
THE MANGA'S GONNA START!!
ZOMBIE BOY
ISAMU
STOMACH

I WON'T LOZE TO THAT COLD NORTH WIND!

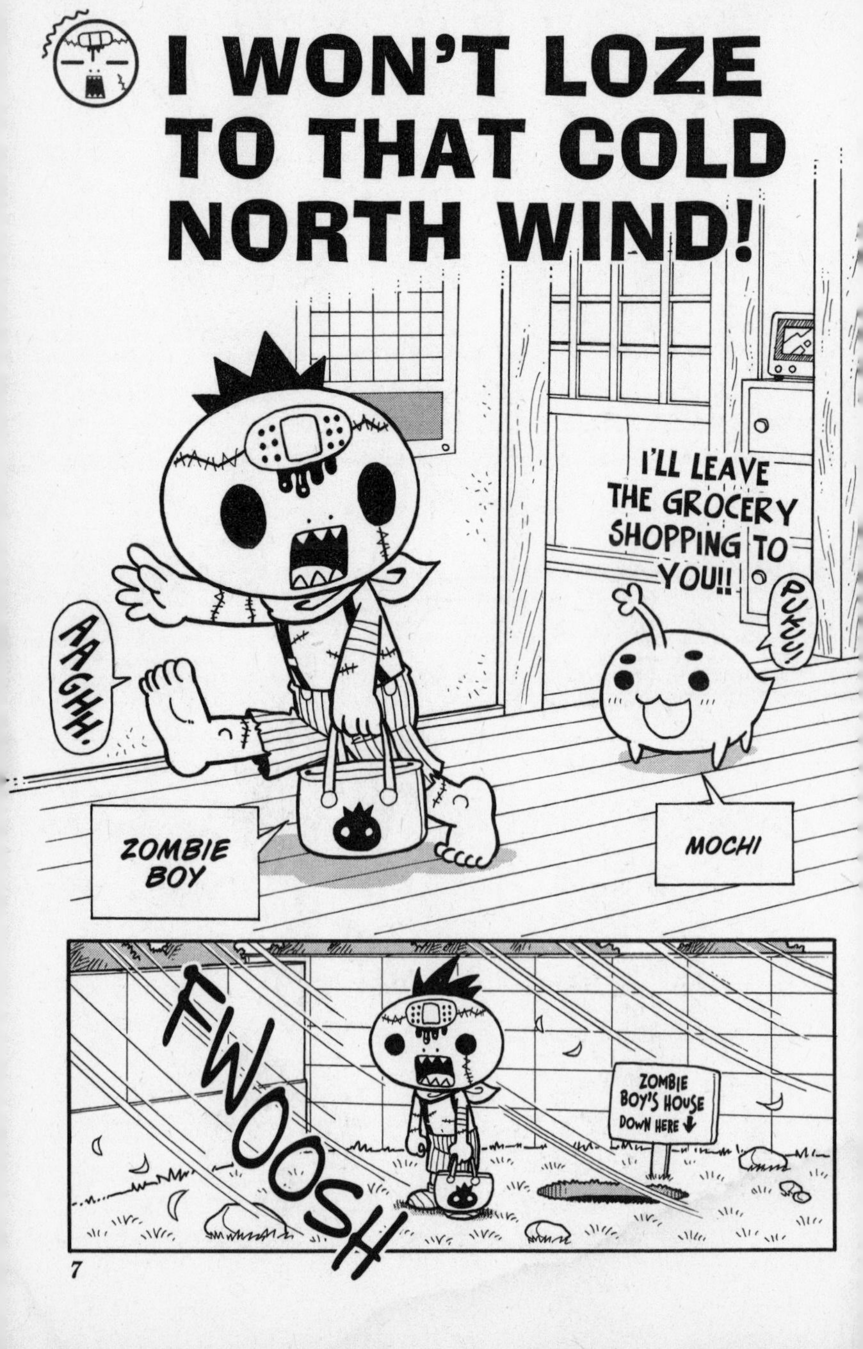
I'LL LEAVE THE GROCERY SHOPPING TO YOU!!
PUKUU!
AAGHH.
MOCHI
ZOMBIE BOY
ZOMBIE BOY'S HOUSE DOWN HERE ↓
FWOOSH

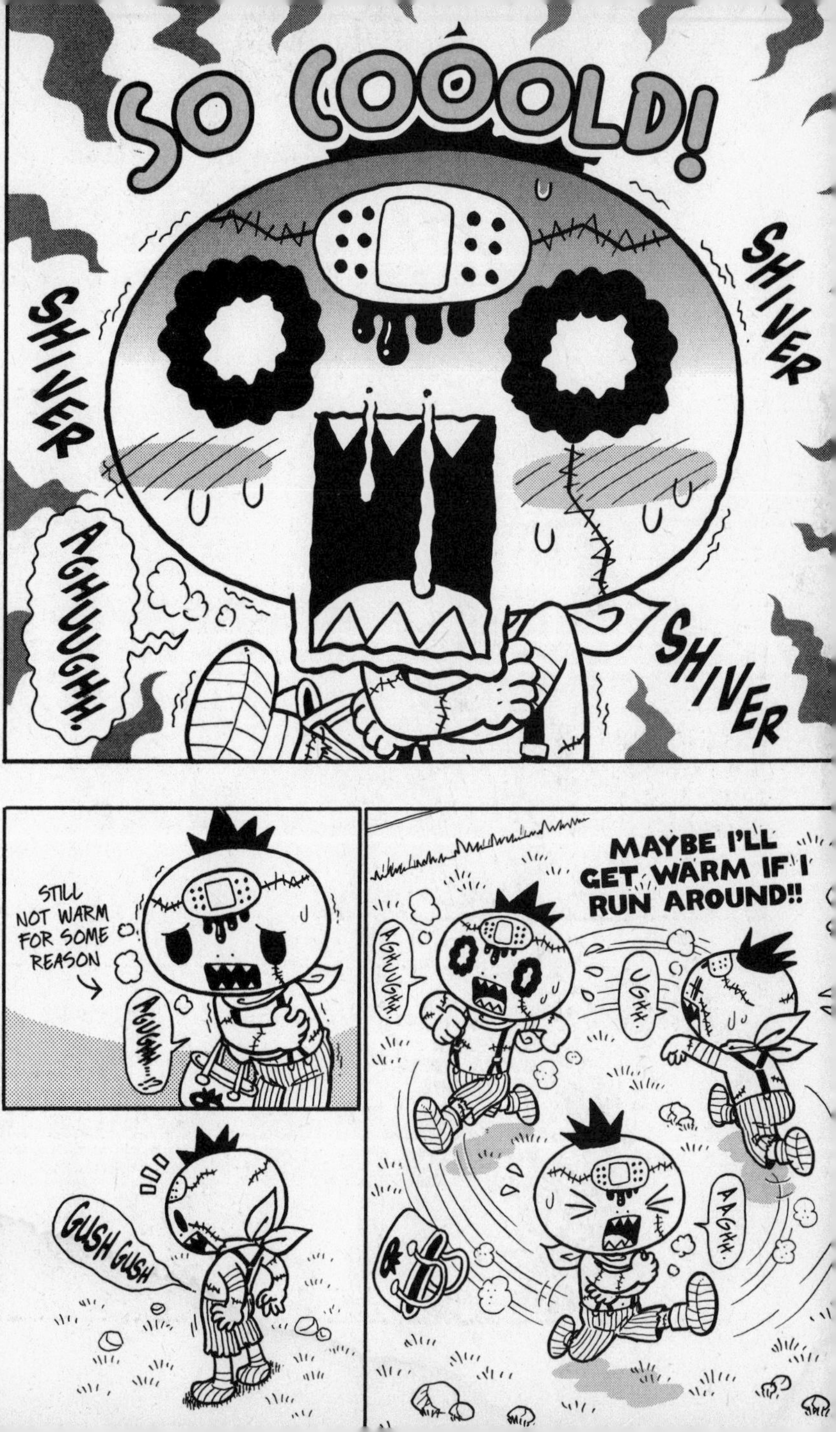

SO COOOLD!
SHIVER
SHIVER
SHIVER
AGHUUUGHH.
MAYBE I'LL GET WARM IF I RUN AROUND!!
UGHH.
AGHUUGHH.
AAGHH.
STILL NOT WARM FOR SOME REASON
AGUGHH...!?
GUSH GUSH

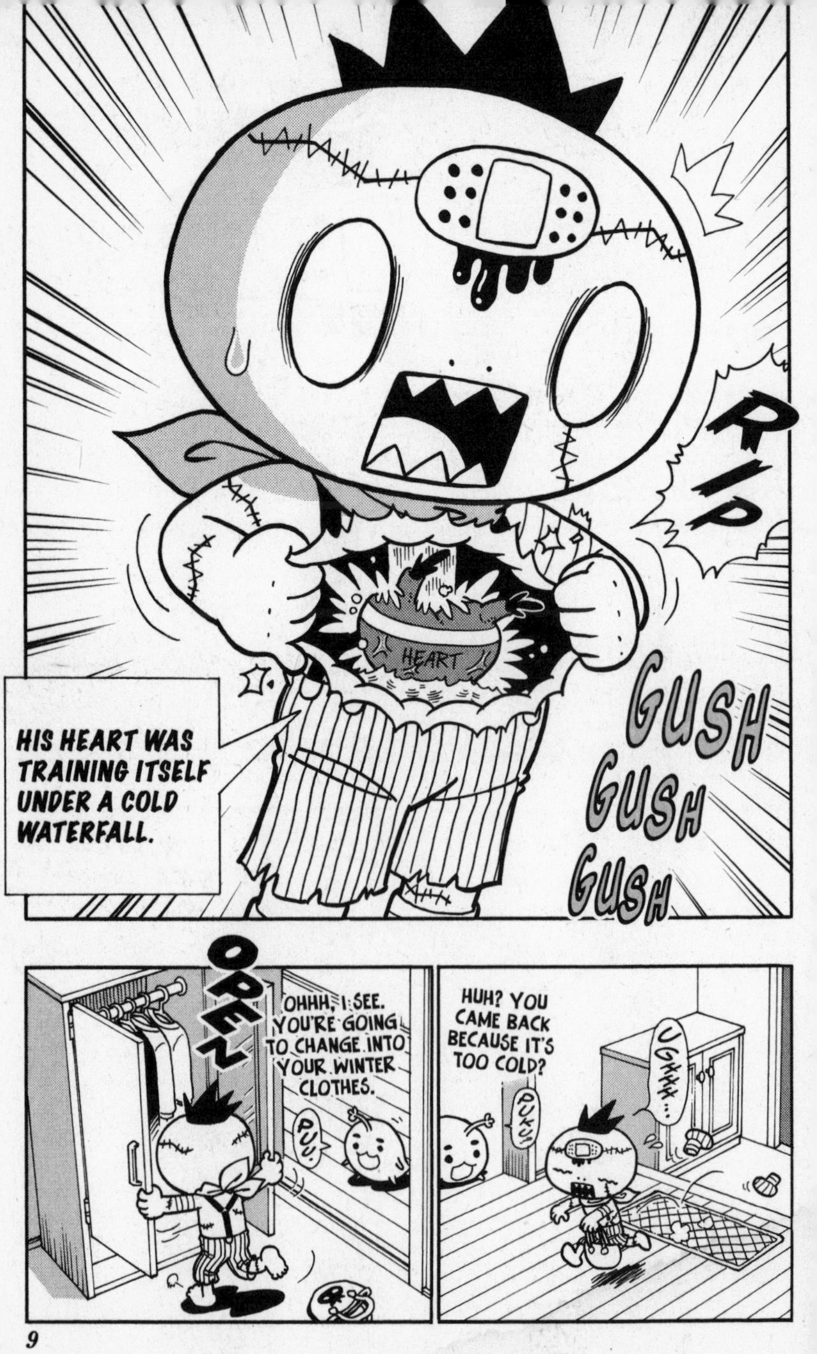
RIP
HEART
GUSH GUSH GUSH
HIS HEART WAS TRAINING ITSELF UNDER A COLD WATERFALL.
HUH? YOU CAME BACK BECAUSE IT'S TOO COLD?
UGHHH...
PUKU!
OPEN
OHHH, I SEE. YOU'RE GOING TO CHANGE INTO YOUR WINTER CLOTHES.
PU!

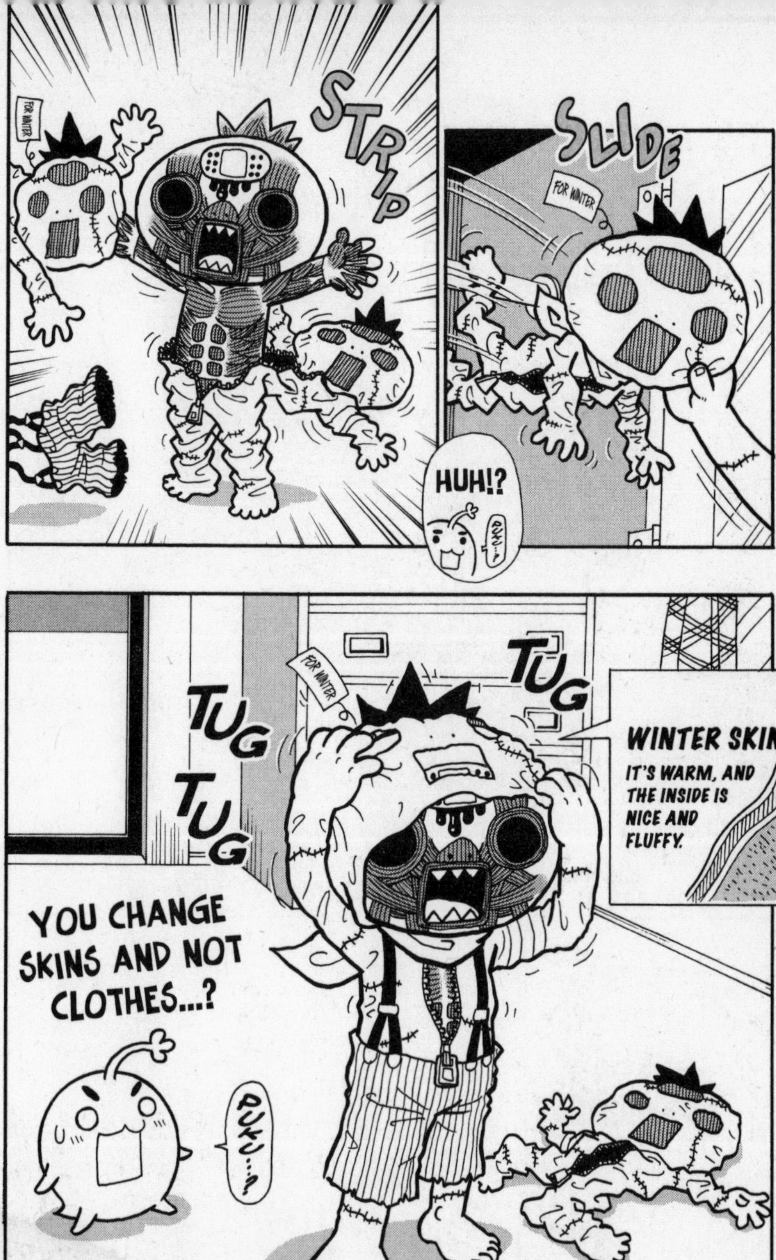
SLIDE
FOR WINTER
HUH!?
PUKU...?
STRIP
FOR WINTER
TUG
WINTER SKIN
IT'S WARM, AND THE INSIDE IS NICE AND FLUFFY.
FOR WINTER
TUG
TUG
YOU CHANGE SKINS AND NOT CLOTHES...?
PUKU...?

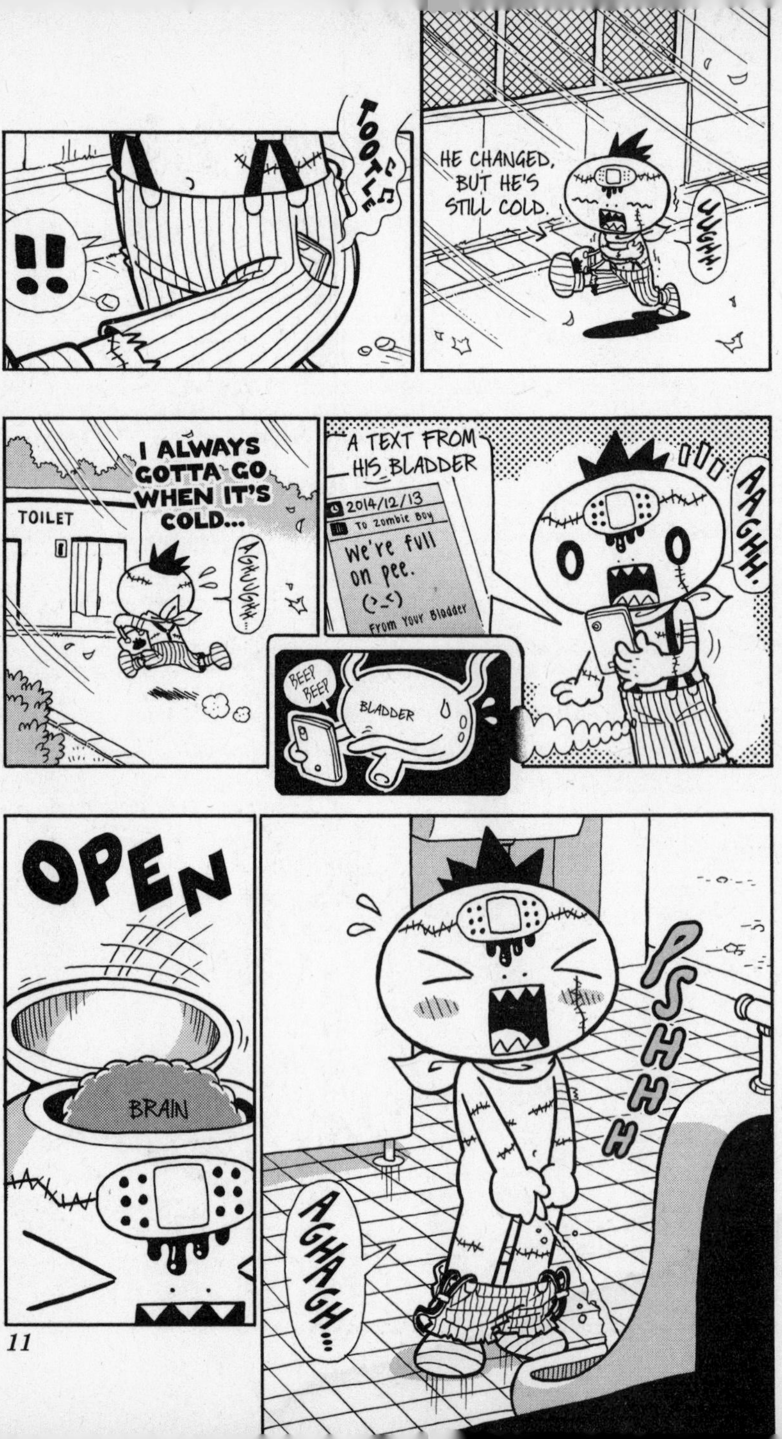

HE CHANGED, BUT HE'S STILL COLD.
UGHH.
TOOTLE ♫
!!
A TEXT FROM HIS BLADDER
2014/12/13
To Zombie Boy
We're full on pee.
(>_<)
From Your Bladder
AAGHH.
BEEP BEEP
BLADDER
I ALWAYS GOTTA GO WHEN IT'S COLD...
TOILET
AGHUGHH...
PSHHHH
AGHAGH...
OPEN
BRAIN

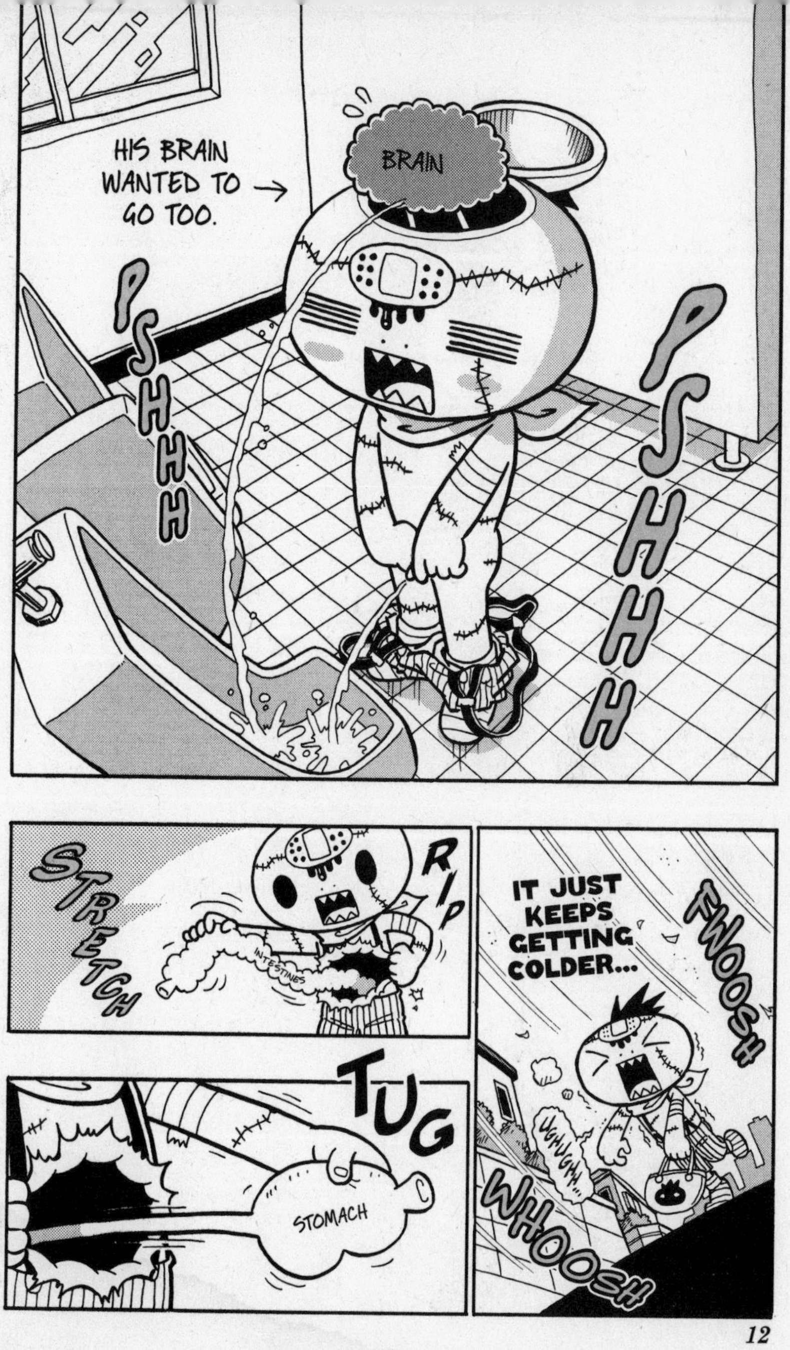
BRAIN
HIS BRAIN WANTED TO GO TOO.
PSHHHH
PSHHHH
FWOOSH
IT JUST KEEPS GETTING COLDER...
UGHUGH
WHOOSH
RIP
STRETCH
INTESTINES
TUG
STOMACH

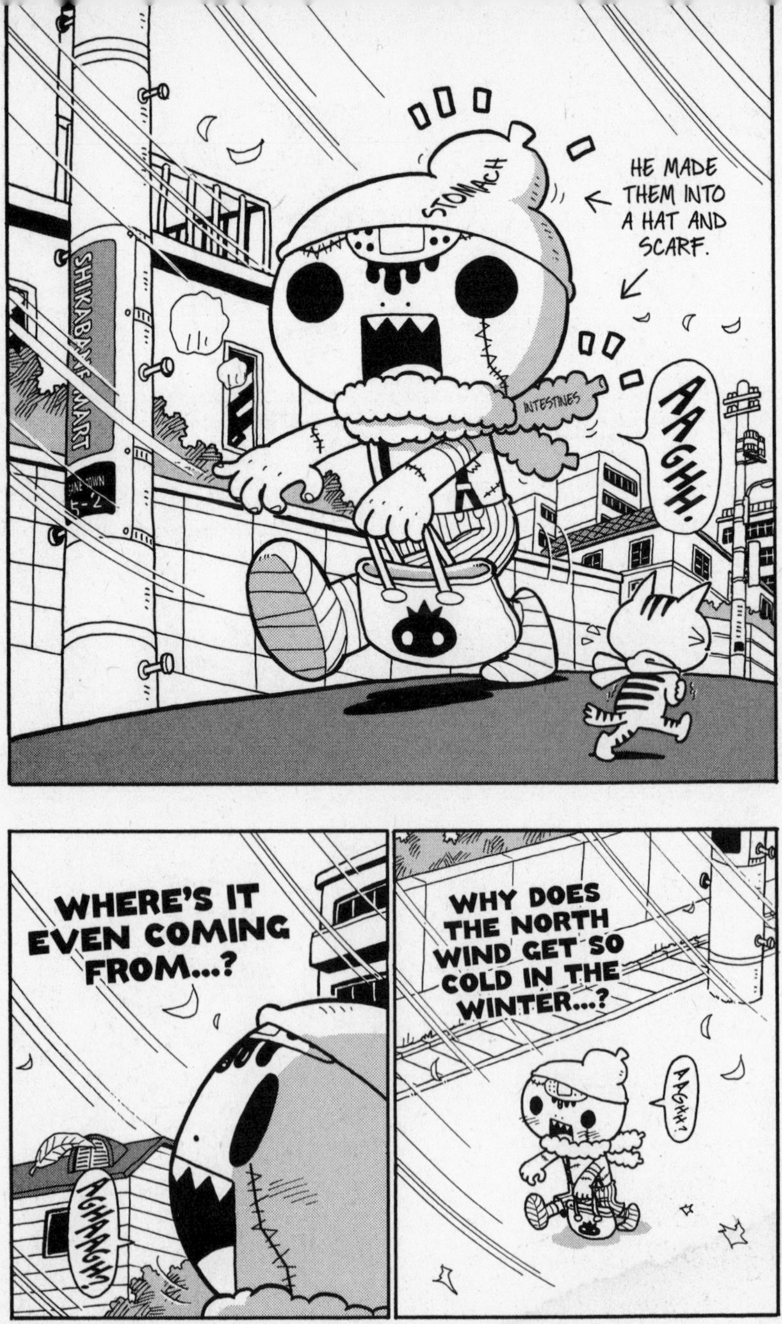
HE MADE THEM INTO A HAT AND SCARF.
STOMACH
INTESTINES
AAGHH.
WHY DOES THE NORTH WIND GET SO COLD IN THE WINTER...?
AAGHH!?
WHERE'S IT EVEN COMING FROM...?
AGHAAGH!?

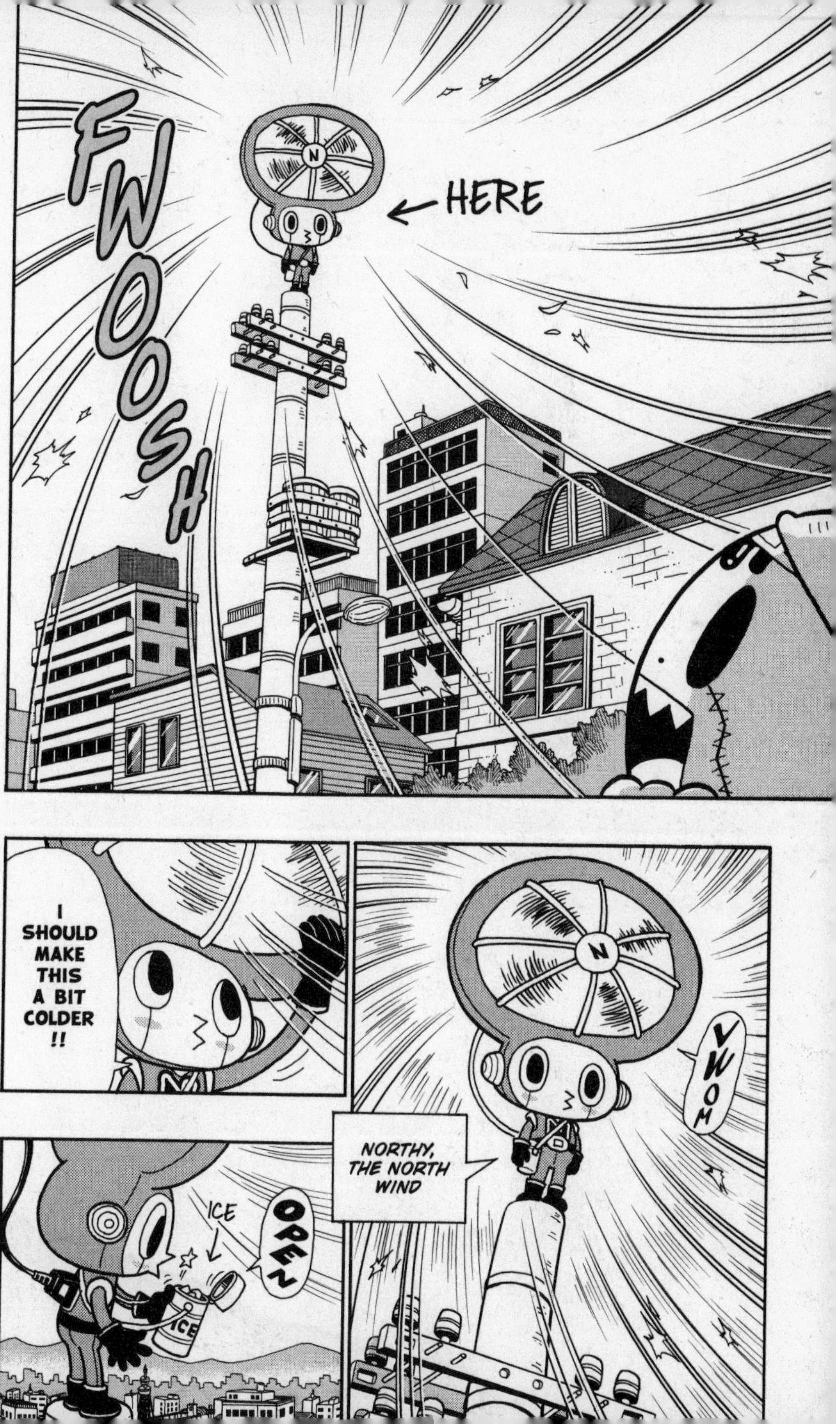
FWOOSH
HERE
VWOOM
NORTHY, THE NORTH WIND
I SHOULD MAKE THIS A BIT COLDER!!
OPEN
ICE
ICE

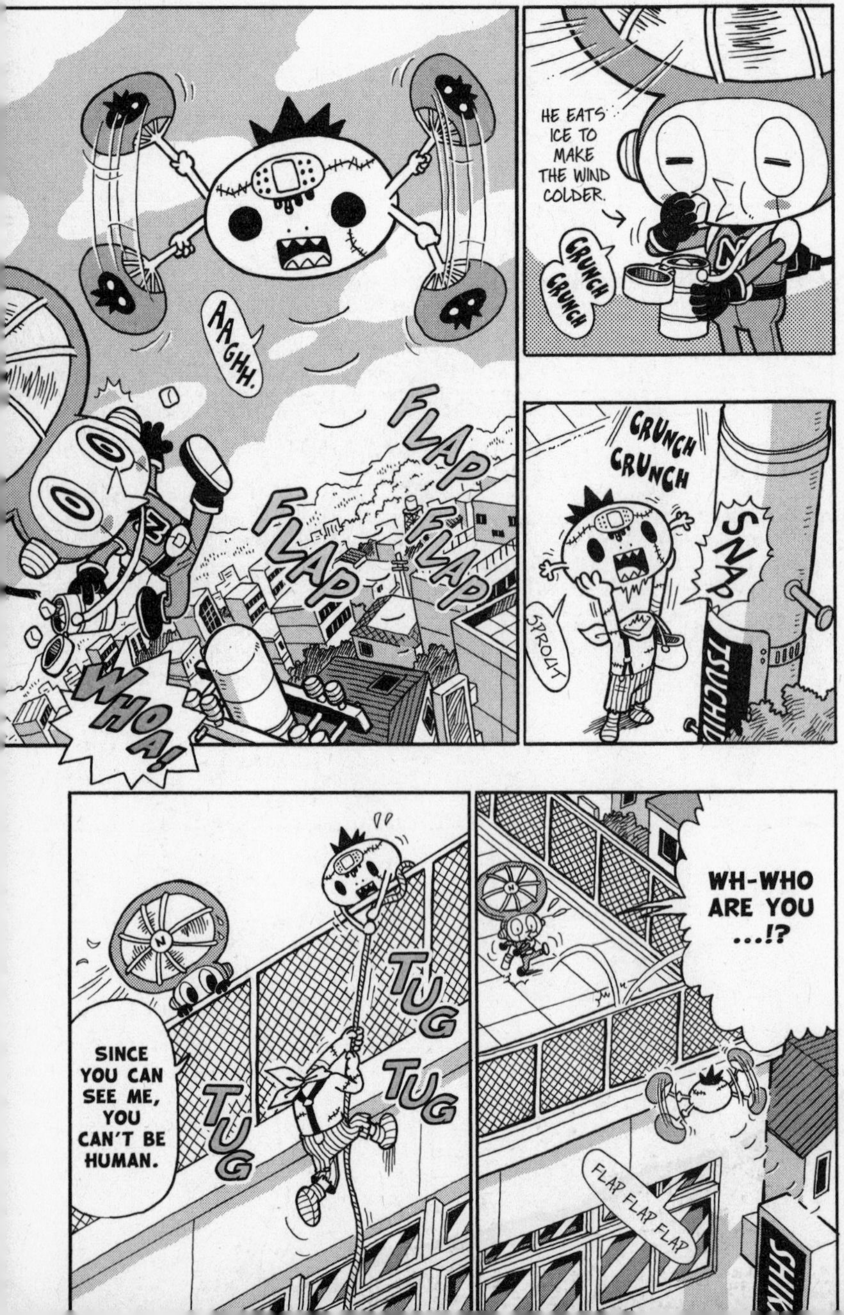
HE EATS ICE TO MAKE THE WIND COLDER.
CRUNCH CRUNCH
CRUNCH CRUNCH
SNAP
STROLL
AAGHH.
FLAP FLAP
FLAP FLAP
WHOA!
WH-WHO ARE YOU ...!?
FLAP FLAP FLAP
TUG TUG
TUG TUG
SINCE YOU CAN SEE ME, YOU CAN'T BE HUMAN.

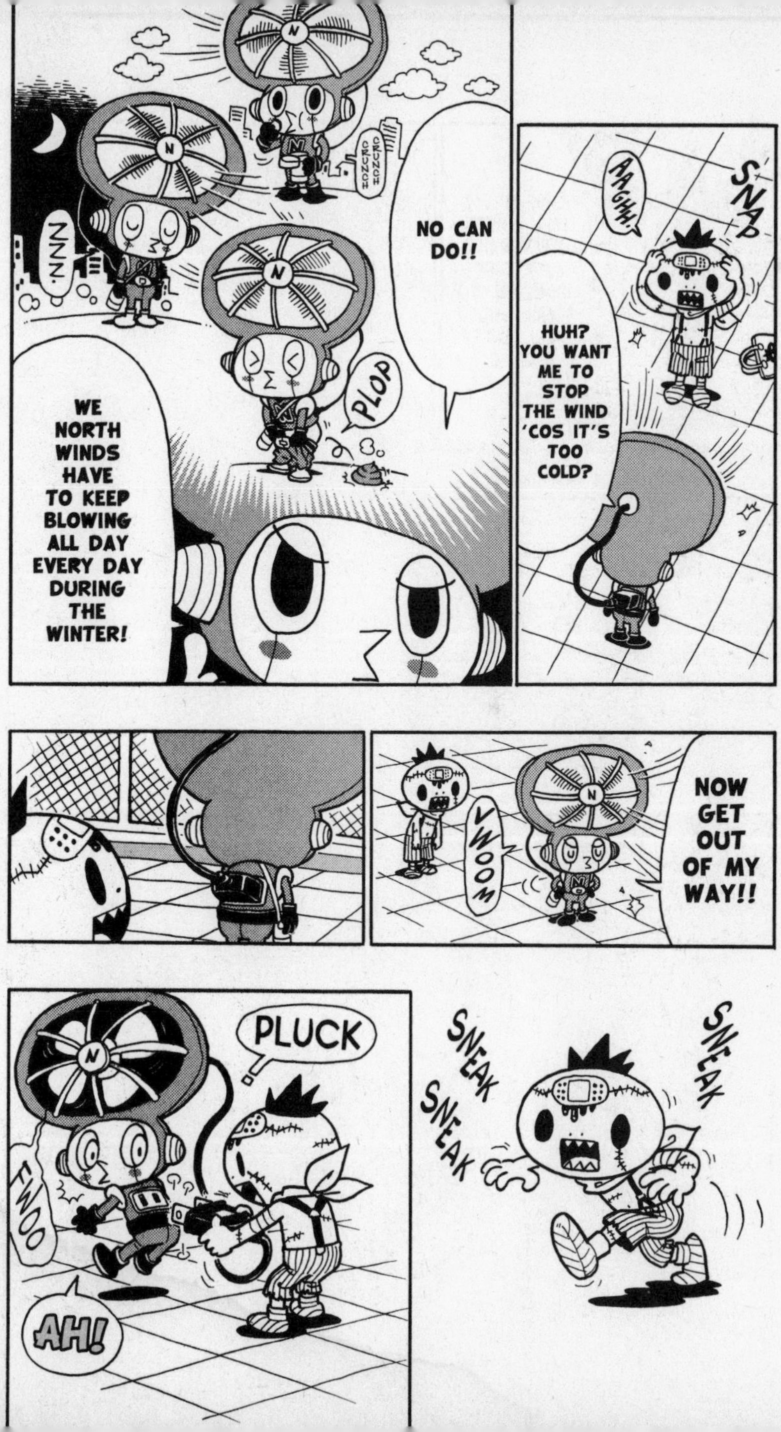
SNAP
AAGHH!
HUH? YOU WANT ME TO STOP THE WIND 'COS IT'S TOO COLD?
NO CAN DO!!
CRUNCH CRUNCH
NNN.
PLOP
WE NORTH WINDS HAVE TO KEEP BLOWING ALL DAY EVERY DAY DURING THE WINTER!
NOW GET OUT OF MY WAY!!
VWOOM
SNEAK
SNEAK
SNEAK
PLUCK
FWOO
AH!

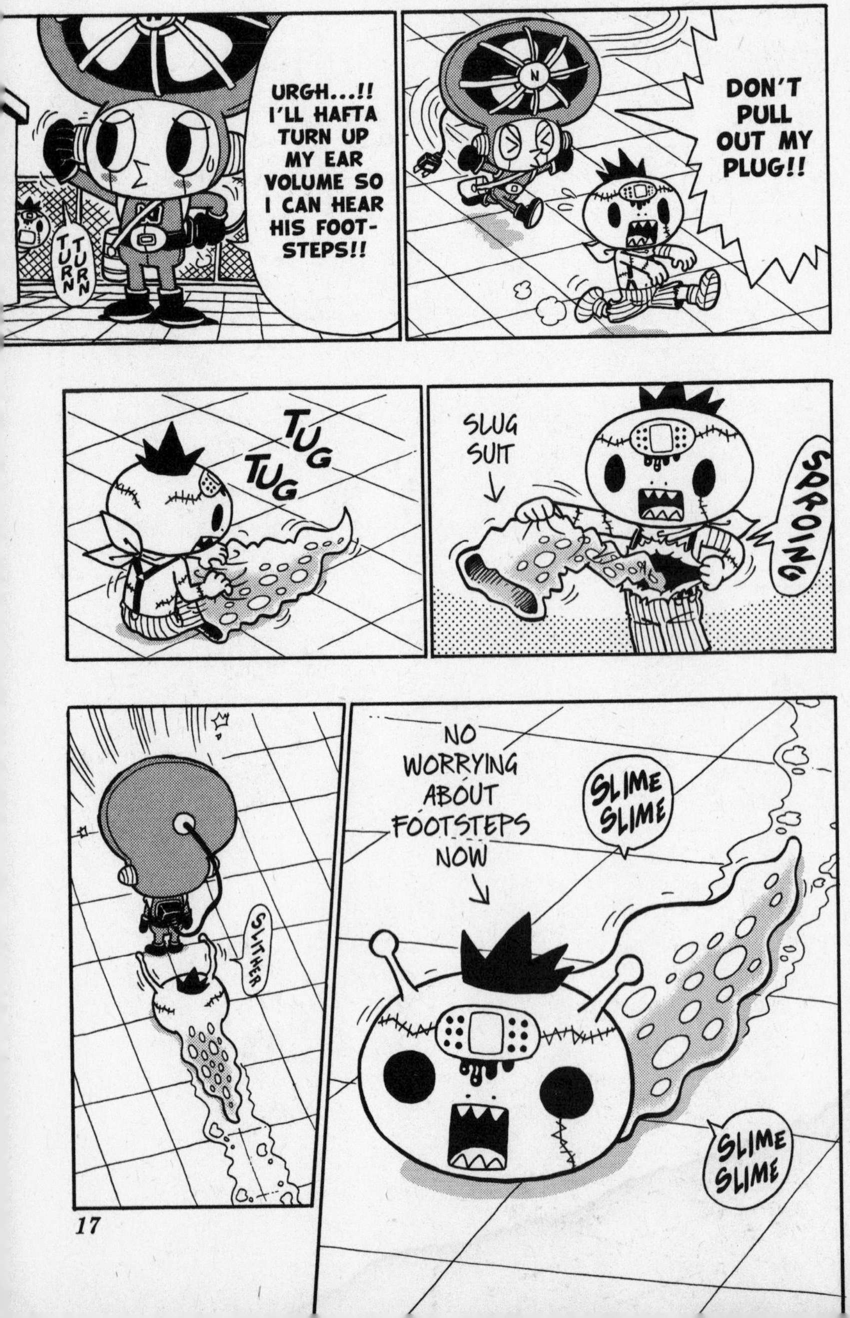
DON'T PULL OUT MY PLUG!!
URGH...!! I'LL HAFTA TURN UP MY EAR VOLUME SO I CAN HEAR HIS FOOTSTEPS!!
TURN TURN
SLUG SUIT
SPROING
TUG TUG
NO WORRYING ABOUT FOOTSTEPS NOW
SLIME SLIME
SLIME SLIME
SLITHER

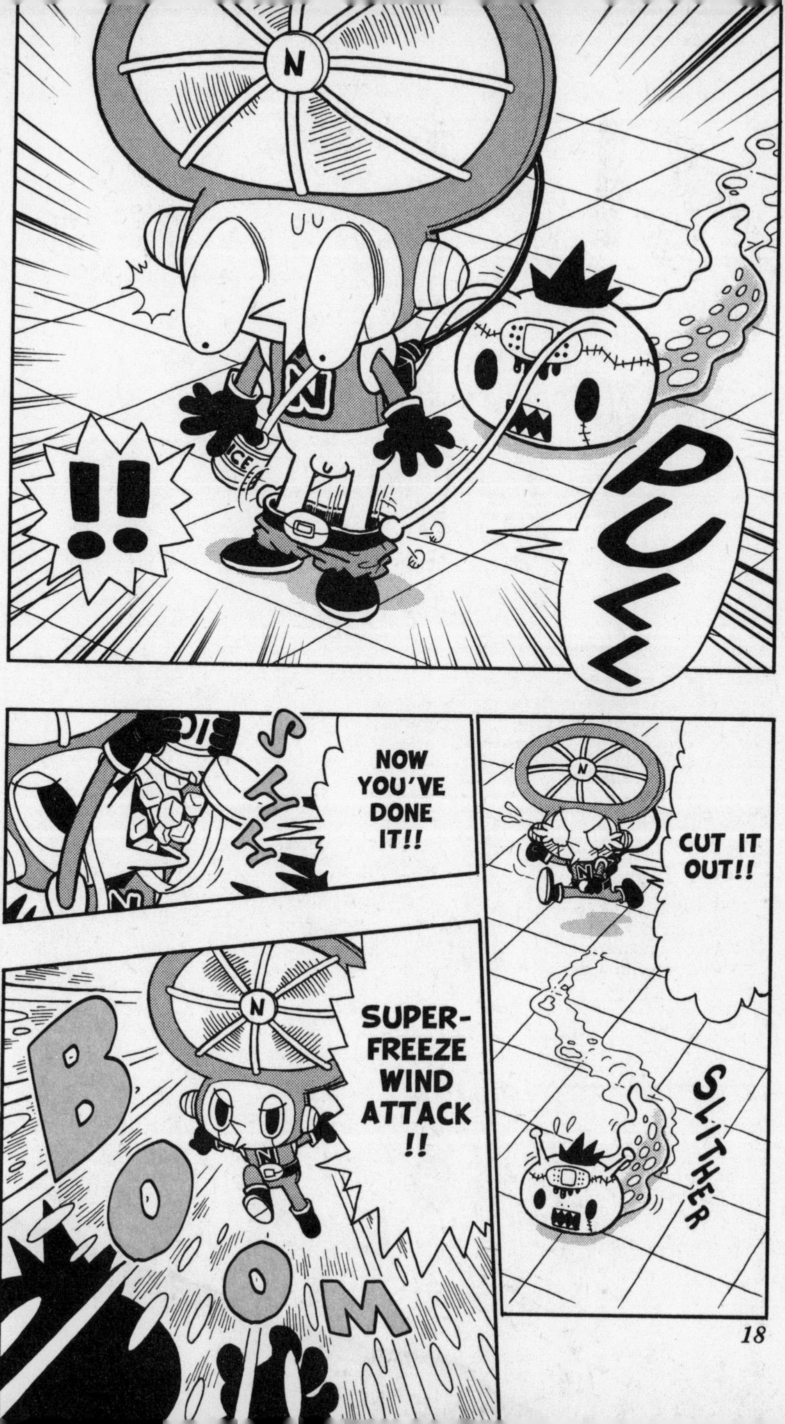
!!
ICE
PULL
CUT IT OUT!!
SLITHER
SHH
NOW YOU'VE DONE IT!!
SUPER-FREEZE WIND ATTACK!!
BOOM

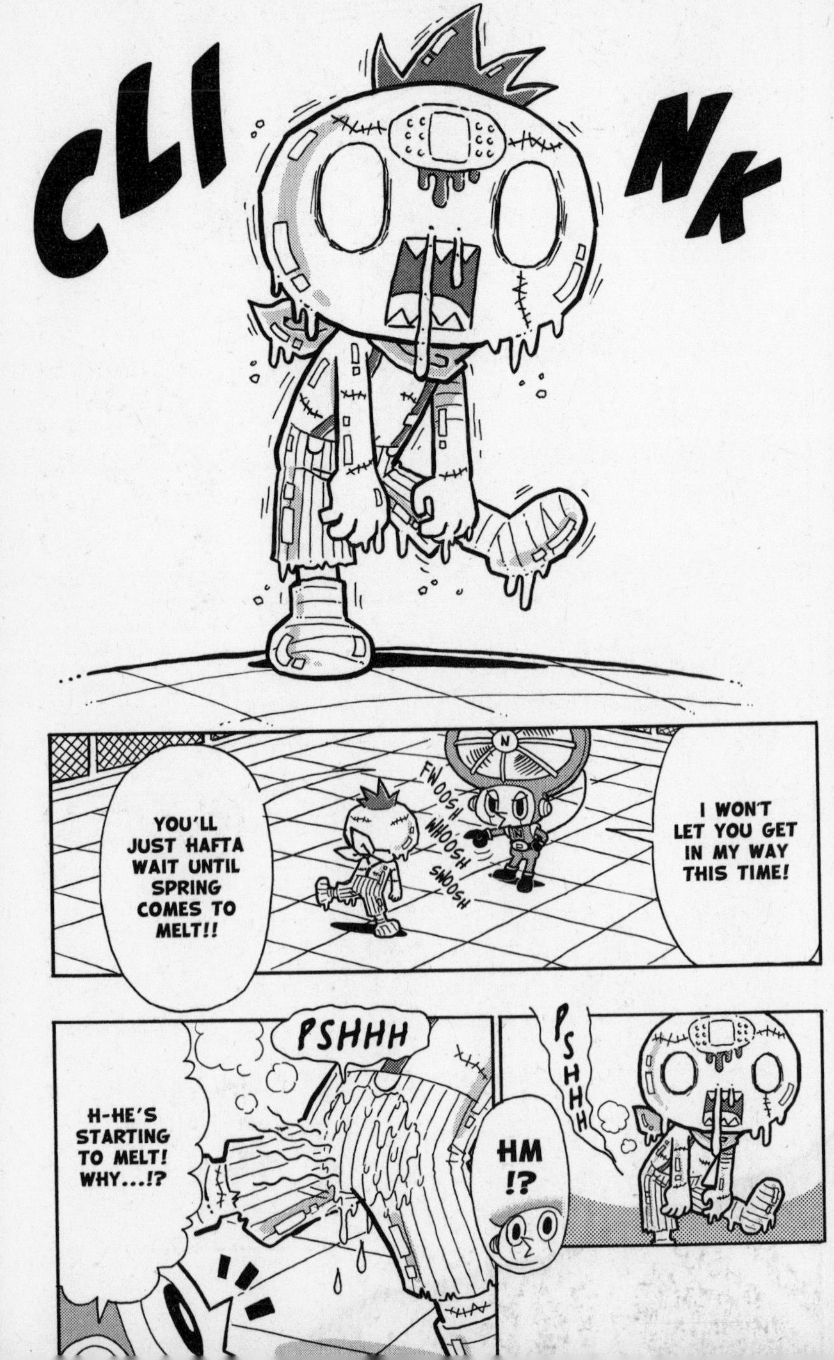
CLINK
I WON'T LET YOU GET IN MY WAY THIS TIME!
FWOOSH
WHOOSH
SWOOSH
YOU'LL JUST HAFTA WAIT UNTIL SPRING COMES TO MELT!!
PSHHH
HM !?
PSHHH
H-HE'S STARTING TO MELT! WHY...!?

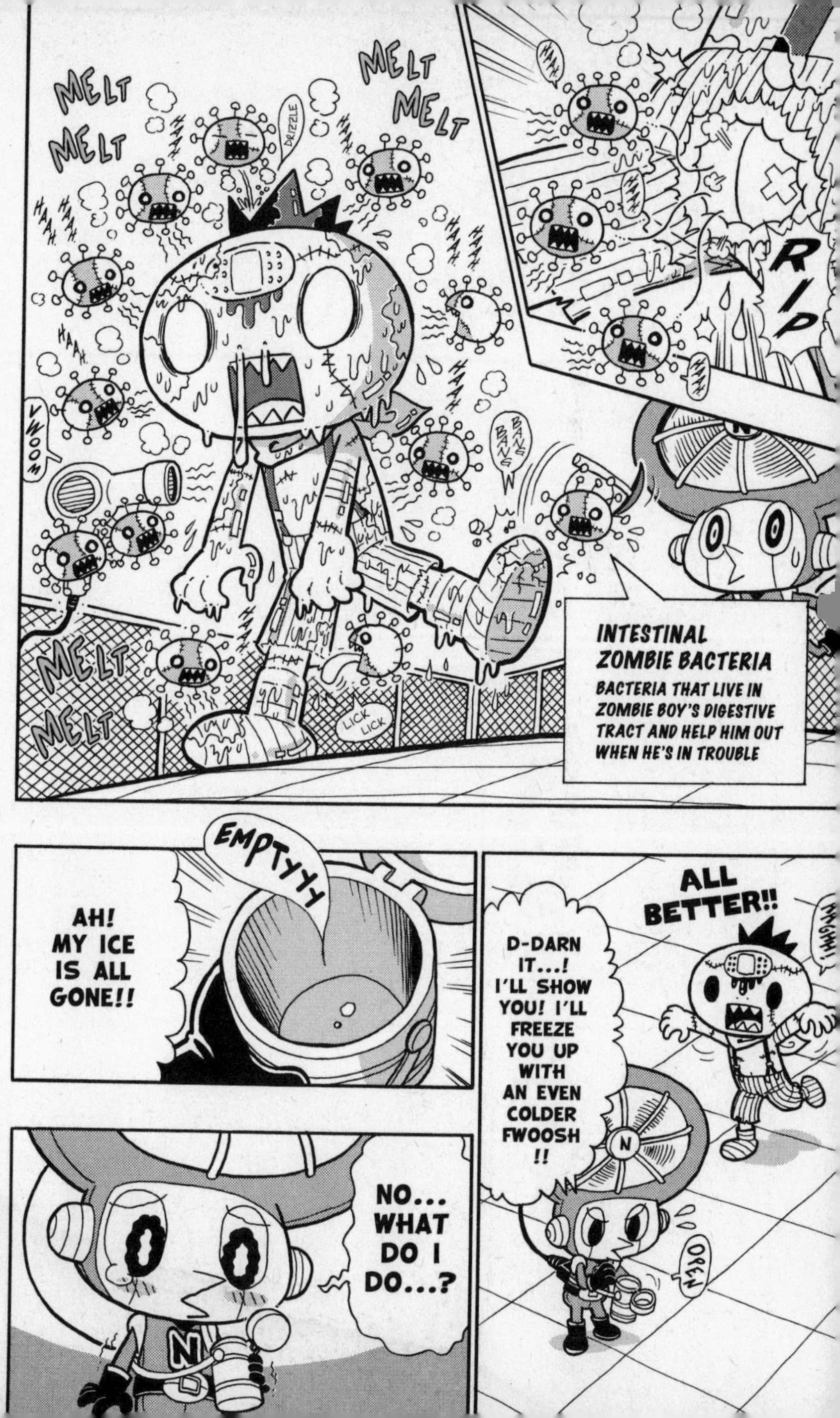
HAAH
HAAH
RIP
MELT
MELT
DRIZZLE
MELT
MELT
HAAH
HAAH
HAAH
HAAH
HAAH
VWOOM
BANG BANG BANG
MELT
MELT
LICK LICK
INTESTINAL ZOMBIE BACTERIA
BACTERIA THAT LIVE IN ZOMBIE BOY'S DIGESTIVE TRACT AND HELP HIM OUT WHEN HE'S IN TROUBLE
ALL BETTER!!
MMGHH!
D-DARN IT...! I'LL SHOW YOU! I'LL FREEZE YOU UP WITH AN EVEN COLDER FWOOSH!!
OPEN
EMPTYYY
AH! MY ICE IS ALL GONE!!
NO... WHAT DO I DO...?

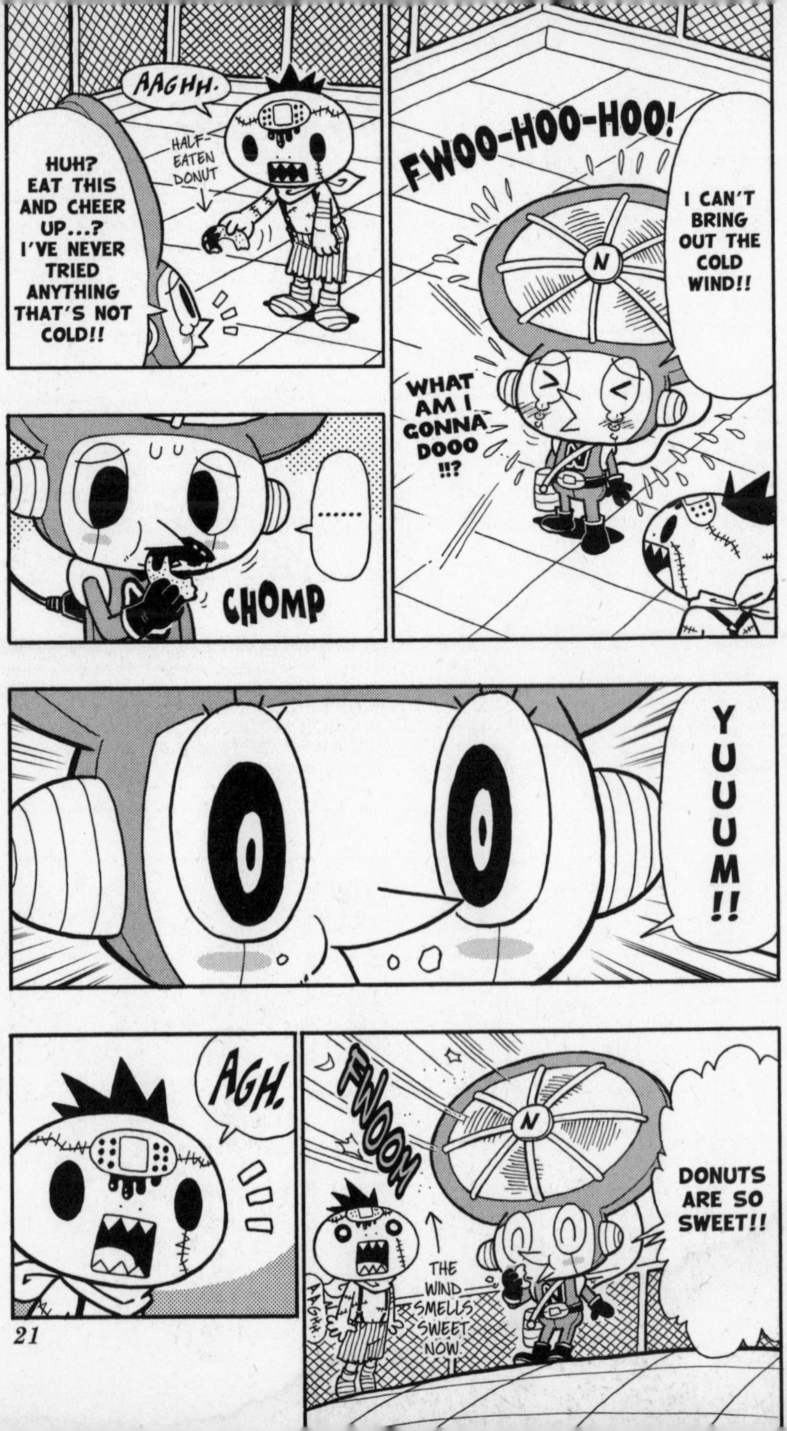
FWOO-HOO-HOO!
I CAN'T BRING OUT THE COLD WIND!!
WHAT AM I GONNA DOOO!!?
AAGHH.
HUH? EAT THIS AND CHEER UP...? I'VE NEVER TRIED ANYTHING THAT'S NOT COLD!!
HALF-EATEN DONUT
......
CHOMP
YUUUM!!
DONUTS ARE SO SWEET!!
FWOOM
THE WIND SMELLS SWEET NOW.
AAGHH
AGH.

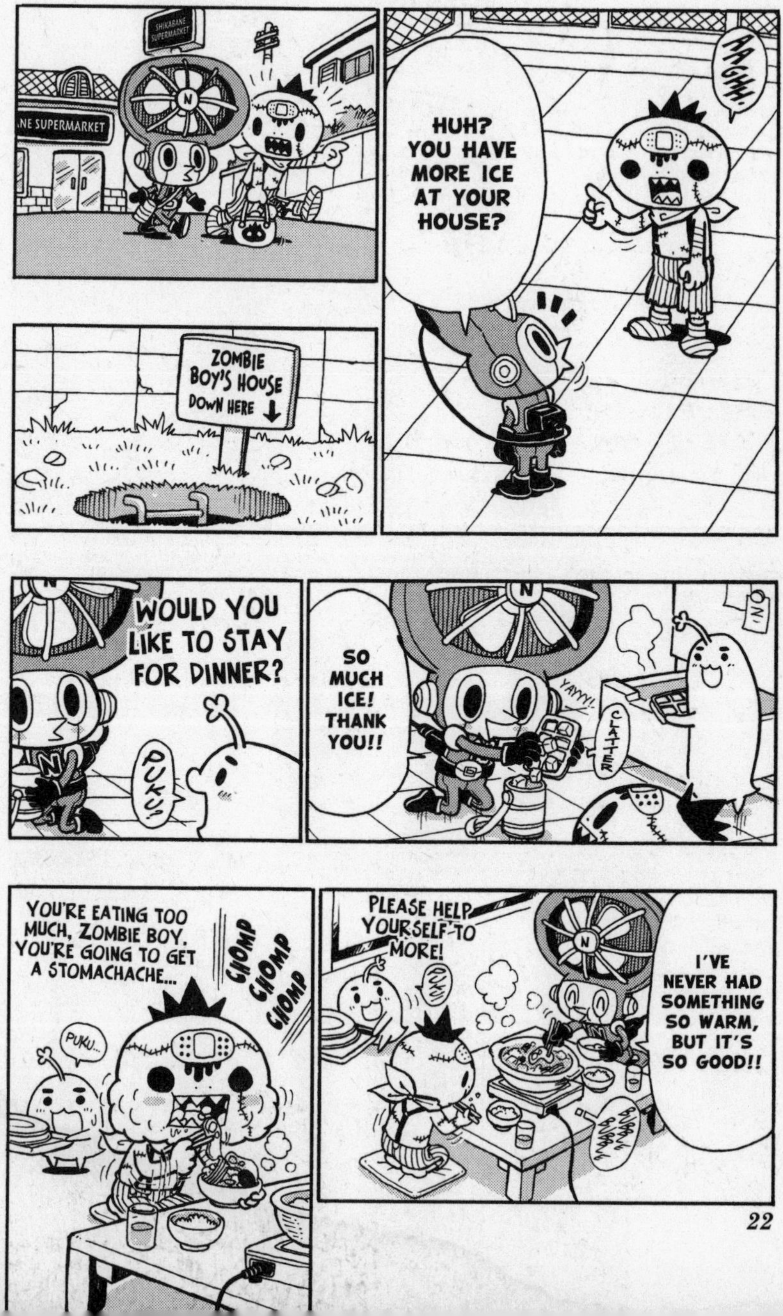
AAGHH.
HUH? YOU HAVE MORE ICE AT YOUR HOUSE?
SHIKABANE SUPERMARKET
..NE SUPERMARKET
ZOMBIE BOY'S HOUSE DOWN HERE ↓
SO MUCH ICE! THANK YOU!!
YAYYY!
CLATTER
WOULD YOU LIKE TO STAY FOR DINNER?
PUKU!
I'VE NEVER HAD SOMETHING SO WARM, BUT IT'S SO GOOD!!
PLEASE HELP YOURSELF TO MORE!
PUKU
BUBBLE BUBBLE
YOU'RE EATING TOO MUCH, ZOMBIE BOY. YOU'RE GOING TO GET A STOMACHACHE...
CHOMP CHOMP CHOMP
PUKU...

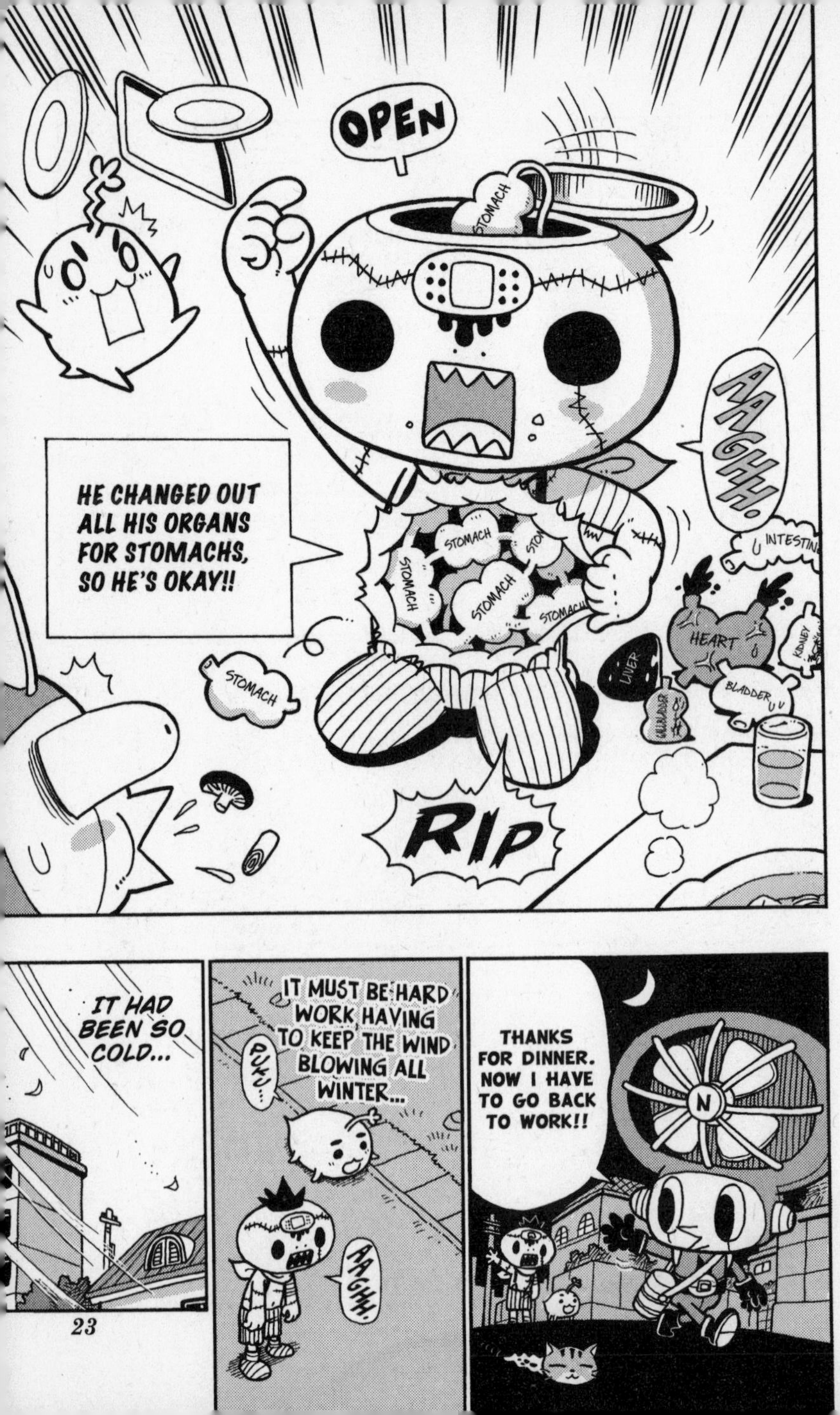
OPEN
STOMACH
AAGHH!
INTESTINE
HE CHANGED OUT ALL HIS ORGANS FOR STOMACHS, SO HE'S OKAY!!
STOMACH
STOMACH
STOMACH
STOMACH
HEART
KIDNEY
LIVER
BLADDER
GALLBLADDER
STOMACH
RIP
THANKS FOR DINNER. NOW I HAVE TO GO BACK TO WORK!!
N
IT MUST BE HARD WORK HAVING TO KEEP THE WIND BLOWING ALL WINTER...
PUKU...
AAGHH.
IT HAD BEEN SO COLD...

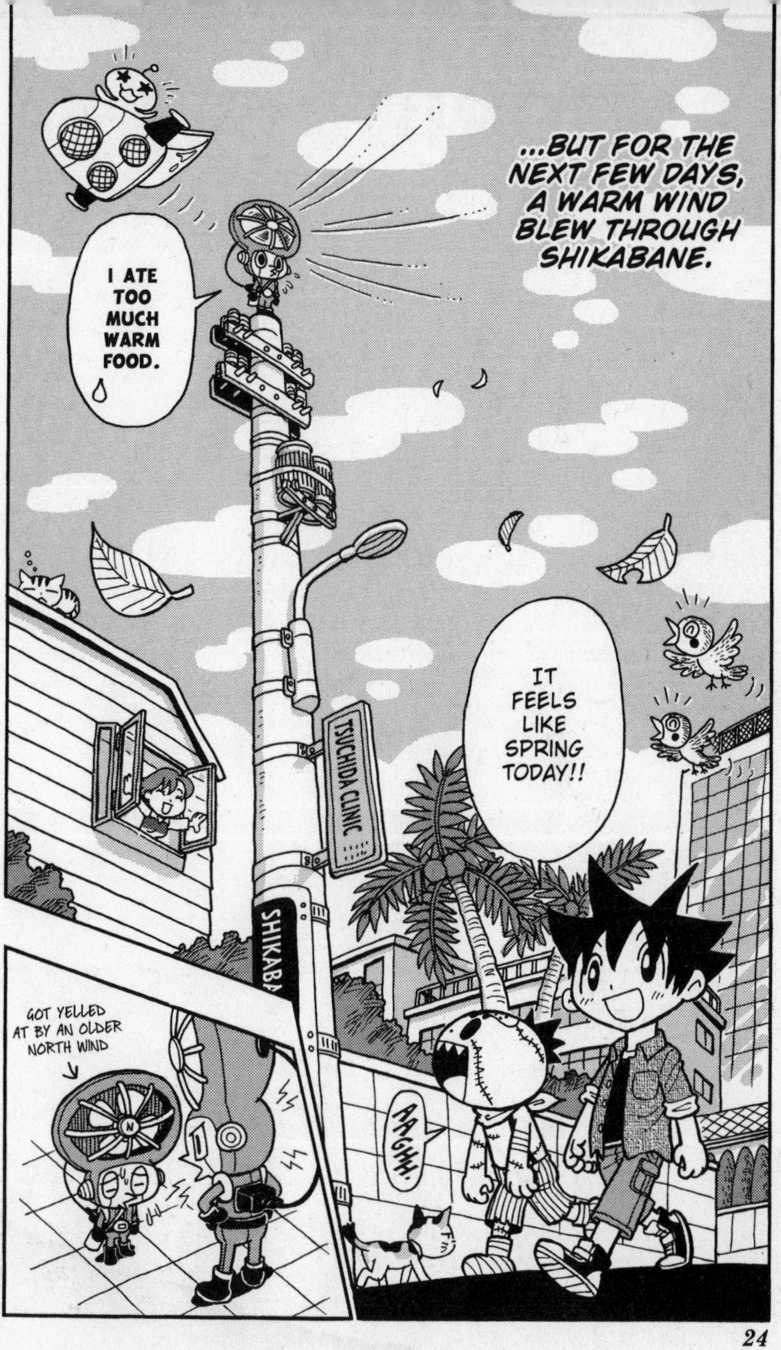
...BUT FOR THE NEXT FEW DAYS, A WARM WIND BLEW THROUGH SHIKABANE.
I ATE TOO MUCH WARM FOOD.
TSUCHIDA CLINIC
IT FEELS LIKE SPRING TODAY!!
AAGHH.
GOT YELLED AT BY AN OLDER NORTH WIND

I SERIOUZLY NEED A DRINK!

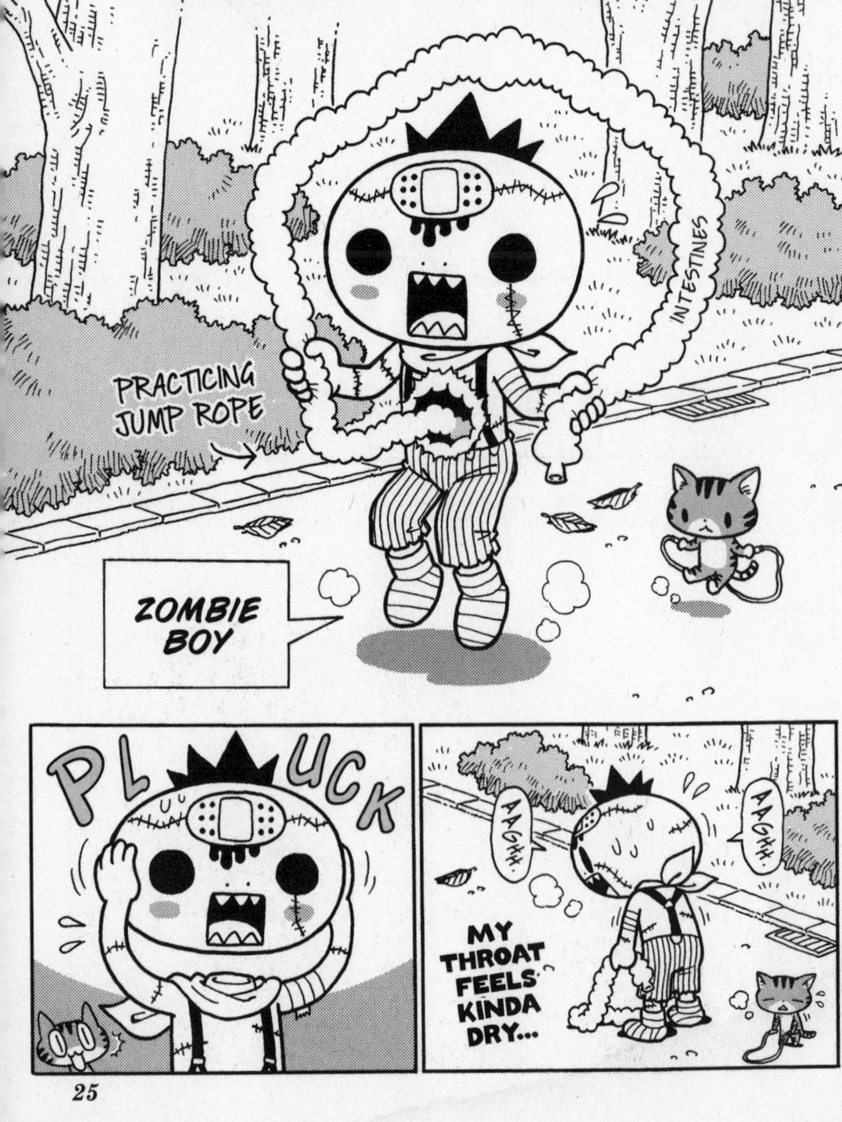
INTESTINES
PRACTICING JUMP ROPE
ZOMBIE BOY
AAGHH.
AAGHH.
MY THROAT FEELS KINDA DRY...
PLUCK

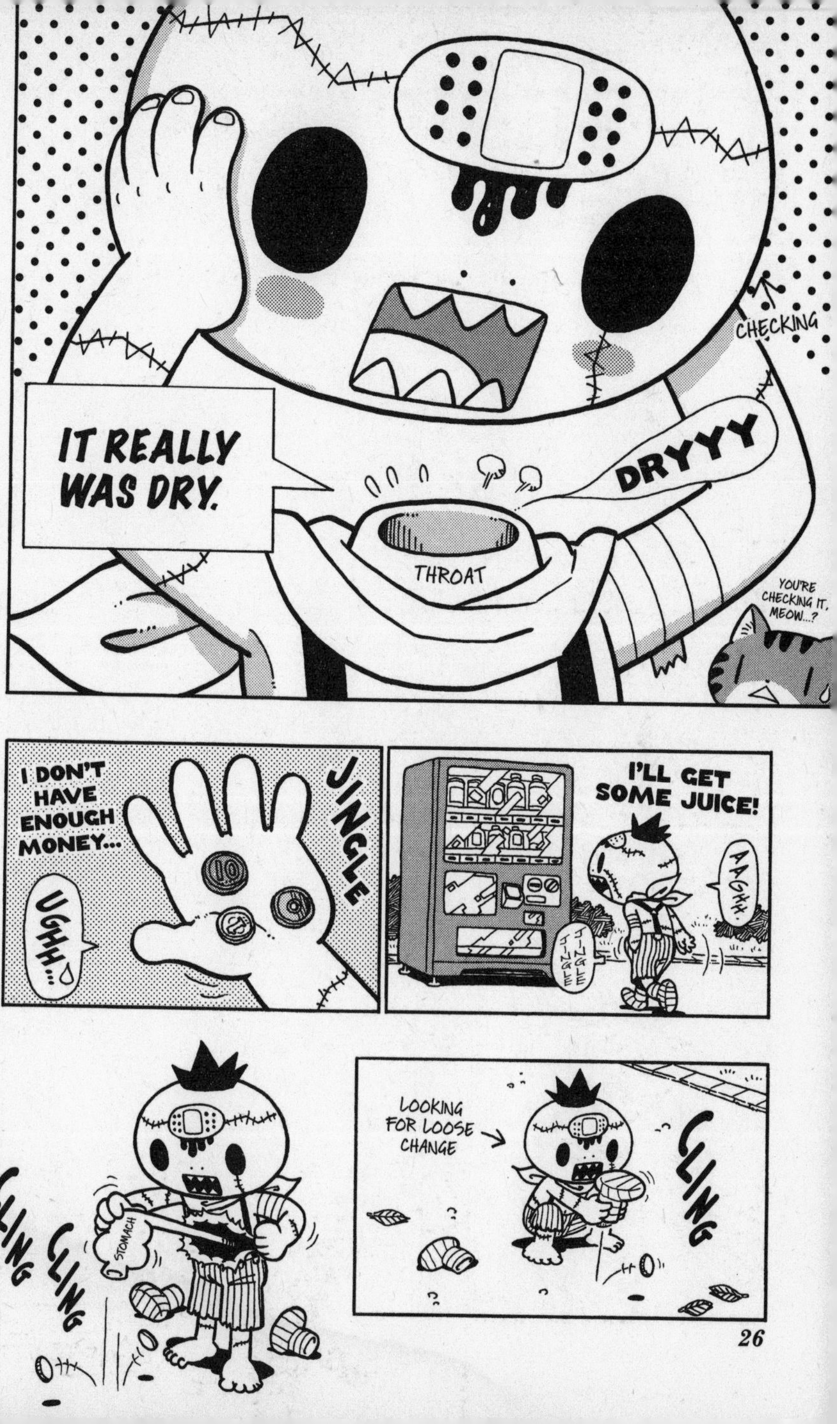
CHECKING
DRYYY
IT REALLY WAS DRY.
THROAT
YOU'RE CHECKING IT, MEOW...?
I'LL GET SOME JUICE!
AAGHH.
JINGLE JINGLE
JINGLE
I DON'T HAVE ENOUGH MONEY...
UGHH...
CLING
LOOKING FOR LOOSE CHANGE
STOMACH
CLING
CLING
CLING

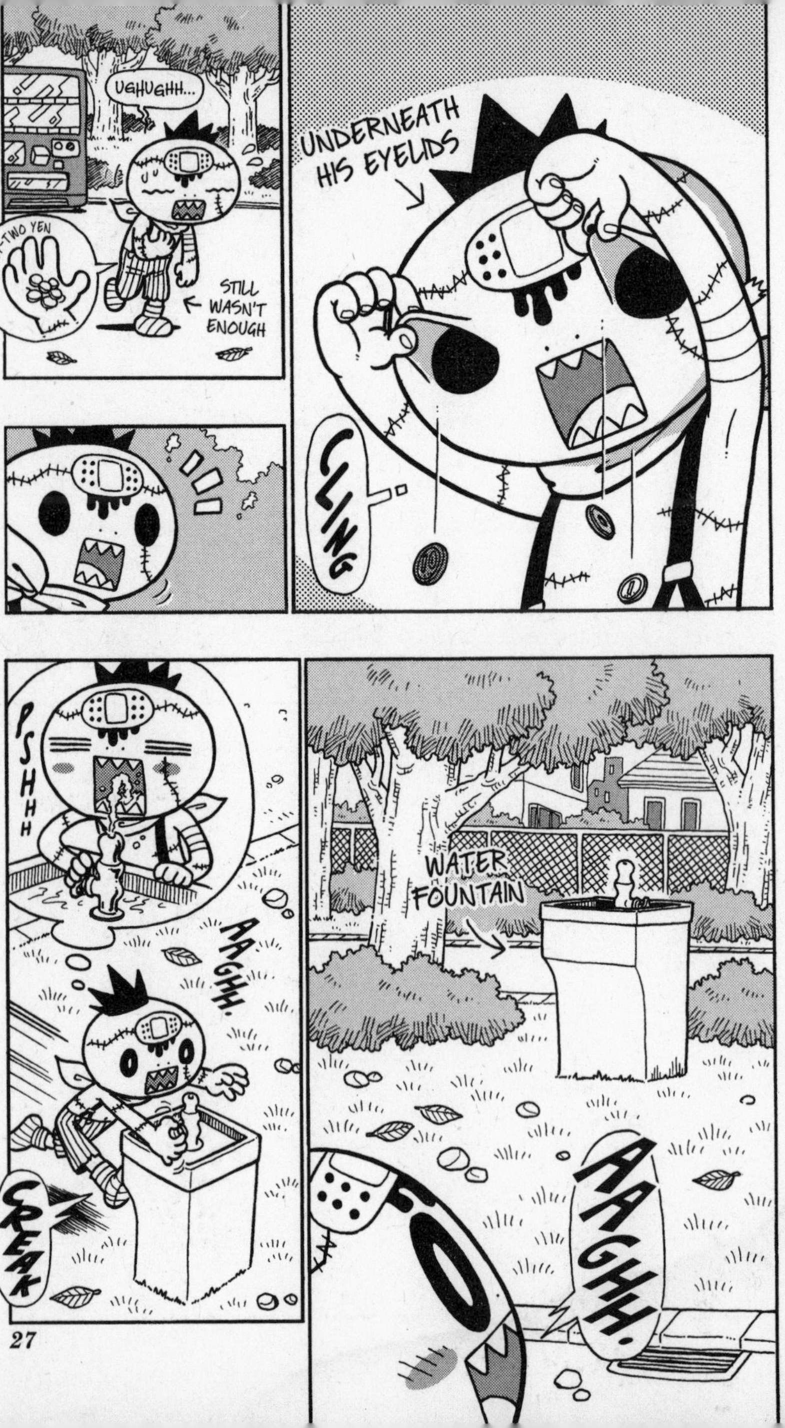
UNDERNEATH HIS EYELIDS
CLING
UGHUGHH...
FIFTY-TWO YEN
STILL WASN'T ENOUGH
WATER FOUNTAIN
AAGHH.
PSHHH
AAGHH.
CREAK

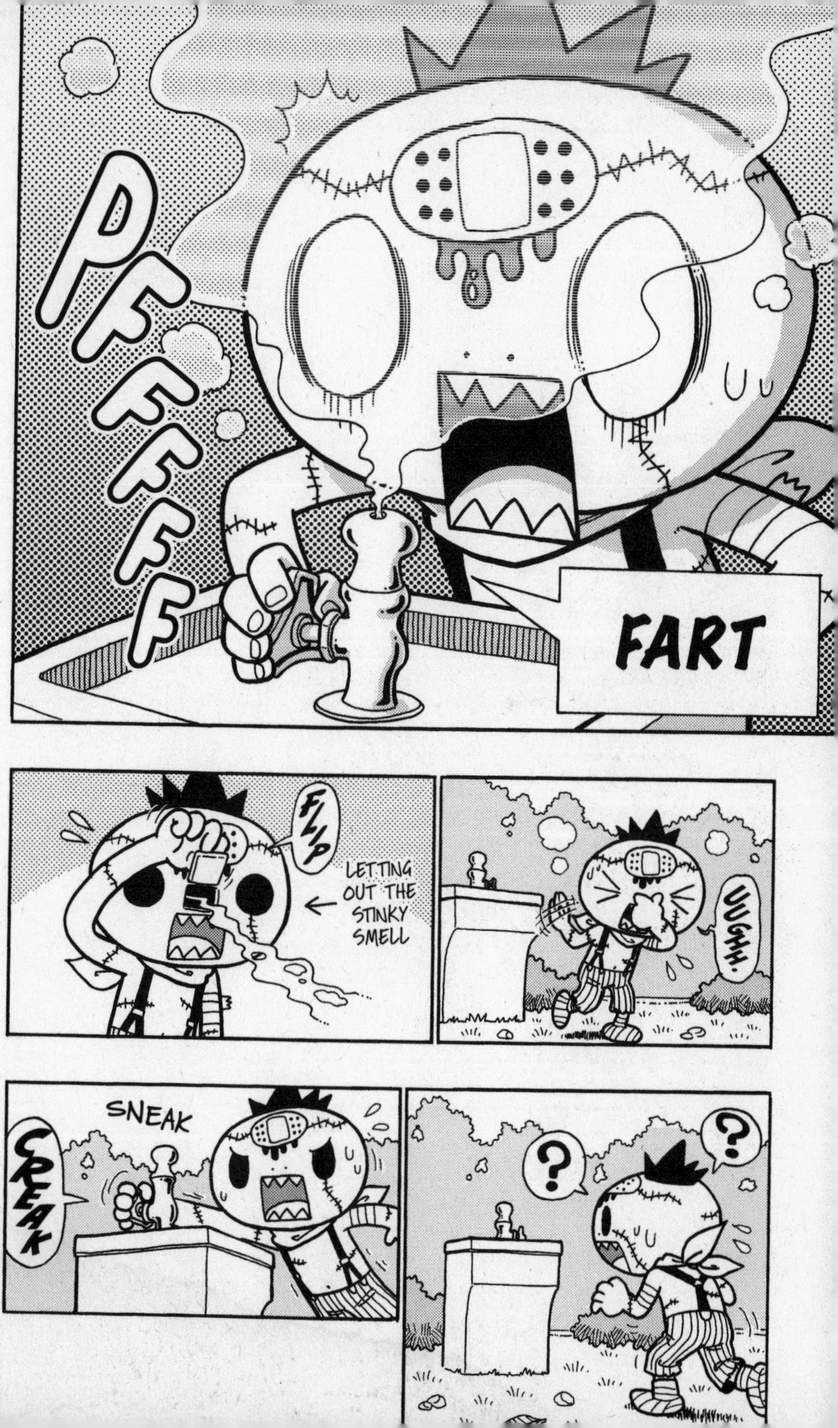
PFFFFFF
FART
UUGHH.
FLIP
LETTING OUT THE STINKY SMELL
?
?
SNEAK
CREAK

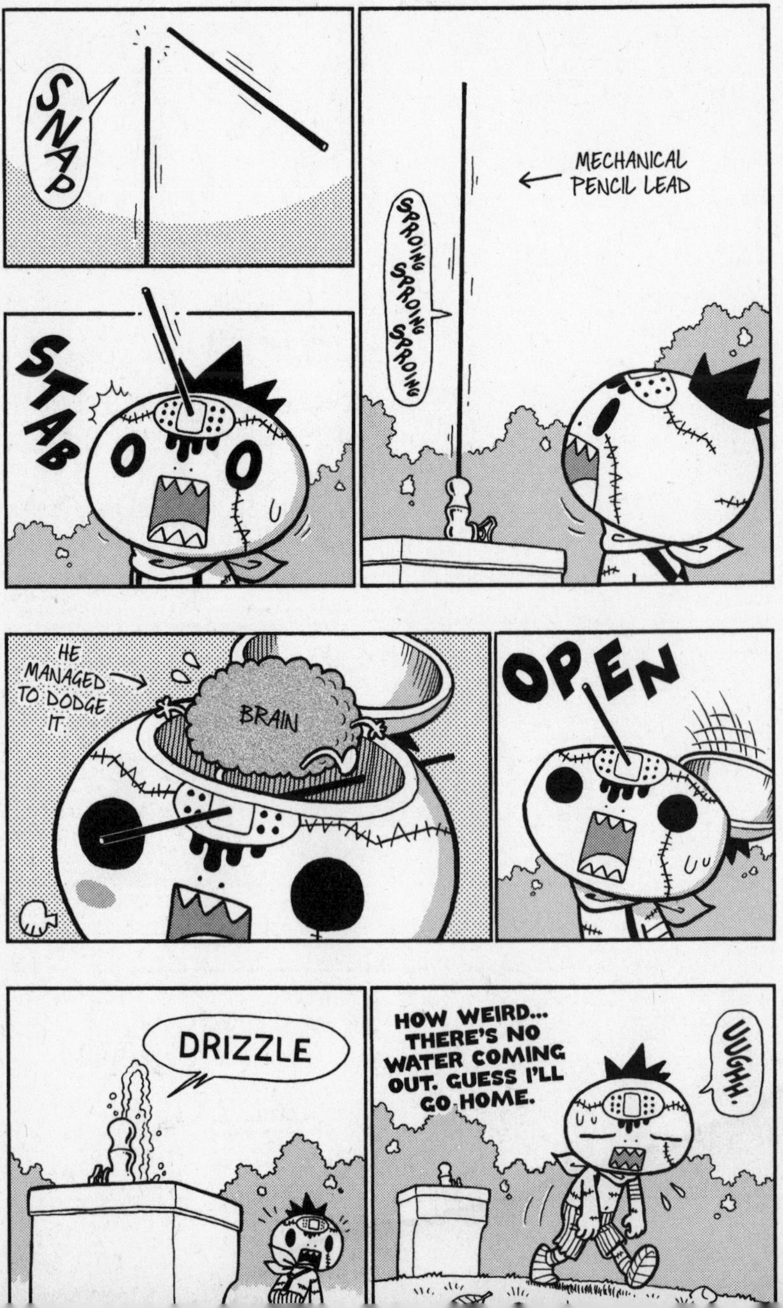
MECHANICAL PENCIL LEAD
SPROING SPROING SPROING
SNAP
STAB
OPEN
HE MANAGED TO DODGE IT.
BRAIN
UUGHH.
HOW WEIRD... THERE'S NO WATER COMING OUT. GUESS I'LL GO HOME.
DRIZZLE

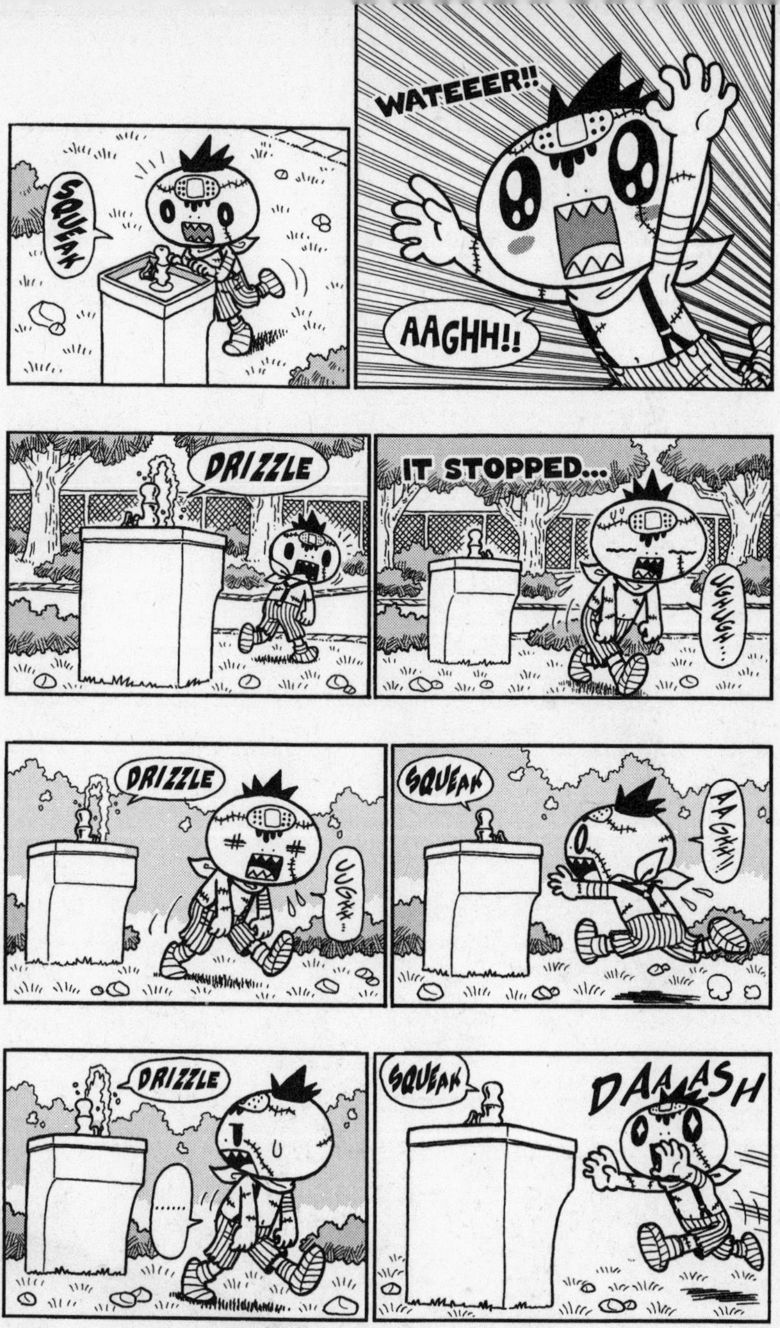
WATEEER!!
AAGHH!!
SQUEAK
IT STOPPED...
UGHUGH...
DRIZZLE
SQUEAK
AAGHH!!
DRIZZLE
UUGHH...
SQUEAK
DAAASH
DRIZZLE
......

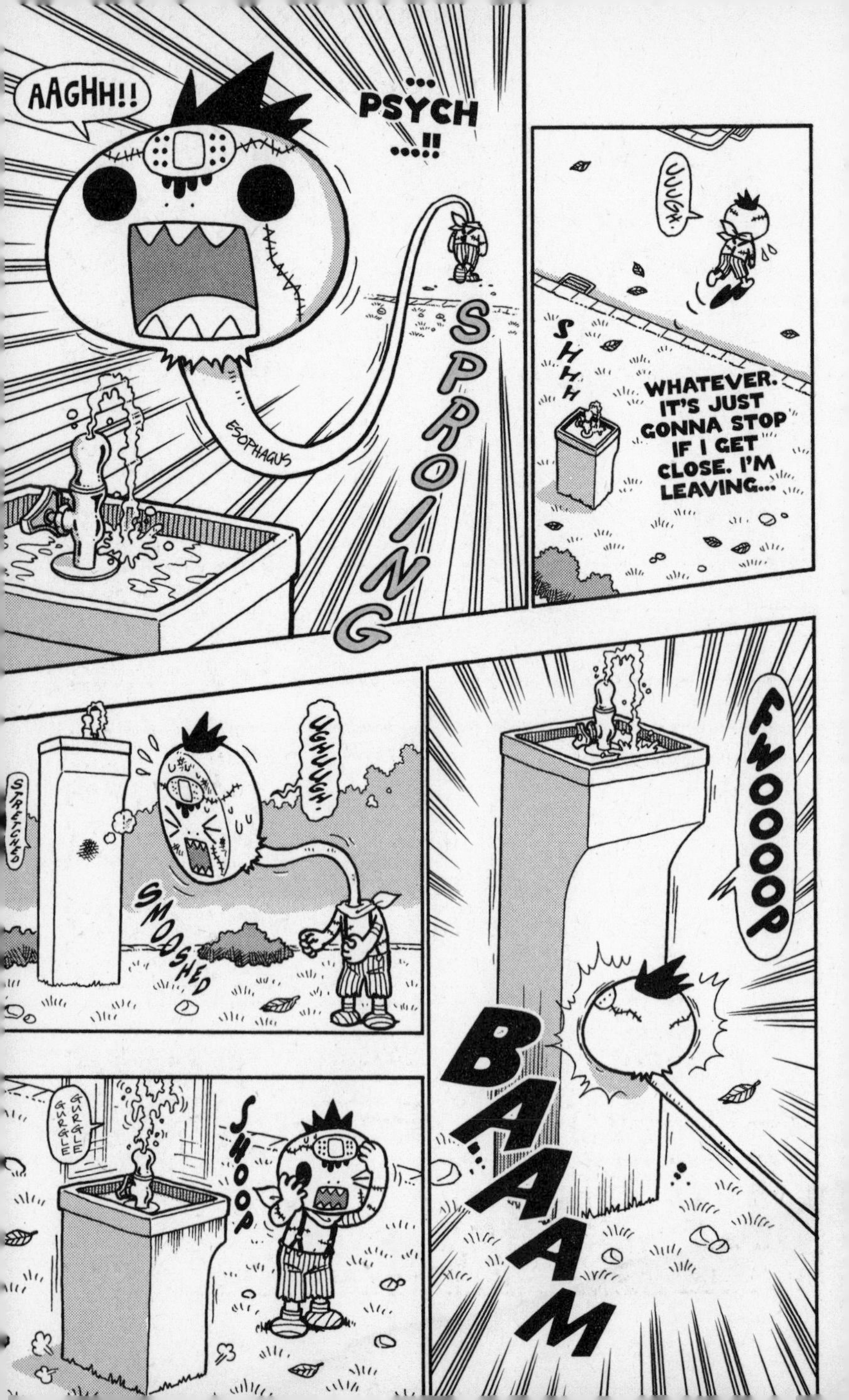
UUUGH.
SHHH
WHATEVER. IT'S JUST GONNA STOP IF I GET CLOSE. I'M LEAVING...
...PSYCH...!!
AAGHH!!
ESOPHAGUS
SPROING
FWOOOOOP
BAAAM
UGHUUGH.
STRETCHED
SMOOSHED
GURGLE GURGLE
SHOOP

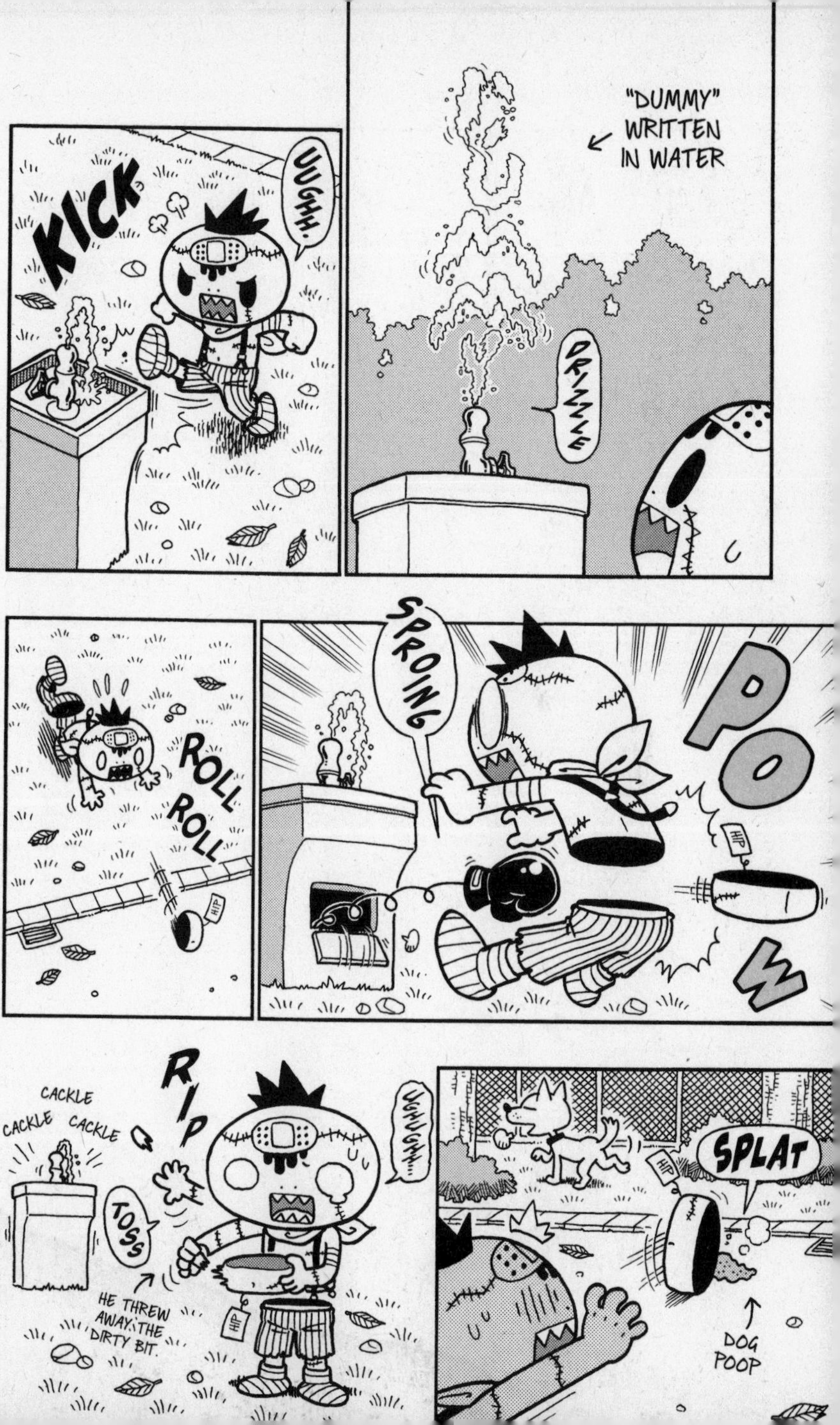
"DUMMY" WRITTEN IN WATER
DRIZZLE
UUGHH.
KICK
SPROING
POW
HIP
ROLL ROLL
HIP
SPLAT
HIP
DOG POOP
RIP
UGHUGHH...
CACKLE CACKLE CACKLE
TOSS
HE THREW AWAY THE DIRTY BIT.
HIP

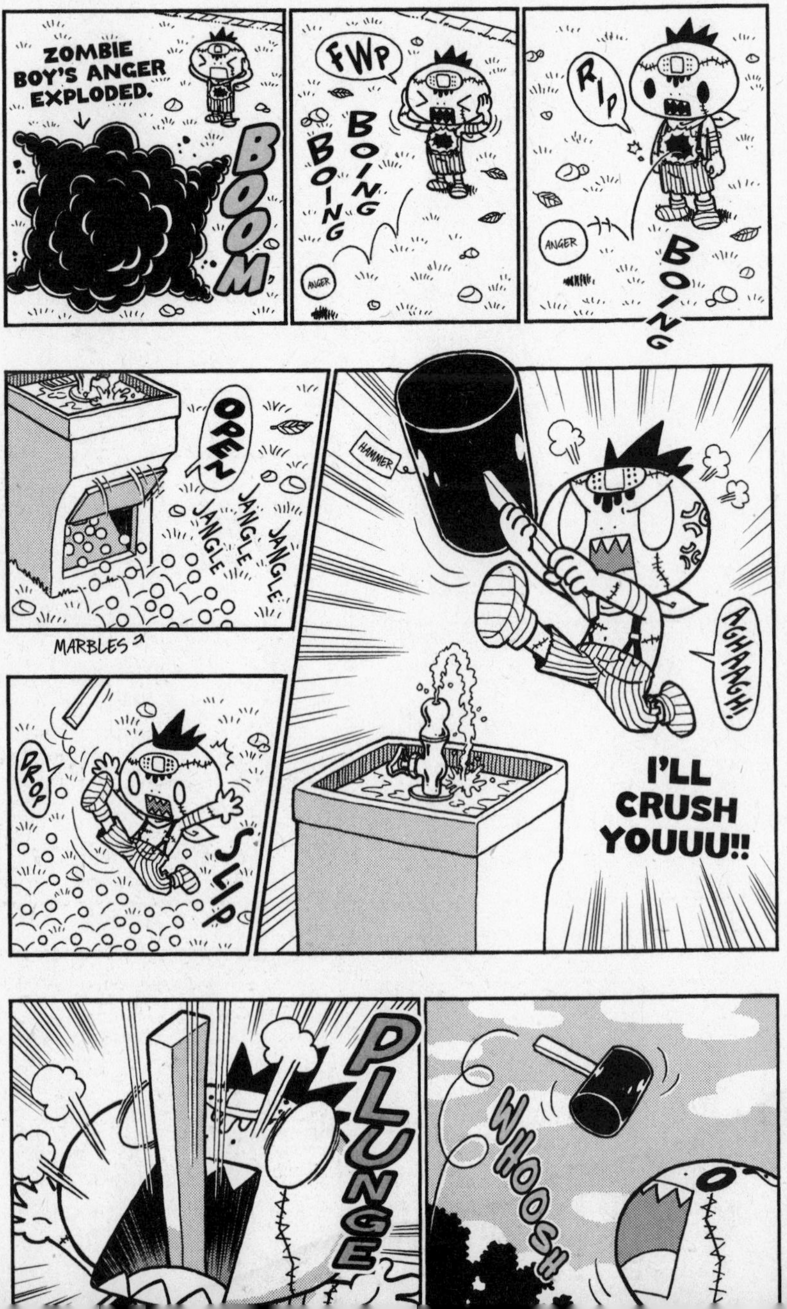
RIP
ANGER
BOING
FWP
BOING
BOING
ANGER
ZOMBIE BOY'S ANGER EXPLODED.
BOOM
HAMMER
AGHAAAGH!
I'LL CRUSH YOUUU!!
OPEN
JANGLE
JANGLE
JANGLE
MARBLES
DROP
SLIP
WHOOSH
O
PLUNGE

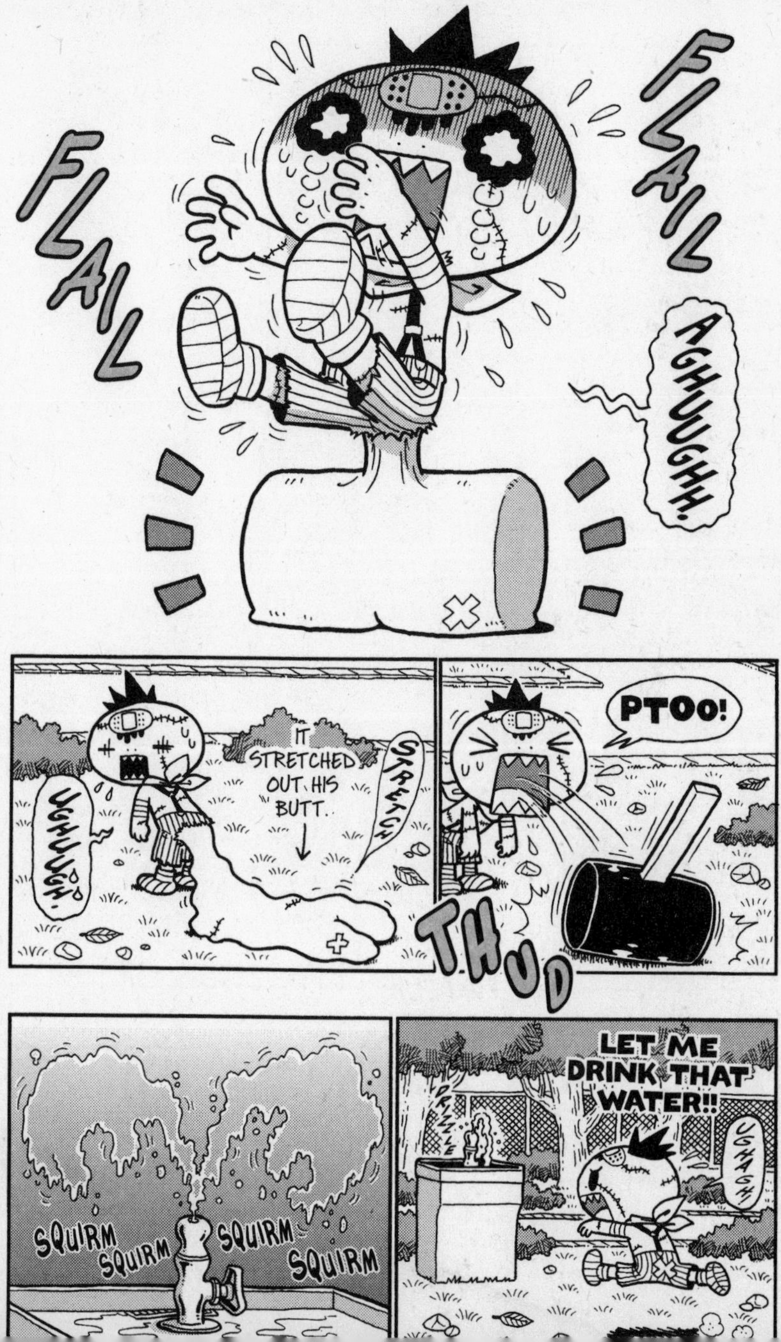
FLAIL
FLAIL
AGHUUGHH.
PTOO!
THUD
IT STRETCHED OUT HIS BUTT.
STRETCH
UGHUUGH.
LET ME DRINK THAT WATER!!
DRIZZLE
UGHAGH!
SQUIRM SQUIRM SQUIRM SQUIRM

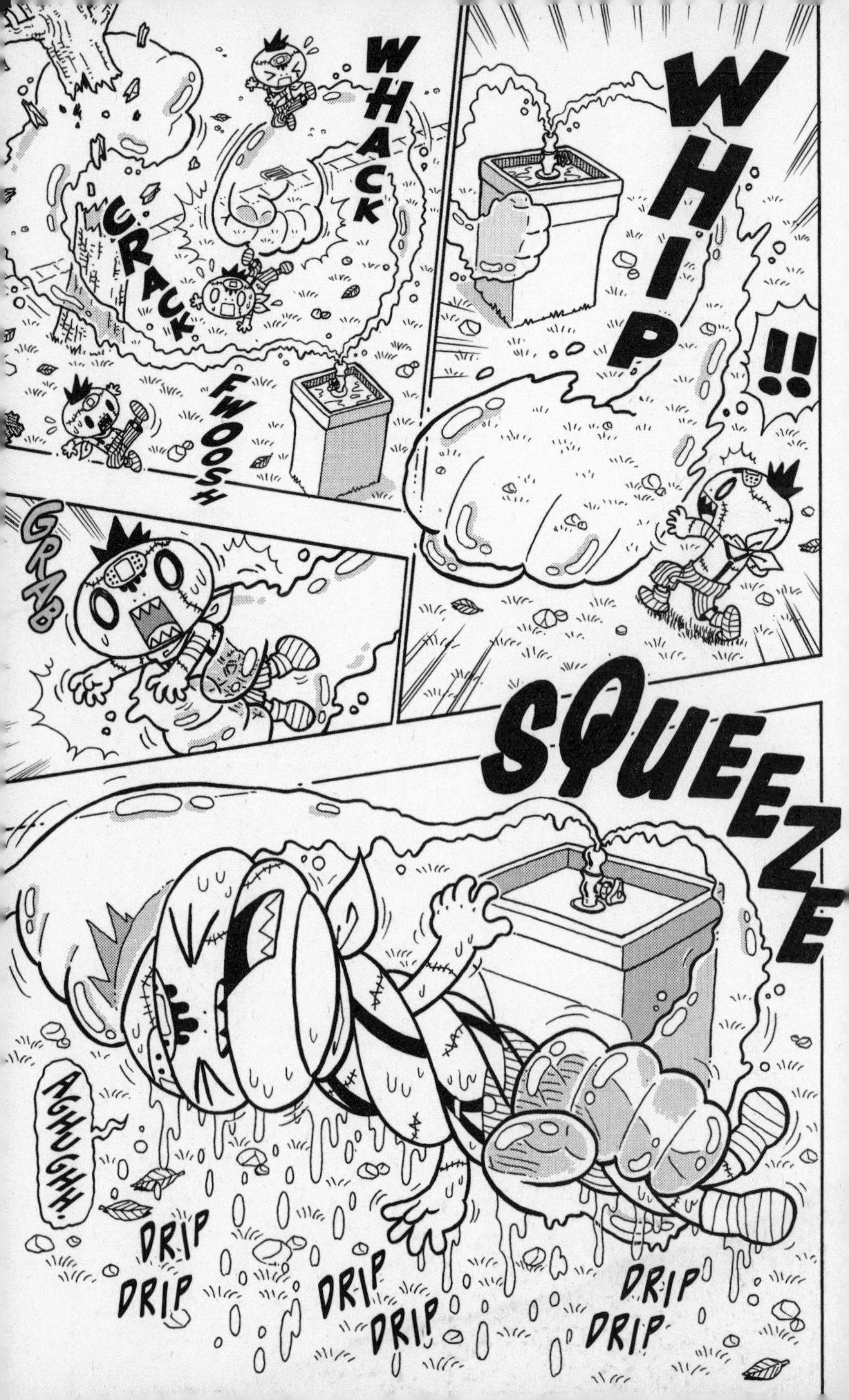
WHIP!!
WHACK
CRACK
FWOOSH
GRAB
SQUEEZE
AGHUGHH.
DRIP DRIP
DRIP DRIP
DRIP DRIP

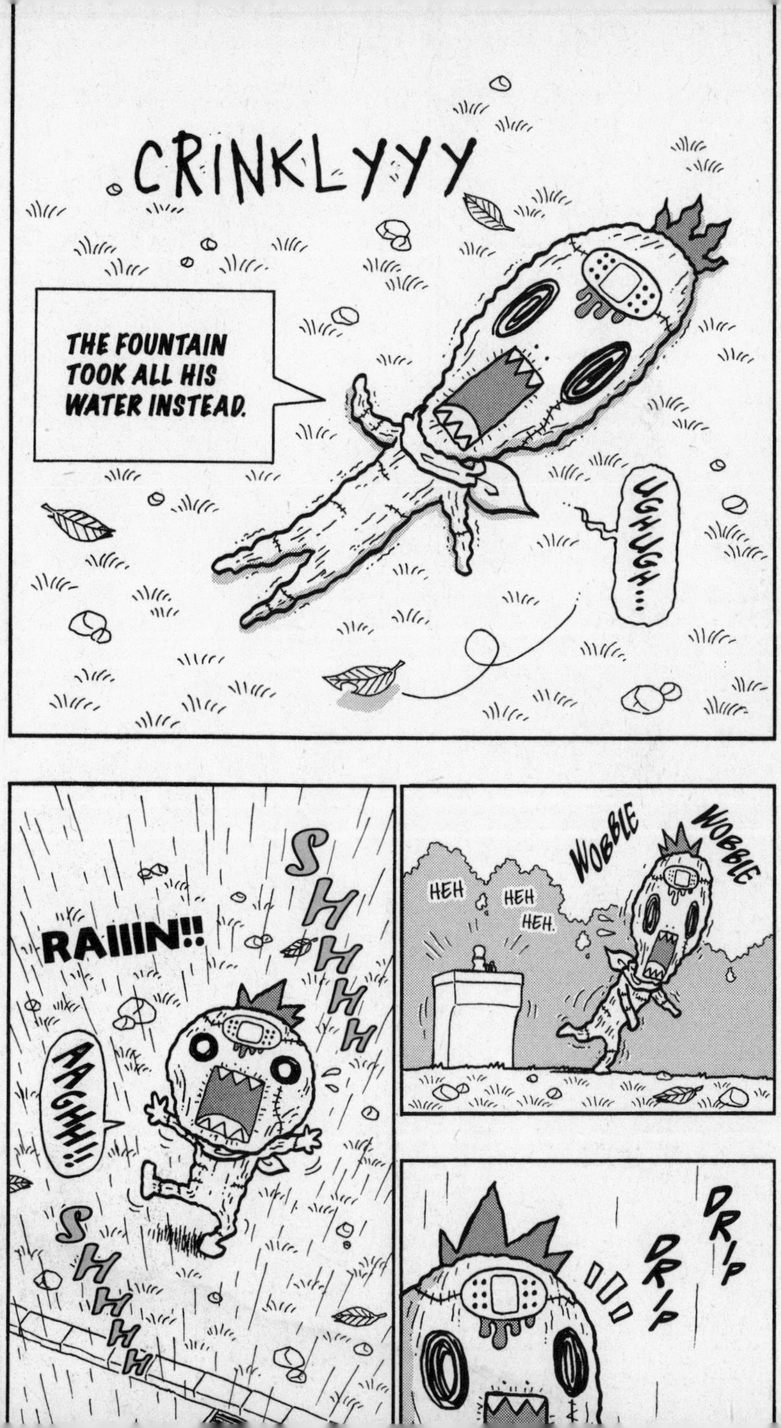
CRINKLYYY
THE FOUNTAIN TOOK ALL HIS WATER INSTEAD.
UGHUGH...
WOBBLE WOBBLE
HEH HEH HEH.
DRIP DRIP
SHHHH
RAIIIN!!
AAGHH!!
SHHHH

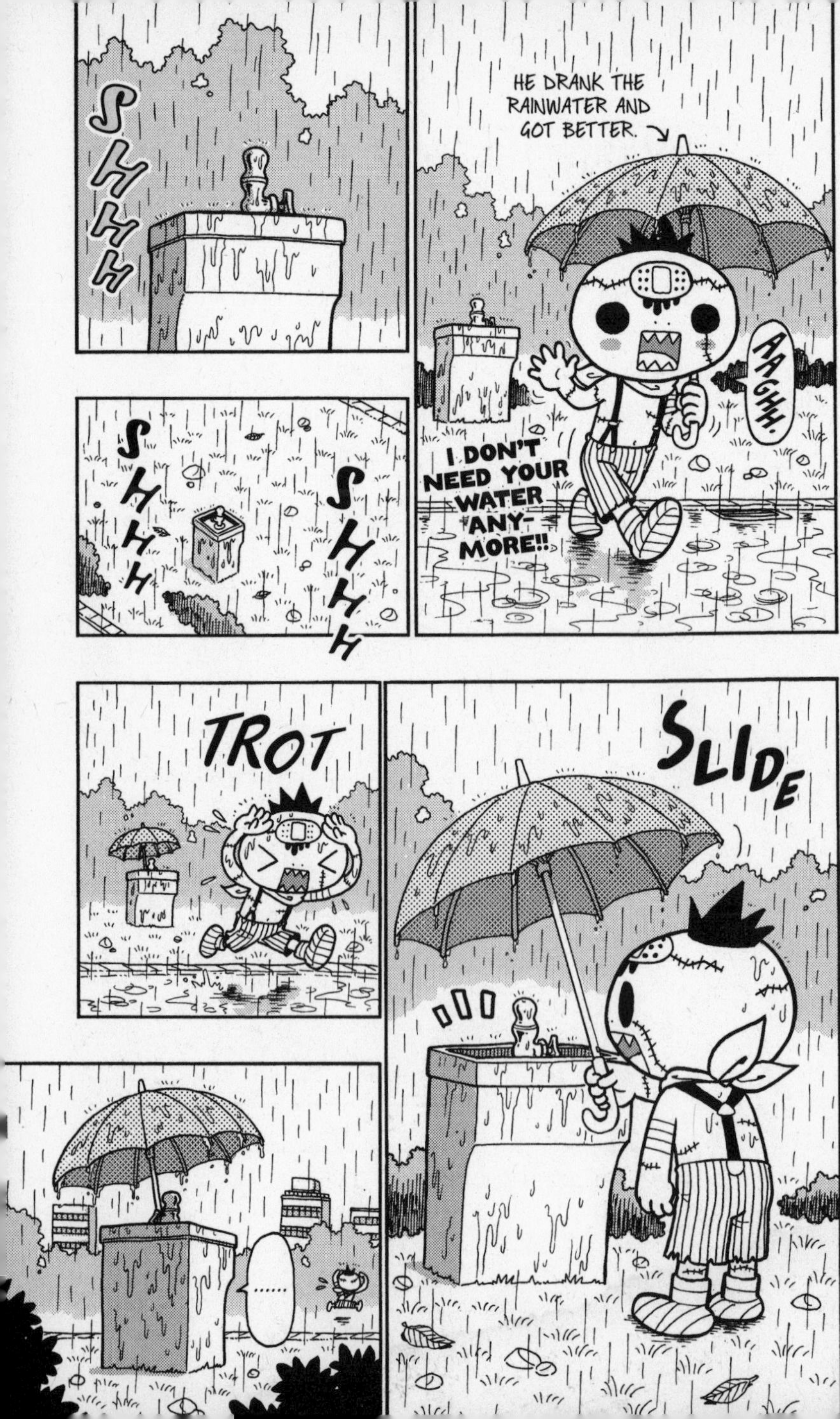
HE DRANK THE RAINWATER AND GOT BETTER.
AAGHH.
I DON'T NEED YOUR WATER ANY-MORE!!
SHHHH
SHHHH
SHHHH
SLIDE
TROT
......

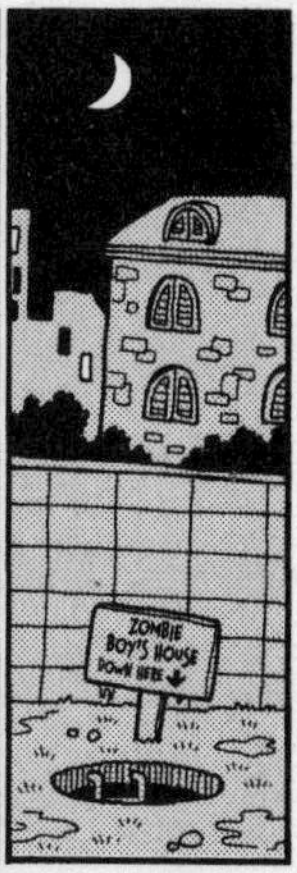
ZOMBIE BOY'S HOUSE DOWN HERE

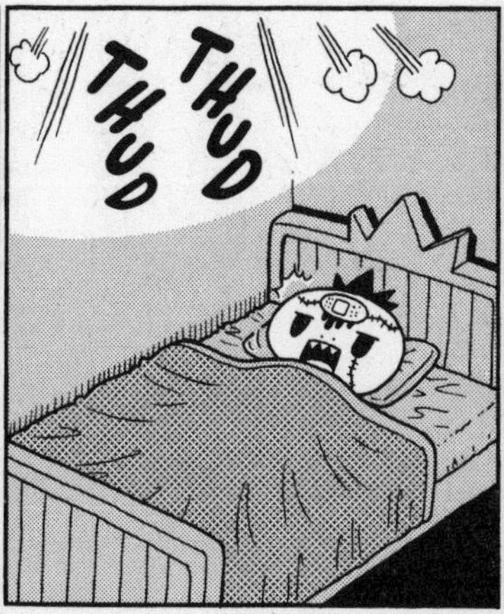
THUD THUD

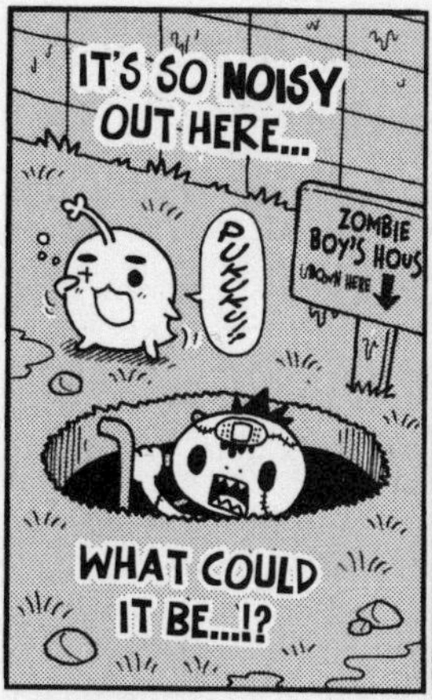
IT'S SO NOISY OUT HERE...
PUKUKU!!
ZOMBIE BOY'S HOUS DOWN HERE
WHAT COULD IT BE...!?

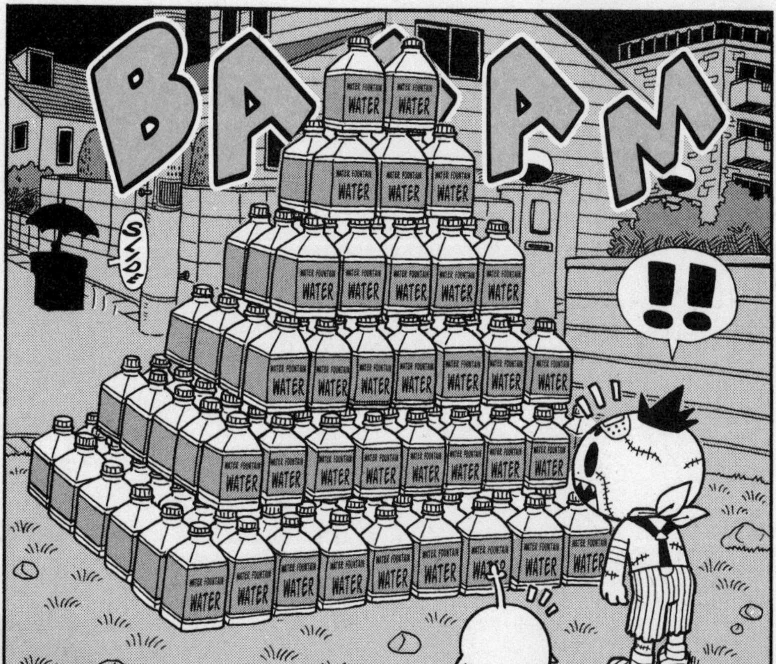
BA AM
SLIDE
WATER FOUNTAIN WATER
!!

PUMPED FOR FUN IN THE ZNOW!

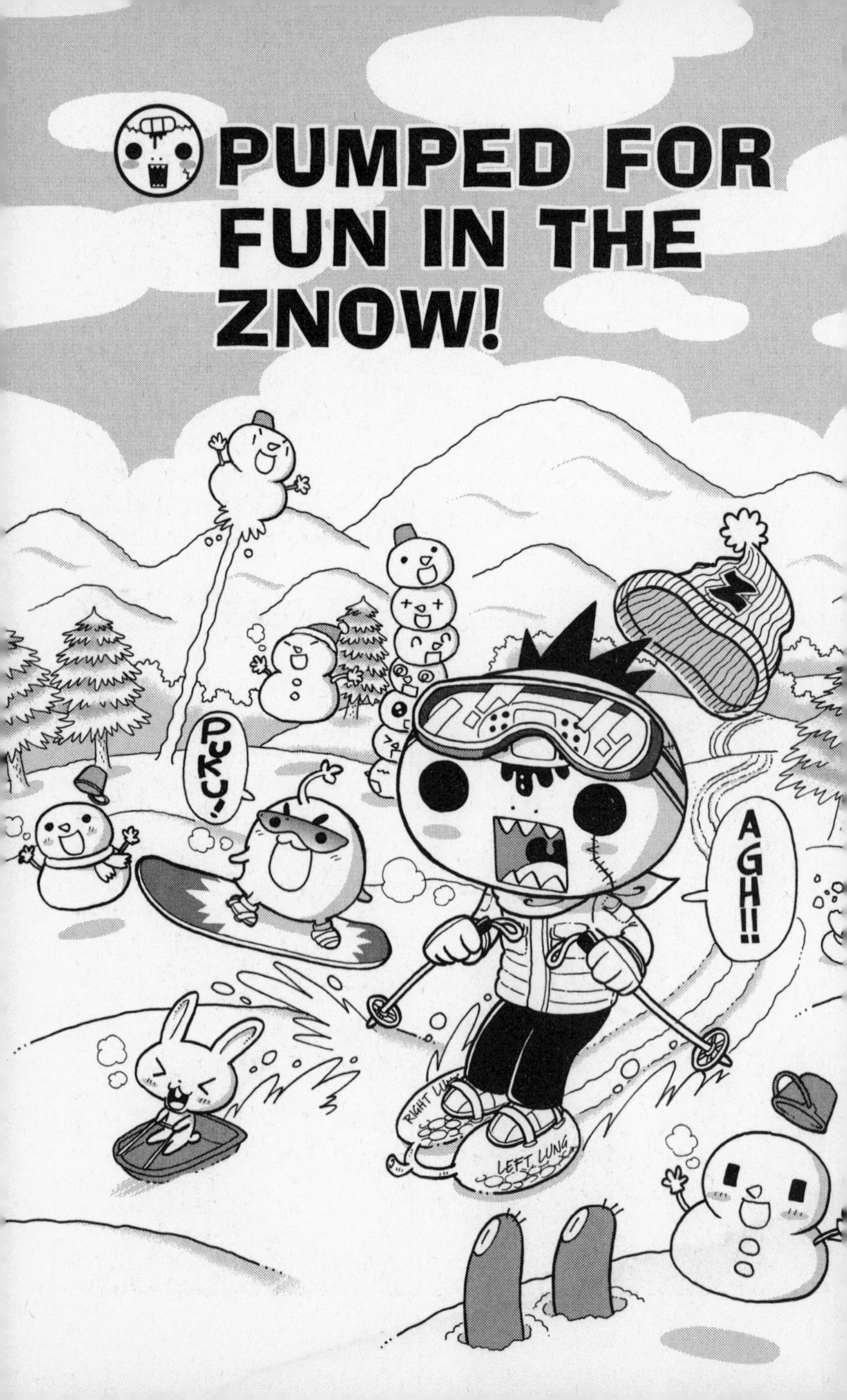
AGH!!
RIGHT LUNG
LEFT LUNG
PUKU!

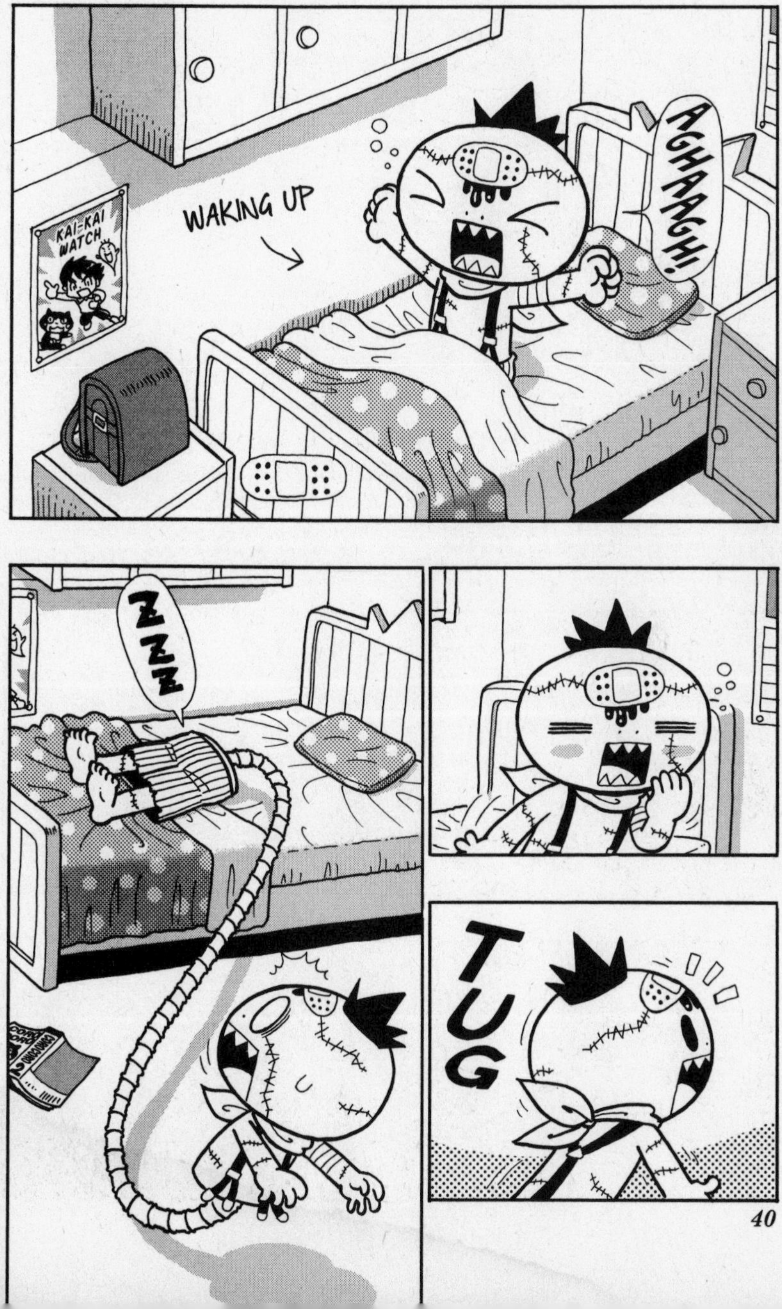
AGHAAAGH!
WAKING UP
KAI-KAI WATCH
TUG
ZZZ

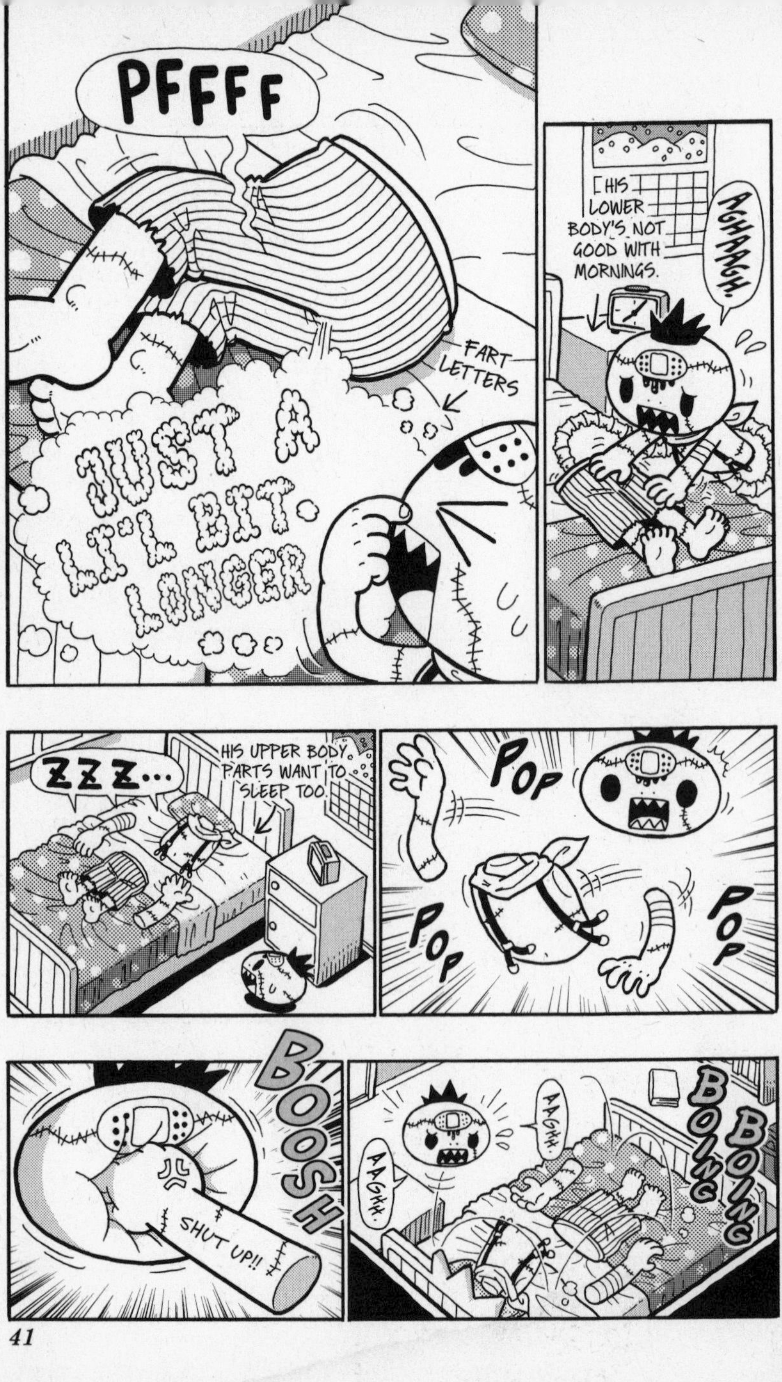
[HIS LOWER BODY'S NOT GOOD WITH MORNINGS.
AGHAAGH.
PFFFF
JUST A LI'L BIT LONGER
FART LETTERS
POP
POP
POP
ZZZ...
HIS UPPER BODY PARTS WANT TO SLEEP TOO.
BOING
BOING
AAGHH.
AAGHH.
BOOSH
SHUT UP!!

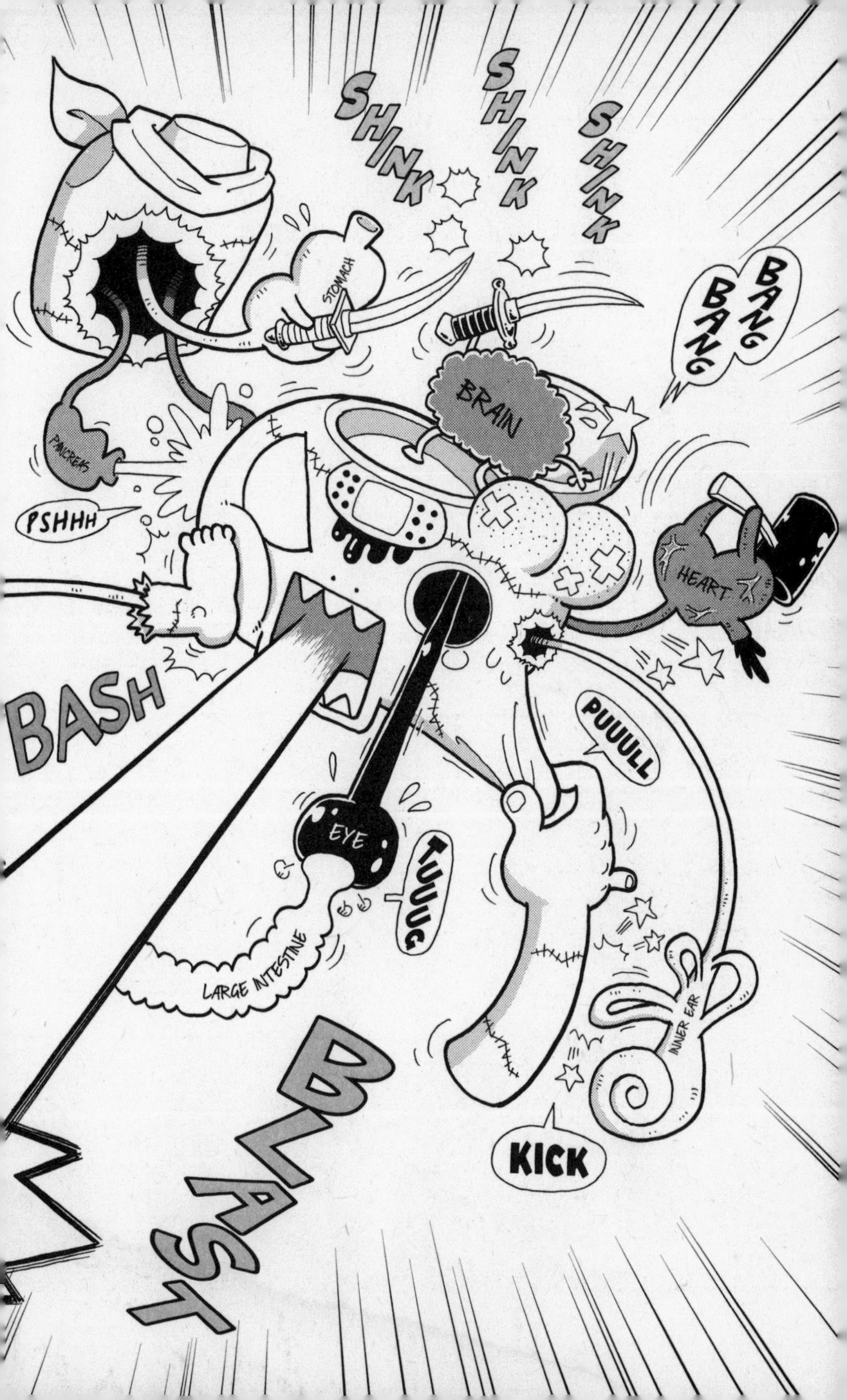
BANG BANG
SHINK
SHINK
SHINK
STOMACH
BRAIN
HEART
PANCREAS
PSHHH
BASH
PUUULL
EYE
TUUUG
INNER EAR
LARGE INTESTINE
KICK
BLAST

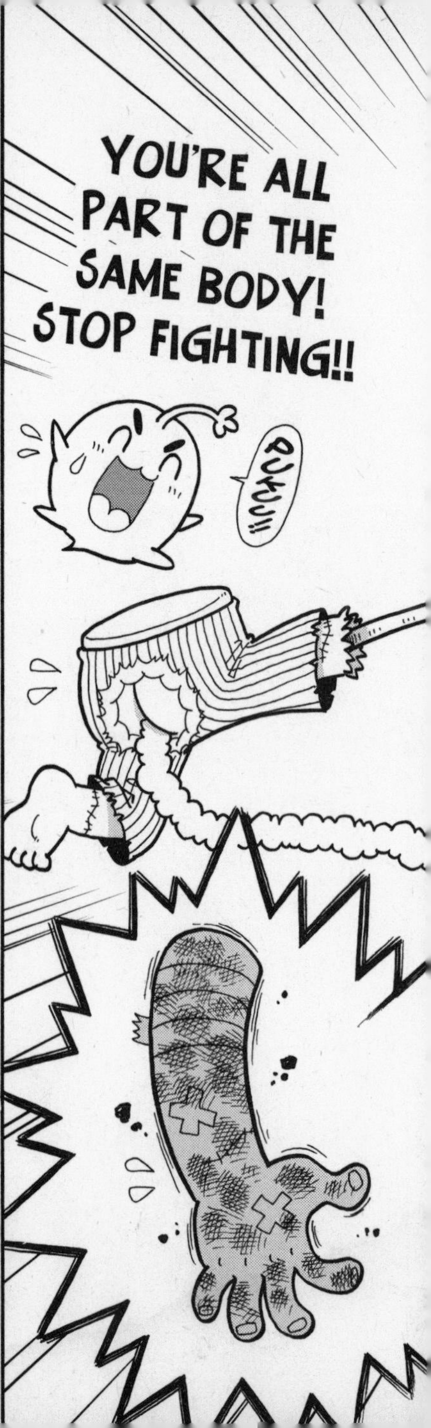
YOU'RE ALL PART OF THE SAME BODY! STOP FIGHTING!!
PUKUU!!

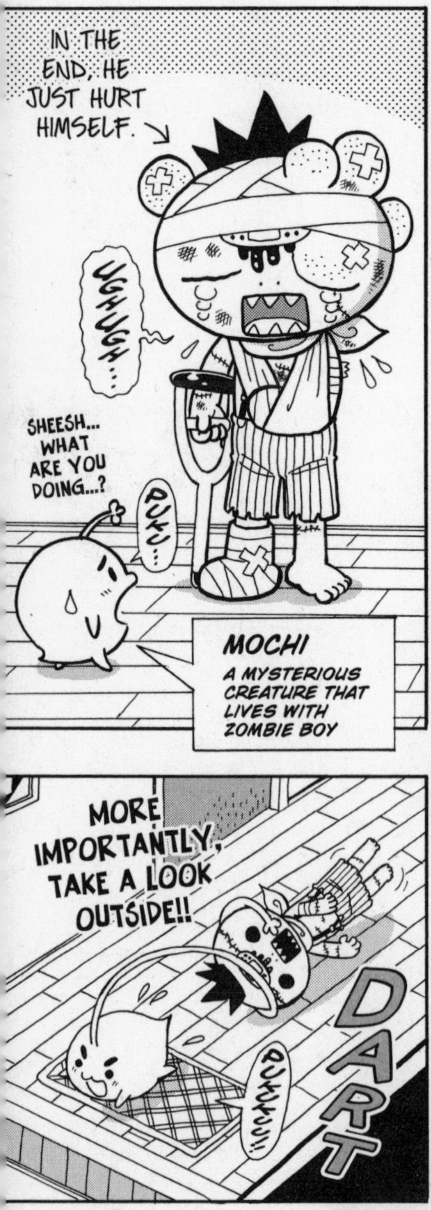
IN THE END, HE JUST HURT HIMSELF.
UGHUGH...
SHEESH... WHAT ARE YOU DOING...?
PUKU...
MOCHI
A MYSTERIOUS CREATURE THAT LIVES WITH ZOMBIE BOY
MORE IMPORTANTLY, TAKE A LOOK OUTSIDE!!
DART
PUKUKU!!

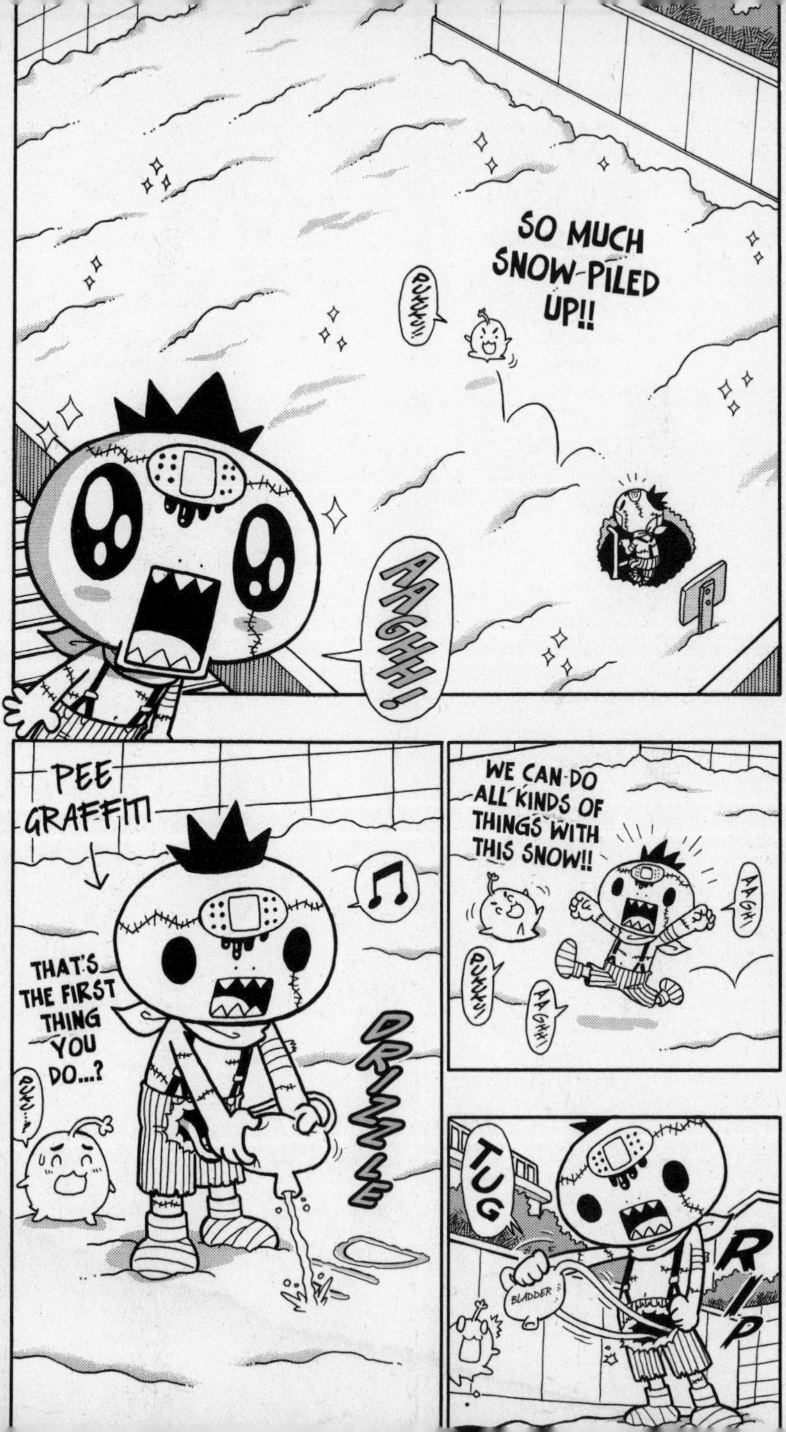
SO MUCH SNOW PILED UP!!
PUKYU!!
AAGHH!
WE CAN DO ALL KINDS OF THINGS WITH THIS SNOW!!
AAGH!
AAGHH!
PUKYU!
TUG
RIP
BLADDER
PEE GRAFFITI
♫
DRIZZLE
THAT'S THE FIRST THING YOU DO...?
PUKYU...?

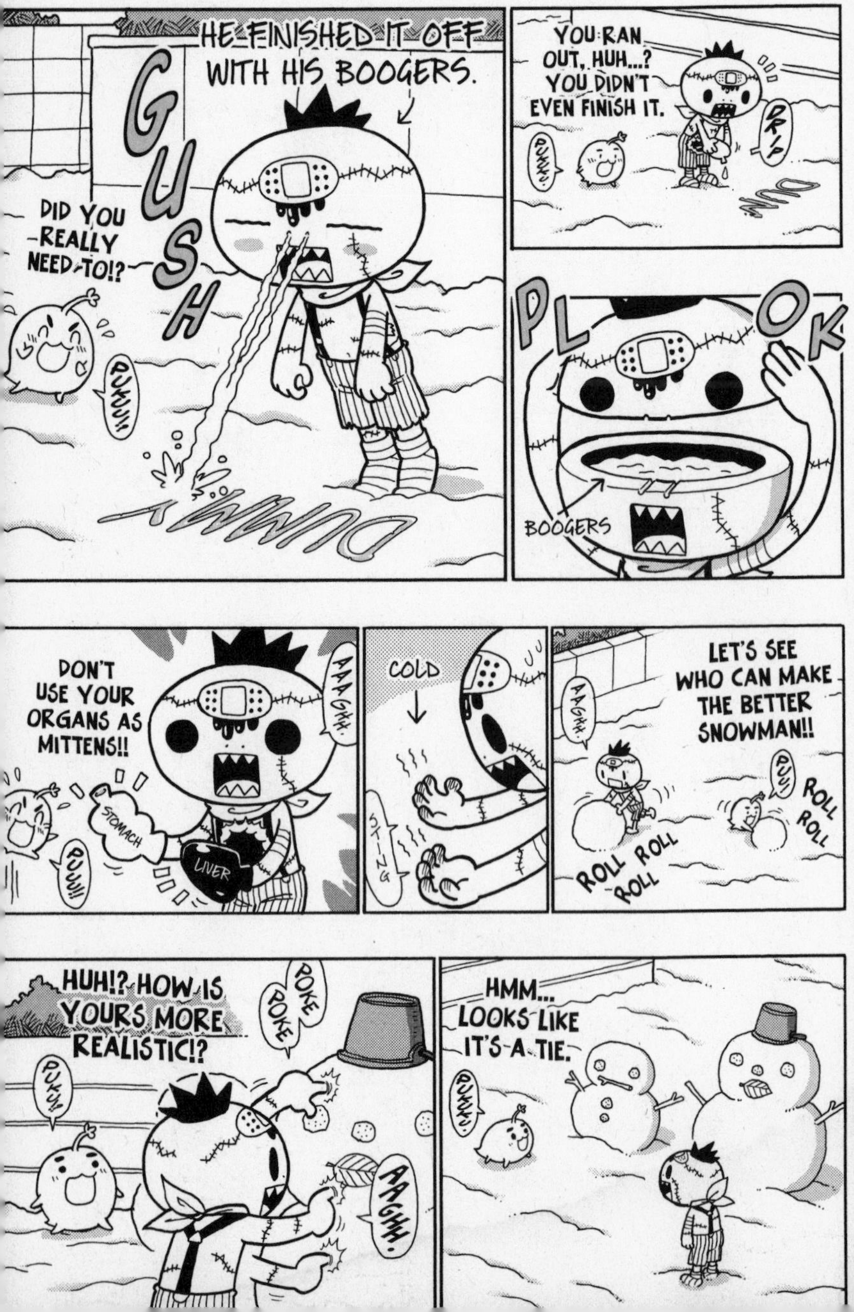
YOU RAN OUT, HUH...? YOU DIDN'T EVEN FINISH IT.
DRIP
PLOK
BOOGERS
HE FINISHED IT OFF WITH HIS BOOGERS.
GUSH
DID YOU REALLY NEED TO!?
LET'S SEE WHO CAN MAKE THE BETTER SNOWMAN!!
ROLL ROLL
ROLL ROLL ROLL
COLD
STING
DON'T USE YOUR ORGANS AS MITTENS!!
STOMACH
LIVER
HMM... LOOKS LIKE IT'S A TIE.
POKE POKE
HUH!? HOW IS YOURS MORE REALISTIC!?

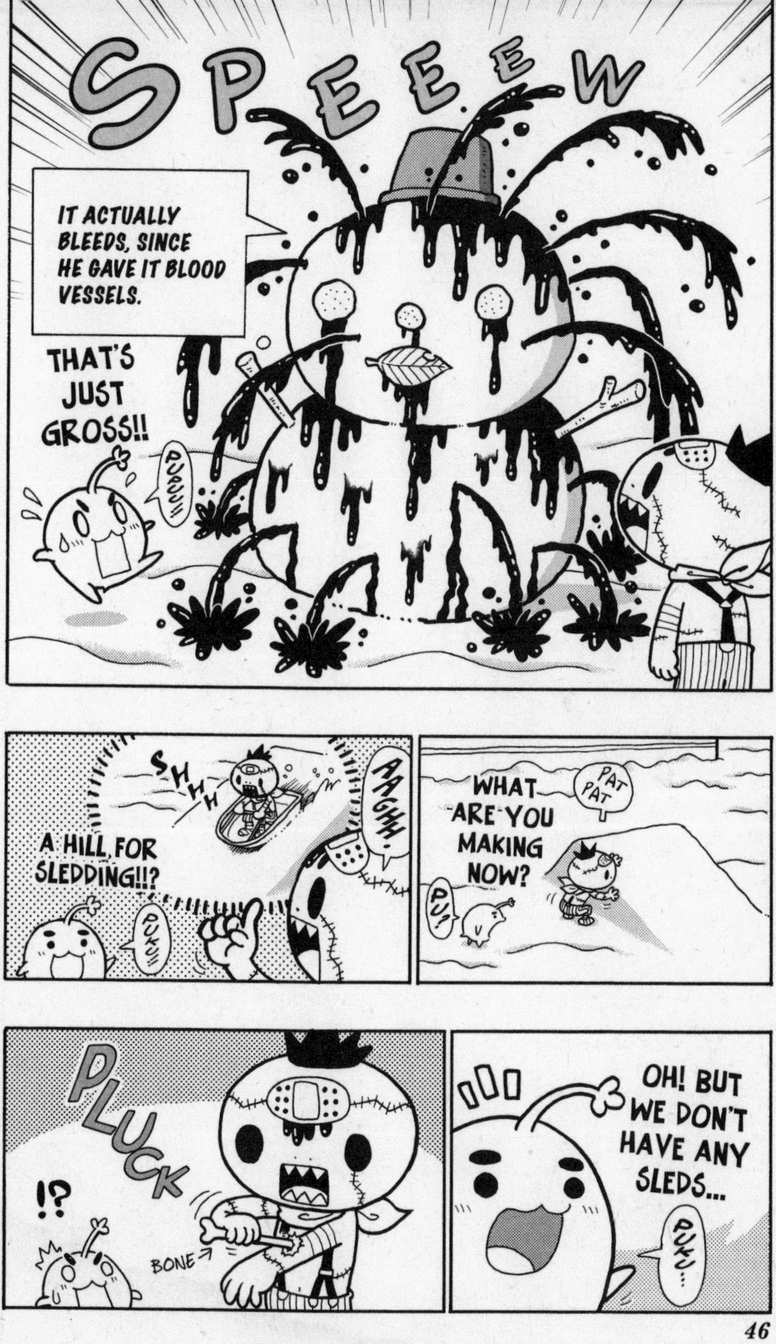
SPEEEW
IT ACTUALLY BLEEDS, SINCE HE GAVE IT BLOOD VESSELS.
THAT'S JUST GROSS!!
WHAT ARE YOU MAKING NOW?
PAT PAT
PU?
A HILL, FOR SLEDDING!!?
AAGHH
SHHH
PUKU!!
OH! BUT WE DON'T HAVE ANY SLEDS...
PUKU...
PLUCK
!?
BONE

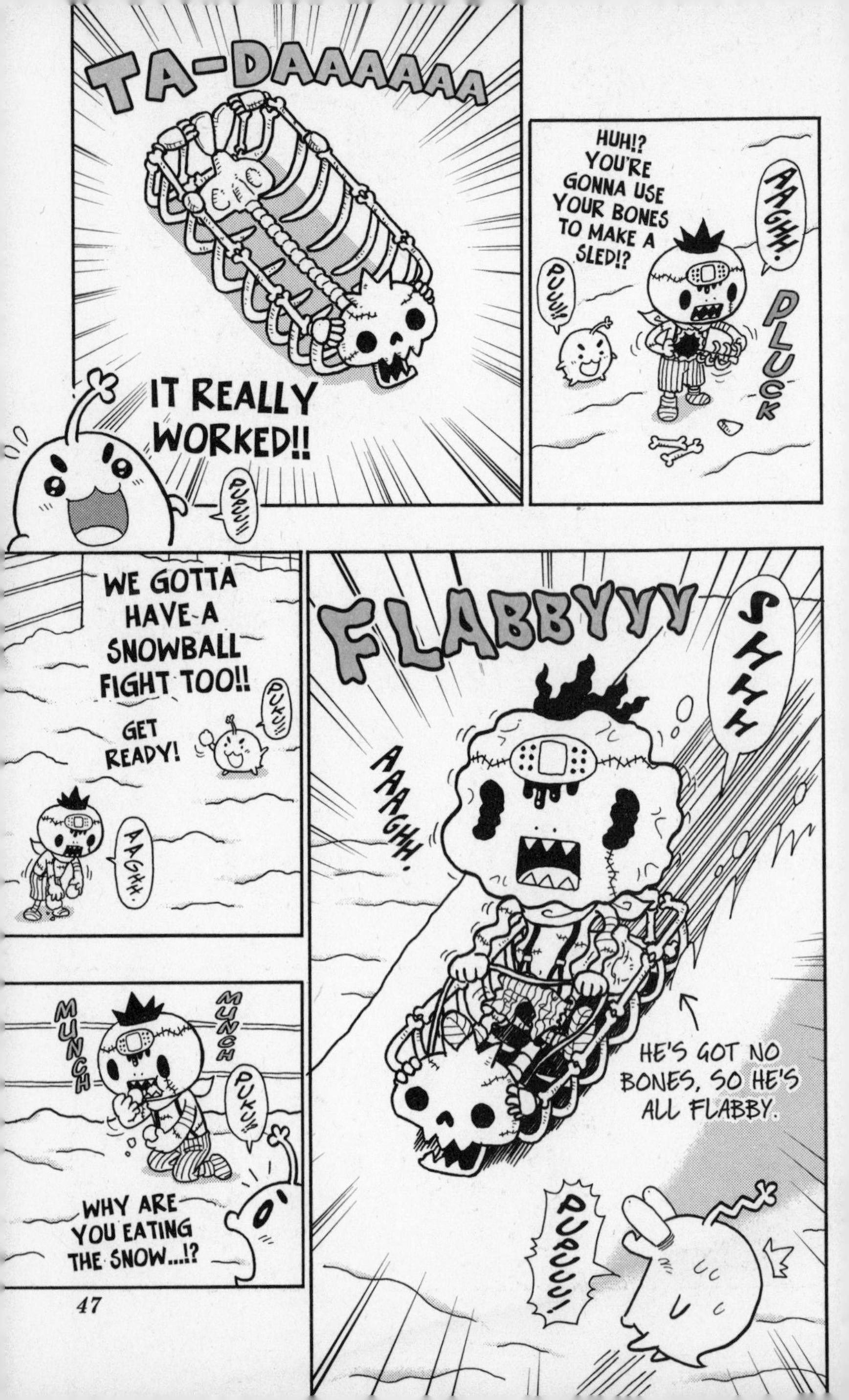
HUH!? YOU'RE GONNA USE YOUR BONES TO MAKE A SLED!?
AAGHH.
PUUU!!
PLUCK
TA-DAAAAAAA
IT REALLY WORKED!!
PUUUU!!
FLABBYYY
SHHHH
AAAAGHH.
HE'S GOT NO BONES, SO HE'S ALL FLABBY.
PUPUUUU!
WE GOTTA HAVE A SNOWBALL FIGHT TOO!!
PUKUU!!
GET READY!
AAGHH.
MUNCH
MUNCH
PUKUU!
WHY ARE YOU EATING THE SNOW...!?

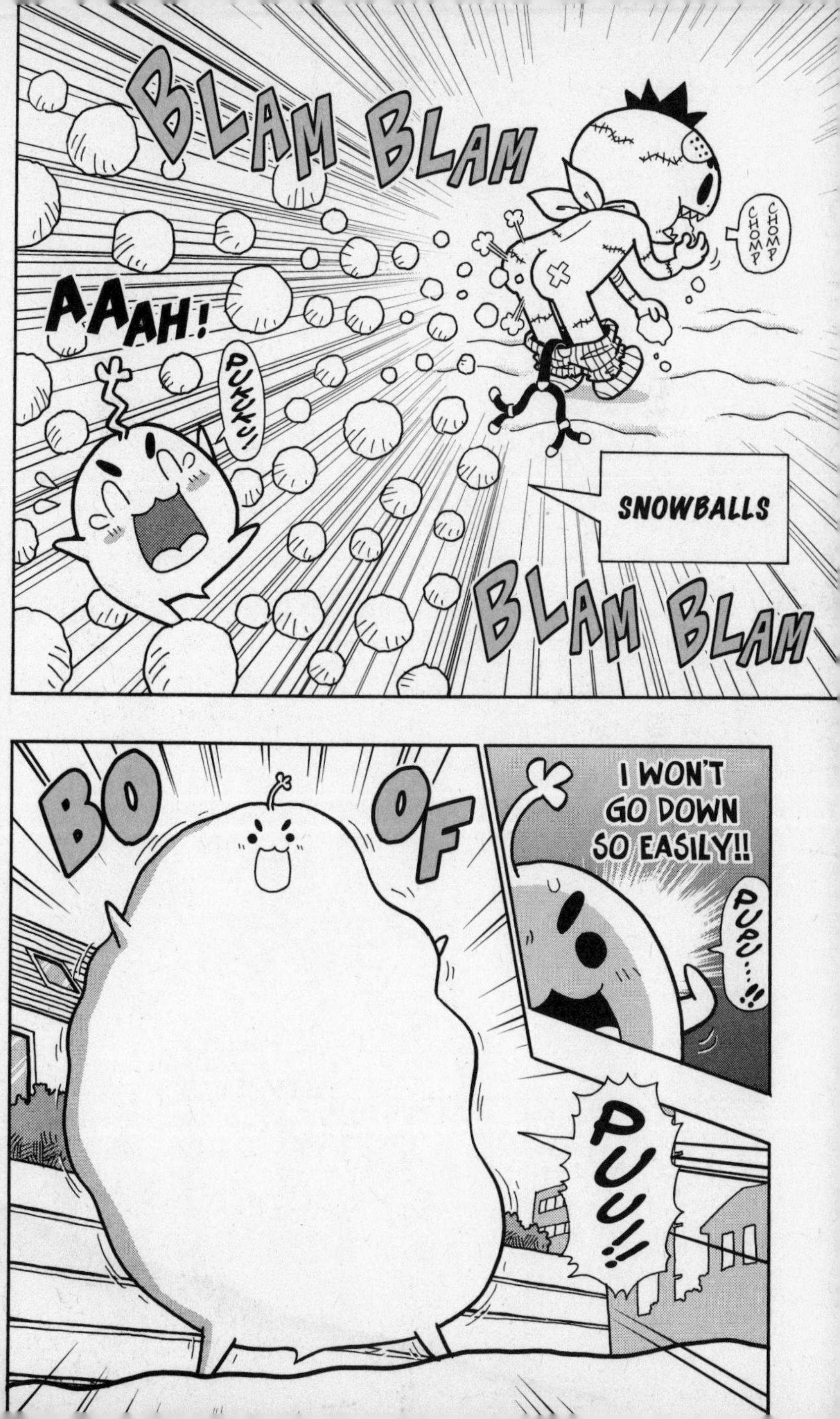
CHOMP CHOMP
BLAM BLAM
SNOWBALLS
PUKUKU!
AAAH!
BLAM BLAM
I WON'T GO DOWN SO EASILY!!
PUPU...!!
BOOF
PUU!!

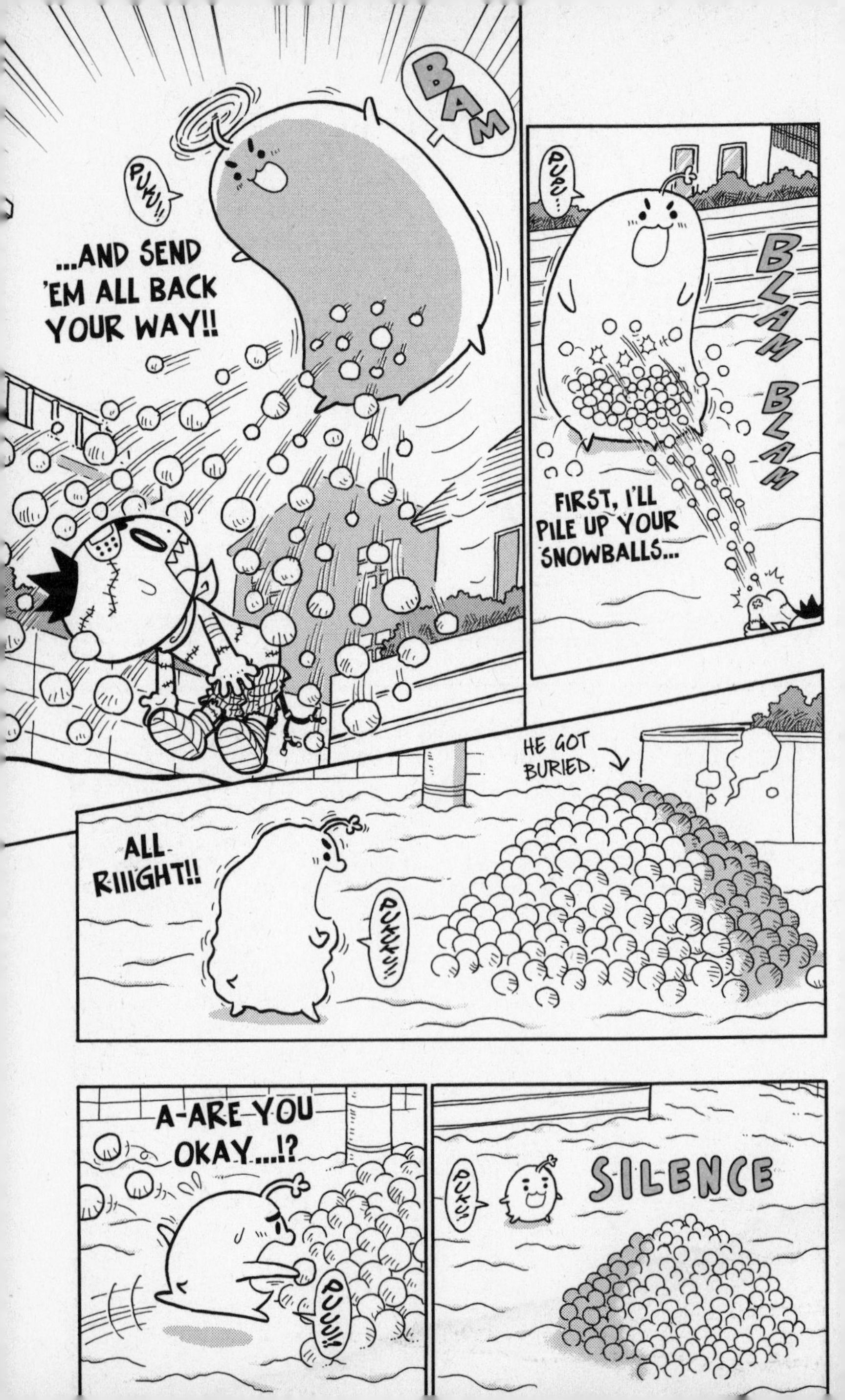
PUKU...
BLAM BLAM
FIRST, I'LL PILE UP YOUR SNOWBALLS...
BAM
PUKU!!
...AND SEND 'EM ALL BACK YOUR WAY!!
HE GOT BURIED.
PUKUKU!!
ALL RIIIGHT!!
SILENCE
PUKU!?
A-ARE YOU OKAY...!?
PUUU!!

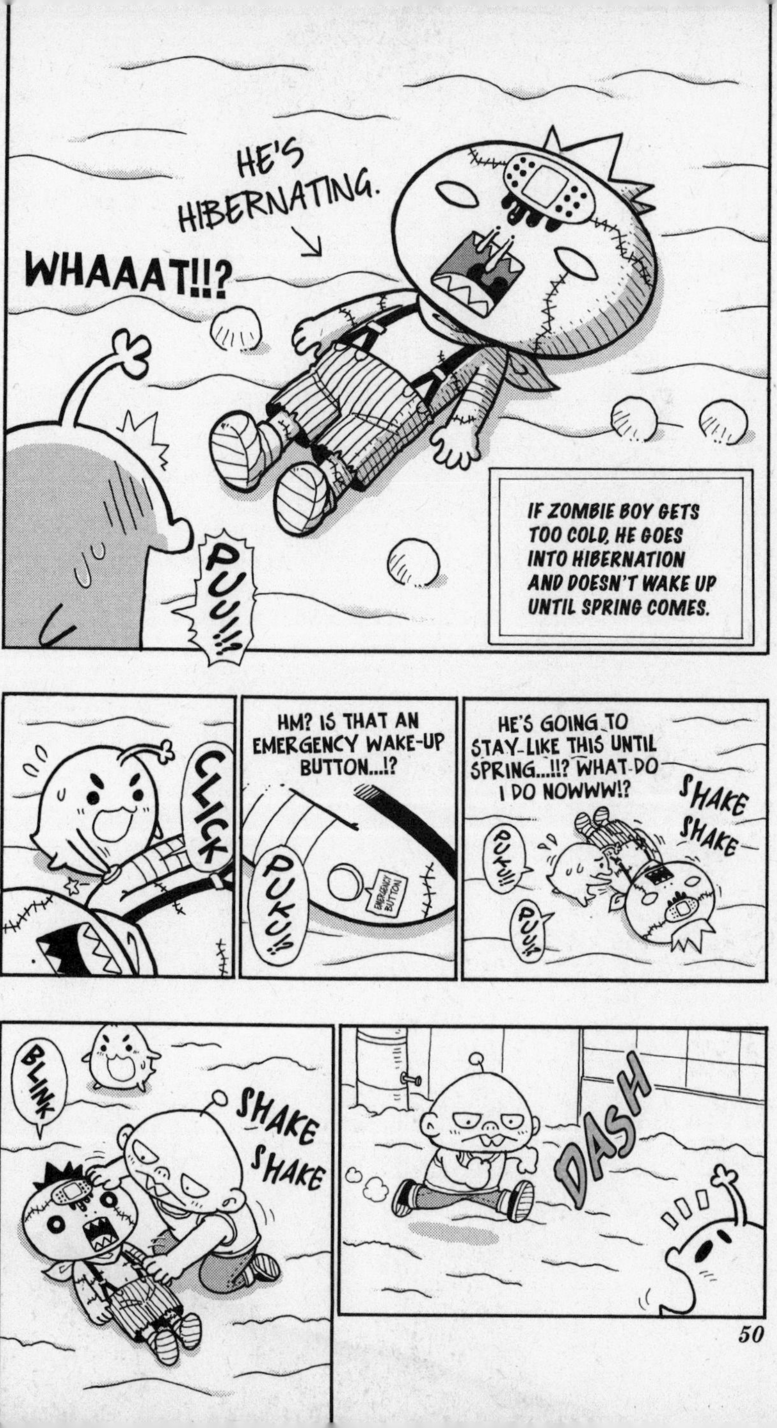
HE'S HIBERNATING.
WHAAAT!!?
IF ZOMBIE BOY GETS TOO COLD, HE GOES INTO HIBERNATION AND DOESN'T WAKE UP UNTIL SPRING COMES.
PUUU!!?
HE'S GOING TO STAY LIKE THIS UNTIL SPRING...!!? WHAT DO I DO NOWWW!?
SHAKE SHAKE
PUKU!!
PUU!?
HM? IS THAT AN EMERGENCY WAKE-UP BUTTON...!?
EMERGENCY BUTTON
PUKU!?
CLICK
DASH
SHAKE SHAKE
BLINK

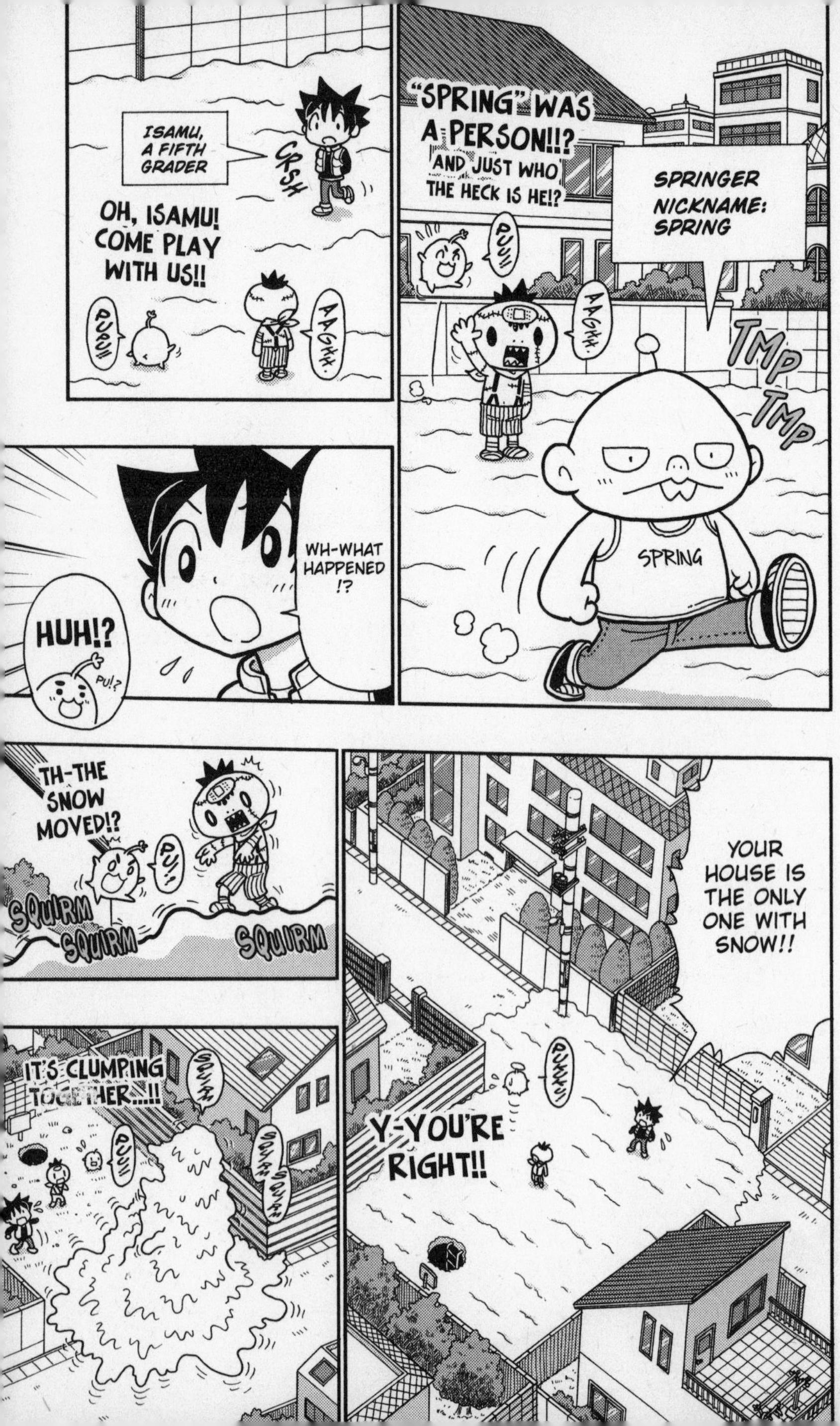

"SPRING" WAS A PERSON!!?
AND JUST WHO THE HECK IS HE!?
SPRINGER NICKNAME: SPRING
PU!!
AAGHH.
TMP TMP
SPRING
ISAMU, A FIFTH GRADER
CRSH
OH, ISAMU! COME PLAY WITH US!!
AAGHH.
PU!!
WH-WHAT HAPPENED!?
HUH!?
PU!?
YOUR HOUSE IS THE ONLY ONE WITH SNOW!!
PUHH!
Y-YOU'RE RIGHT!!
TH-THE SNOW MOVED!?
PU!?
SQUIRM
SQUIRM
SQUIRM
IT'S CLUMPING TOGETHER...!!
SQUIRM
PU!!
SQUIRM
SQUIRM

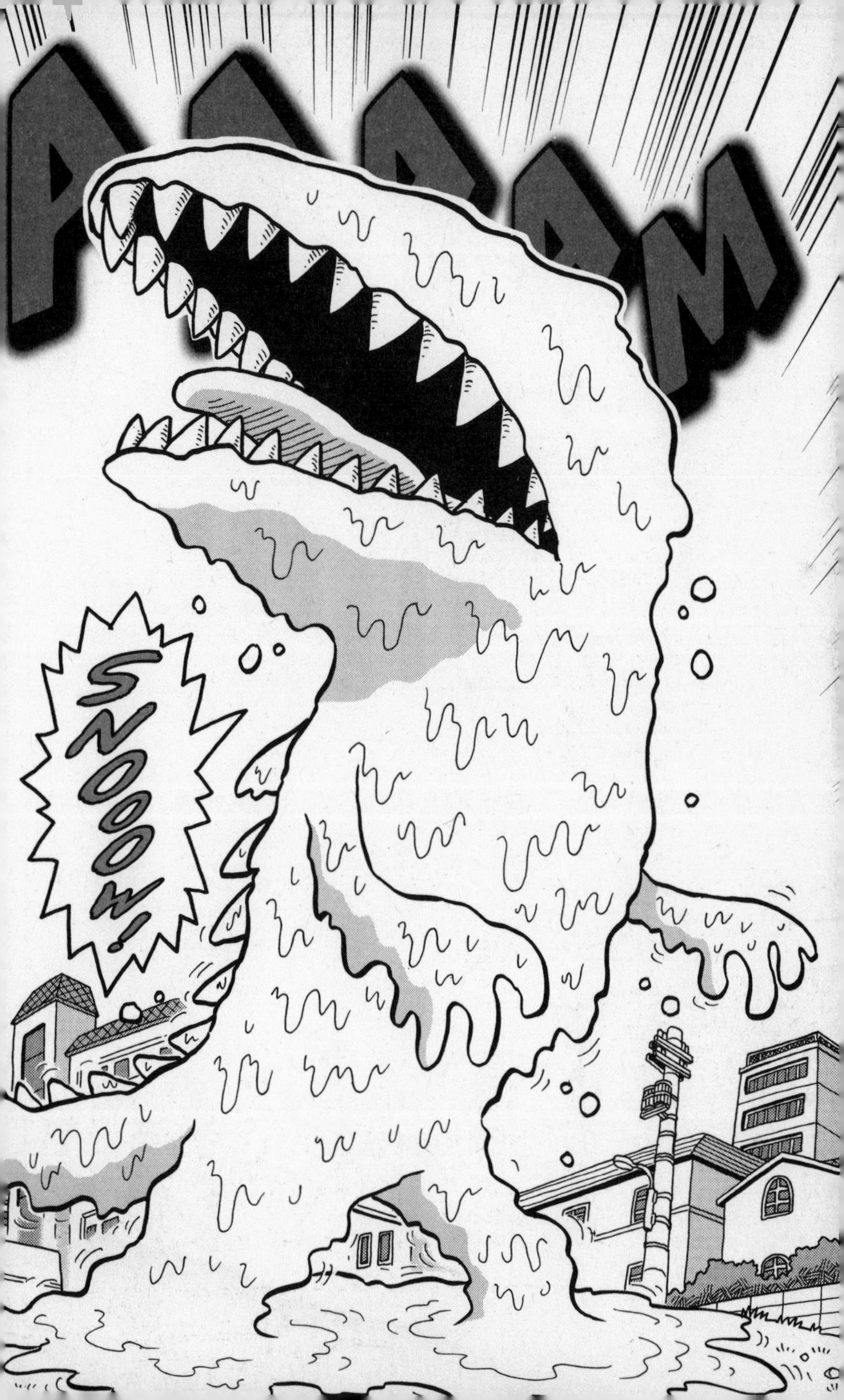

PAPAM
SNOOOW!

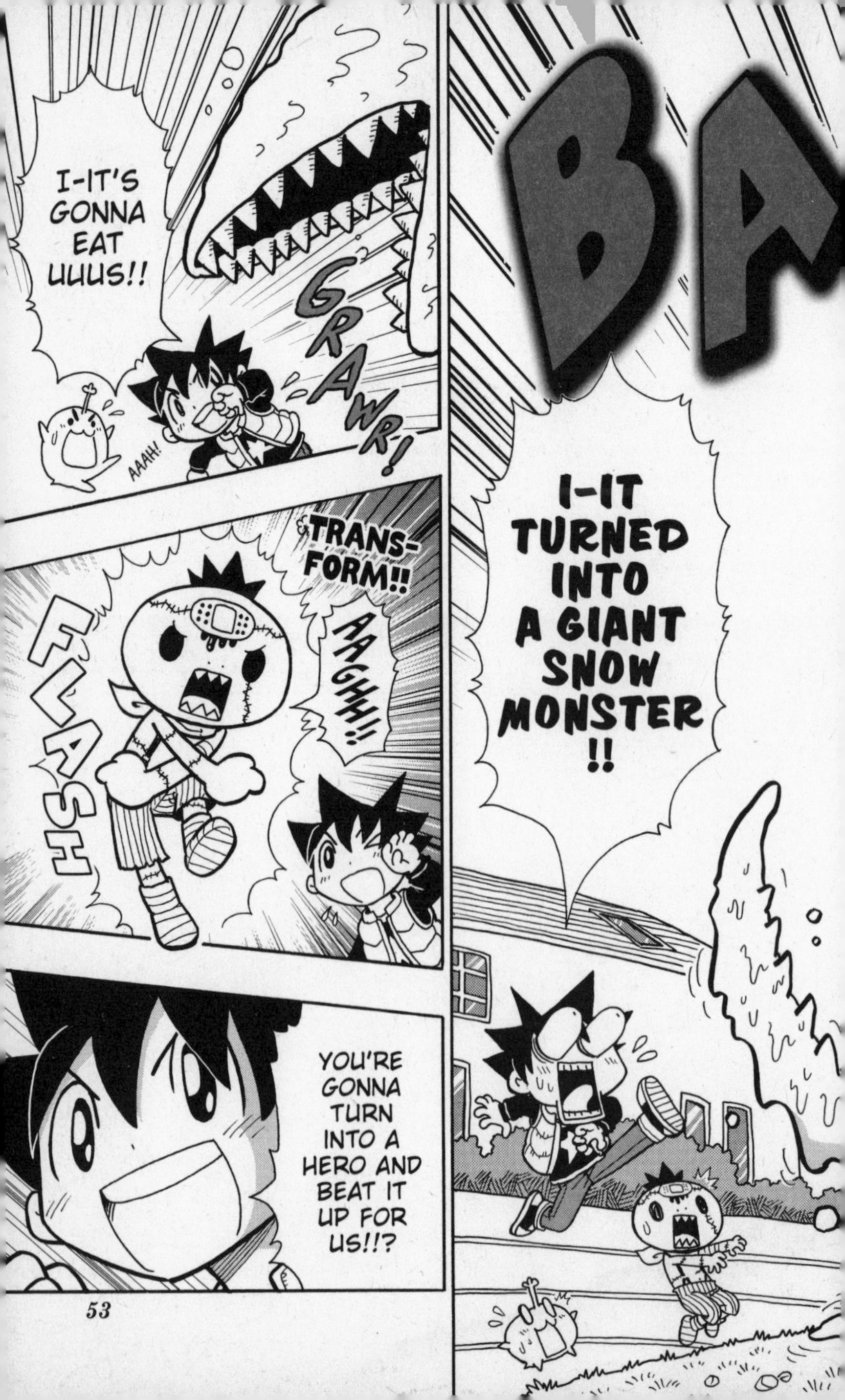
BA
I-IT TURNED INTO A GIANT SNOW MONSTER !!
GRAWR!
I-IT'S GONNA EAT UUUS!!
AAAH!
TRANS-FORM!!
AAGHH!!
FLASH
YOU'RE GONNA TURN INTO A HERO AND BEAT IT UP FOR US!!?

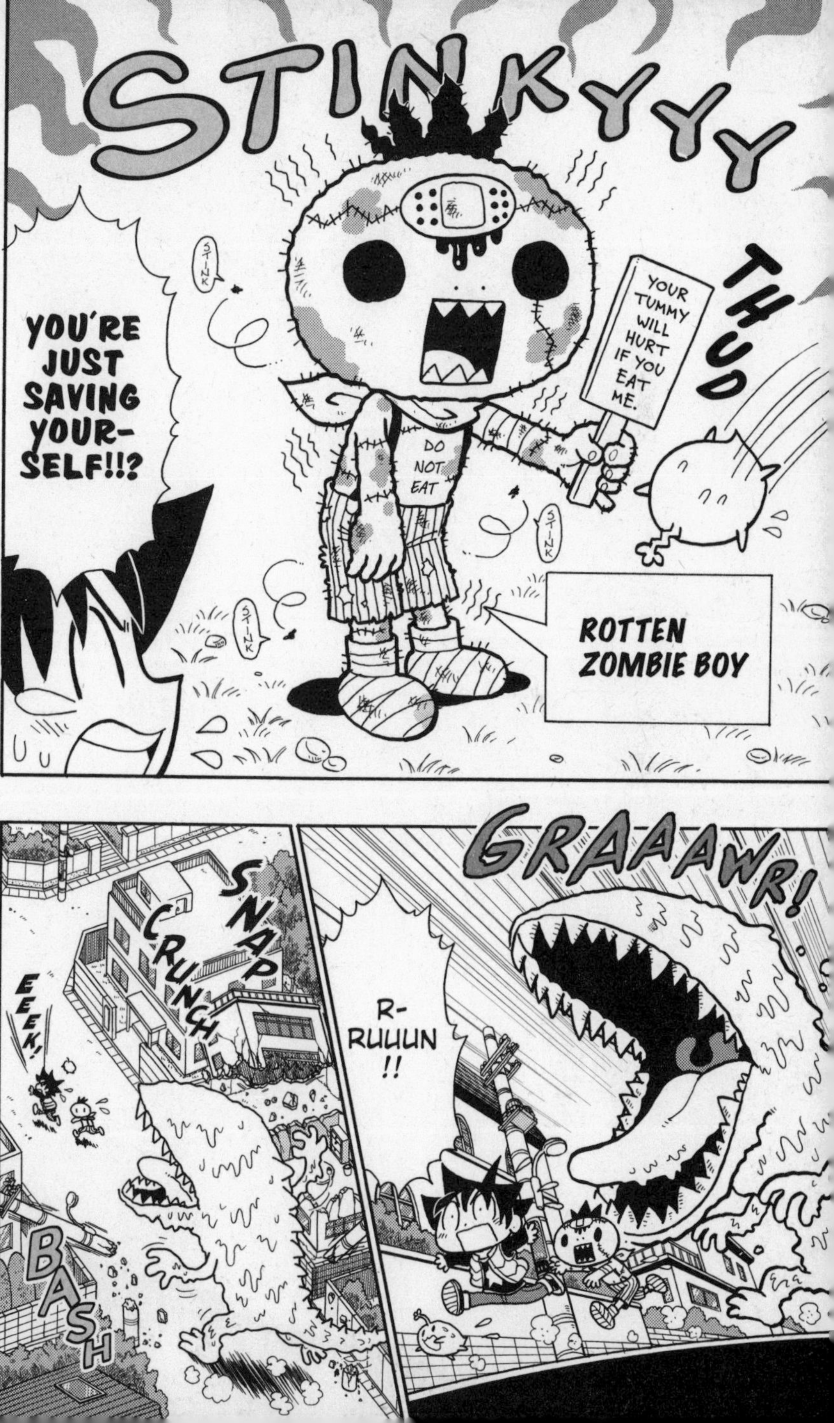
STINKYYY
THUD
YOUR TUMMY WILL HURT IF YOU EAT ME.
STINK
ROTTEN ZOMBIE BOY
DO NOT EAT
STINK
STINK
YOU'RE JUST SAVING YOUR-SELF!!?
GRAAAWR!
R-RUUUN!!
SNAP
CRUNCH
EEEK!
BASH

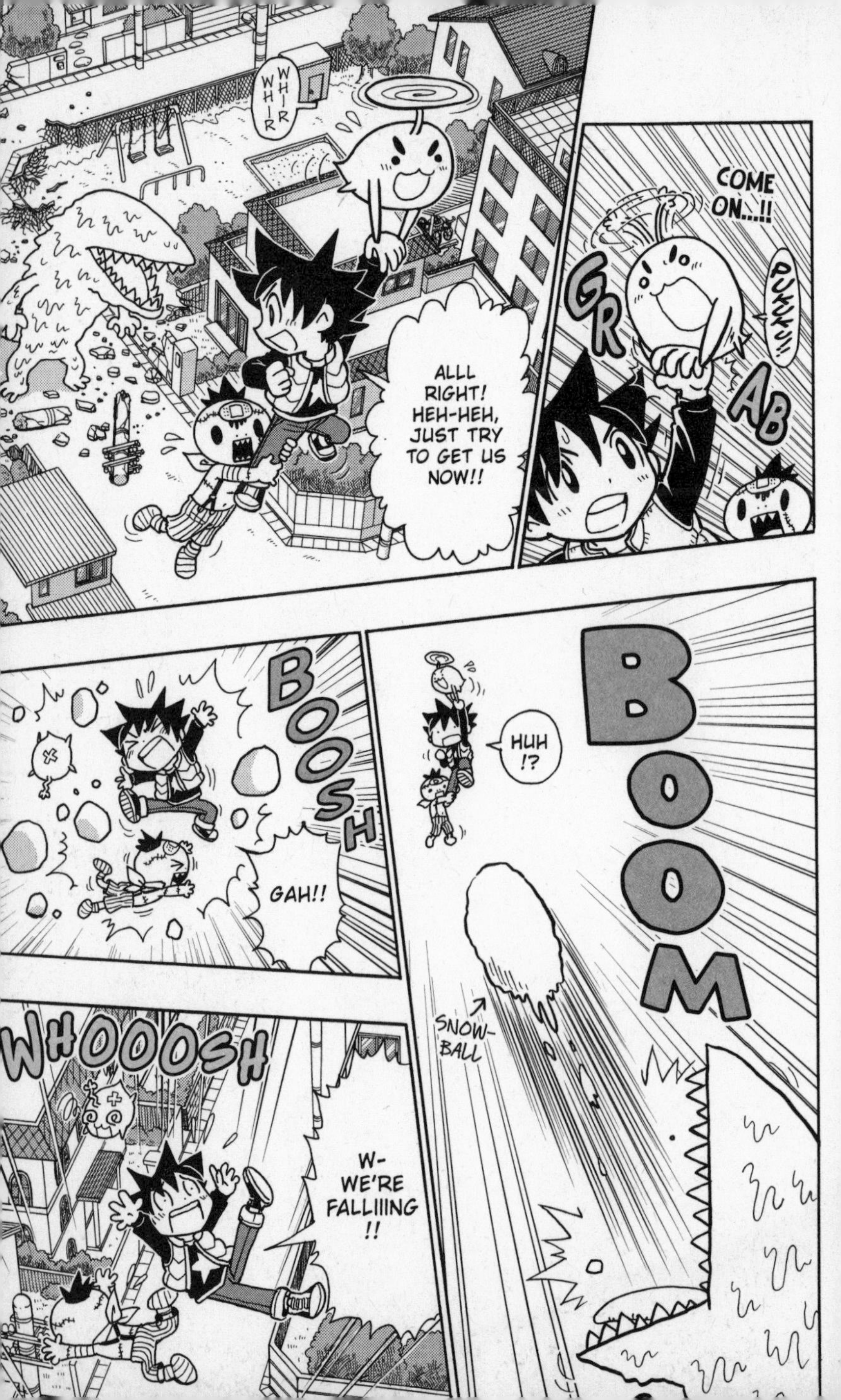
COME ON...!!
GRAB
PUKUU!!
WHIR WHIR
ALLL RIGHT! HEH-HEH, JUST TRY TO GET US NOW!!
BOOM
HUH!?
SNOW-BALL
BOOSH
GAH!!
WHOOOSH
W- WE'RE FALLIIING!!

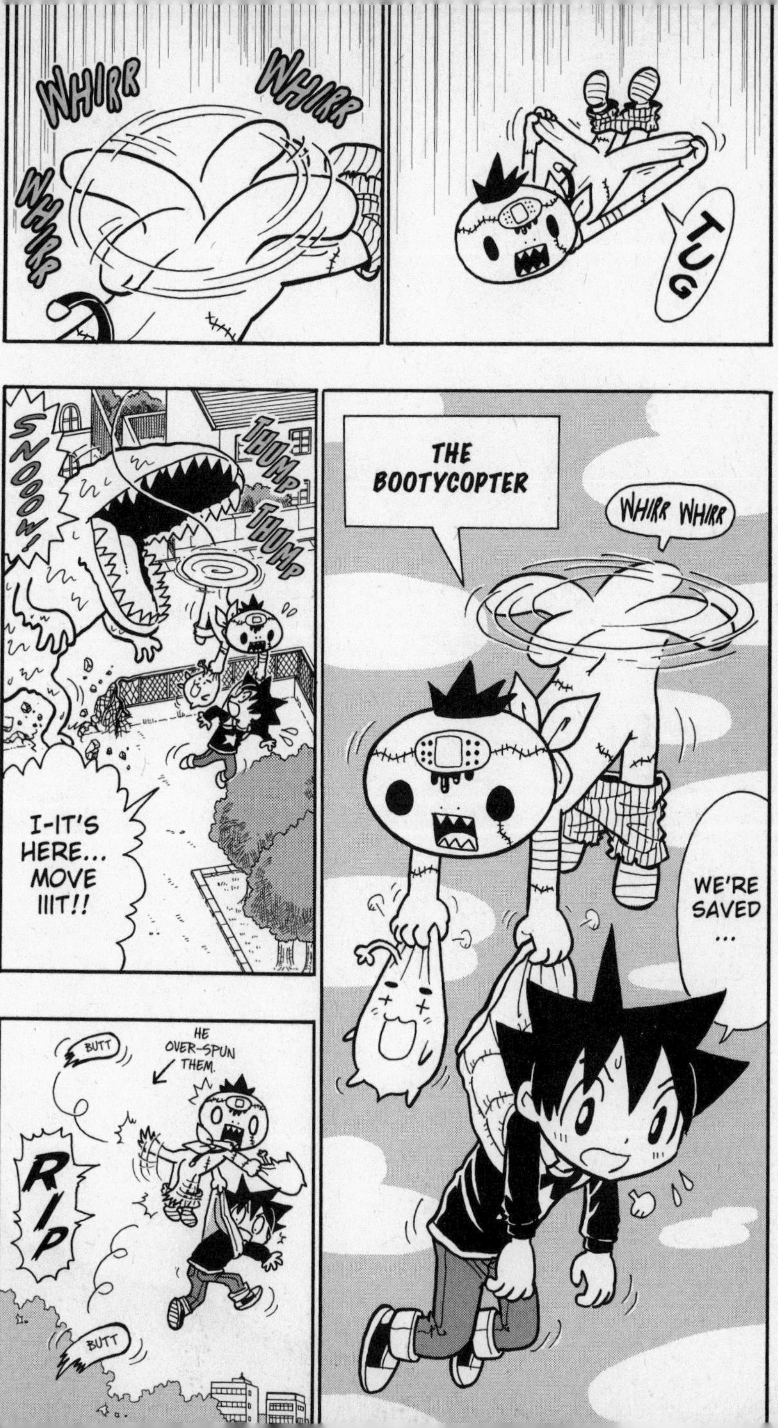
TUG
WHIRR
WHIRR
WHIRR
THE BOOTYCOPTER
WHIRR WHIRR
WE'RE SAVED...
SNOOOOW!
THUMP THUMP
I-IT'S HERE... MOVE IIIT!!
BUTT
HE OVER-SPUN THEM.
RIP
BUTT

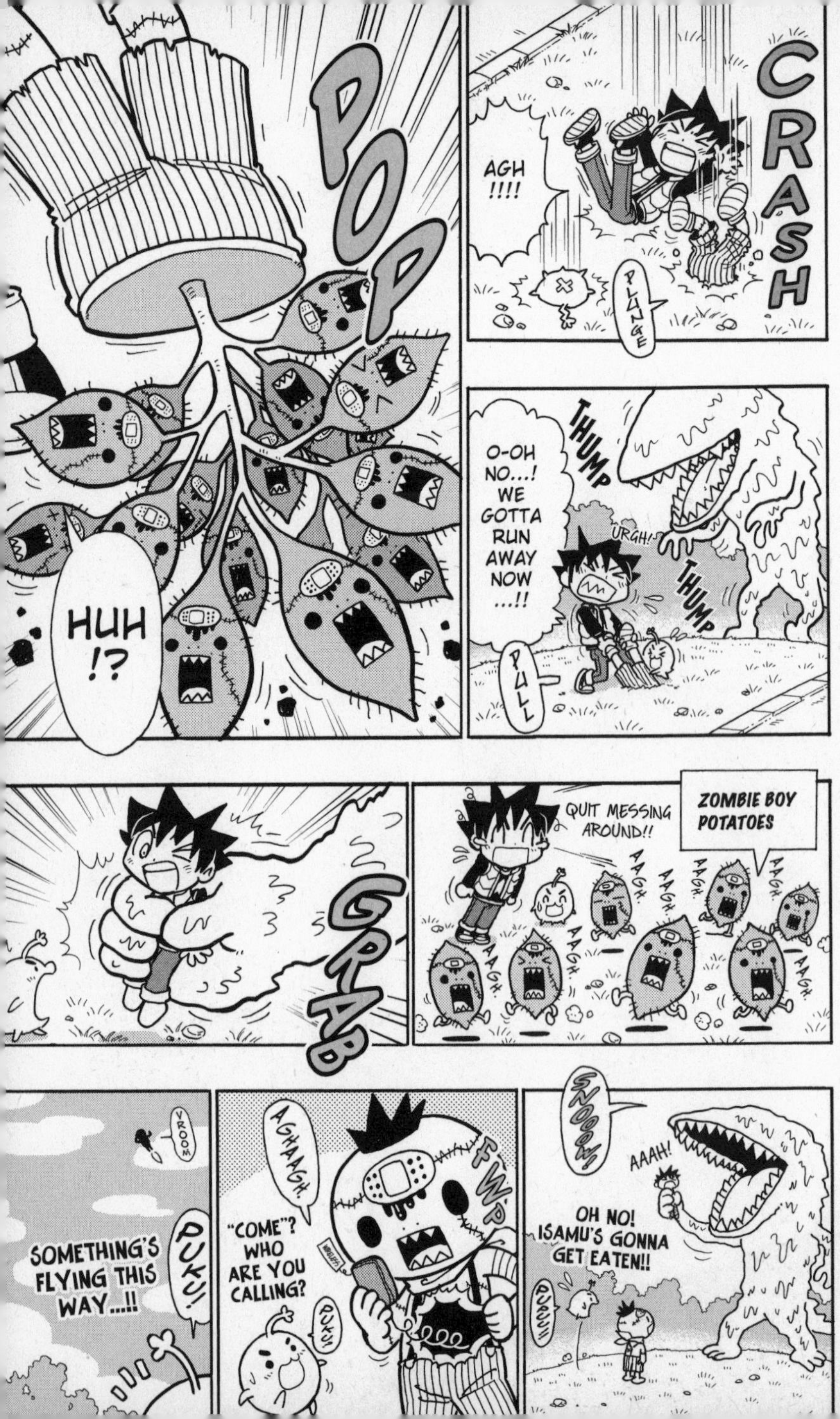
CRASH
AGH !!!!
PLUNGE
O-OH NO...! WE GOTTA RUN AWAY NOW ...!!
THUMP
URGH!
THUMP
PULL
POP
HUH !?
ZOMBIE BOY POTATOES
QUIT MESSING AROUND!!
AAGH.
AAGH.
AAGH.
AAGH.
AAGH.
AAGH.
AAGH.
GRAB
GNOOOW!
AAAH!
OH NO! ISAMU'S GONNA GET EATEN!!
PUKUU!!
AGHAAGH.
FWP
"COME"? WHO ARE YOU CALLING?
PUKU!
VROOM
SOMETHING'S FLYING THIS WAY...!!
PUKU!

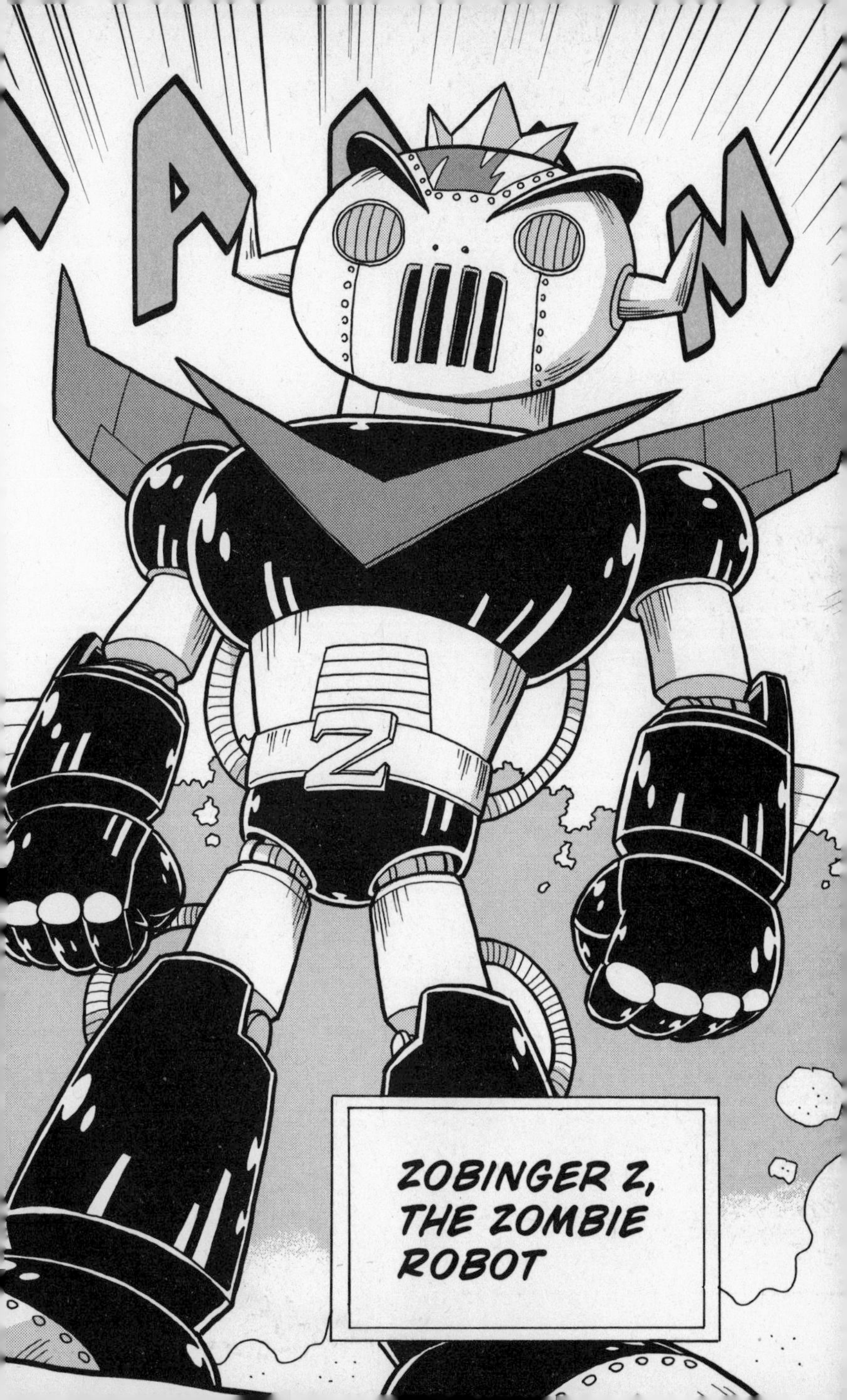
AAM
ZOBINGER Z, THE ZOMBIE ROBOT

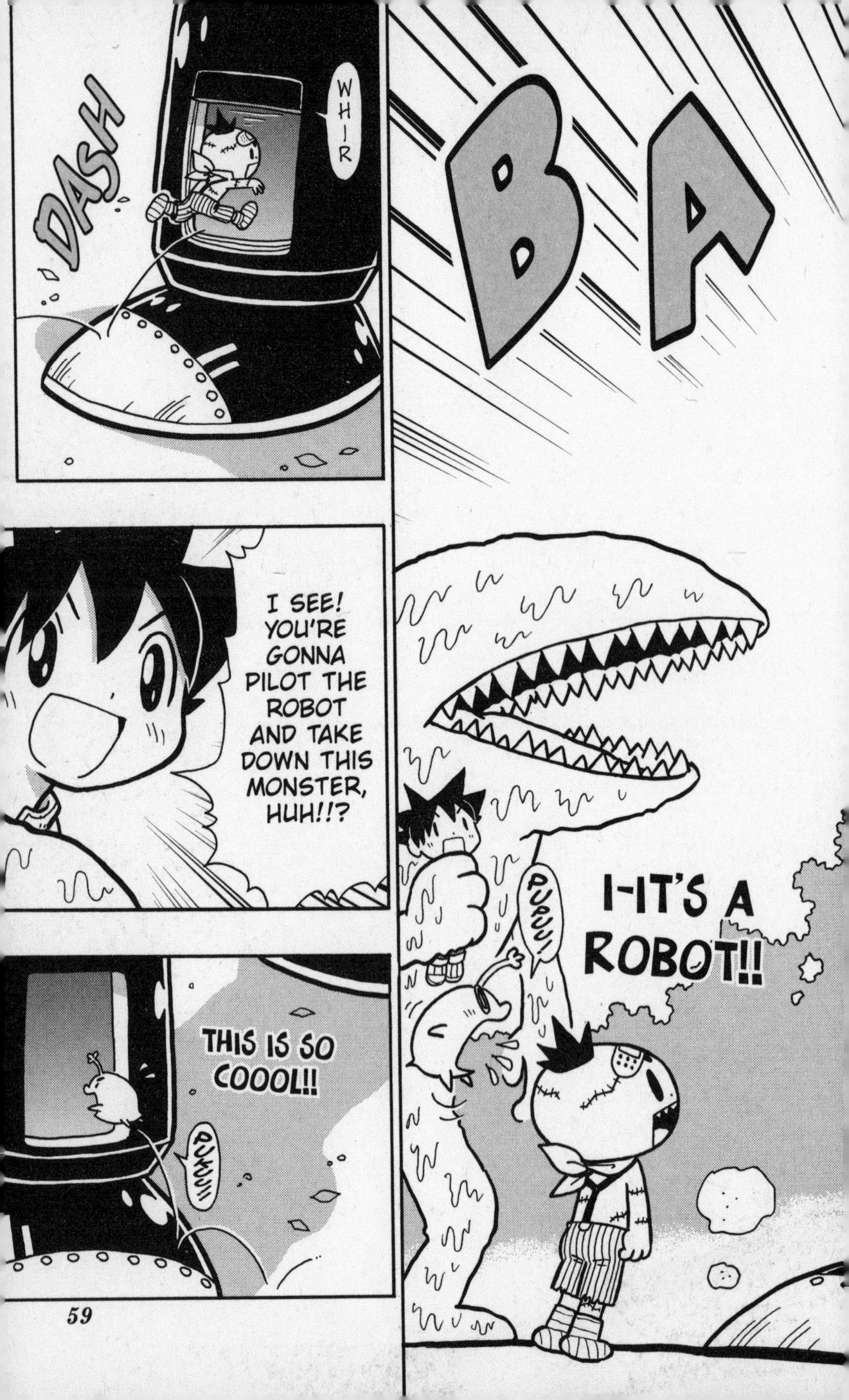
BA
PUPUU!
I-IT'S A ROBOT!!
WHIR
DASH
I SEE! YOU'RE GONNA PILOT THE ROBOT AND TAKE DOWN THIS MONSTER, HUH!!?
THIS IS SO COOOL!!
PUKUU!!

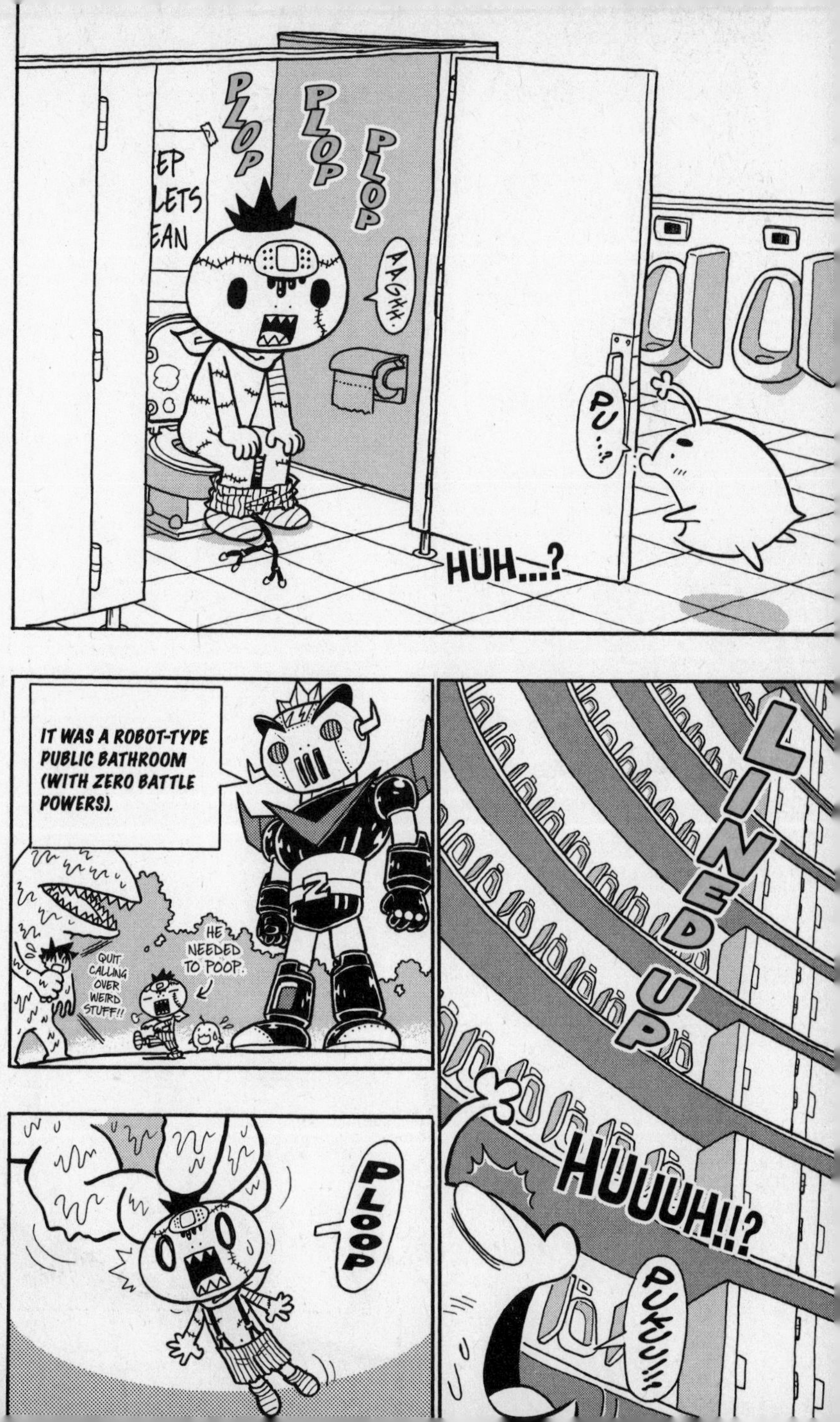

EP
LETS
EAN
PLOP
PLOP
PLOP
AAGHX.
PU...?
HUH...?
LINED UP
HUUUH!!?
PUKUU!!?
IT WAS A ROBOT-TYPE PUBLIC BATHROOM (WITH ZERO BATTLE POWERS).
HE NEEDED TO POOP.
QUIT CALLING OVER WEIRD STUFF!!
PLOOP

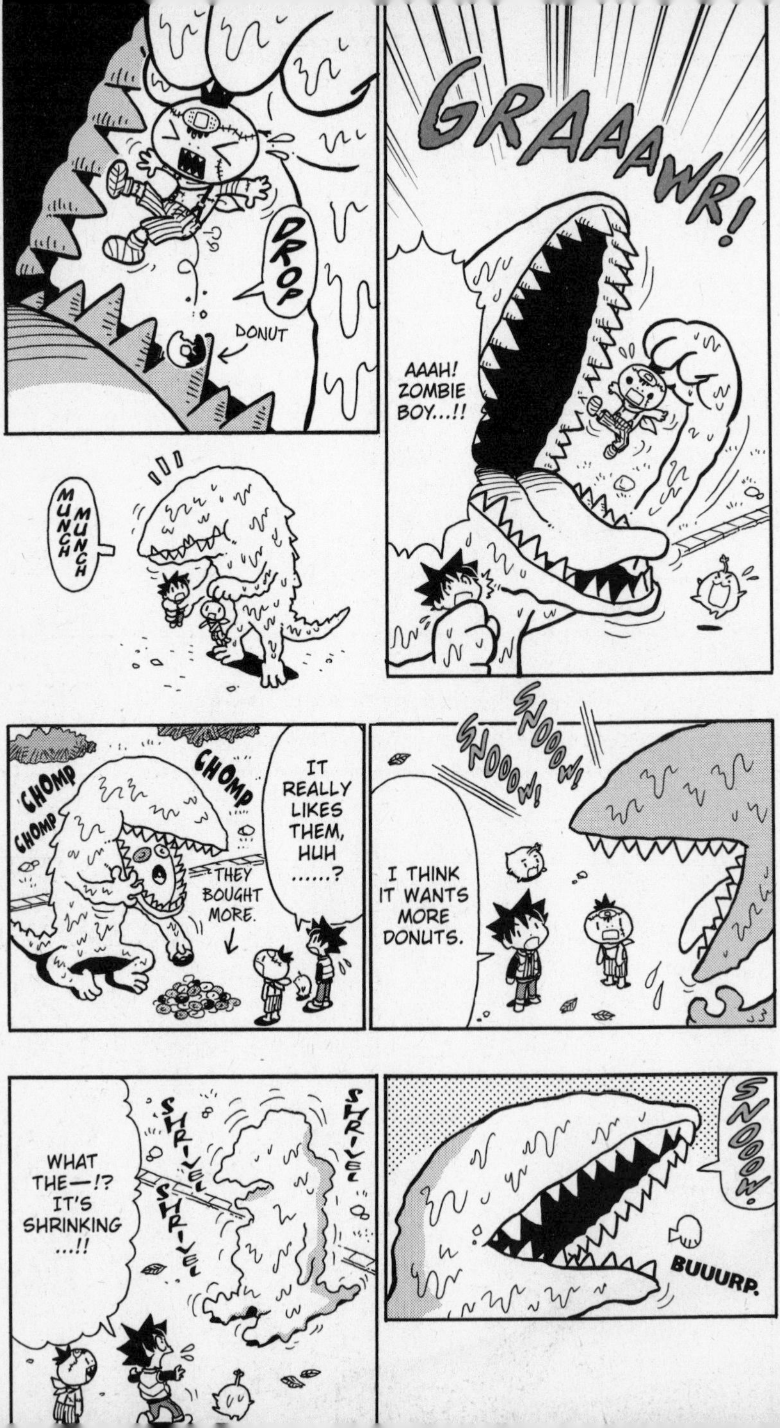
GRAAAAWR!
AAAH! ZOMBIE BOY...!!
DROP
DONUT
MUNCH MUNCH
SNOOOW! SNOOOW!
I THINK IT WANTS MORE DONUTS.
CHOMP CHOMP CHOMP
IT REALLY LIKES THEM, HUH ......?
THEY BOUGHT MORE.
SNOOOW.
BUUURP.
SHRIVEL SHRIVEL SHRIVEL
WHAT THE—!? IT'S SHRINKING ...!!

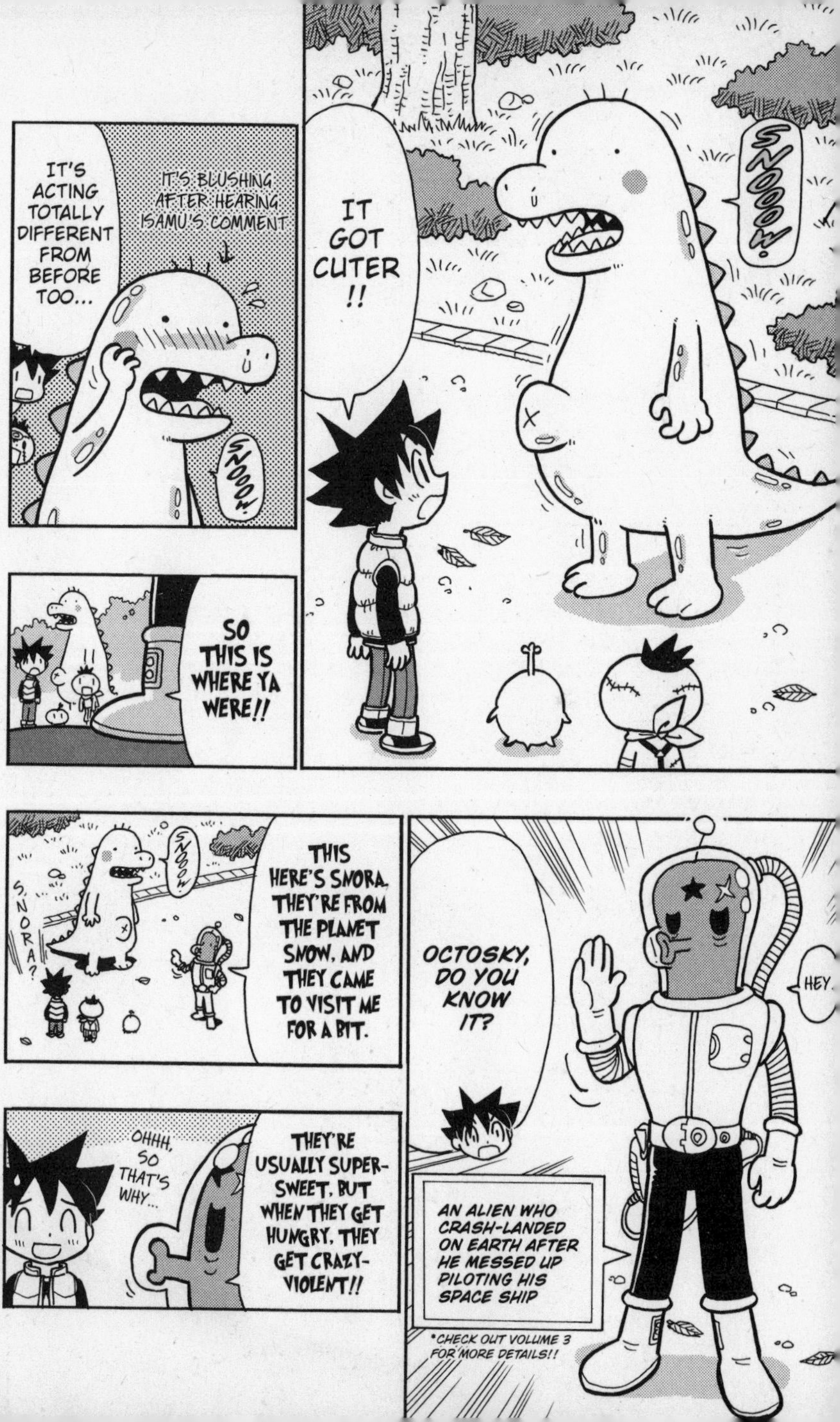
SNOOOW!
IT GOT CUTER!!
IT'S ACTING TOTALLY DIFFERENT FROM BEFORE TOO...
IT'S BLUSHING AFTER HEARING ISAMU'S COMMENT
SNOOOW!
SO THIS IS WHERE YA WERE!!
HEY.
OCTOSKY, DO YOU KNOW IT?
AN ALIEN WHO CRASH-LANDED ON EARTH AFTER HE MESSED UP PILOTING HIS SPACE SHIP
*CHECK OUT VOLUME 3 FOR MORE DETAILS!!
SNOOOW
THIS HERE'S SNORA. THEY'RE FROM THE PLANET SNOW, AND THEY CAME TO VISIT ME FOR A BIT.
SNORA?
THEY'RE USUALLY SUPER-SWEET, BUT WHEN THEY GET HUNGRY, THEY GET CRAZY-VIOLENT!!
OHHH, SO THAT'S WHY...

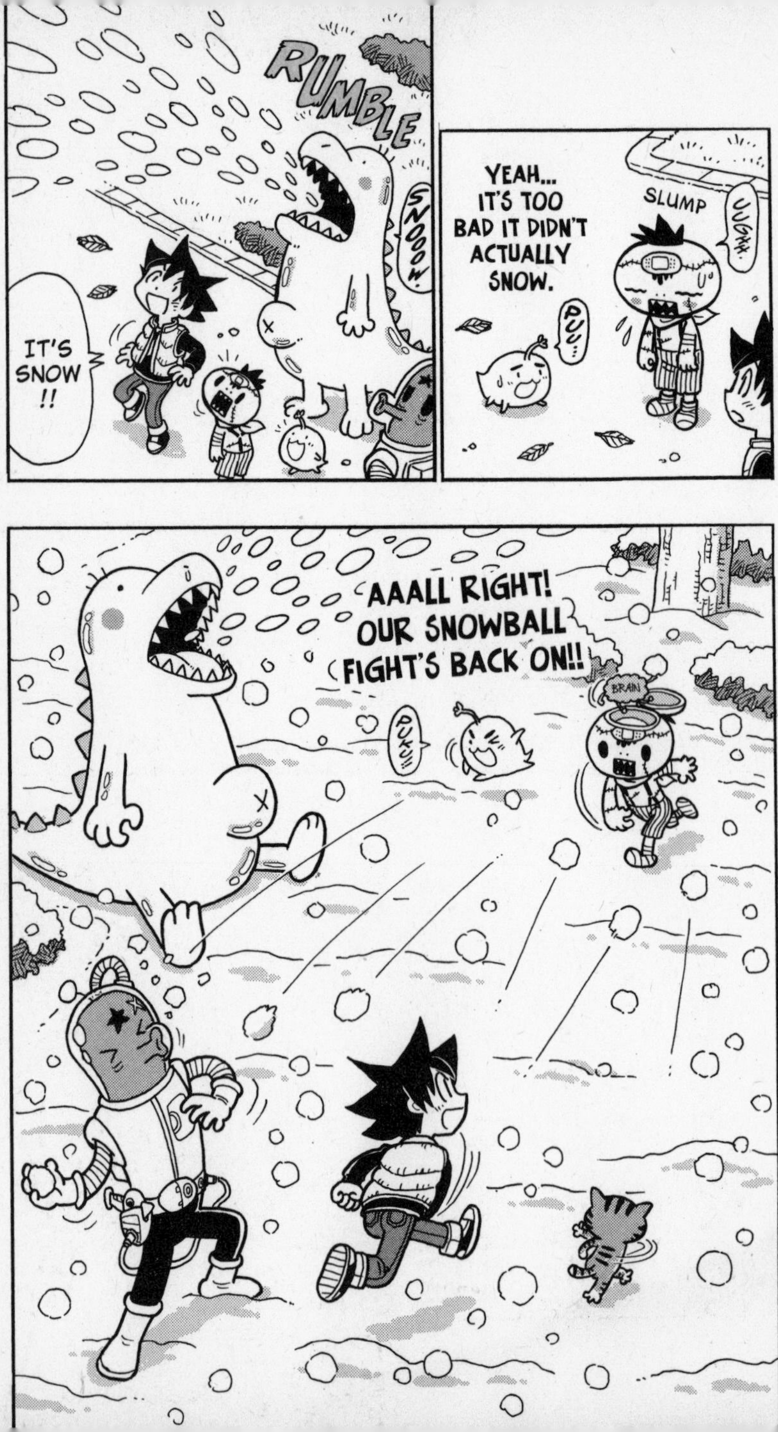
SLUMP
UUGHH.
YEAH... IT'S TOO BAD IT DIDN'T ACTUALLY SNOW.
PUU...
RUMBLE
SNOOOOW!
IT'S SNOW!!
AAALL RIGHT! OUR SNOWBALL FIGHT'S BACK ON!!
BRAIN
PUKU!!

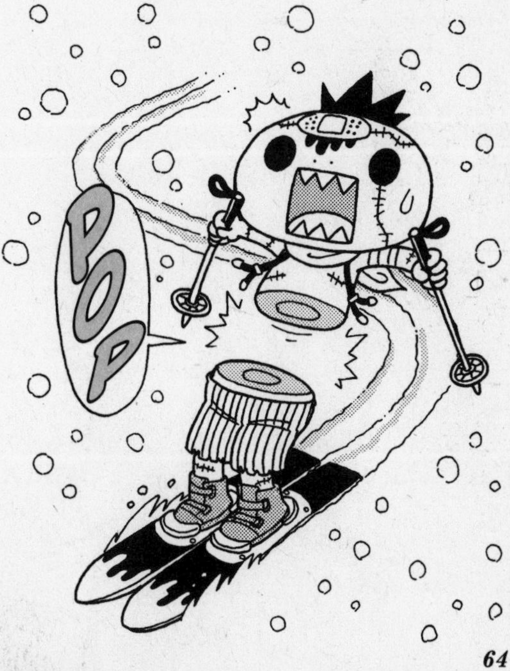
POP

FOURTEEN SHORT JOKEZ IN A ROW!

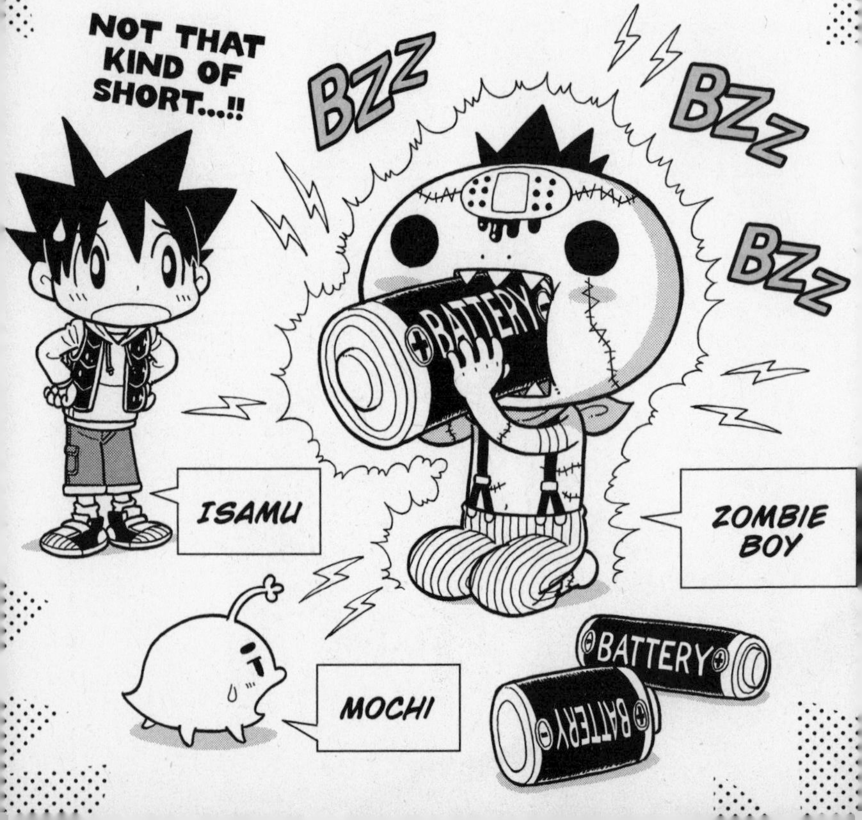
NOT THAT KIND OF SHORT...!!
BZZ
BZZ
BZZ
BATTERY
ISAMU
ZOMBIE BOY
MOCHI
BATTERY
BATTERY

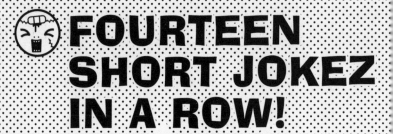

BLOOD TYPES

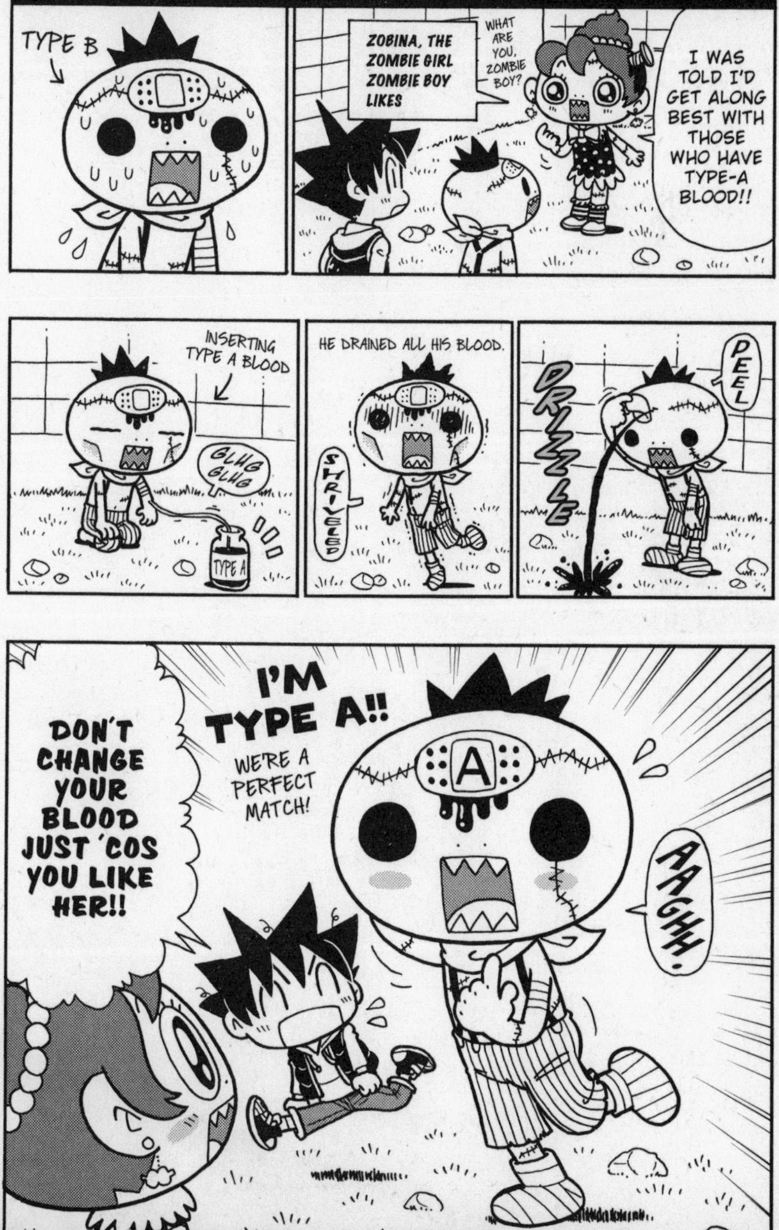
I WAS TOLD I'D GET ALONG BEST WITH THOSE WHO HAVE TYPE-A BLOOD!!
WHAT ARE YOU, ZOMBIE BOY?
ZOBINA, THE ZOMBIE GIRL ZOMBIE BOY LIKES
TYPE B
PEEL
DRIZZLE
HE DRAINED ALL HIS BLOOD.
SHRIVELED
INSERTING TYPE A BLOOD
GLUG GLUG
TYPE A
I'M TYPE A!!
WE'RE A PERFECT MATCH!
AAGHH.
DON'T CHANGE YOUR BLOOD JUST 'COS YOU LIKE HER!!

MEASUREMENTS

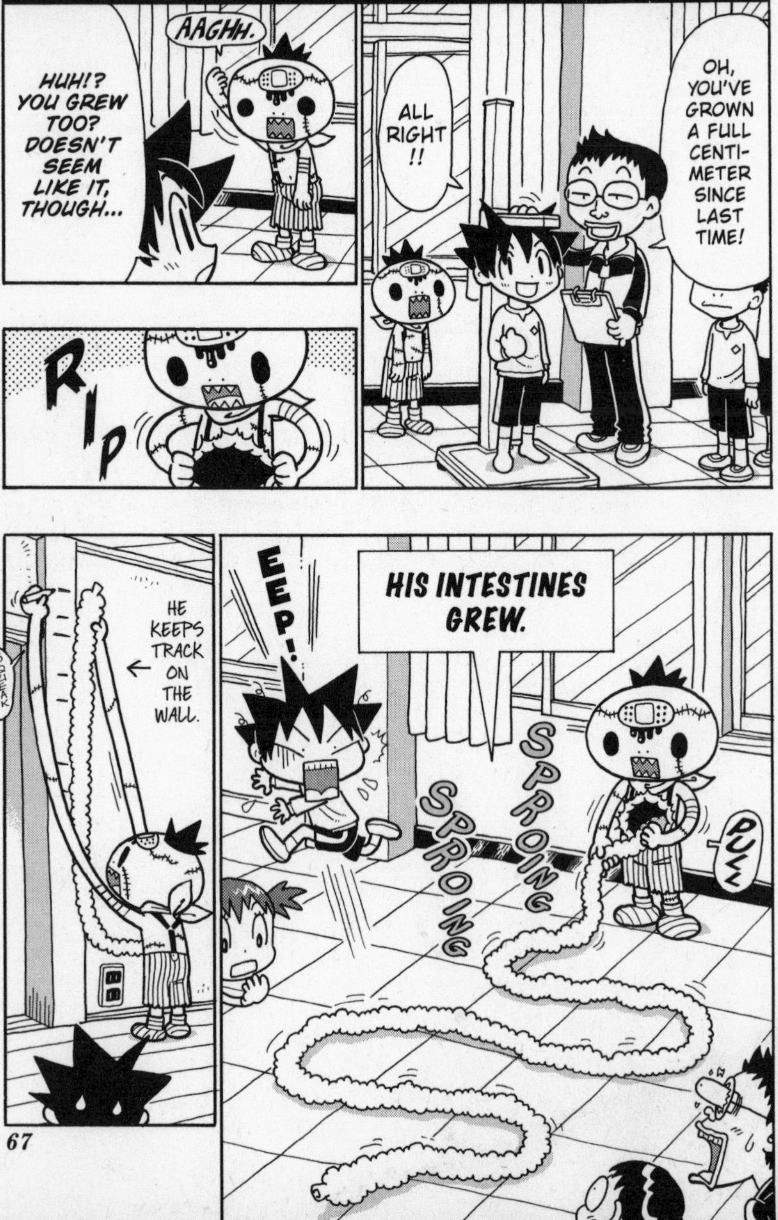
OH, YOU'VE GROWN A FULL CENTI-METER SINCE LAST TIME!
ALL RIGHT!!
AAGHH.
HUH!? YOU GREW TOO? DOESN'T SEEM LIKE IT, THOUGH...
RIP
HIS INTESTINES GREW.
EEP!
SPROING
SPROING
PULL
HE KEEPS TRACK ON THE WALL.
SQUEAK SQUEAK

MEASUREMENTS ②

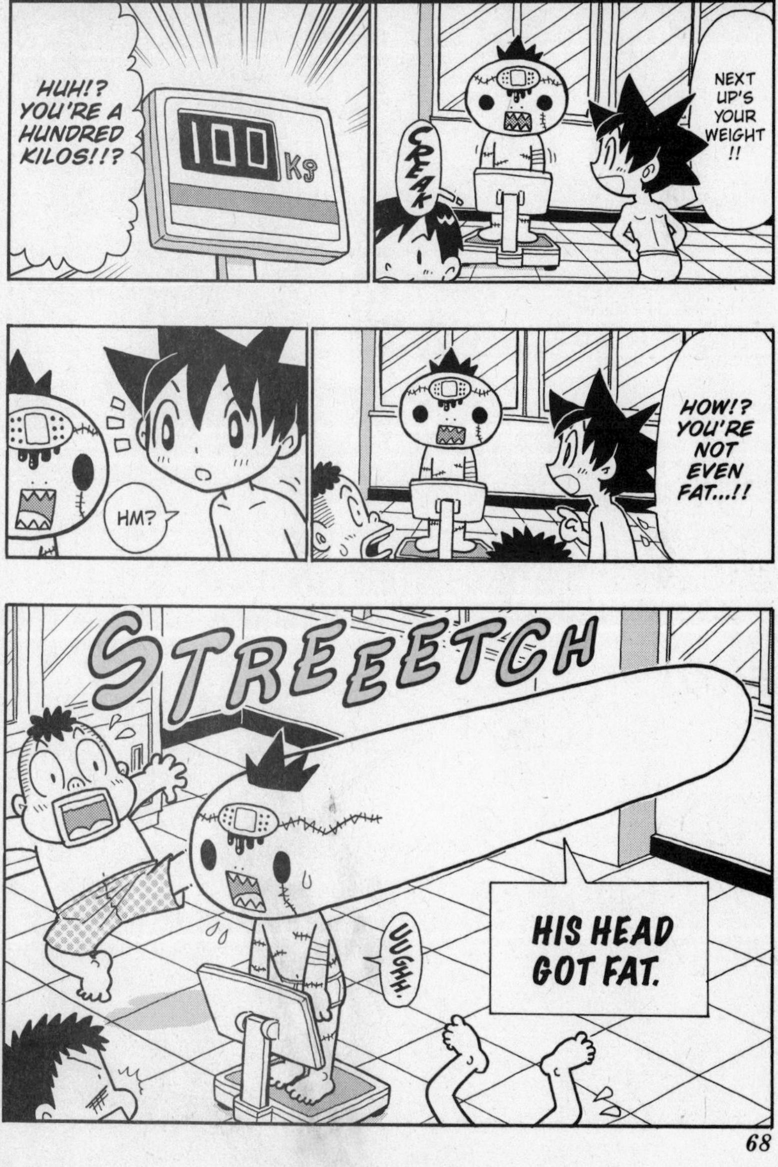
NEXT UP'S YOUR WEIGHT !!
CREAK
HUH!? YOU'RE A HUNDRED KILOS!!?
HOW!? YOU'RE NOT EVEN FAT...!!
HM?
STREEETCH
UUGHH.
HIS HEAD GOT FAT.

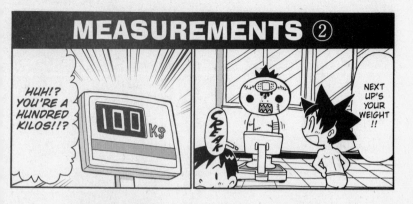

SNOT

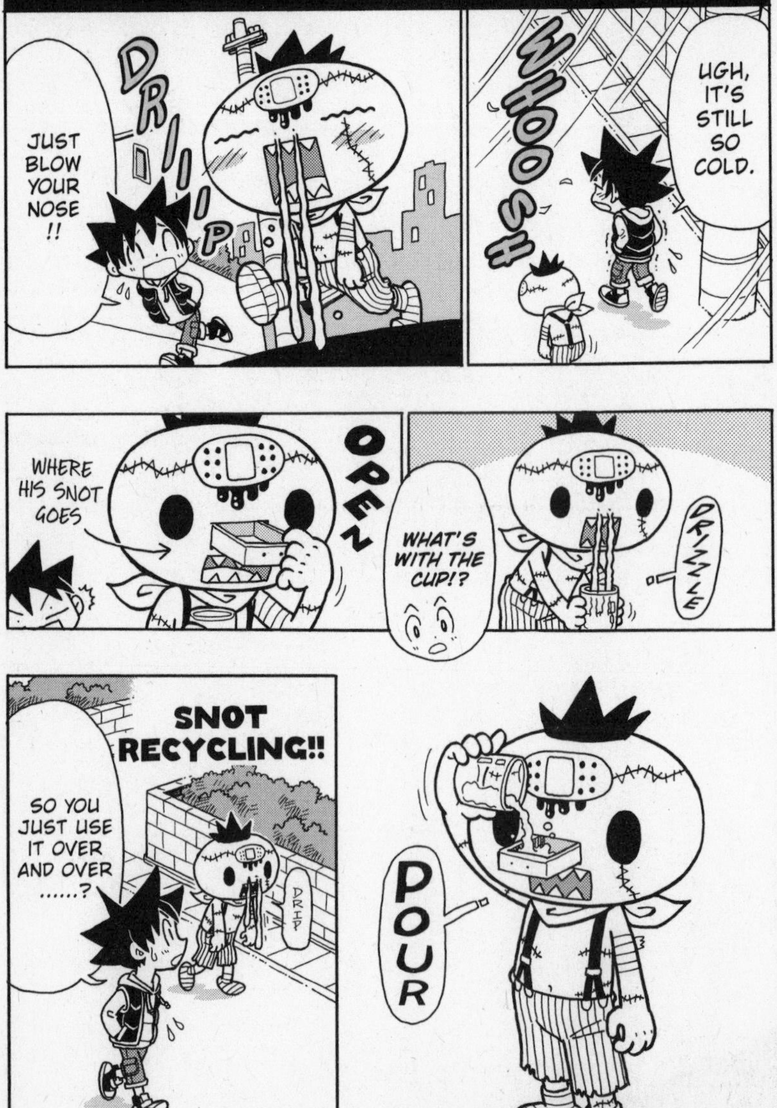
UGH, IT'S STILL SO COLD.
WHOOSH
DRIIIP
JUST BLOW YOUR NOSE !!
WHAT'S WITH THE CUP!?
DRIZZLE
OPEN
WHERE HIS SNOT GOES
POUR
SNOT RECYCLING!!
SO YOU JUST USE IT OVER AND OVER ......?
DRIP

HEADACHES

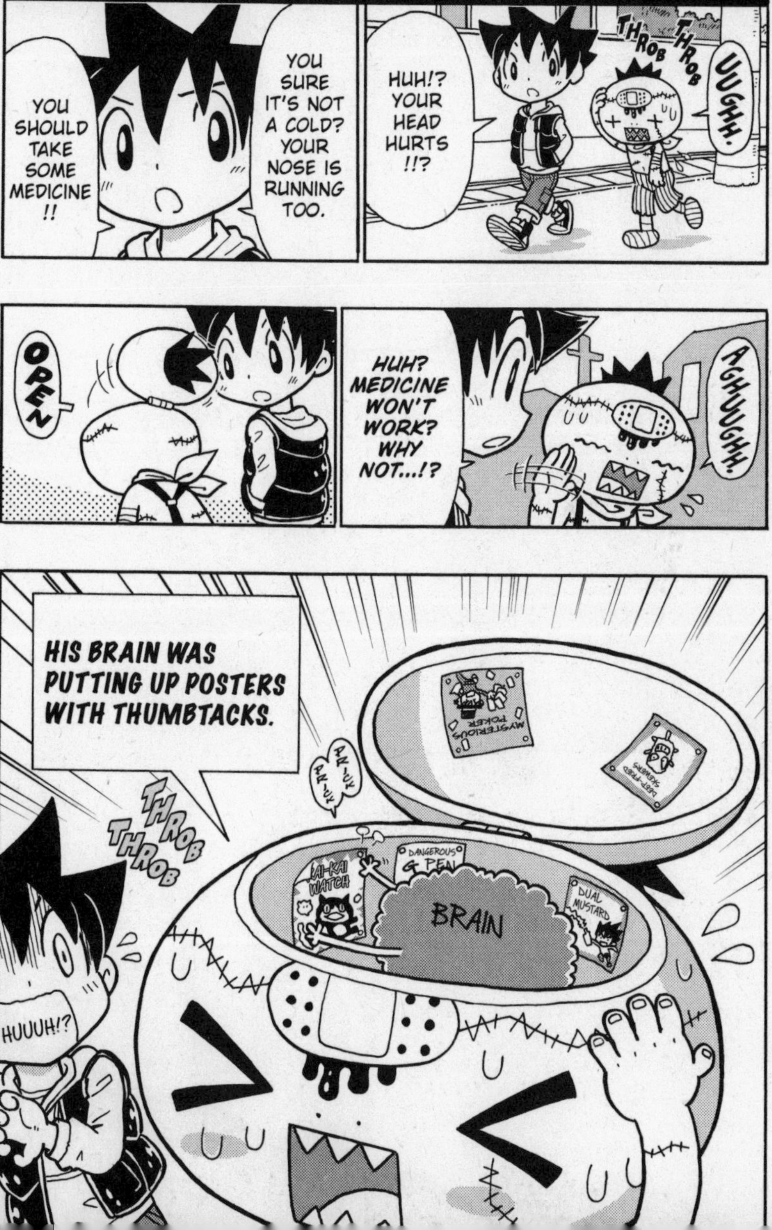
UUGHH.
THROB THROB
HUH!? YOUR HEAD HURTS!!?
YOU SURE IT'S NOT A COLD? YOUR NOSE IS RUNNING TOO.
YOU SHOULD TAKE SOME MEDICINE!!
AGHUUGHH.
HUH? MEDICINE WON'T WORK? WHY NOT...!?
OPEN
DEEP-FRIED SKEWERS
MYSTERIOUS POKER
PRICK PRICK
HIS BRAIN WAS PUTTING UP POSTERS WITH THUMBTACKS.
DUAL MUSTARD
DANGEROUS G PEN
KAI-KAI WATCH
BRAIN
THROB THROB
HUUUH!?

LINING UP

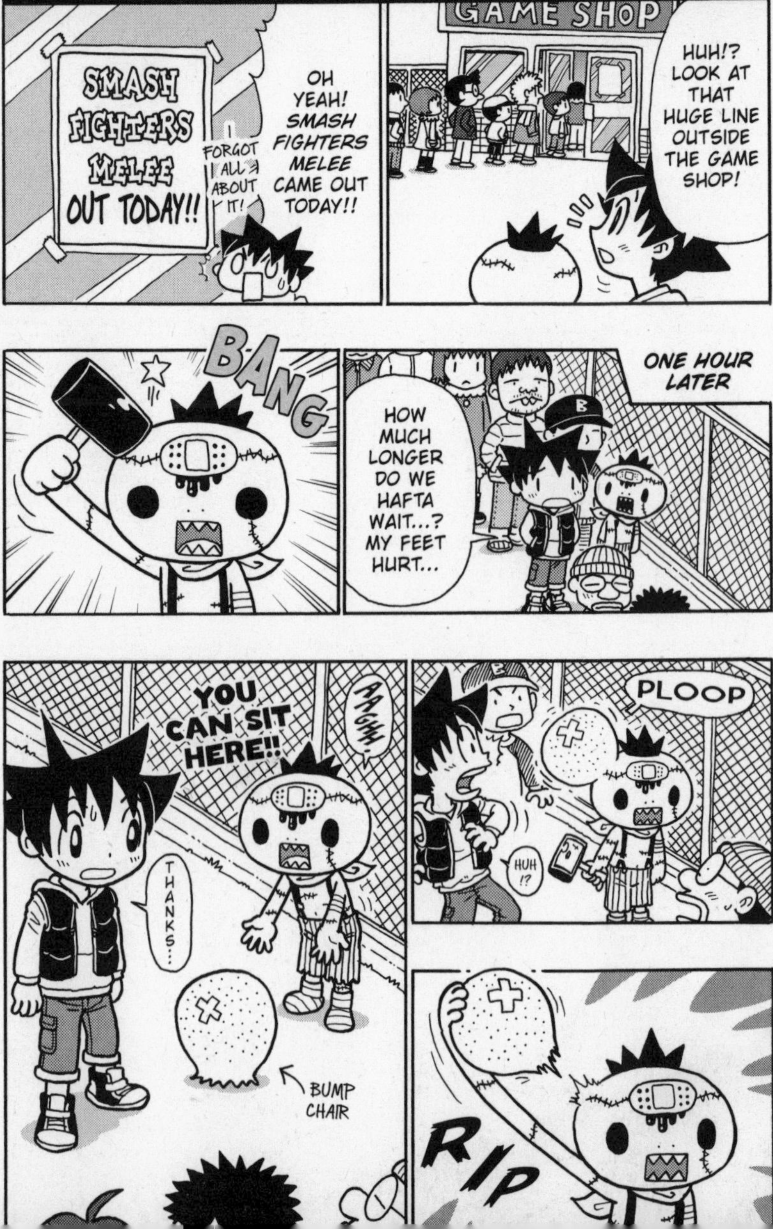
GAME SHOP
HUH!? LOOK AT THAT HUGE LINE OUTSIDE THE GAME SHOP!
OH YEAH! SMASH FIGHTERS MELEE CAME OUT TODAY!!
SMASH FIGHTERS MELEE OUT TODAY!!
I FORGOT ALL ABOUT IT!
ONE HOUR LATER
HOW MUCH LONGER DO WE HAFTA WAIT...? MY FEET HURT...
BANG
PLOOP
HUH!?
RIP
AAGHH
YOU CAN SIT HERE!!
THANKS...
BUMP CHAIR

LINING UP ②

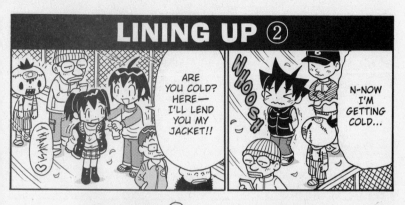

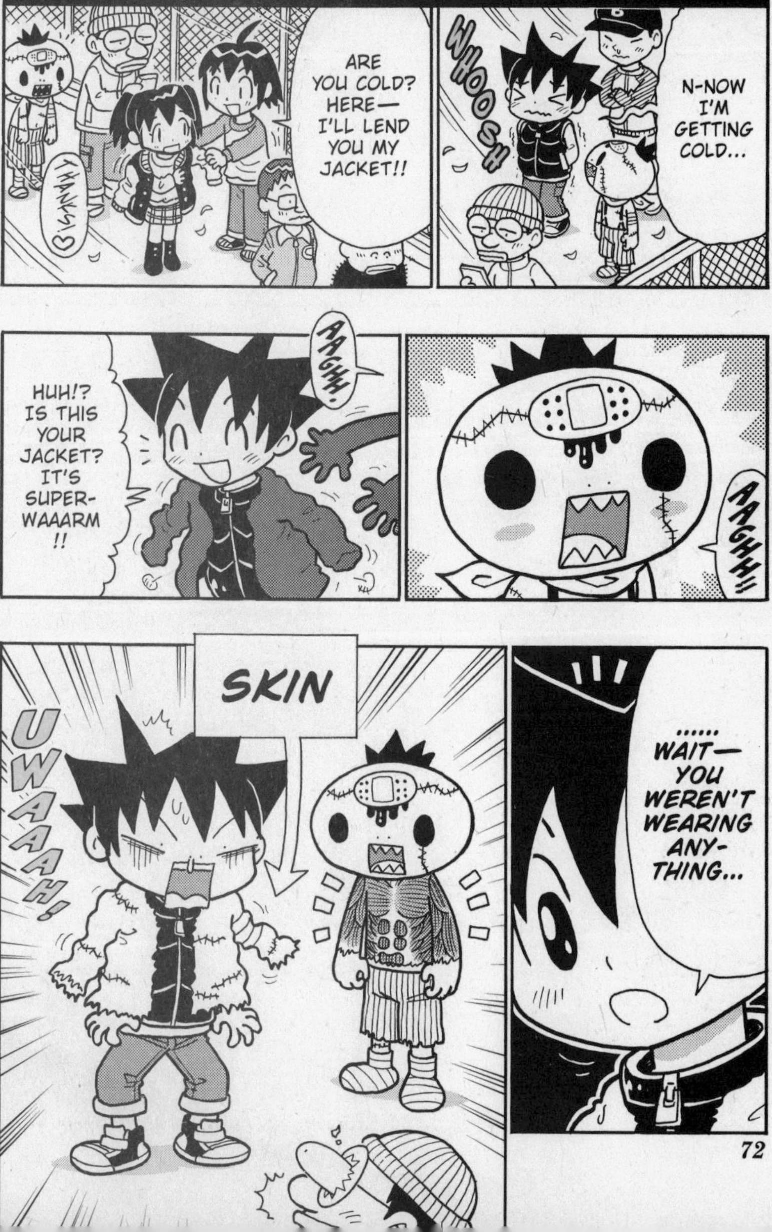
ARE YOU COLD? HERE— I'LL LEND YOU MY JACKET!!
THANKS!♡
WHOOSH
N-NOW I'M GETTING COLD...
HUH!? IS THIS YOUR JACKET? IT'S SUPER-WAAARM!!
AAGHH.
AAGHH!!
SKIN
UWAAAAH!
...... WAIT— YOU WEREN'T WEARING ANY-THING...

'NUTS

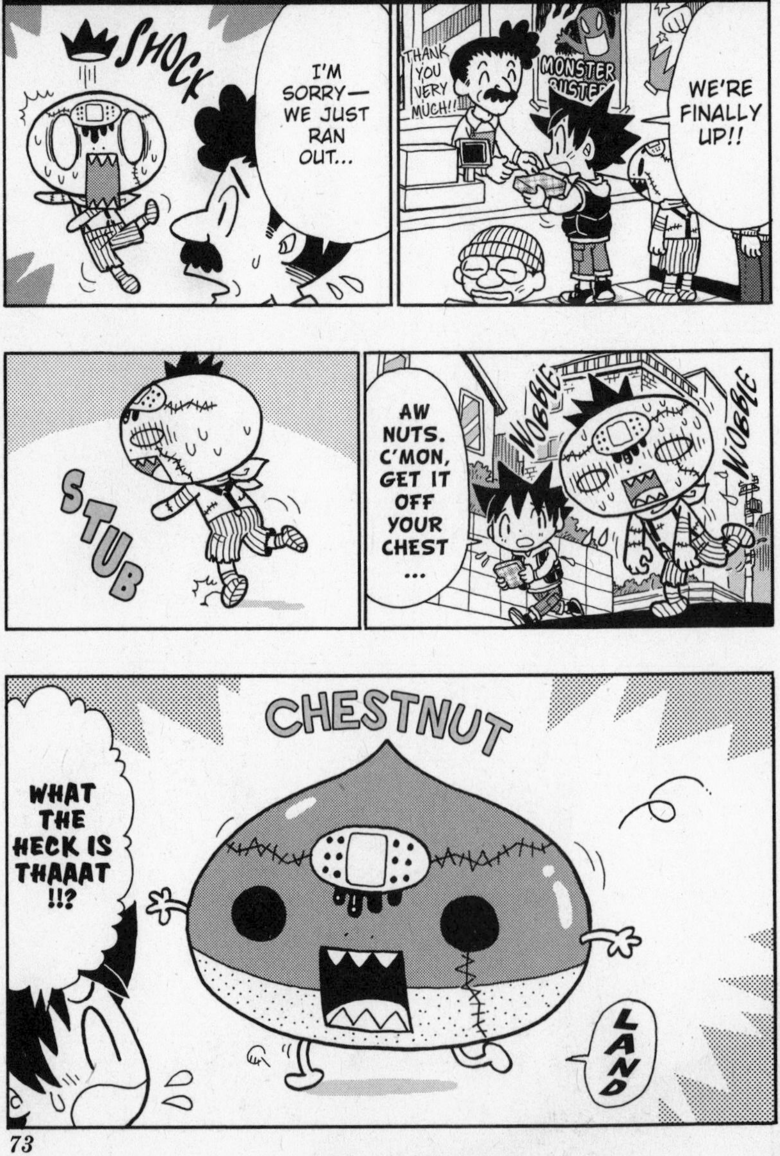
WE'RE FINALLY UP!!
MONSTER
THANK YOU VERY MUCH!!
I'M SORRY—WE JUST RAN OUT...
SHOCK
WOBBLE
WOBBLE
AW NUTS. C'MON, GET IT OFF YOUR CHEST ...
STUB
CHESTNUT
WHAT THE HECK IS THAAAT!!?
LAND

A FEVER!!

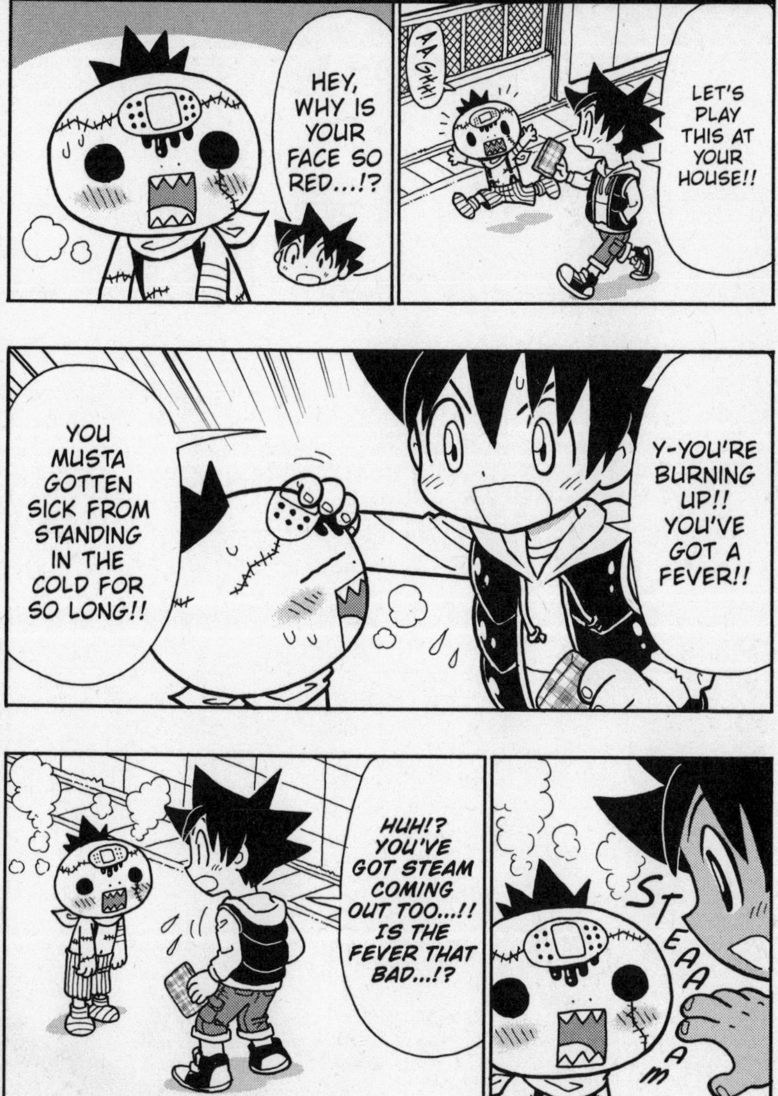
LET'S PLAY THIS AT YOUR HOUSE!!
AAGHH!
HEY, WHY IS YOUR FACE SO RED...!?
Y-YOU'RE BURNING UP!! YOU'VE GOT A FEVER!!
YOU MUSTA GOTTEN SICK FROM STANDING IN THE COLD FOR SO LONG!!
STEAAAAM
HUH!? YOU'VE GOT STEAM COMING OUT TOO...!! IS THE FEVER THAT BAD...!?

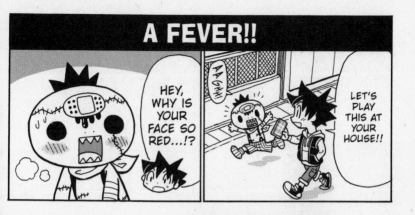

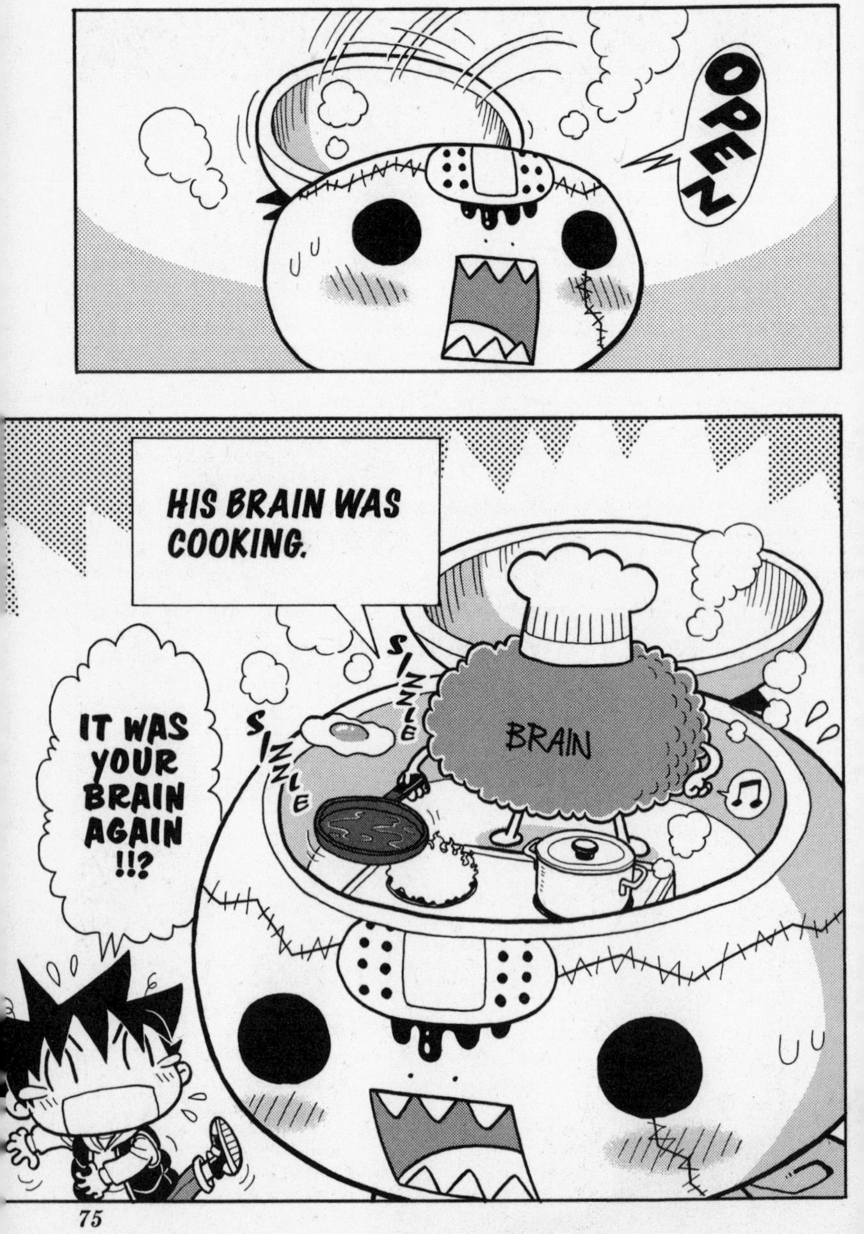
OPEN
HIS BRAIN WAS COOKING.
SIZZLE
SIZZLE
BRAIN
IT WAS YOUR BRAIN AGAIN!!?

HEART-POUNDING!!

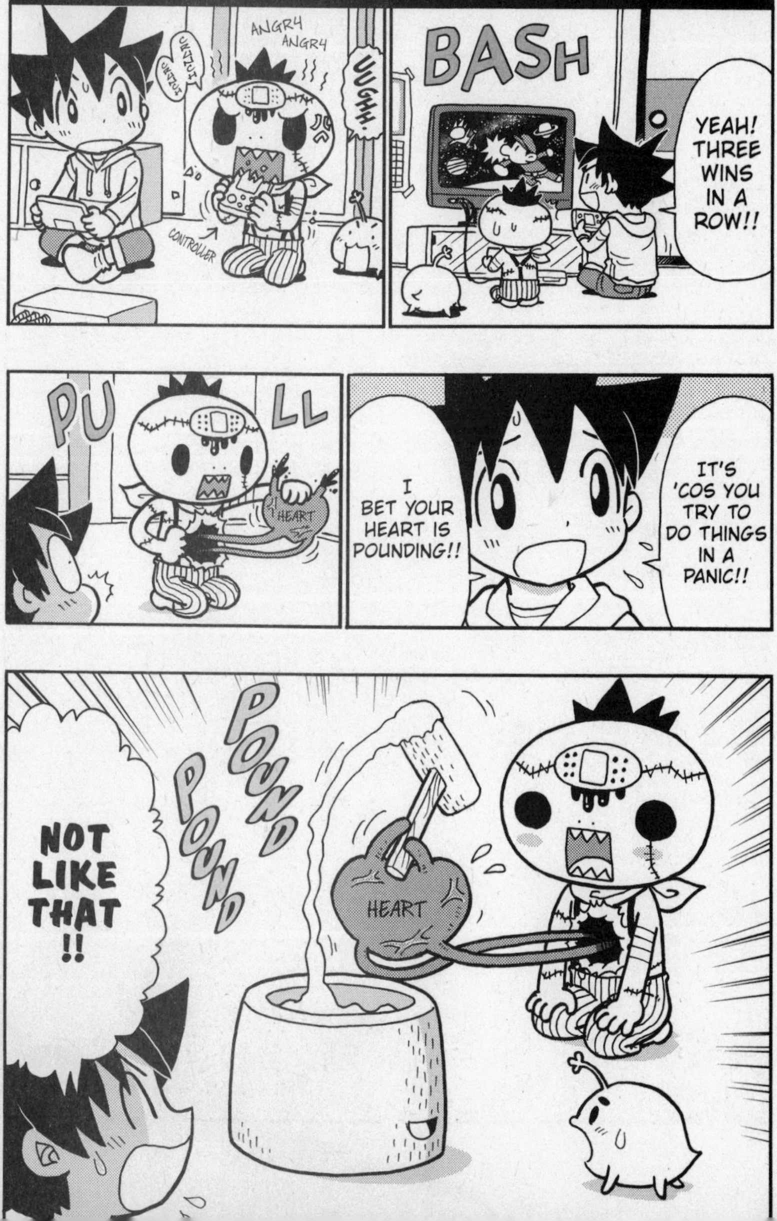

BASH
YEAH! THREE WINS IN A ROW!!
ANGRY ANGRY
UUGHH.
CONTROLLER
IT'S 'COS YOU TRY TO DO THINGS IN A PANIC!!
I BET YOUR HEART IS POUNDING!!
PULL
HEART
POUND
POUND
HEART
NOT LIKE THAT!!

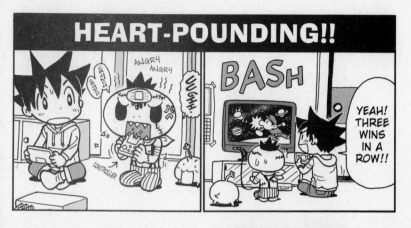

YOUR EYES WILL GO BAD

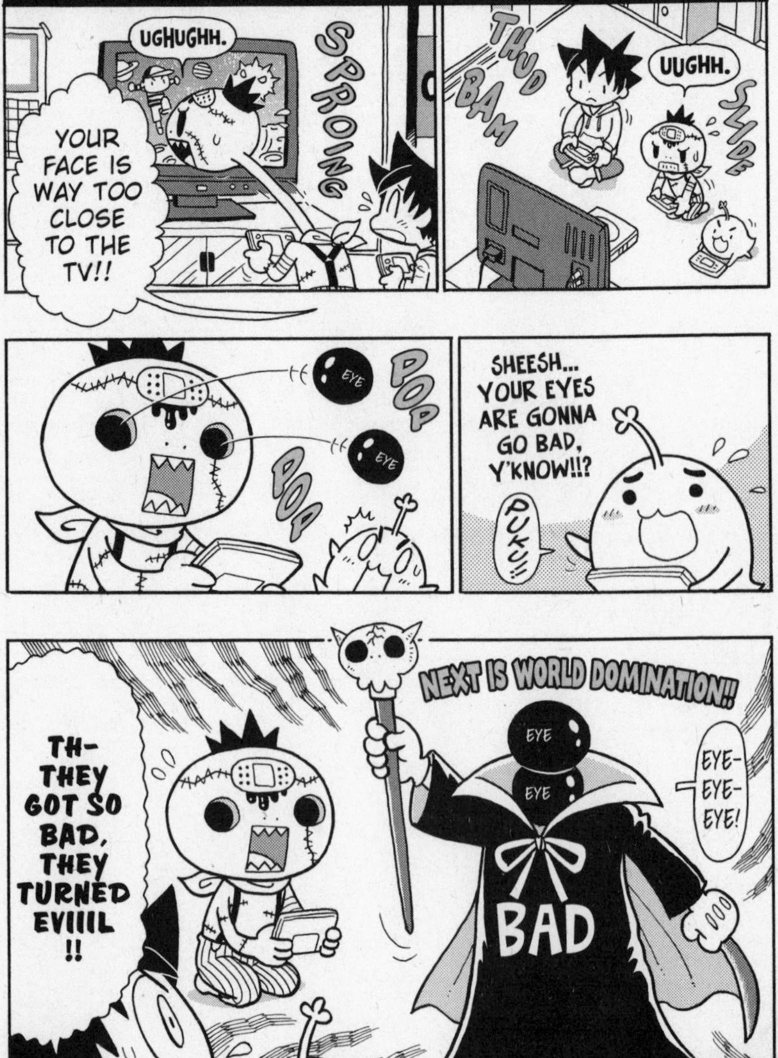
THUD
BAM
UUGHH.
SLIDE
UGHUGHH.
SPROING
YOUR FACE IS WAY TOO CLOSE TO THE TV!!
SHEESH... YOUR EYES ARE GONNA GO BAD, Y'KNOW!!?
PUKU!!
POP
POP
EYE
EYE
EYE-EYE-EYE!
NEXT IS WORLD DOMINATION!!
EYE
EYE
BAD
TH-THEY GOT SO BAD, THEY TURNED EVIIIL!!

ALL KINDS OF "UP"

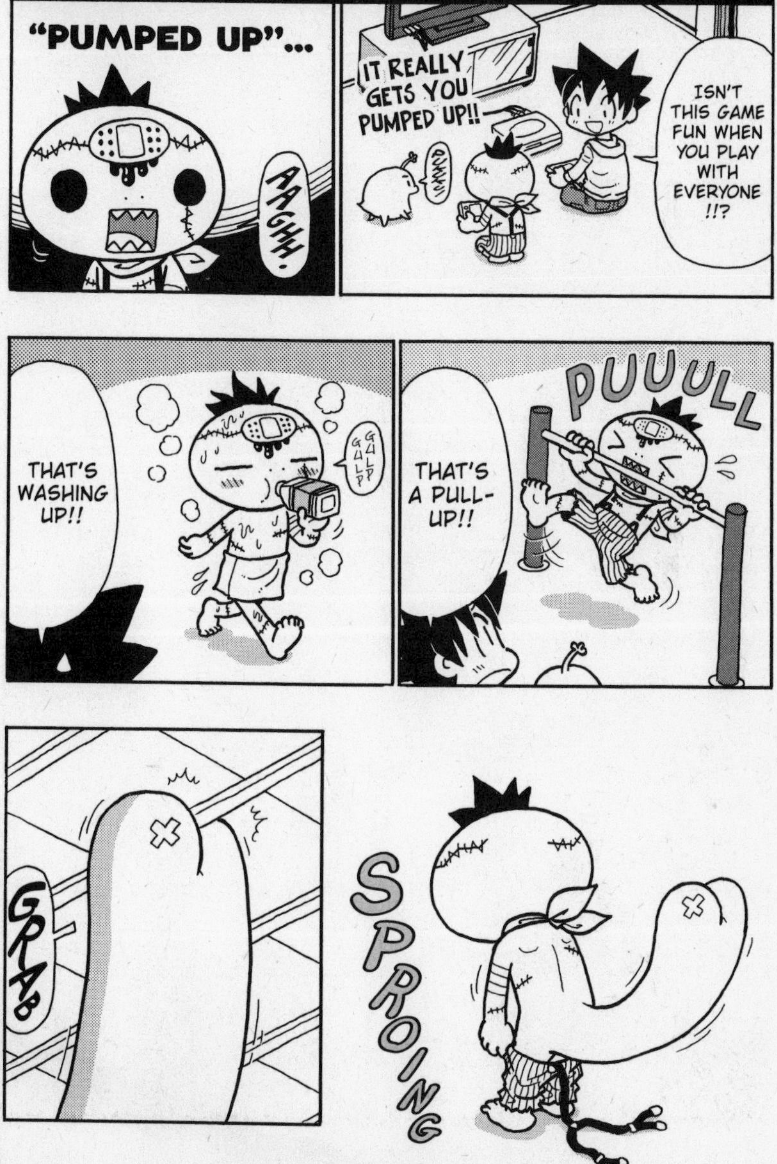
ISN'T THIS GAME FUN WHEN YOU PLAY WITH EVERYONE !!?
IT REALLY GETS YOU PUMPED UP!!
"PUMPED UP"...
AAGHH.
PUUUULL
THAT'S A PULL-UP!!
GULP GULP
THAT'S WASHING UP!!
SPROING
GRAB

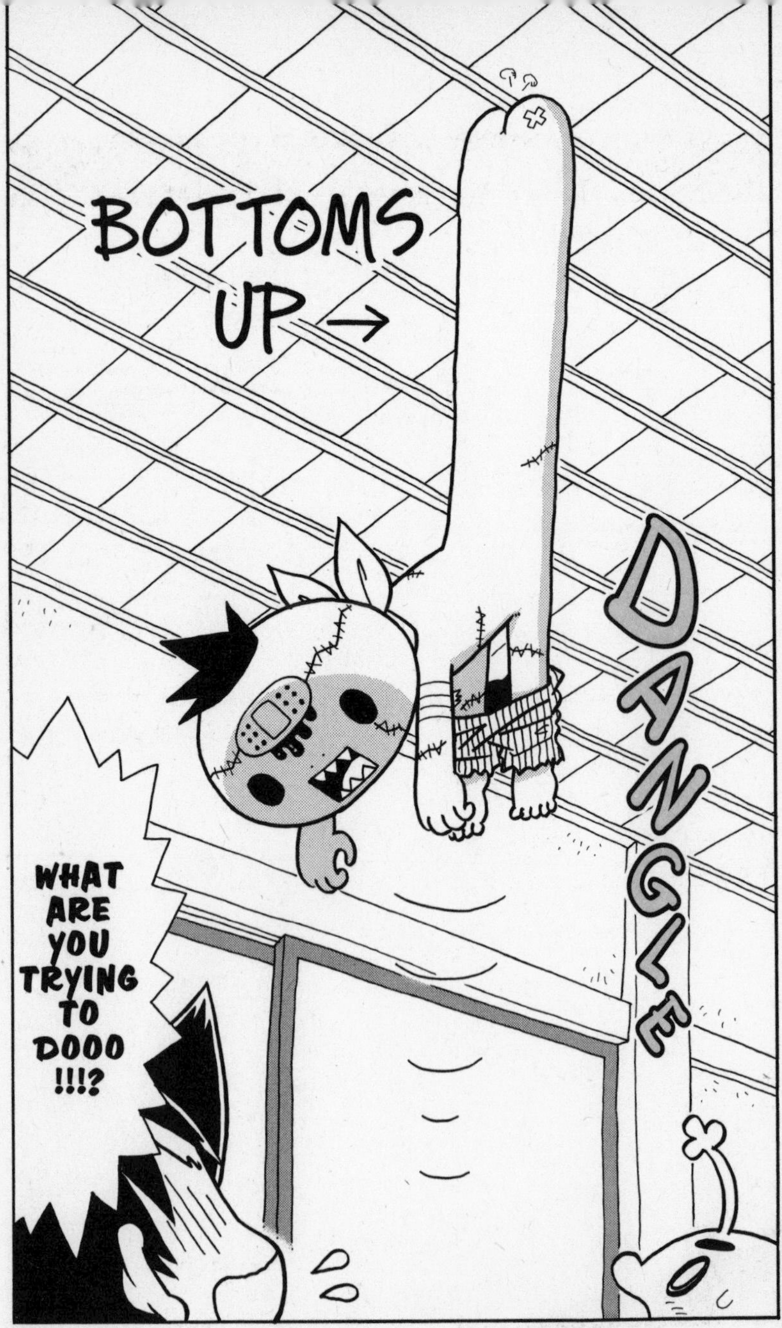
BOTTOMS UP →
DANGLE
WHAT ARE YOU TRYING TO DOOO !!!?

ALL TOGETHER NOW

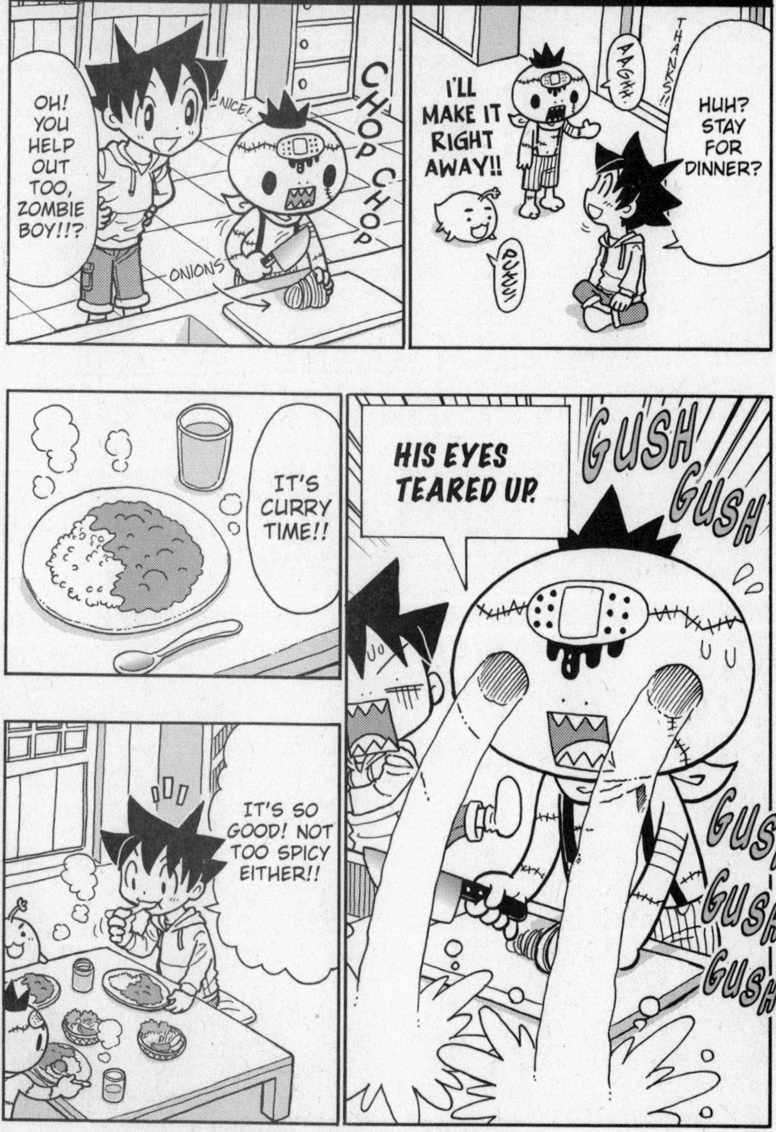
HUH? STAY FOR DINNER?
THANKS!!
AAGHH.
I'LL MAKE IT RIGHT AWAY!!
PUKUU
OH! YOU HELP OUT TOO, ZOMBIE BOY!!?
NICE!
CHOP CHOP CHOP CHOP
ONIONS
HIS EYES TEARED UP.
GUSH GUSH
GUSH GUSH GUSH
IT'S CURRY TIME!!
IT'S SO GOOD! NOT TOO SPICY EITHER!!

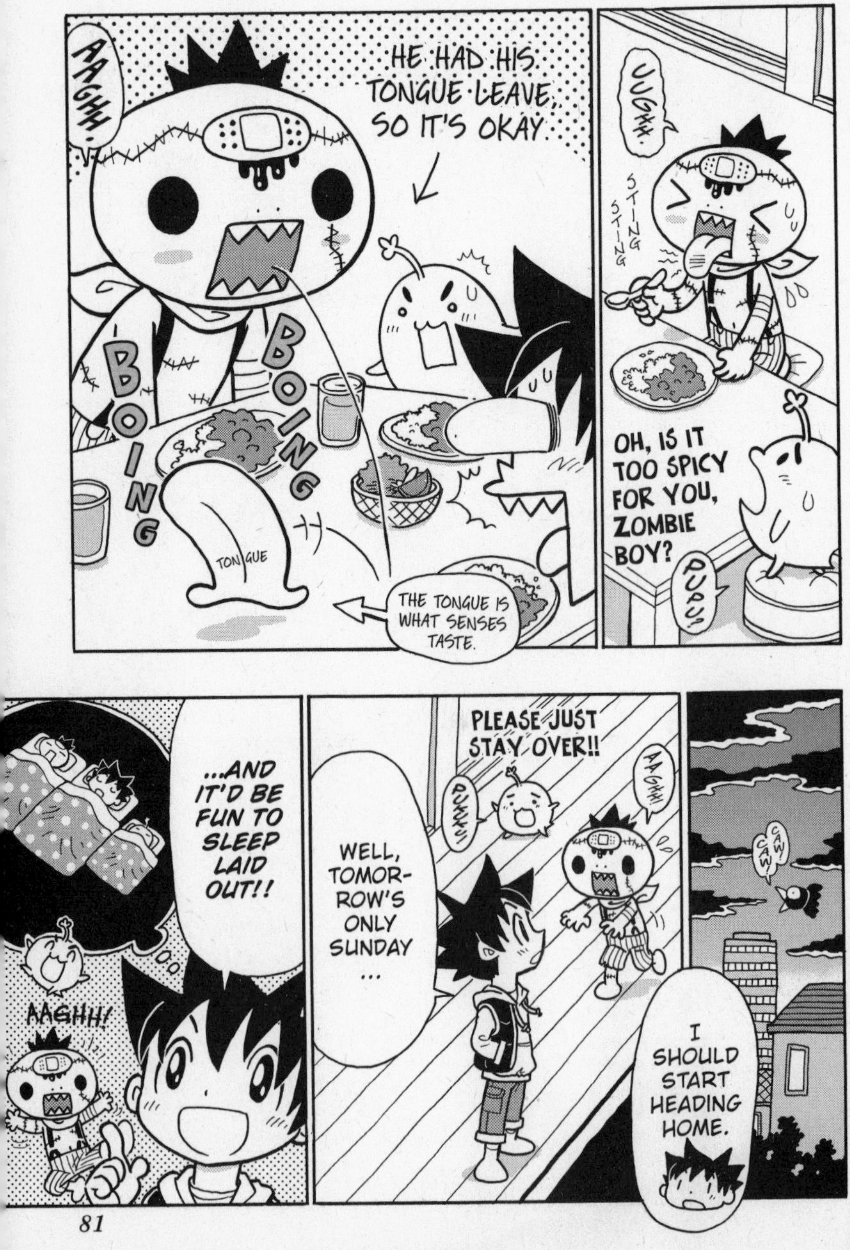
UUGHH.
STING STING
OH, IS IT TOO SPICY FOR YOU, ZOMBIE BOY?
PUPU!
AAGHH.
HE HAD HIS TONGUE LEAVE, SO IT'S OKAY
BOING BOING
TONGUE
THE TONGUE IS WHAT SENSES TASTE.
CAW! CAW!
I SHOULD START HEADING HOME.
PLEASE JUST STAY OVER!!
AAGHH!
PUPUU!
WELL, TOMORROW'S ONLY SUNDAY ...
...AND IT'D BE FUN TO SLEEP LAID OUT!!
AAGHH!

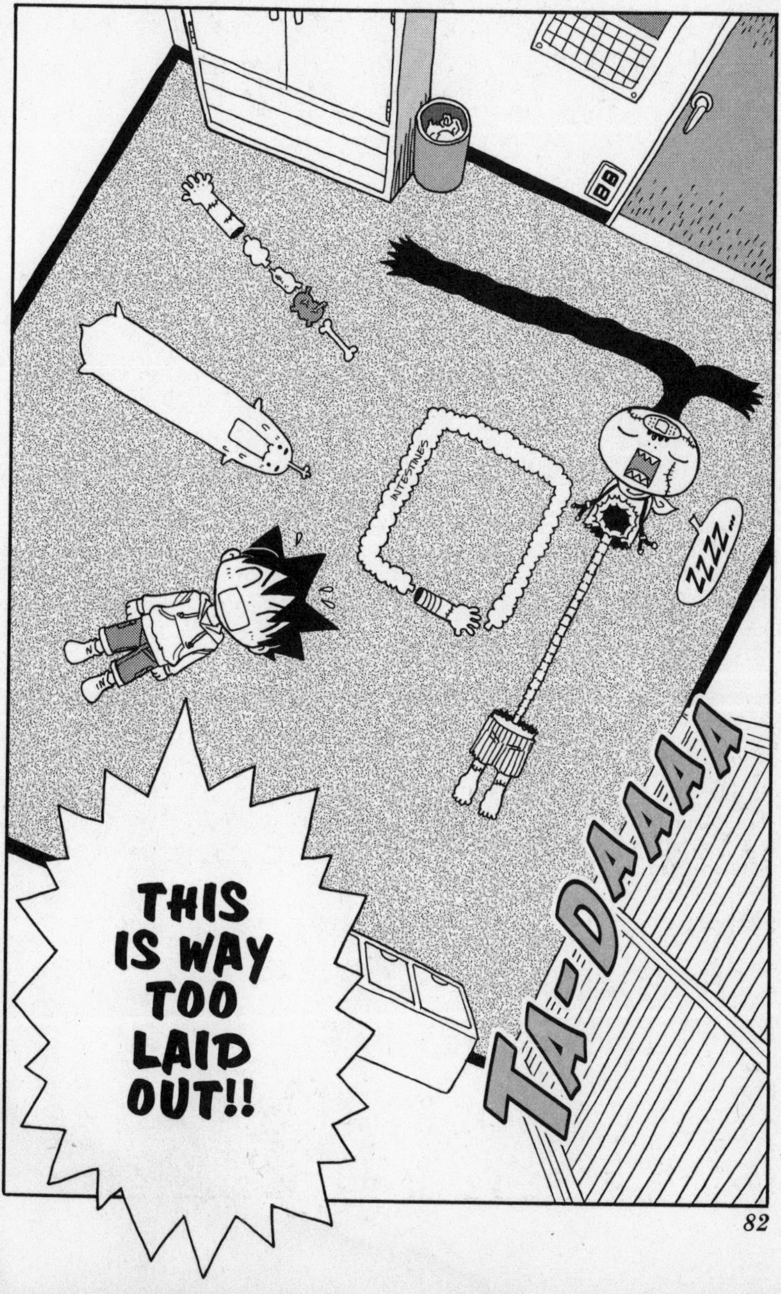
ZZZZZ...
INTESTINES
TA-DAAAA
THIS IS WAY TOO LAID OUT!!

ZO MUCH TO BLOW UP!

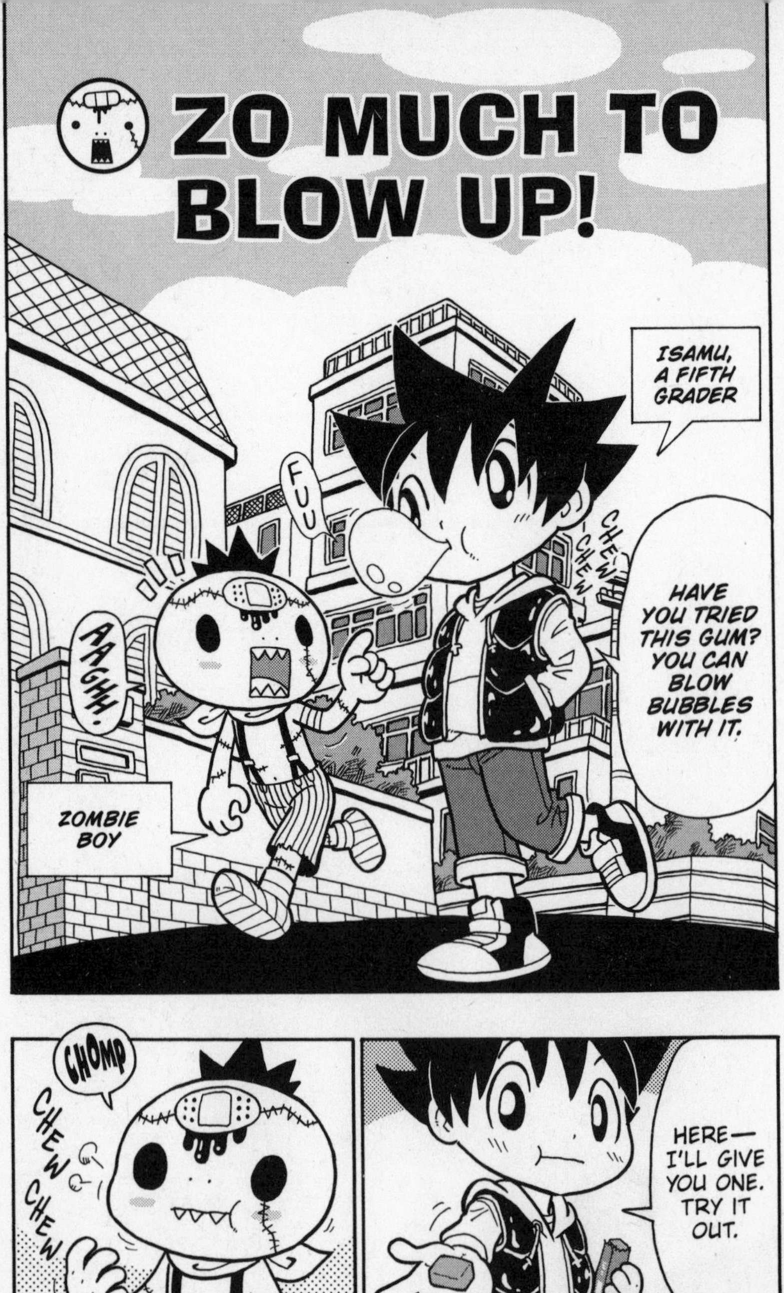
ISAMU, A FIFTH GRADER
CHEW CHEW
HAVE YOU TRIED THIS GUM? YOU CAN BLOW BUBBLES WITH IT.
FUU
AAGHH
ZOMBIE BOY
HERE— I'LL GIVE YOU ONE. TRY IT OUT.
CHOMP
CHEW CHEW CHEW

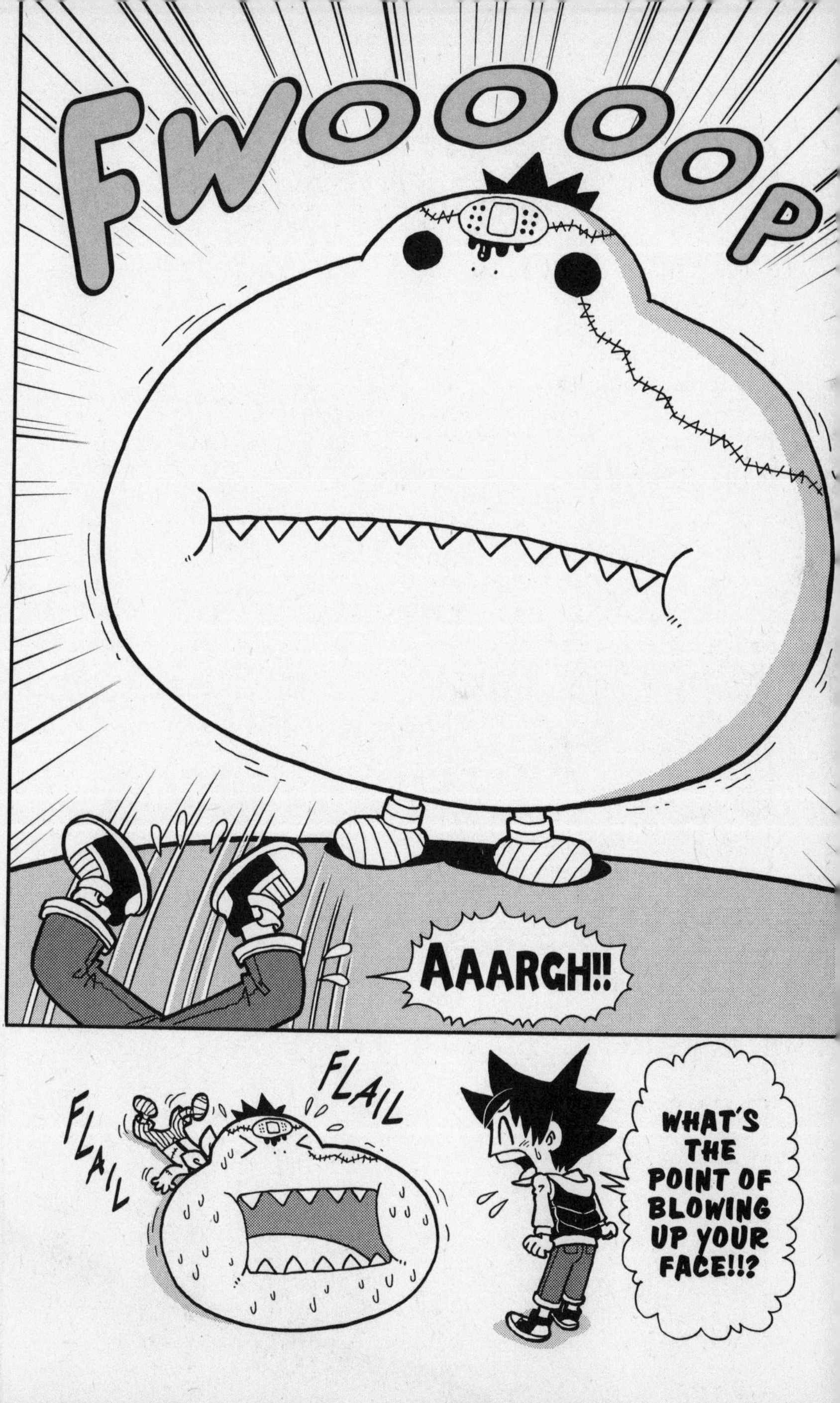
FWOOOOOP
AAARGH!!
WHAT'S THE POINT OF BLOWING UP YOUR FACE!!?
FLAIL
FLAIL

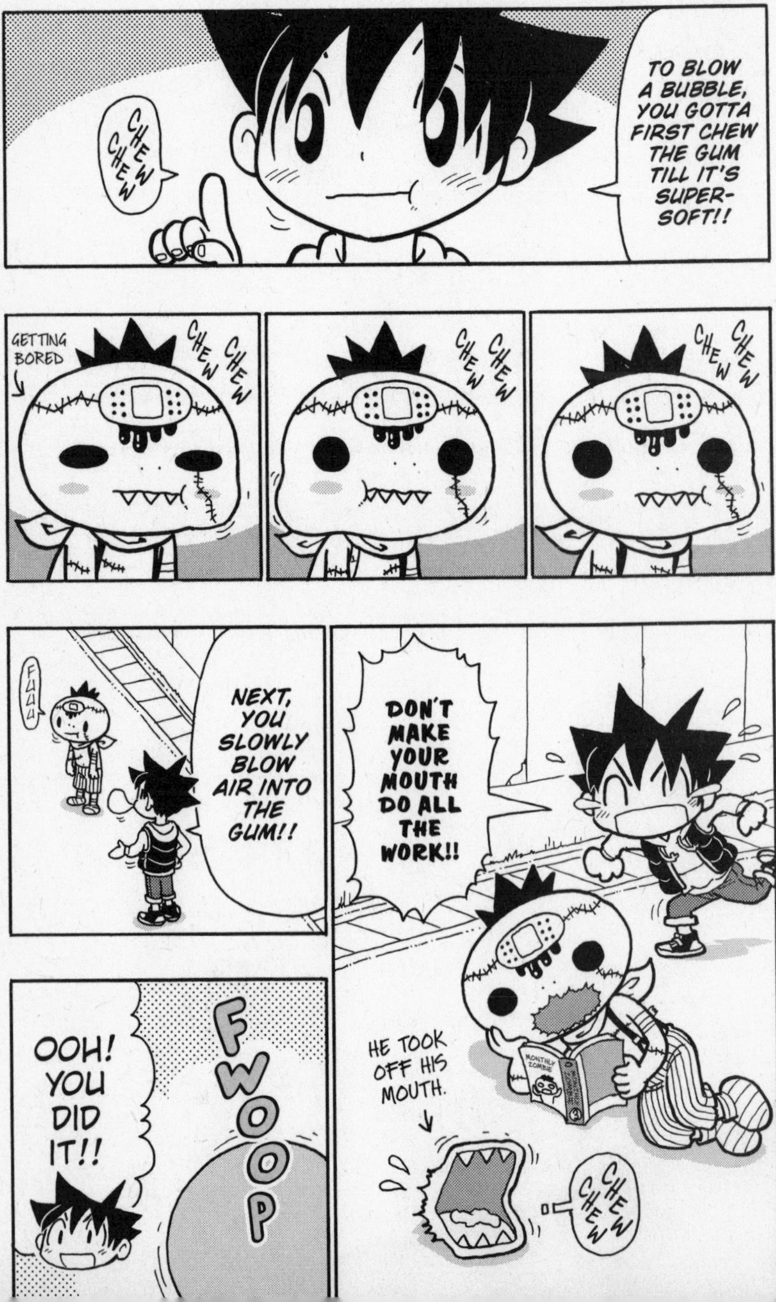
TO BLOW A BUBBLE, YOU GOTTA FIRST CHEW THE GUM TILL IT'S SUPER-SOFT!!
CHEW CHEW
CHEW CHEW
CHEW CHEW
CHEW CHEW
GETTING BORED
DON'T MAKE YOUR MOUTH DO ALL THE WORK!!
HE TOOK OFF HIS MOUTH.
CHEW CHEW
NEXT, YOU SLOWLY BLOW AIR INTO THE GUM!!
FUUU
FWOOP
OOH! YOU DID IT!!

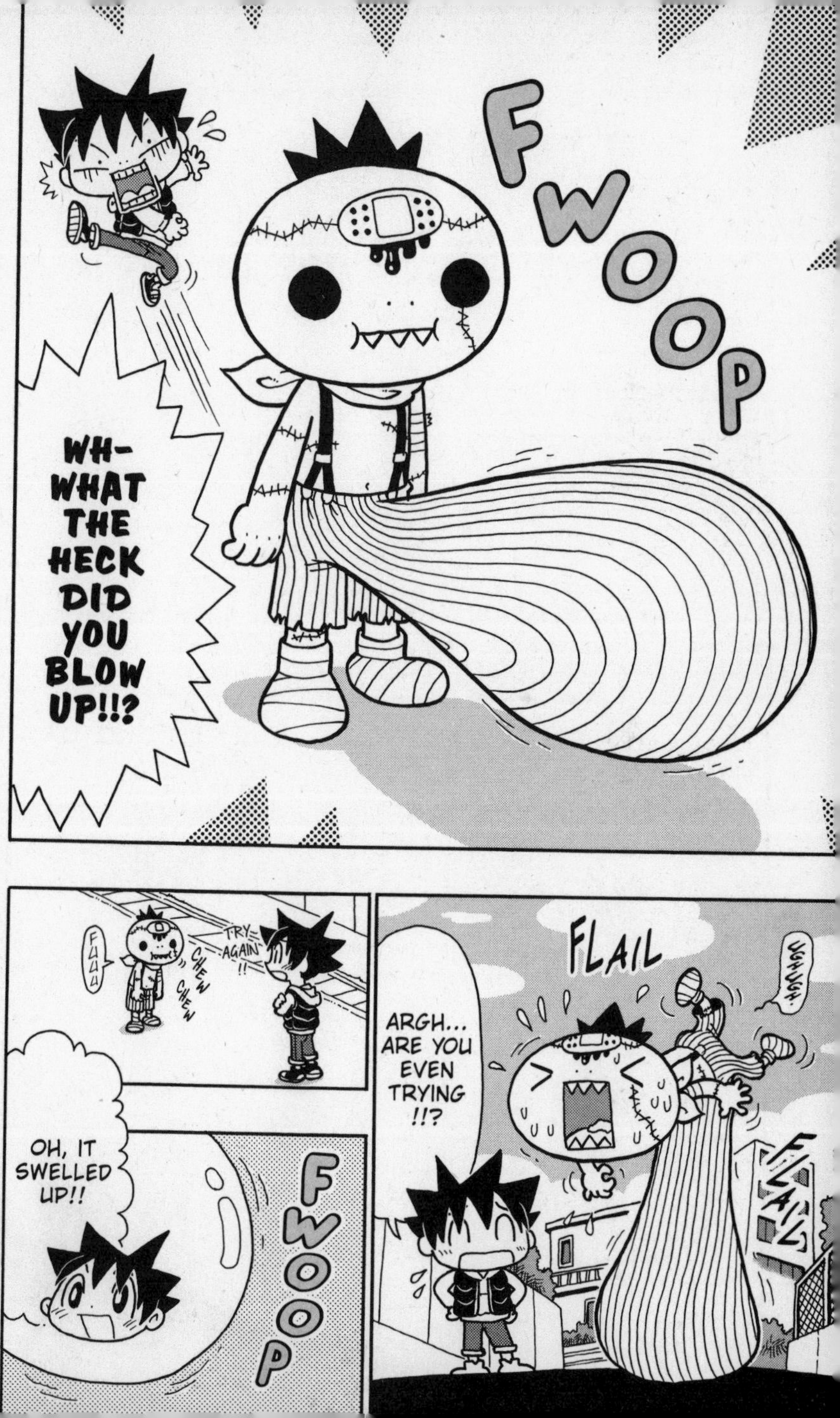
FWOOP
WH-WHAT THE HECK DID YOU BLOW UP!!?
FLAIL
UGHUGH.
ARGH... ARE YOU EVEN TRYING!!?
FLAIL
T·R·Y AGAIN!!
CHEW CHEW
FUUU
OH, IT SWELLED UP!!
FWOOP

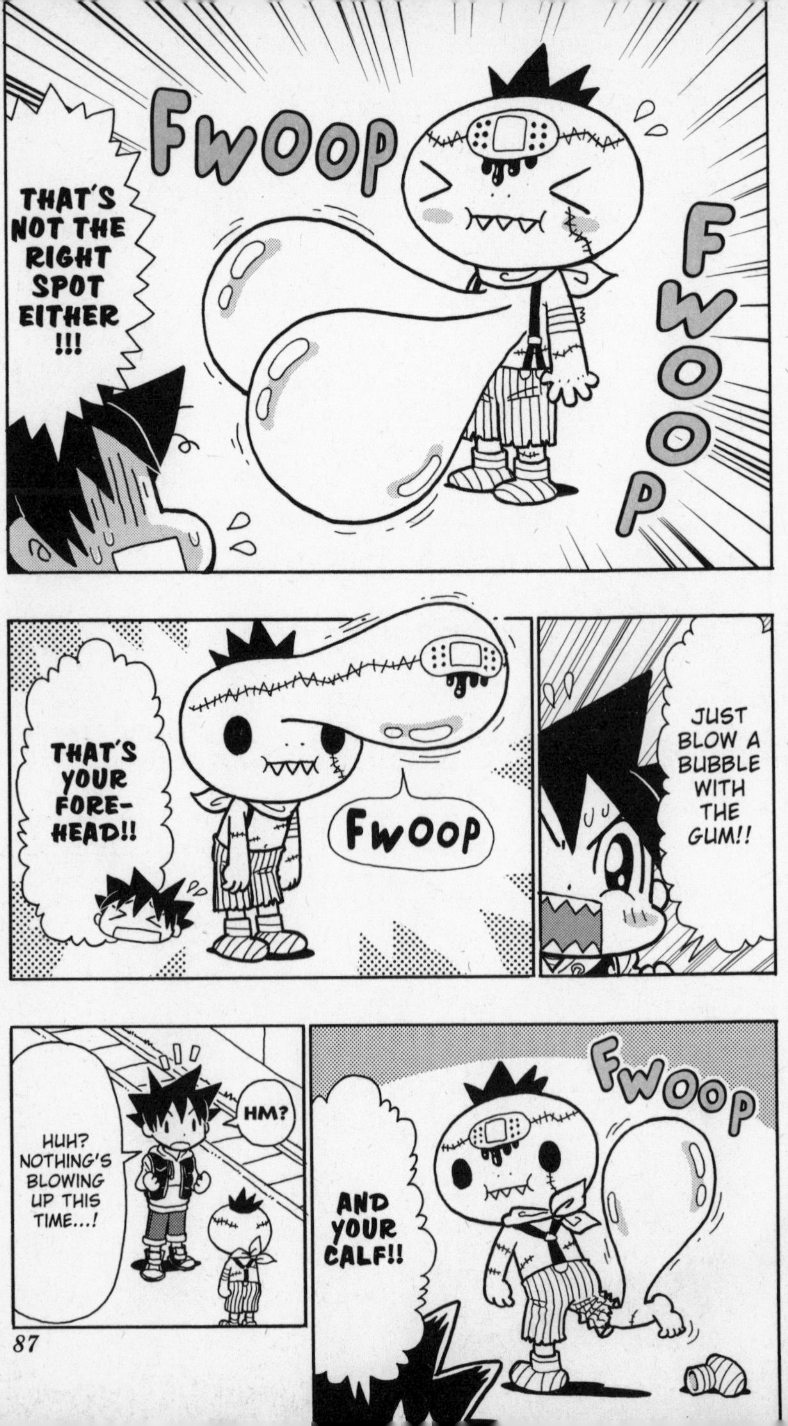
FWOOP
FWOOP
THAT'S NOT THE RIGHT SPOT EITHER!!!
JUST BLOW A BUBBLE WITH THE GUM!!
FWOOP
THAT'S YOUR FORE-HEAD!!
FWOOP
AND YOUR CALF!!
HM?
HUH? NOTHING'S BLOWING UP THIS TIME...!

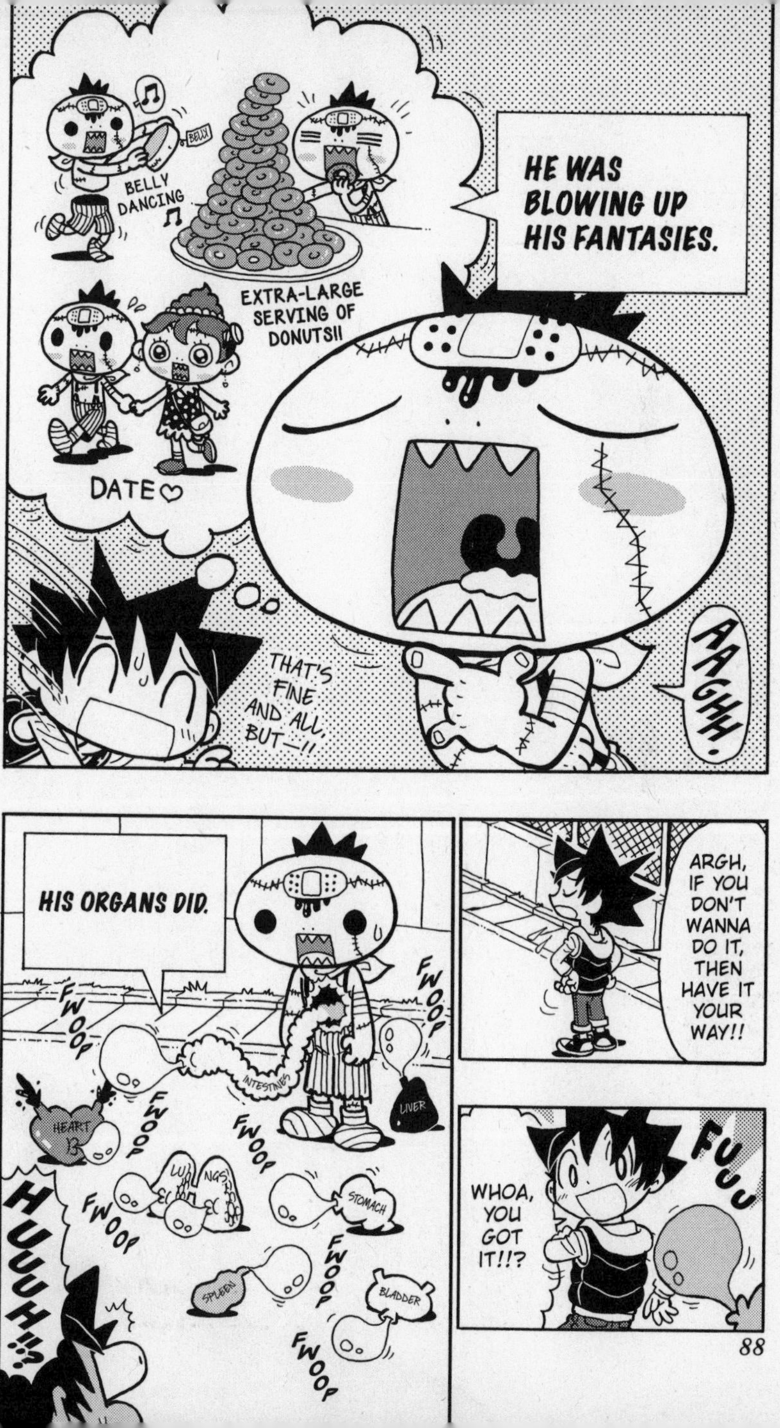
HE WAS BLOWING UP HIS FANTASIES.
BELLY
BELLY DANCING
EXTRA-LARGE SERVING OF DONUTS!!
DATE♡
AAGHH.
THAT'S FINE AND ALL, BUT—!!
ARGH, IF YOU DON'T WANNA DO IT, THEN HAVE IT YOUR WAY!!
FUUU
WHOA, YOU GOT IT!!?
HIS ORGANS DID.
FWOOP
FWOOP
INTESTINES
LIVER
HEART
FWOOP
FWOOP
LUNGS
STOMACH
FWOOP
FWOOP
SPLEEN
BLADDER
FWOOP
HUUUH!!!?

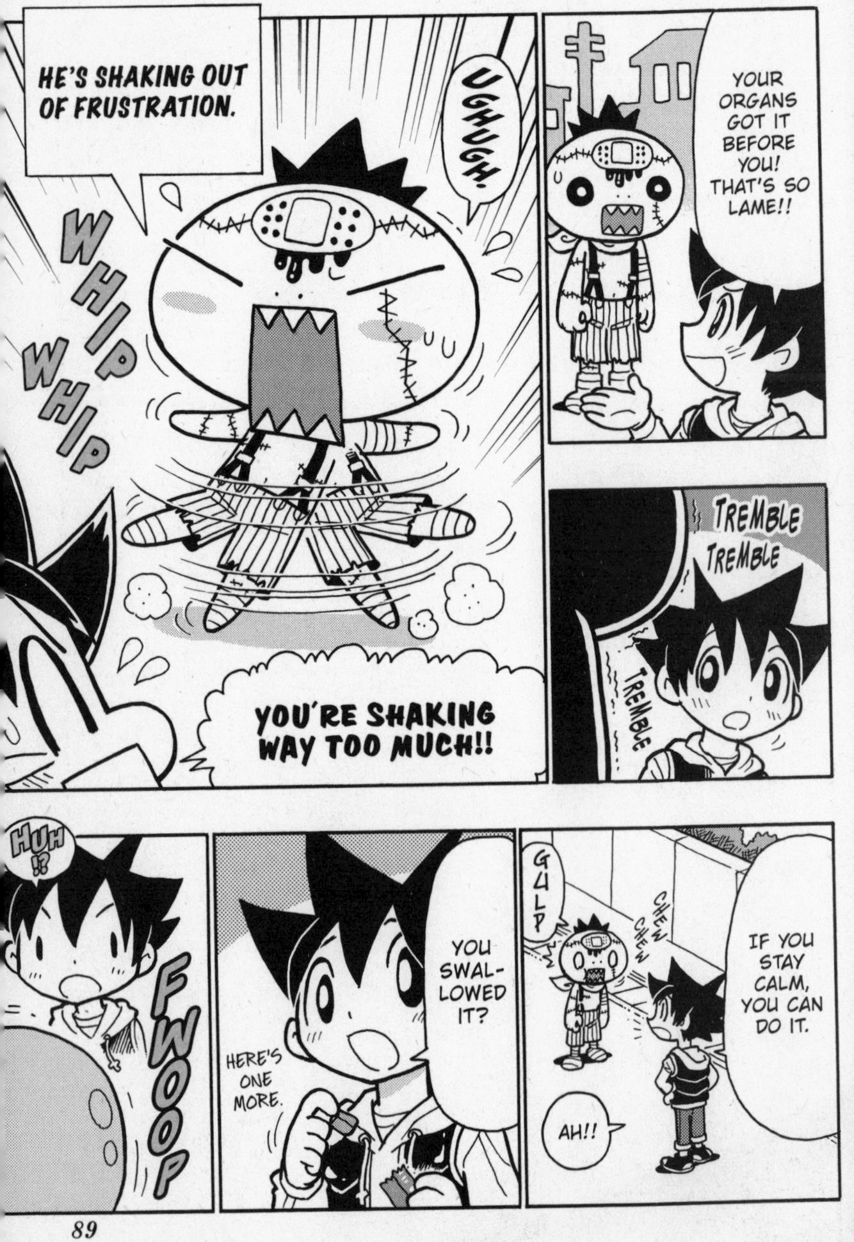
YOUR ORGANS GOT IT BEFORE YOU! THAT'S SO LAME!!
TREMBLE
TREMBLE
TREMBLE
HE'S SHAKING OUT OF FRUSTRATION.
UGHUGH.
WHIP
WHIP
YOU'RE SHAKING WAY TOO MUCH!!
IF YOU STAY CALM, YOU CAN DO IT.
GULP
CHEW CHEW
AH!!
YOU SWAL-LOWED IT?
HERE'S ONE MORE.
HUH!?
FWOOP

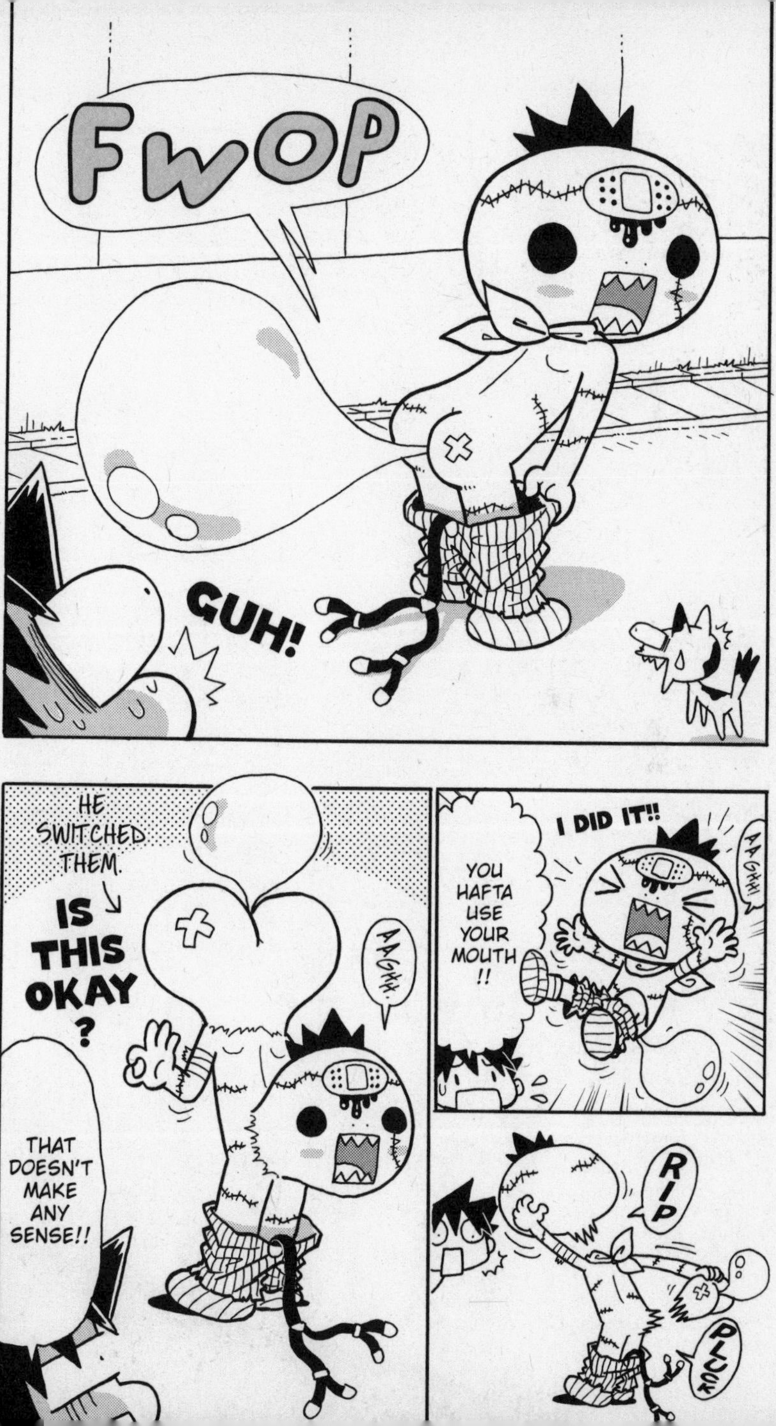
FWOP
GUH!
I DID IT!!
AAGHH!
YOU HAFTA USE YOUR MOUTH!!
RIP
PLUCK
HE SWITCHED THEM.
IS THIS OKAY?
AAGHH.
THAT DOESN'T MAKE ANY SENSE!!

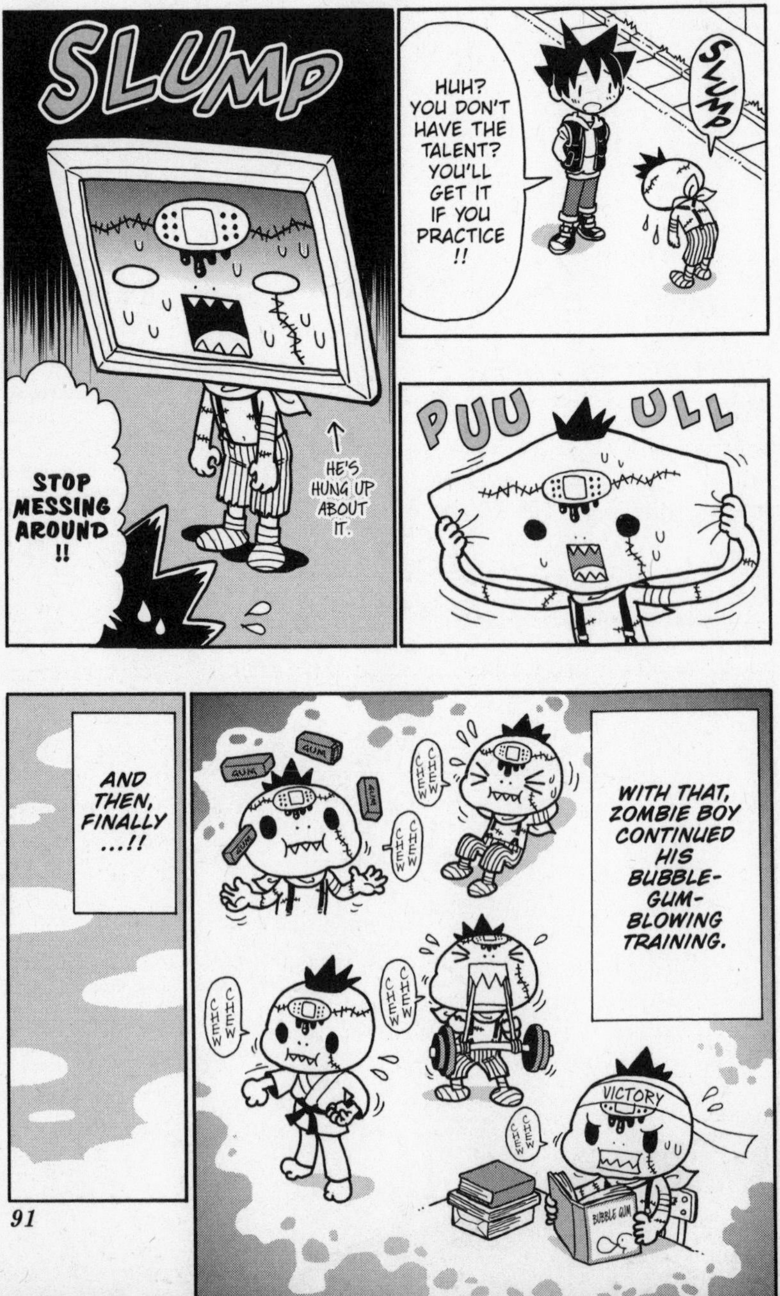

SLUMP
HUH? YOU DON'T HAVE THE TALENT? YOU'LL GET IT IF YOU PRACTICE !!
PUU ULL
SLUMP
STOP MESSING AROUND !!
HE'S HUNG UP ABOUT IT.
WITH THAT, ZOMBIE BOY CONTINUED HIS BUBBLE-GUM-BLOWING TRAINING.
CHEW CHEW
GUM
GUM
GUM
GUM
CHEW CHEW
VICTORY
CHEW CHEW
BUBBLE GUM
CHEW CHEW
CHEW CHEW
AND THEN, FINALLY ...!!

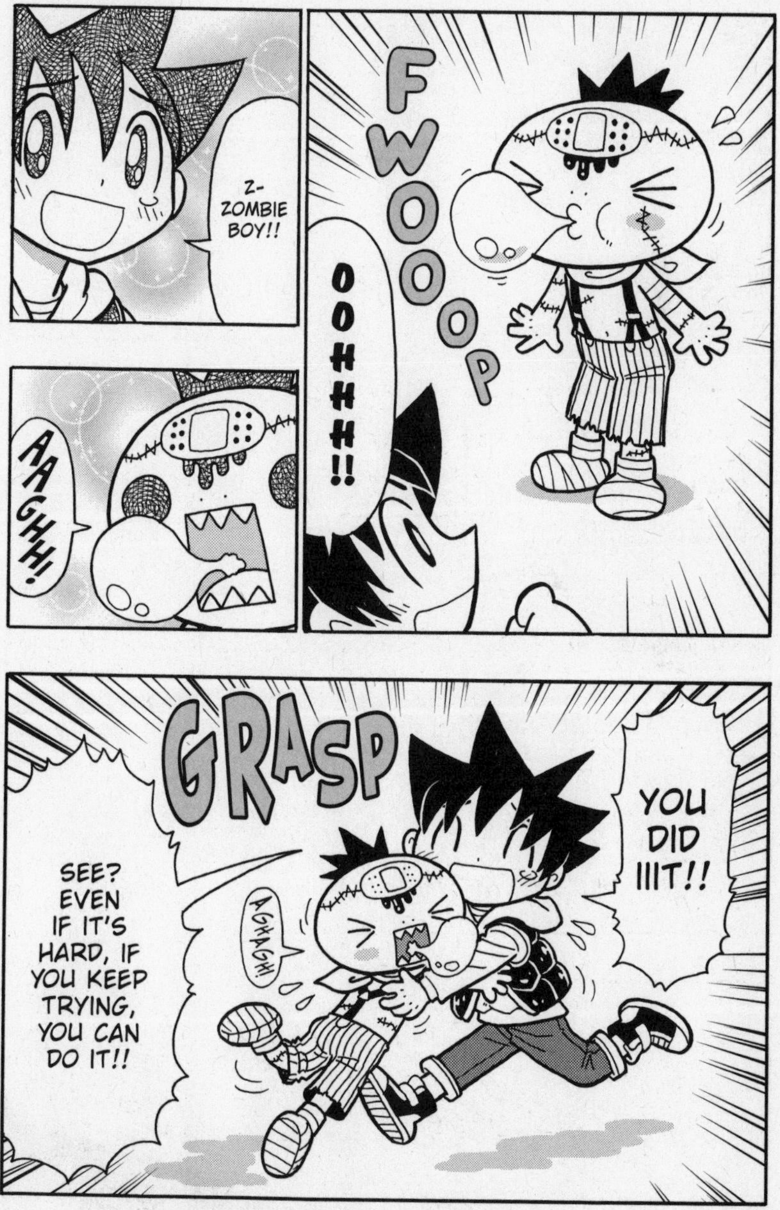
FWOOOOP
OOHHHH!!
Z-ZOMBIE BOY!!
AAGHH!
GRASP
YOU DID IIIT!!
AGHAGH!
SEE? EVEN IF IT'S HARD, IF YOU KEEP TRYING, YOU CAN DO IT!!

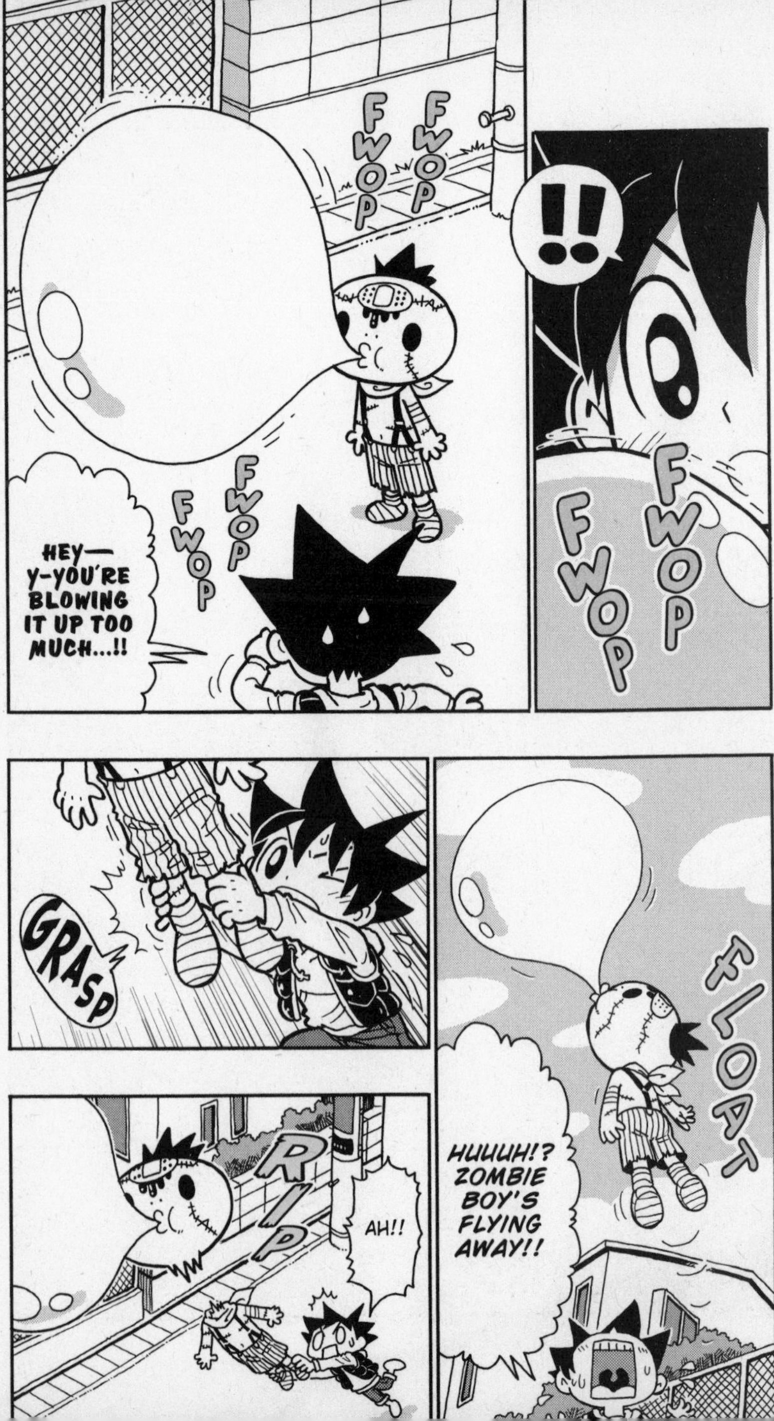
!!
FWOP FWOP
FWOP FWOP
FWOP FWOP
FWOP FWOP
HEY— Y-YOU'RE BLOWING IT UP TOO MUCH...!!
FLOAT
HUUUH!? ZOMBIE BOY'S FLYING AWAY!!
GRASP
RIP
AH!!

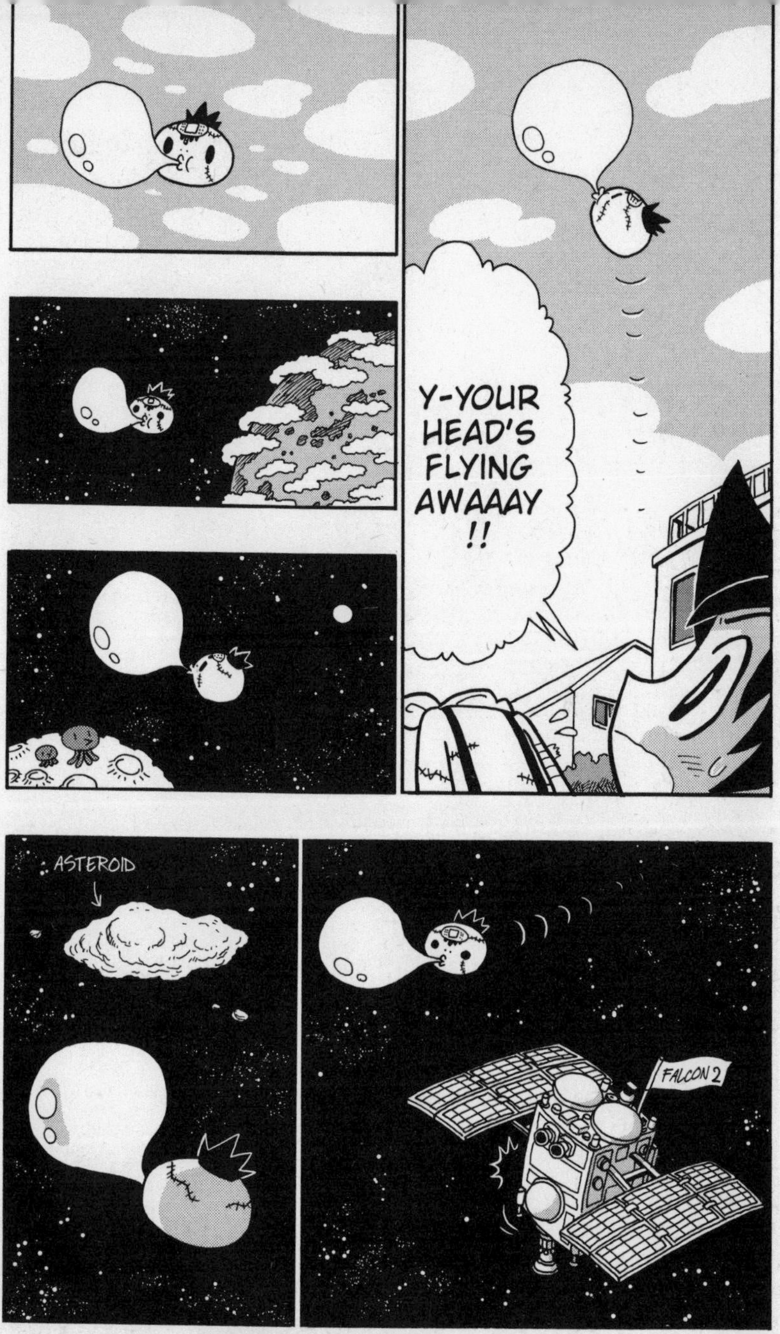
Y-YOUR HEAD'S FLYING AWAAAY!!
FALCON 2
ASTEROID

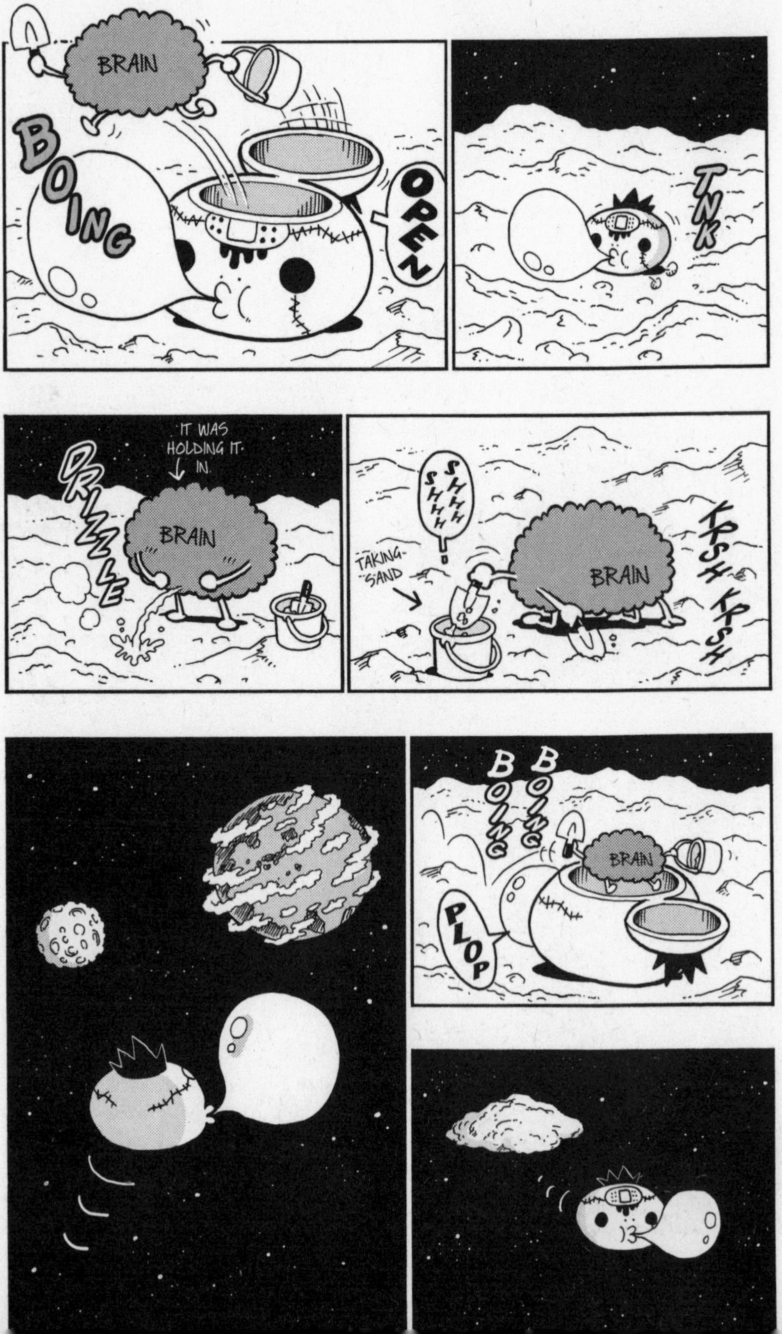
TNK
BRAIN
OPEN
BOING
KRSH KRSH
SHHHH
SHHHH
TAKING SAND
BRAIN
IT WAS HOLDING IT IN.
BRAIN
DRIZZLE
BOING
BOING
BRAIN
PLOP

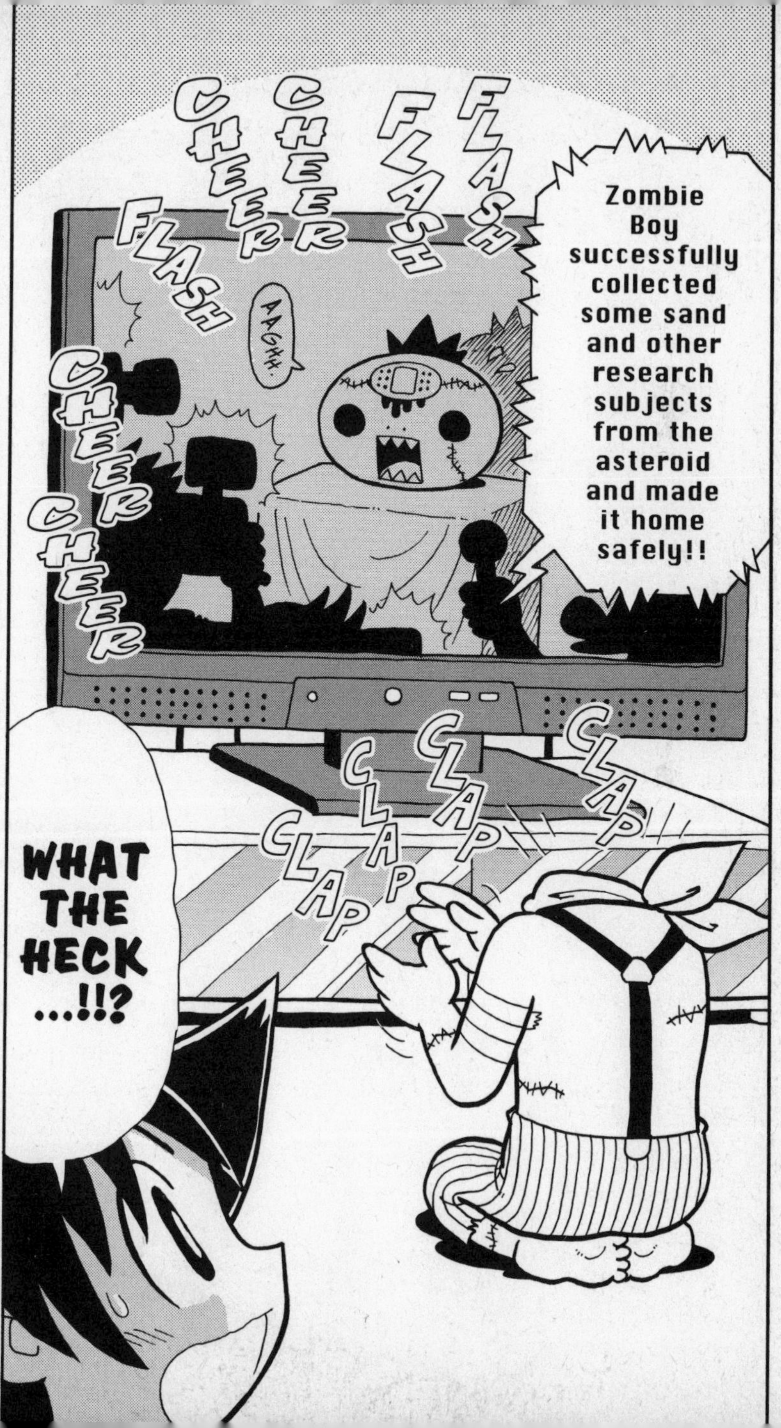
FLASH
FLASH
CHEER
CHEER
Zombie Boy successfully collected some sand and other research subjects from the asteroid and made it home safely!!
FLASH
AAGHH.
CHEER
CHEER
CLAP
CLAP
CLAP
CLAP
WHAT THE HECK ...!!?

LET'Z LEARN SOME ZOMBIE GAMEZ!

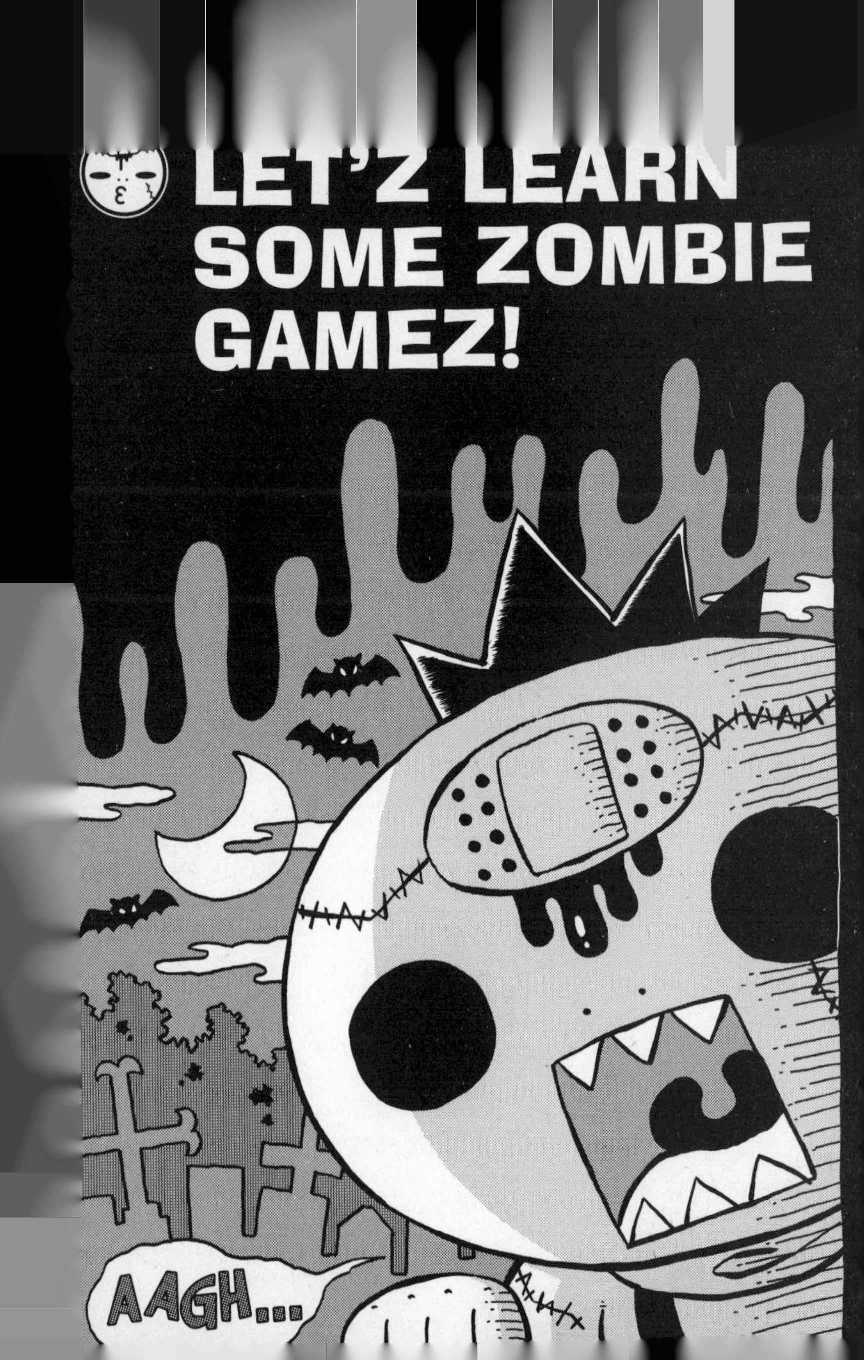
AAGH...

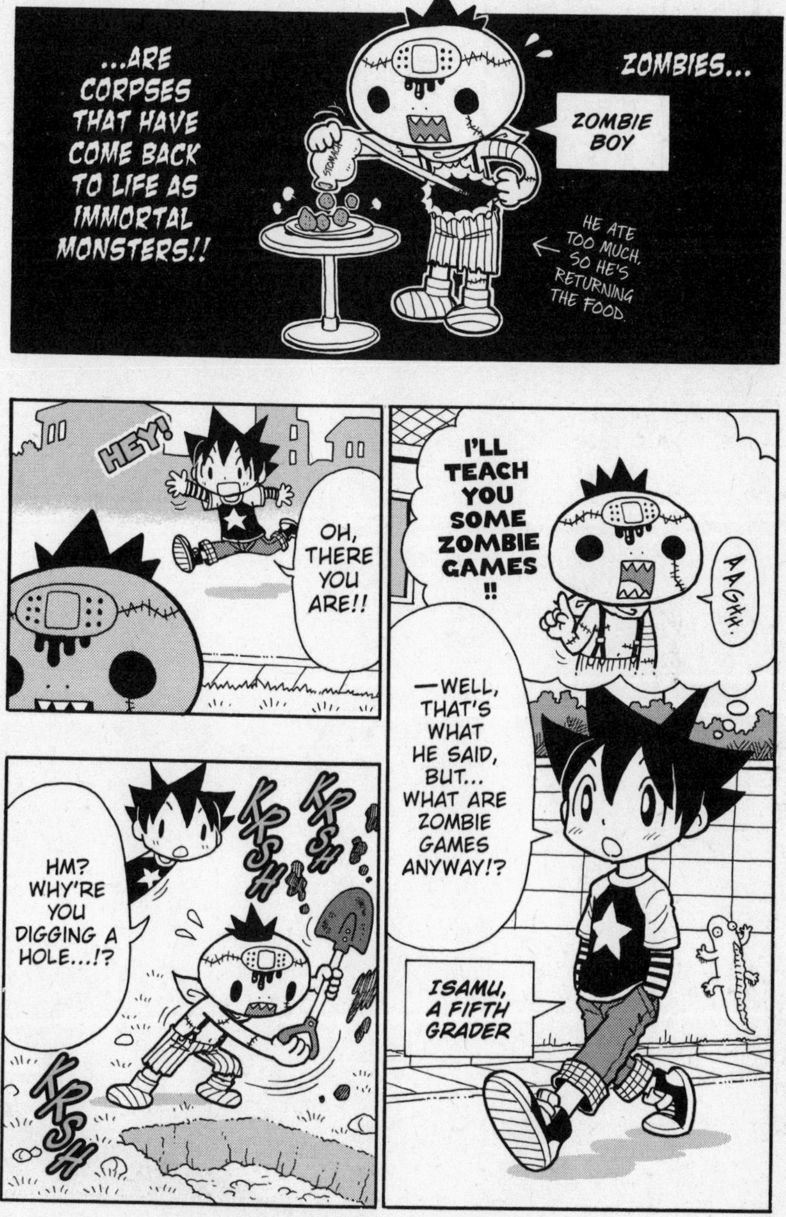
ZOMBIES...
ZOMBIE BOY
STOMACH
HE ATE TOO MUCH, SO HE'S RETURNING THE FOOD.
...ARE CORPSES THAT HAVE COME BACK TO LIFE AS IMMORTAL MONSTERS!!
I'LL TEACH YOU SOME ZOMBIE GAMES!!
AAGHH.
—WELL, THAT'S WHAT HE SAID, BUT... WHAT ARE ZOMBIE GAMES ANYWAY!?
ISAMU, A FIFTH GRADER
HEY!
OH, THERE YOU ARE!!
KRSH
KRSH
HM? WHY'RE YOU DIGGING A HOLE...!?
KRSH

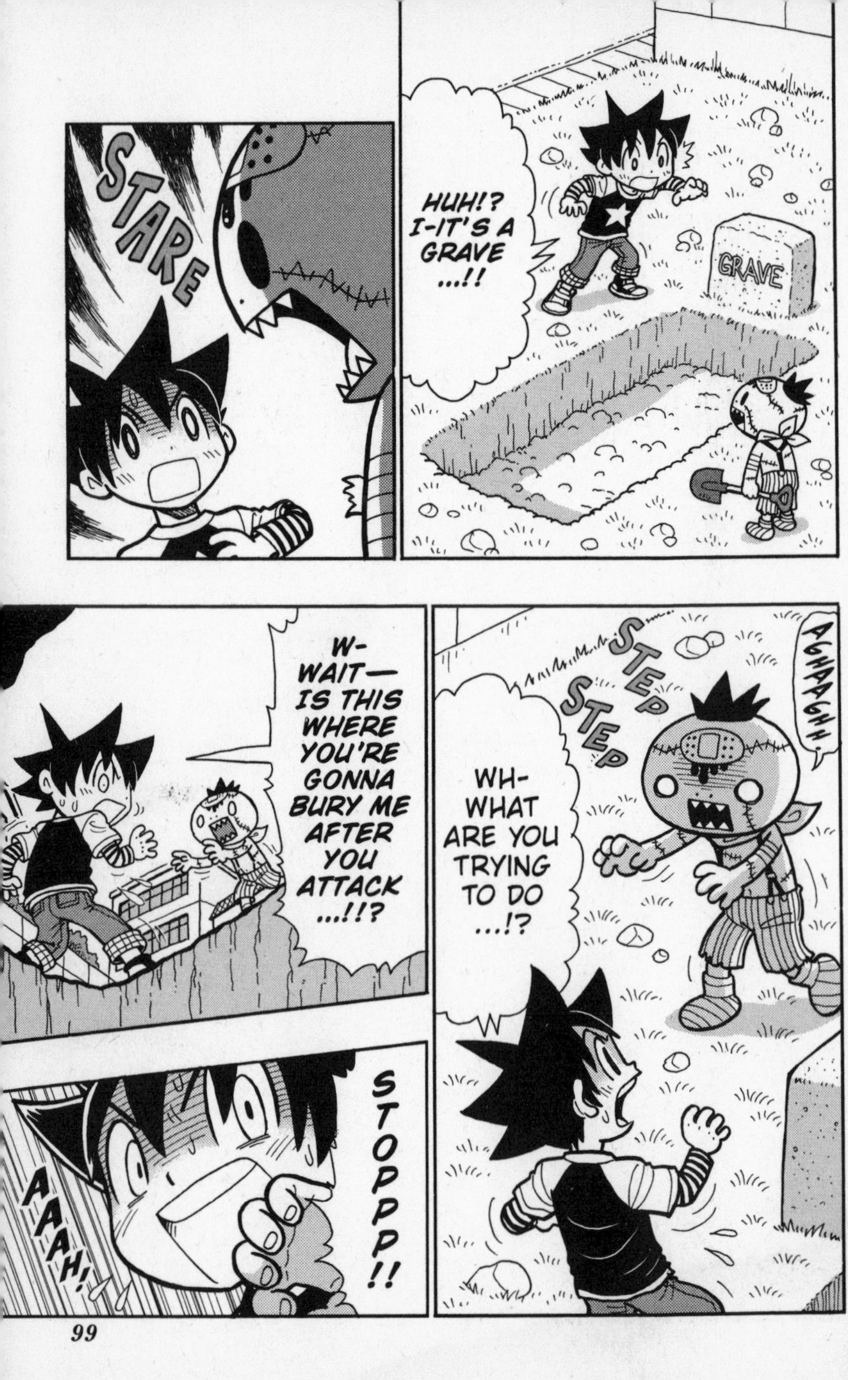
HUH!? I-IT'S A GRAVE ...!!
GRAVE
STARE
STEP STEP
AGHAAGHH
WH-WHAT ARE YOU TRYING TO DO ...!?
W-WAIT— IS THIS WHERE YOU'RE GONNA BURY ME AFTER YOU ATTACK ...!!?
STOPPP!!
AAAH!

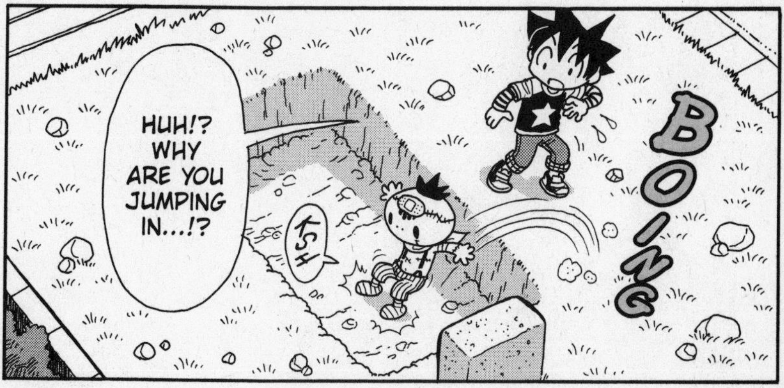
BOING
KSH
HUH!? WHY ARE YOU JUMPING IN...!?

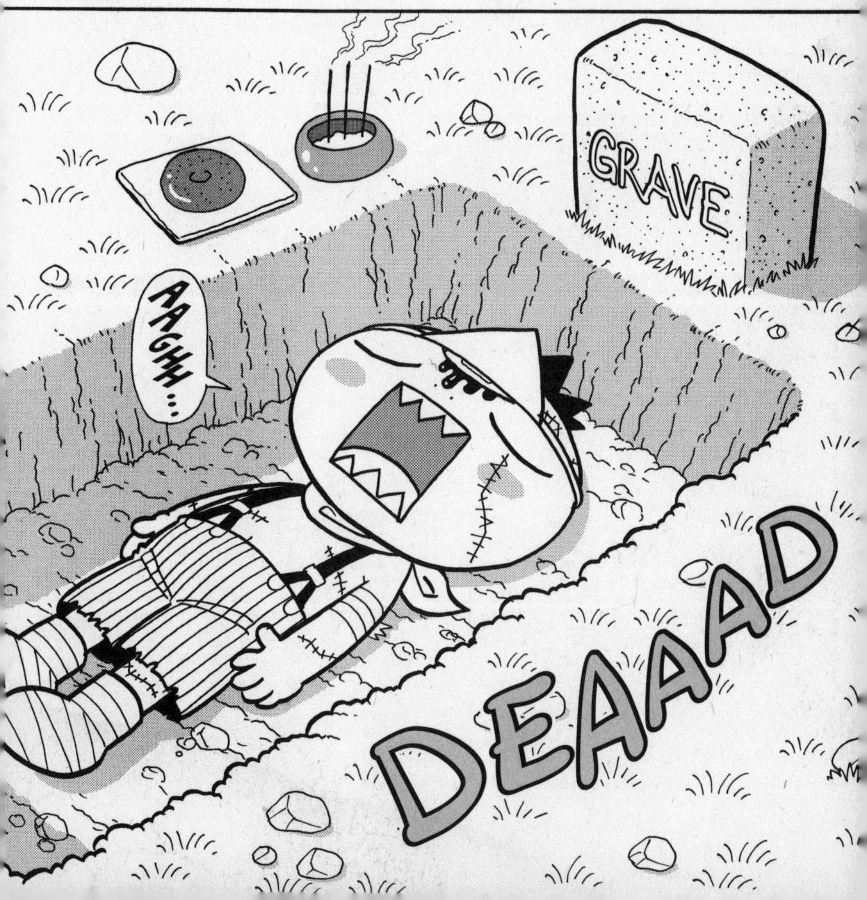
GRAVE
AAGHH...
DEAAAD

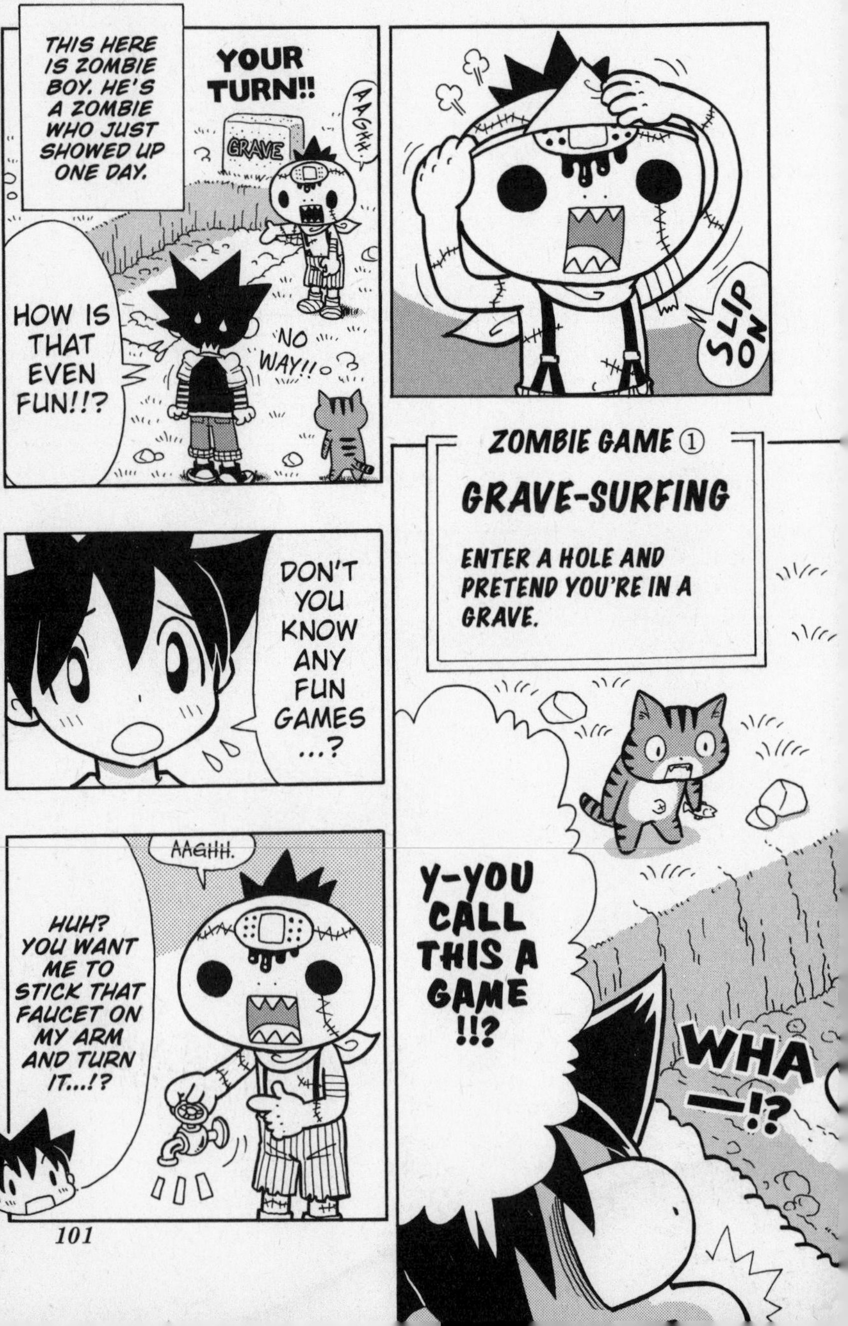
SLIP ON
ZOMBIE GAME ①
GRAVE-SURFING
ENTER A HOLE AND PRETEND YOU'RE IN A GRAVE.
Y-YOU CALL THIS A GAME!!?
WHA—!?
THIS HERE IS ZOMBIE BOY. HE'S A ZOMBIE WHO JUST SHOWED UP ONE DAY.
YOUR TURN!!
AAGHH.
GRAVE
NO WAY!!
HOW IS THAT EVEN FUN!!?
DON'T YOU KNOW ANY FUN GAMES...?
AAGHH.
HUH? YOU WANT ME TO STICK THAT FAUCET ON MY ARM AND TURN IT...!?

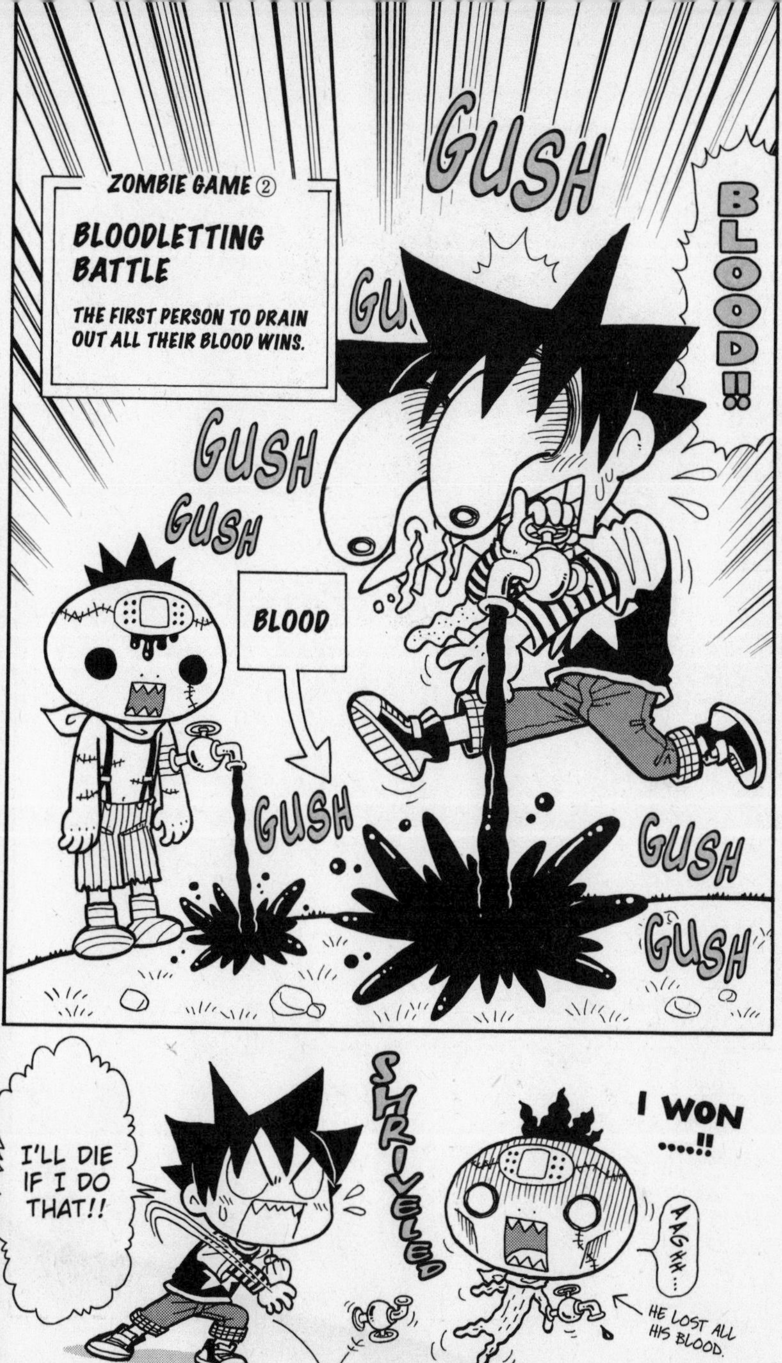
GUSH
BLOOD!!
ZOMBIE GAME ②
BLOODLETTING BATTLE
THE FIRST PERSON TO DRAIN OUT ALL THEIR BLOOD WINS.
GUSH
GUSH
BLOOD
GUSH
GUSH
GUSH
I WON ....!!
AAGHH...
HE LOST ALL HIS BLOOD.
SHRIVELED
I'LL DIE IF I DO THAT!!

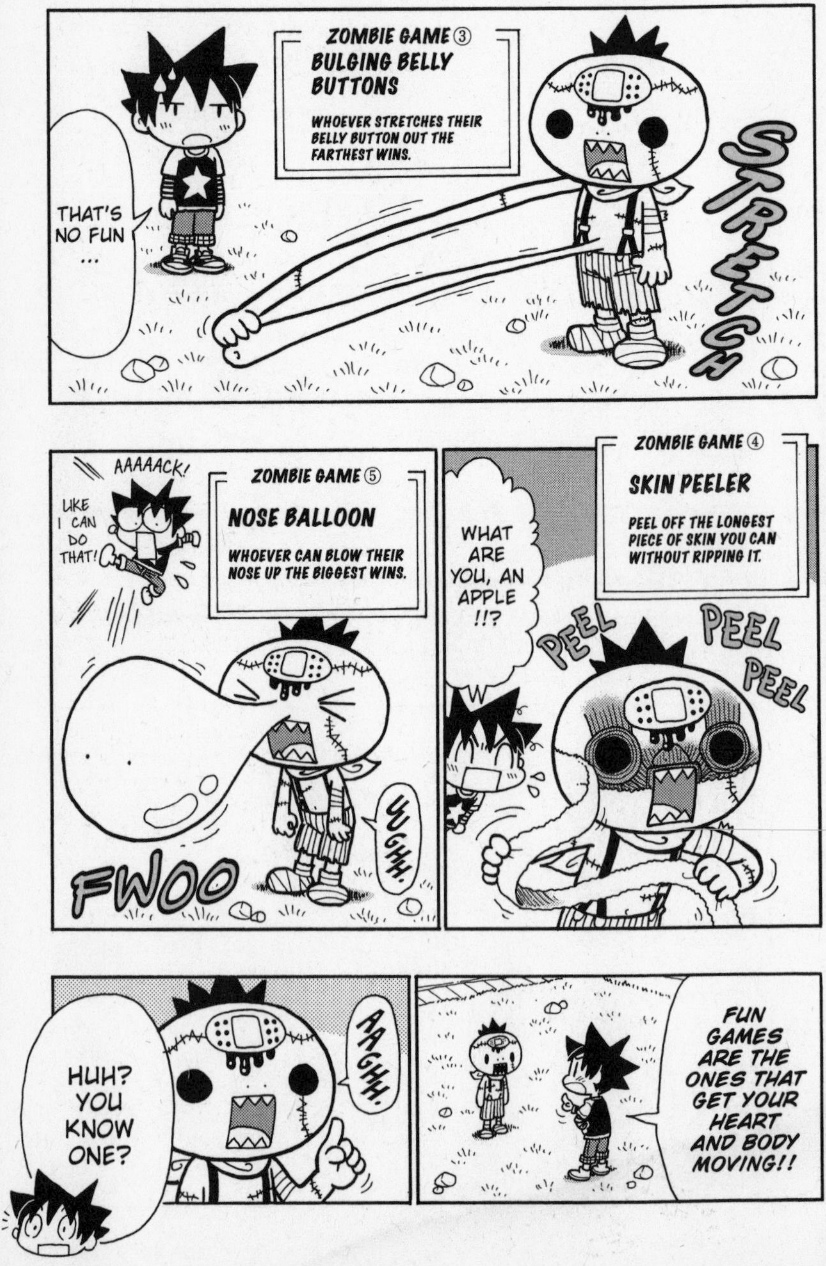
ZOMBIE GAME ③
BULGING BELLY BUTTONS
WHOEVER STRETCHES THEIR BELLY BUTTON OUT THE FARTHEST WINS.
STRETCH
THAT'S NO FUN ...
ZOMBIE GAME ④
SKIN PEELER
PEEL OFF THE LONGEST PIECE OF SKIN YOU CAN WITHOUT RIPPING IT.
PEEL
PEEL
PEEL
WHAT ARE YOU, AN APPLE !!?
ZOMBIE GAME ⑤
NOSE BALLOON
WHOEVER CAN BLOW THEIR NOSE UP THE BIGGEST WINS.
UGHH.
FWOO
AAAAACK!
LIKE I CAN DO THAT!
FUN GAMES ARE THE ONES THAT GET YOUR HEART AND BODY MOVING!!
AAGHH.
HUH? YOU KNOW ONE?

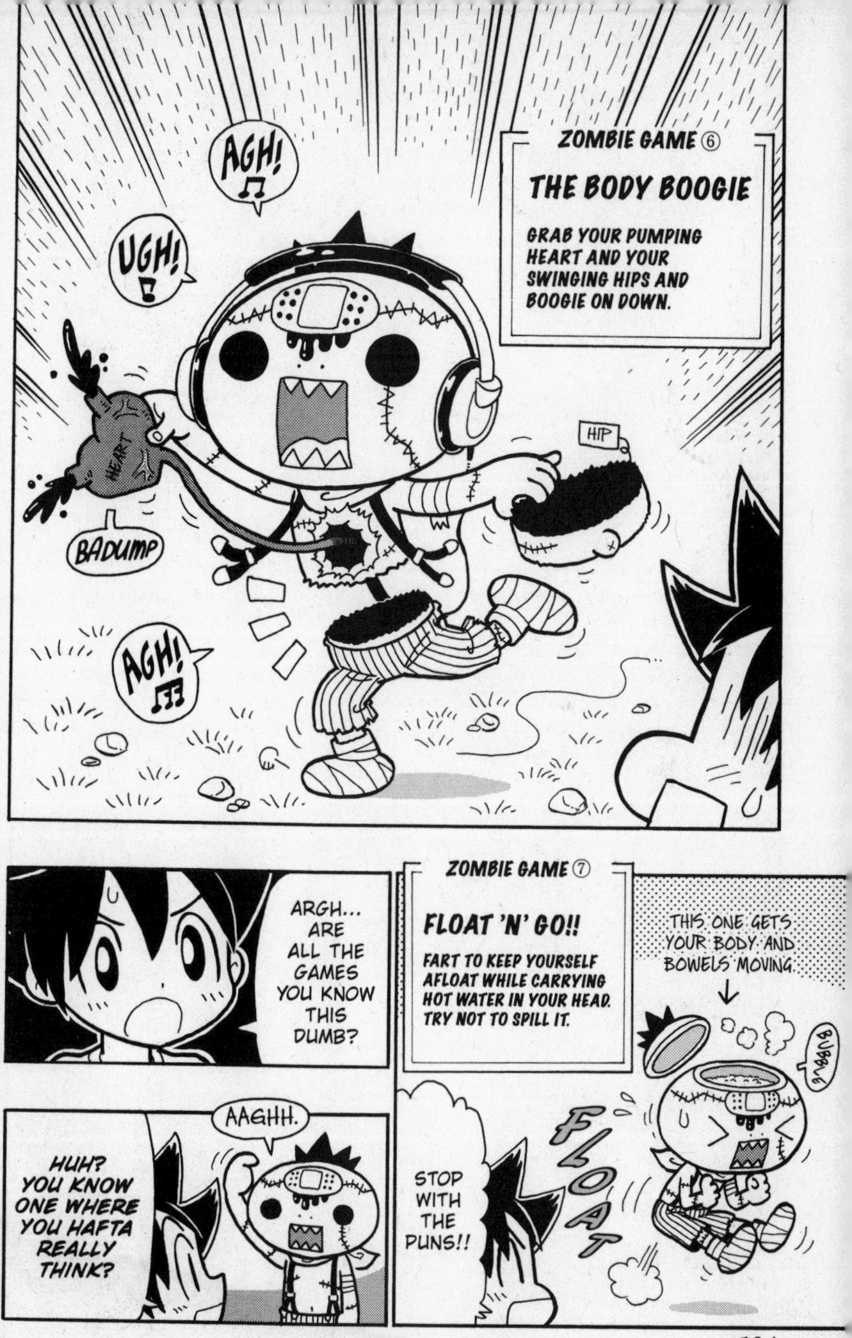
ZOMBIE GAME ⑥
THE BODY BOOGIE
GRAB YOUR PUMPING HEART AND YOUR SWINGING HIPS AND BOOGIE ON DOWN.
AGH! ♫
UGH! ♪
HIP
HEART
BADUMP
AGH! ♫♫
ZOMBIE GAME ⑦
FLOAT 'N' GO!!
FART TO KEEP YOURSELF AFLOAT WHILE CARRYING HOT WATER IN YOUR HEAD. TRY NOT TO SPILL IT.
THIS ONE GETS YOUR BODY AND BOWELS MOVING.
BUBBLE
FLOAT
STOP WITH THE PUNS!!
ARGH... ARE ALL THE GAMES YOU KNOW THIS DUMB?
AAGHH.
HUH? YOU KNOW ONE WHERE YOU HAFTA REALLY THINK?

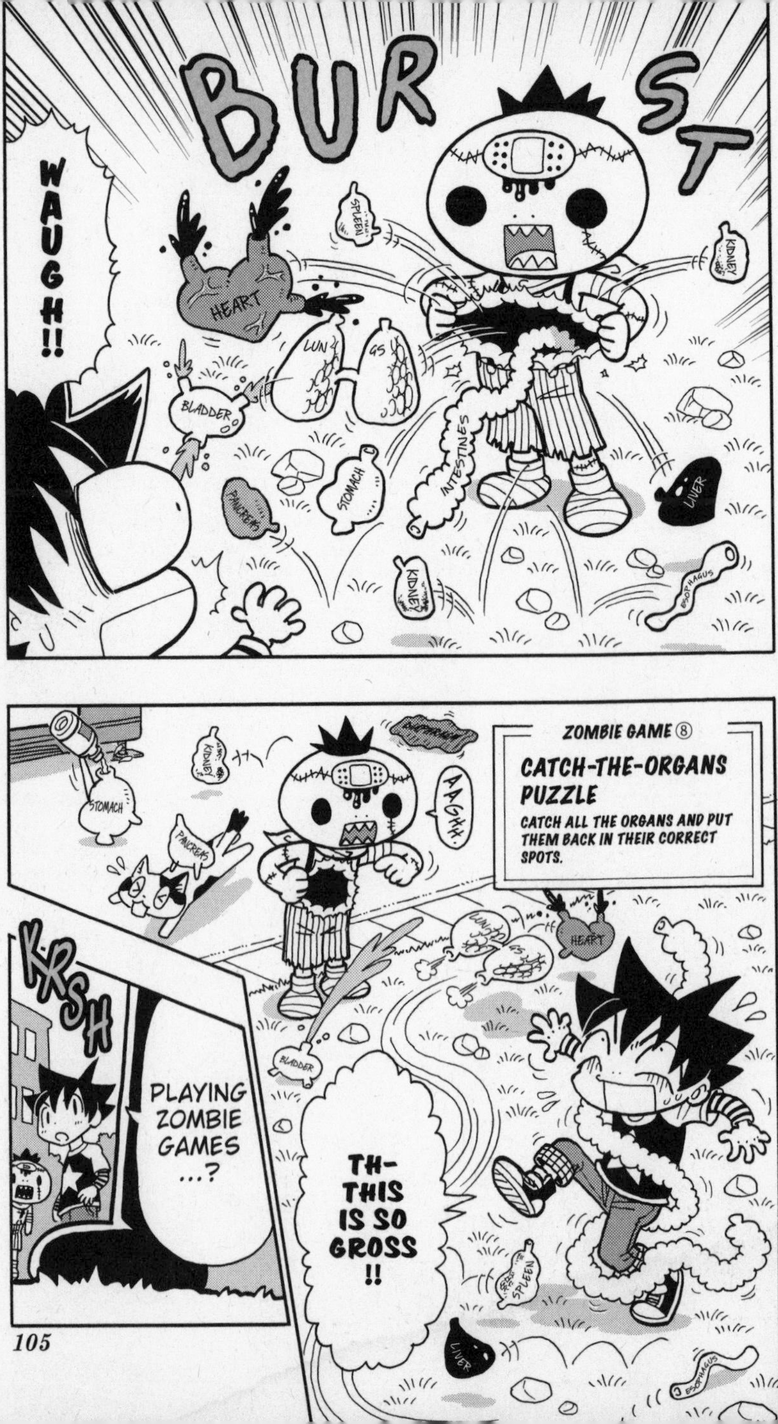
BURST
KIDNEY
SPLEEN
WAUGH!!
HEART
LUN GS
BLADDER
INTESTINES
LIVER
STOMACH
PANCREAS
KIDNEY
ESOPHAGUS
ZOMBIE GAME ⑧
CATCH-THE-ORGANS PUZZLE
CATCH ALL THE ORGANS AND PUT THEM BACK IN THEIR CORRECT SPOTS.
AAGHH.
KIDNEY
STOMACH
PANCREAS
HEART
LUN GS
BLADDER
TH-THIS IS SO GROSS!!
SPLEEN
LIVER
ESOPHAGUS
K-RSH
PLAYING ZOMBIE GAMES ...?

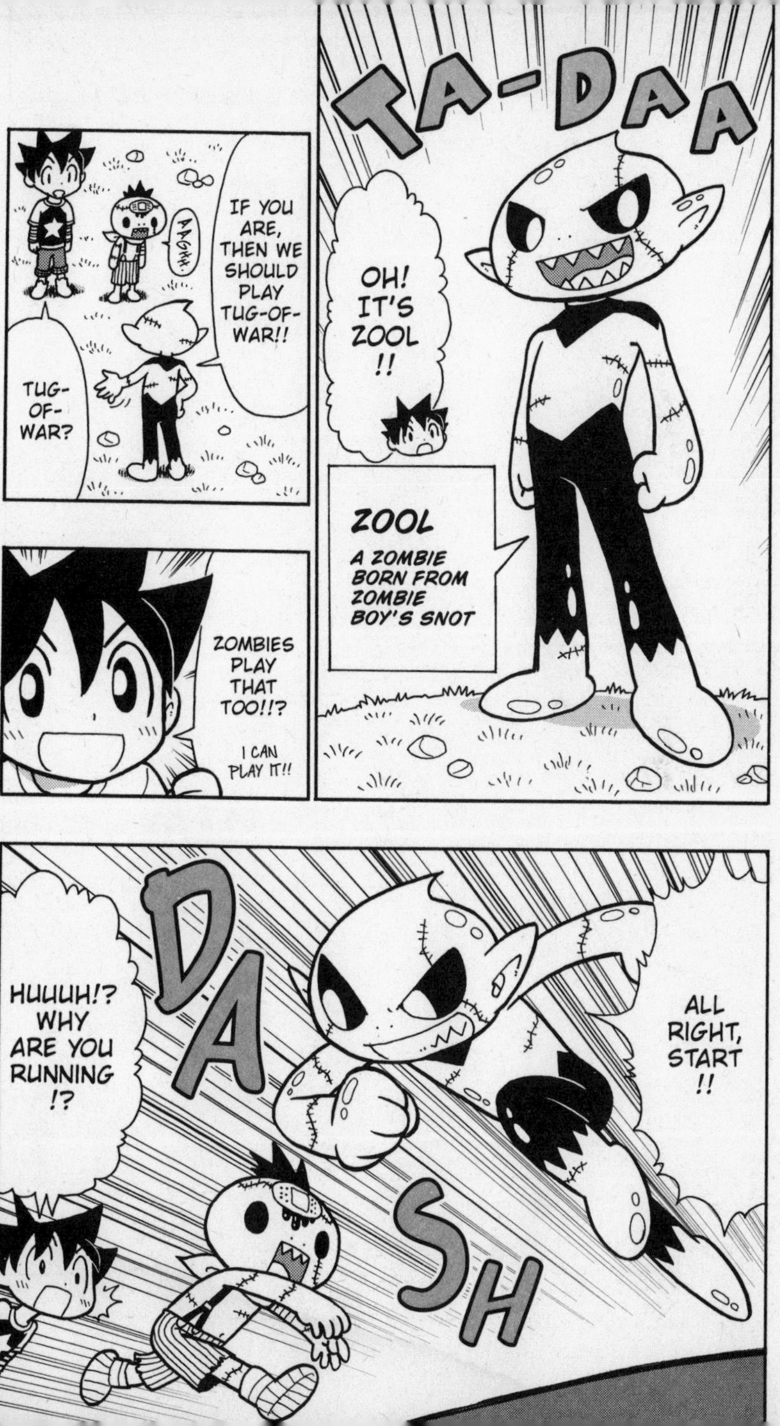
TA-DAA
OH! IT'S ZOOL!!
ZOOL
A ZOMBIE BORN FROM ZOMBIE BOY'S SNOT
IF YOU ARE, THEN WE SHOULD PLAY TUG-OF-WAR!!
AAGHH.
TUG-OF-WAR?
ZOMBIES PLAY THAT TOO!!?
I CAN PLAY IT!!
ALL RIGHT, START!!
DASH
HUUUH!? WHY ARE YOU RUNNING!?

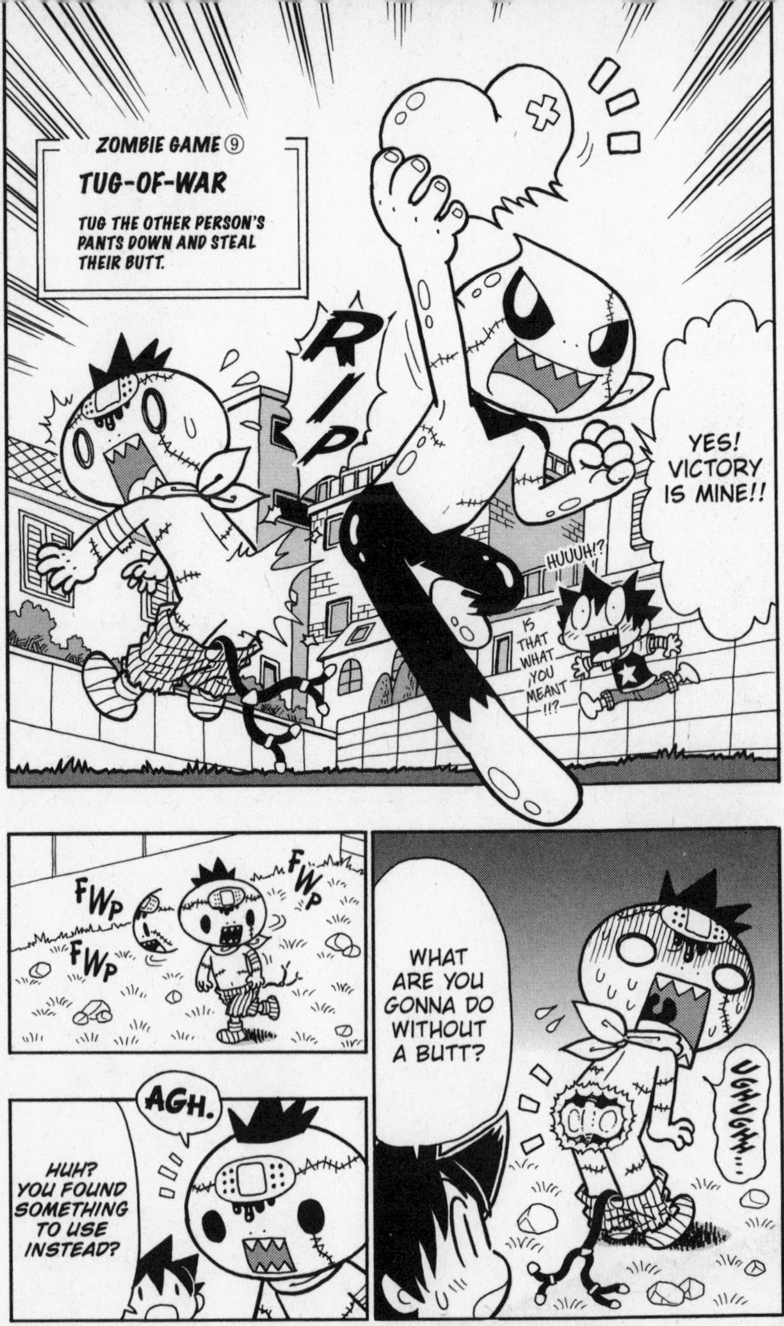
ZOMBIE GAME ⑨
TUG-OF-WAR
TUG THE OTHER PERSON'S PANTS DOWN AND STEAL THEIR BUTT.
RIP
YES! VICTORY IS MINE!!
HUUUH!?
IS THAT WHAT YOU MEANT!!?
WHAT ARE YOU GONNA DO WITHOUT A BUTT?
UGHUGH...
FWP
FWP
FWP
AGH.
HUH? YOU FOUND SOMETHING TO USE INSTEAD?

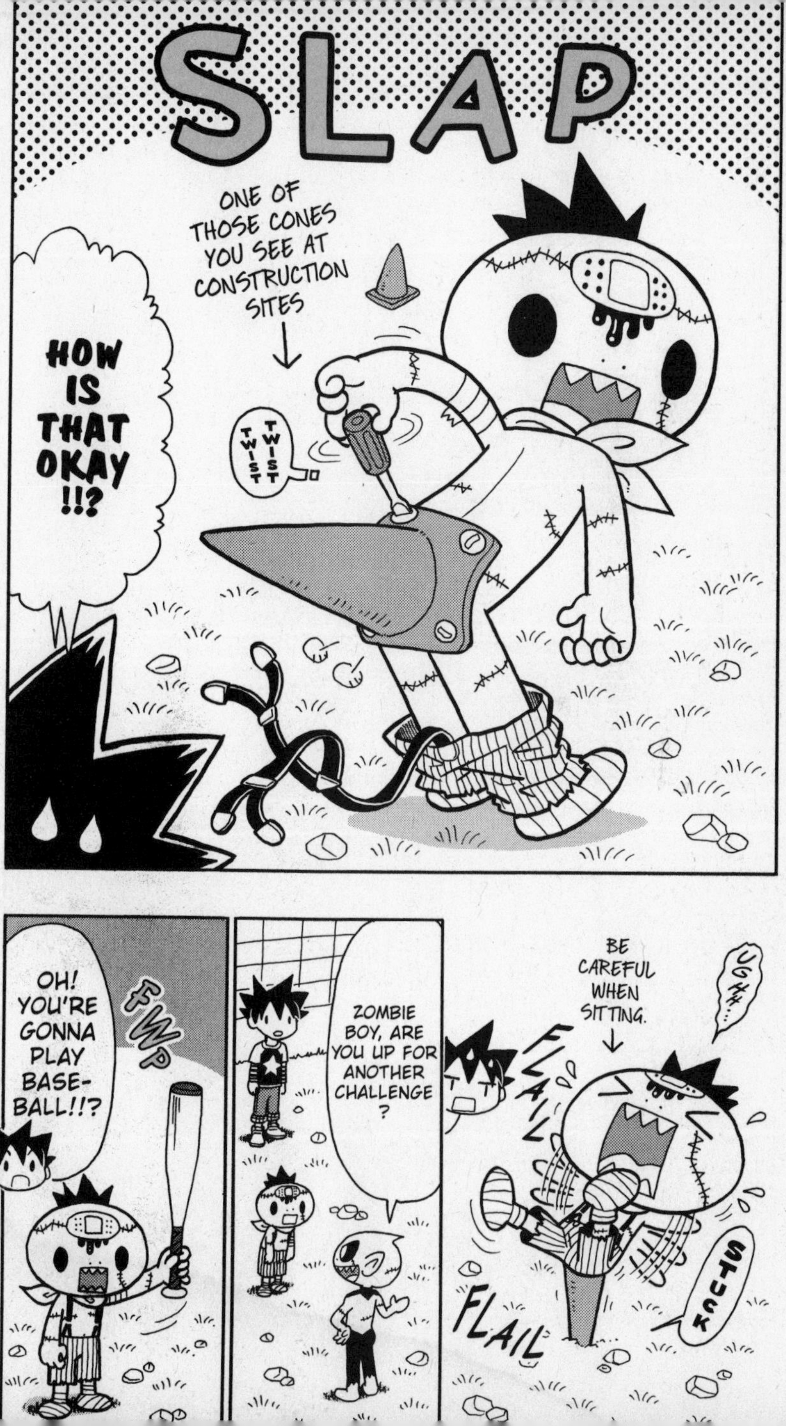
SLAP
ONE OF THOSE CONES YOU SEE AT CONSTRUCTION SITES
TWIST TWIST
HOW IS THAT OKAY!!?
BE CAREFUL WHEN SITTING.
UGHH...
FLAIL
FLAIL
STUCK
ZOMBIE BOY, ARE YOU UP FOR ANOTHER CHALLENGE?
OH! YOU'RE GONNA PLAY BASE-BALL!!?
FWP

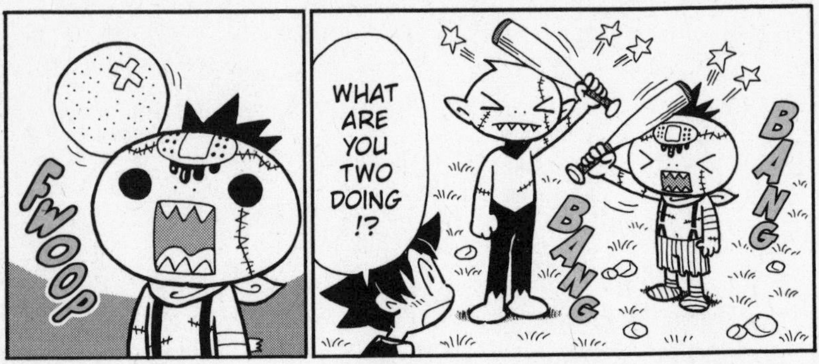
WHAT ARE YOU TWO DOING !?
BANG
BANG
FWOOP

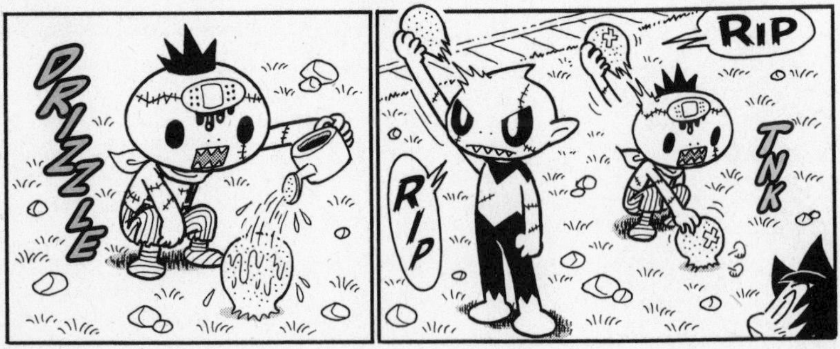
RIP
RIP
TNK
DRIZZLE

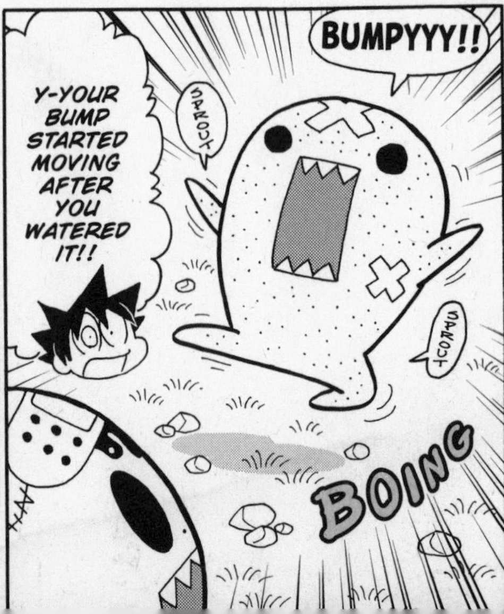
BUMPYYY!!
Y-YOUR BUMP STARTED MOVING AFTER YOU WATERED IT!!
SPROUT
SPROUT
BOING

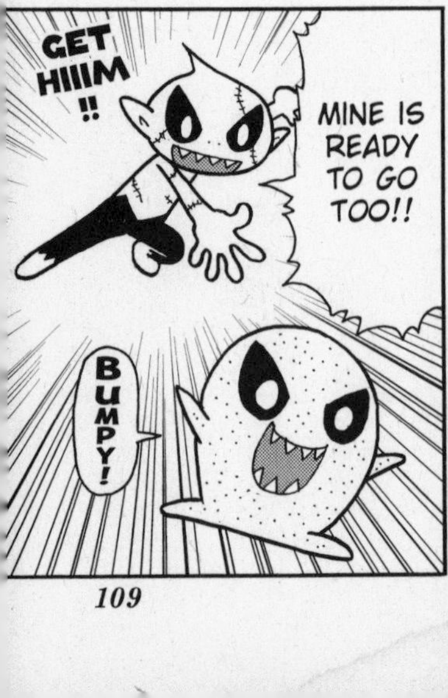
GET HIIIM !!
MINE IS READY TO GO TOO!!
BUMPY!

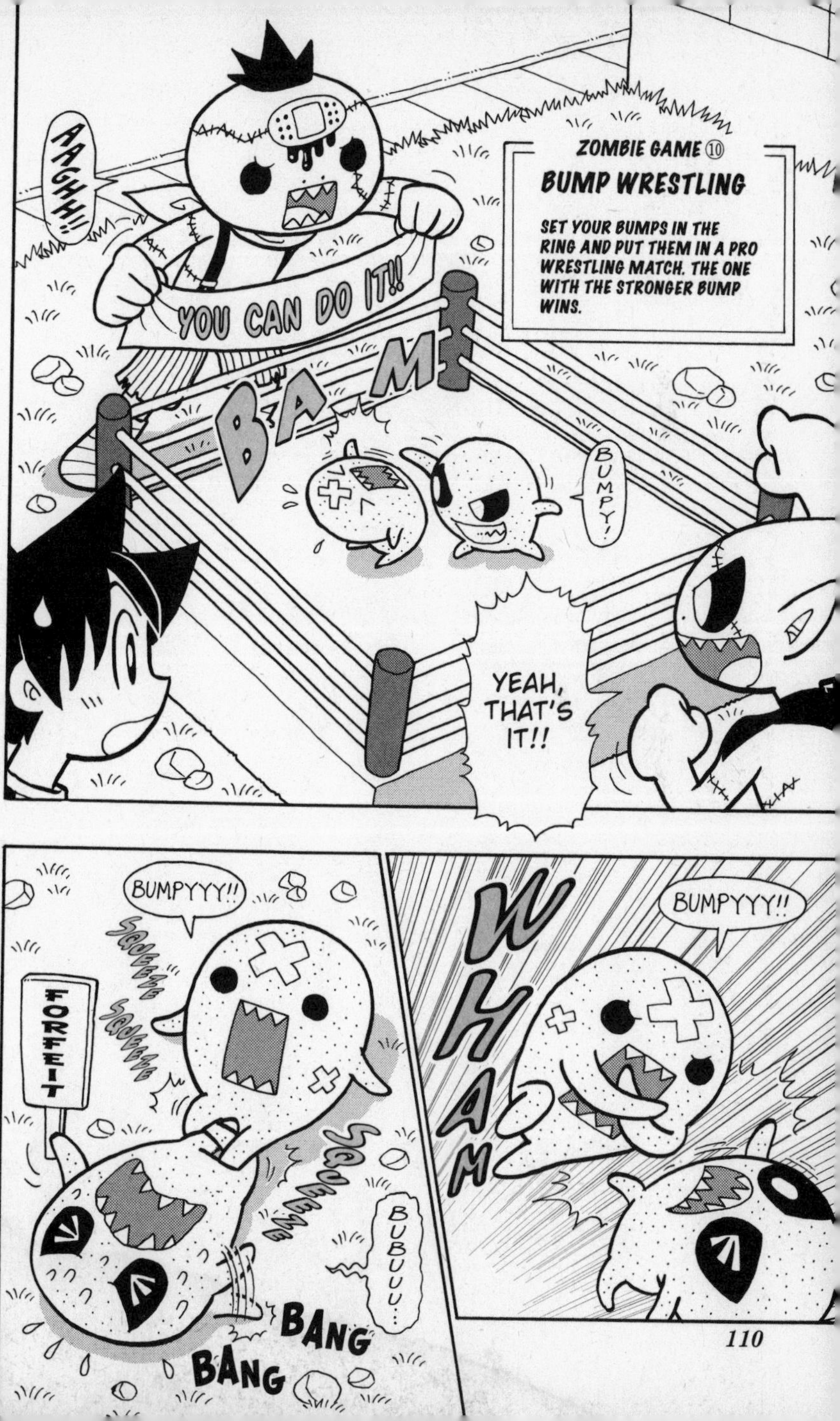
ZOMBIE GAME ⑩
BUMP WRESTLING
SET YOUR BUMPS IN THE RING AND PUT THEM IN A PRO WRESTLING MATCH. THE ONE WITH THE STRONGER BUMP WINS.
AAGHH!!
YOU CAN DO IT!!
BAM
BUMPY!
YEAH, THAT'S IT!!
BUMPYYY!!
WHAM
BUMPYYY!!
SQUEEE
SQUEEE
FORFEIT
SQUEEEE
BUBUUU...
BANG
BANG

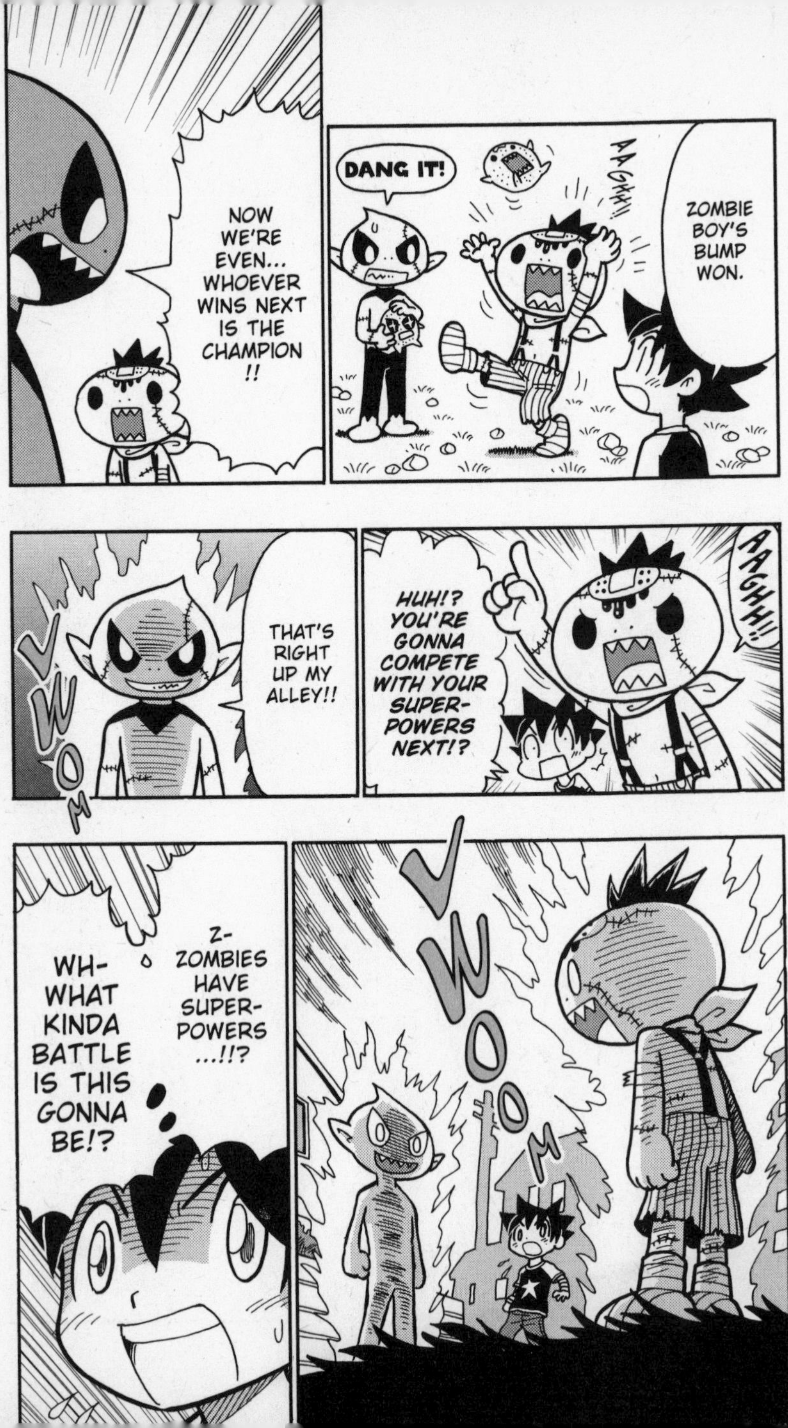
ZOMBIE BOY'S BUMP WON.
AAGHH!!
DANG IT!
NOW WE'RE EVEN... WHOEVER WINS NEXT IS THE CHAMPION!!
AAGHH!!
HUH!? YOU'RE GONNA COMPETE WITH YOUR SUPER-POWERS NEXT!?
THAT'S RIGHT UP MY ALLEY!!
VWOOM
VWOOOM
Z-ZOMBIES HAVE SUPER-POWERS...!!?
WH-WHAT KINDA BATTLE IS THIS GONNA BE!?

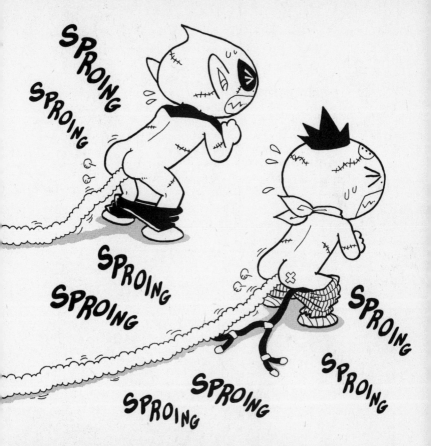

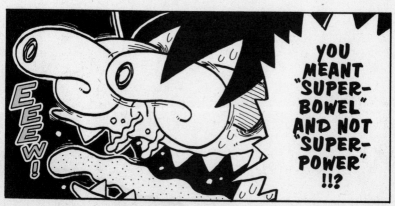

112

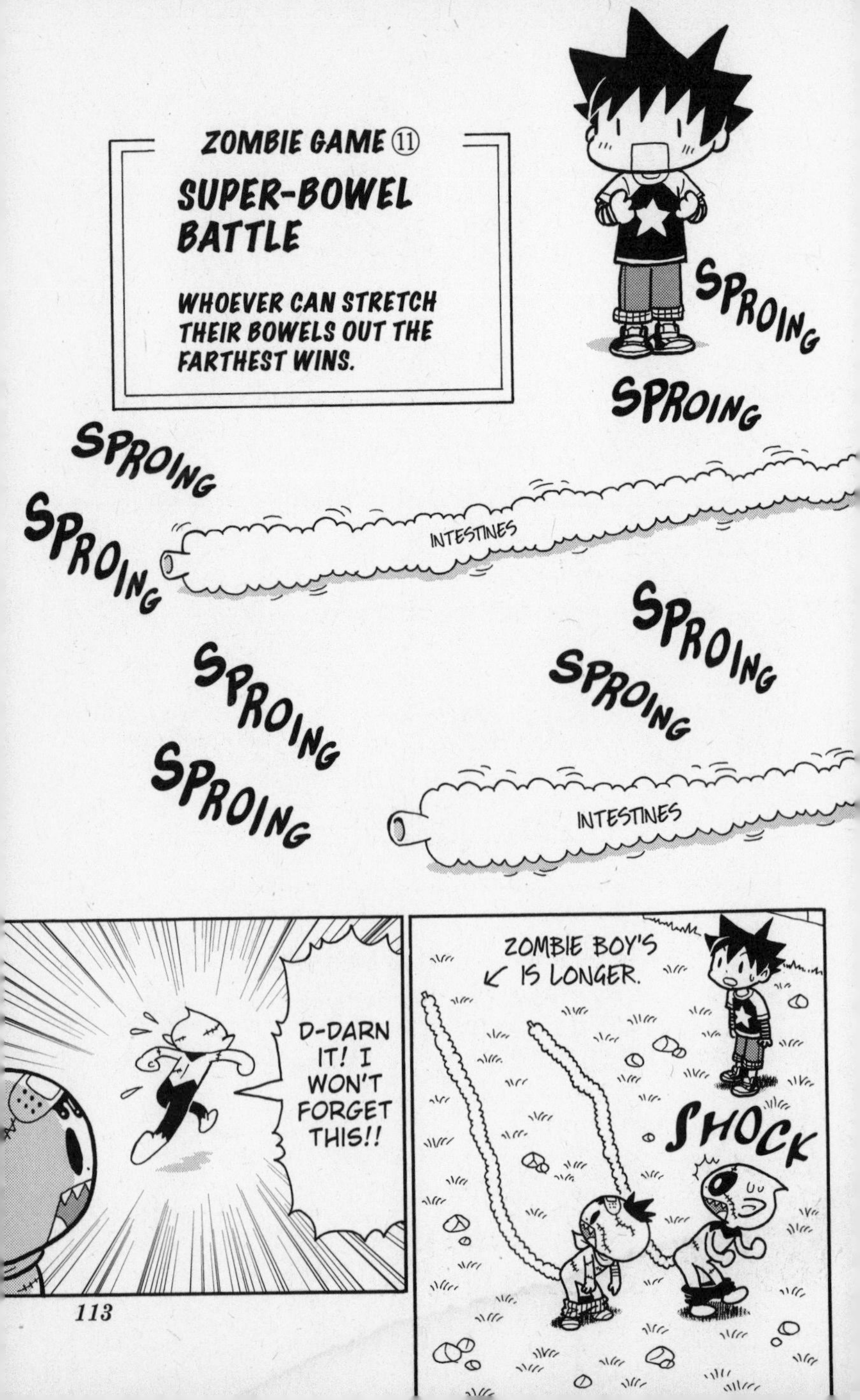
ZOMBIE GAME ⑪
SUPER-BOWEL BATTLE
WHOEVER CAN STRETCH THEIR BOWELS OUT THE FARTHEST WINS.
SPROING
SPROING
SPROING
SPROING
INTESTINES
SPROING
SPROING
SPROING
SPROING
INTESTINES
ZOMBIE BOY'S ↙ IS LONGER.
SHOCK
D-DARN IT! I WON'T FORGET THIS!!

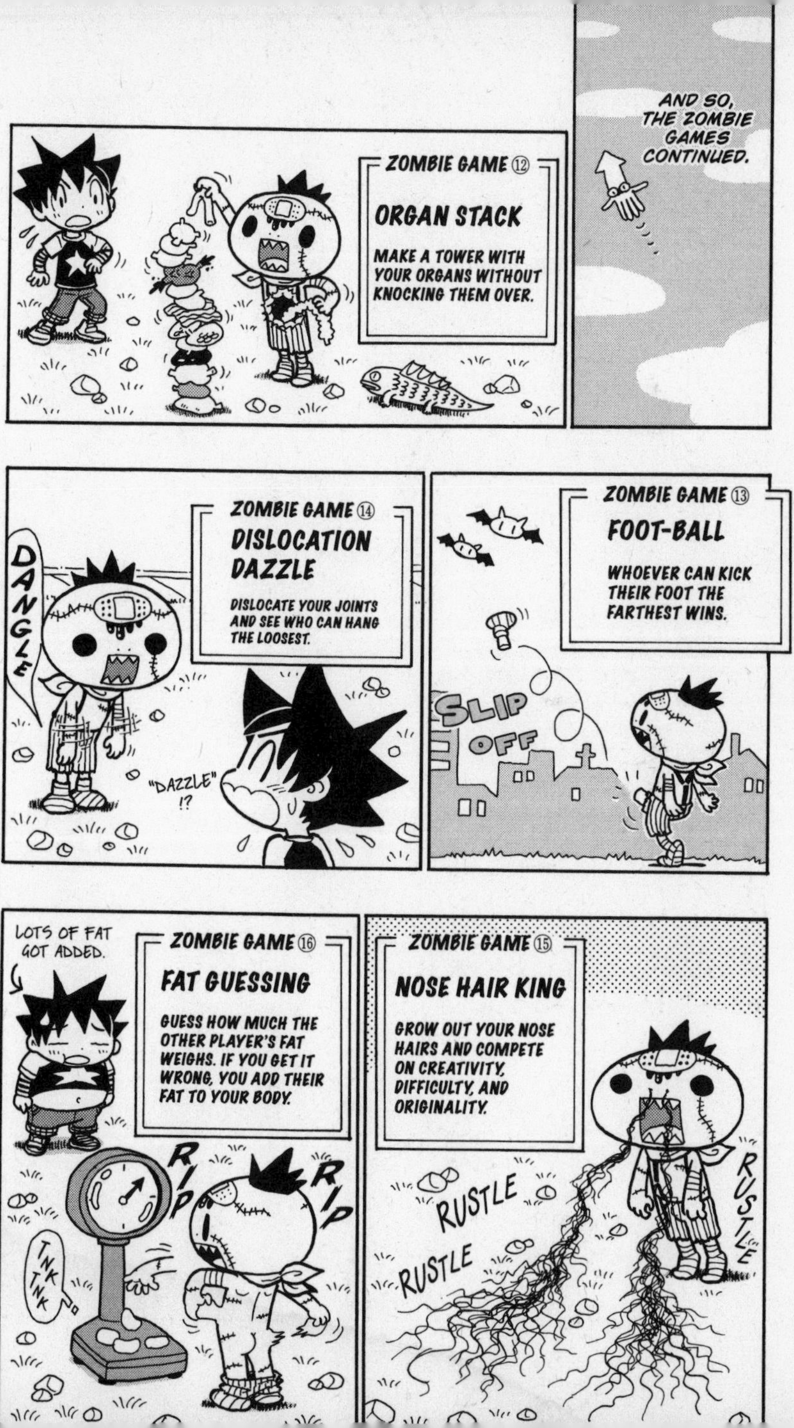

AND SO, THE ZOMBIE GAMES CONTINUED.
ZOMBIE GAME ⑫
ORGAN STACK
MAKE A TOWER WITH YOUR ORGANS WITHOUT KNOCKING THEM OVER.
ZOMBIE GAME ⑬
FOOT-BALL
WHOEVER CAN KICK THEIR FOOT THE FARTHEST WINS.
SLIP OFF
ZOMBIE GAME ⑭
DISLOCATION DAZZLE
DISLOCATE YOUR JOINTS AND SEE WHO CAN HANG THE LOOSEST.
DANGLE
"DAZZLE" !?
ZOMBIE GAME ⑮
NOSE HAIR KING
GROW OUT YOUR NOSE HAIRS AND COMPETE ON CREATIVITY, DIFFICULTY, AND ORIGINALITY.
RUSTLE
RUSTLE
RUSTLE
ZOMBIE GAME ⑯
FAT GUESSING
GUESS HOW MUCH THE OTHER PLAYER'S FAT WEIGHS. IF YOU GET IT WRONG, YOU ADD THEIR FAT TO YOUR BODY.
LOTS OF FAT GOT ADDED.
RIP
RIP
TNK TNK

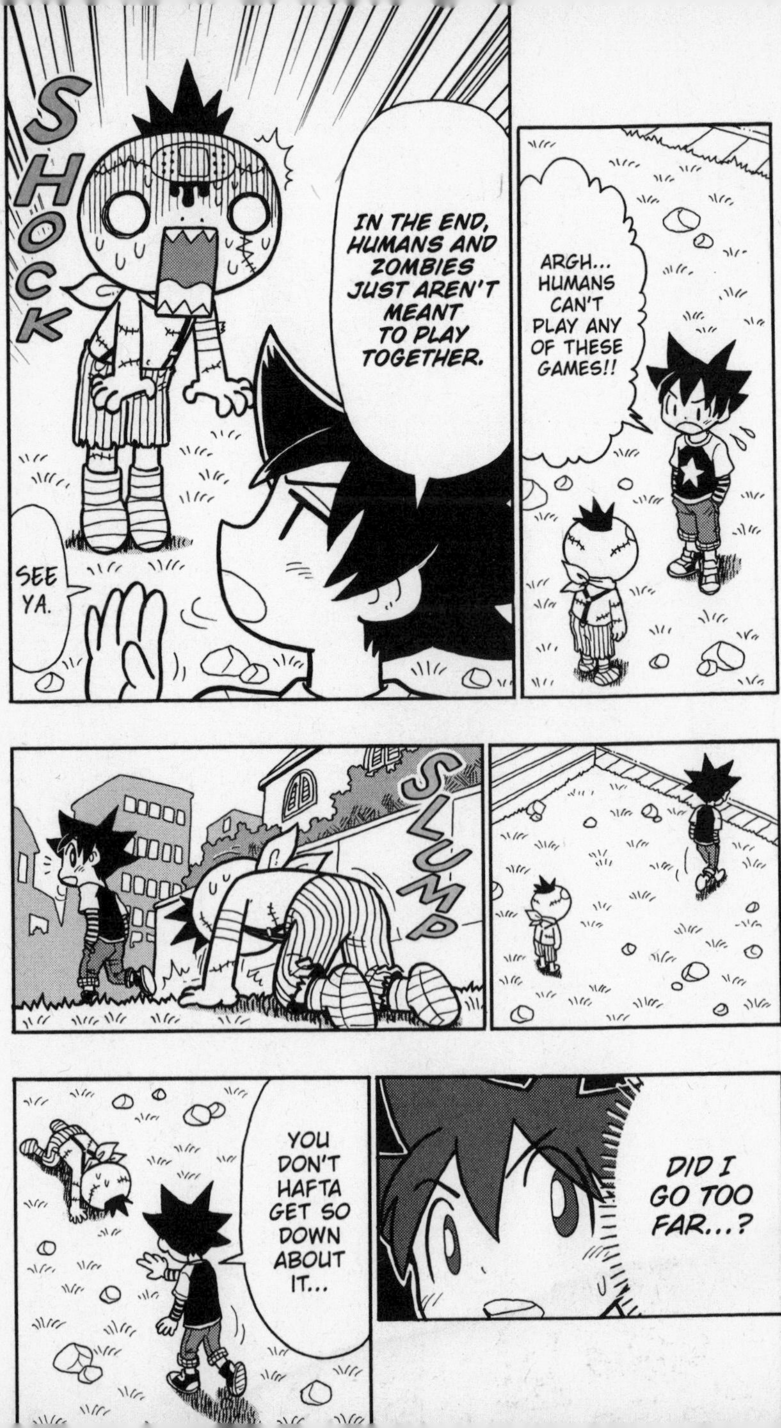
ARGH... HUMANS CAN'T PLAY ANY OF THESE GAMES!!
IN THE END, HUMANS AND ZOMBIES JUST AREN'T MEANT TO PLAY TOGETHER.
SHOCK
SEE YA.
SLUMP
DID I GO TOO FAR...?
YOU DON'T HAFTA GET SO DOWN ABOUT IT...

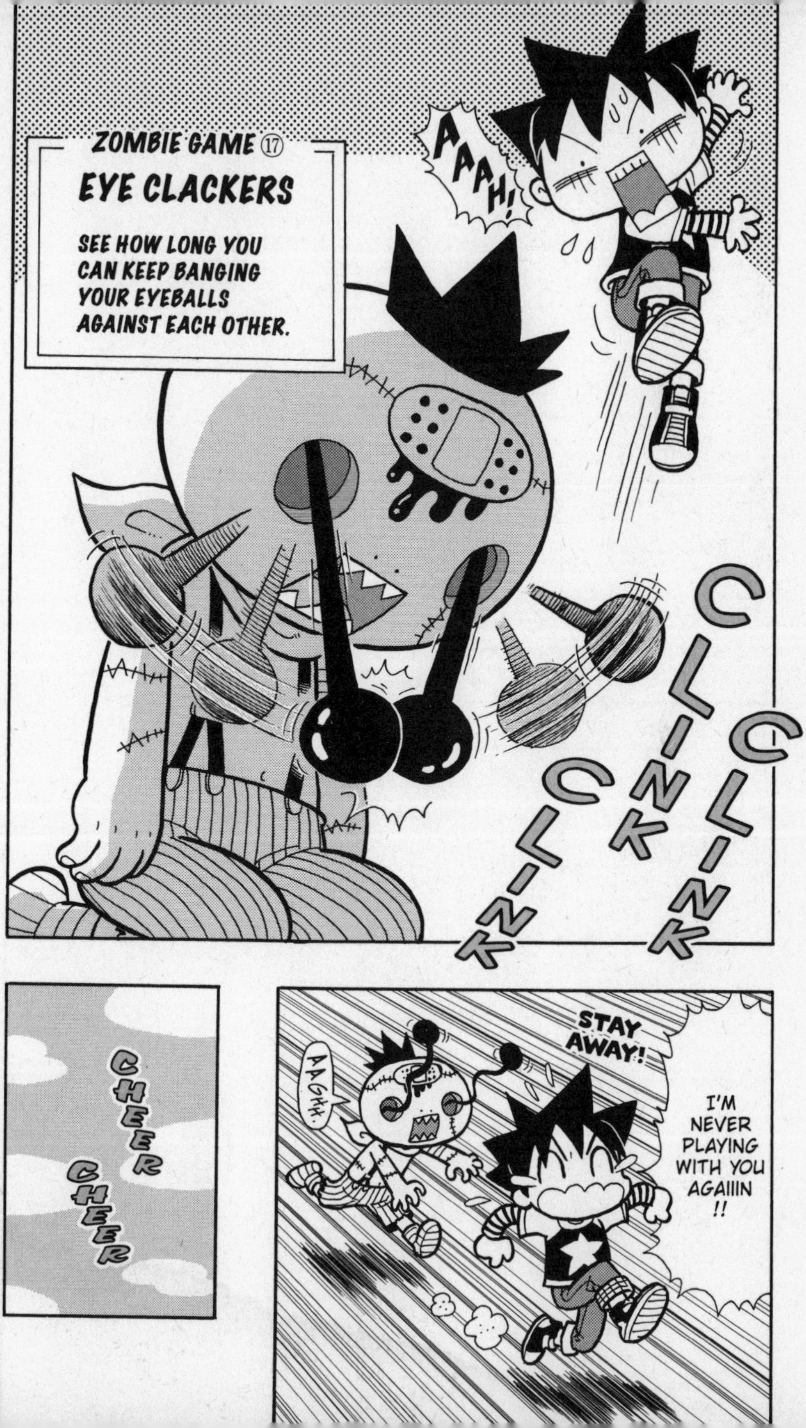
AAAH!
ZOMBIE GAME 17
EYE CLACKERS
SEE HOW LONG YOU CAN KEEP BANGING YOUR EYEBALLS AGAINST EACH OTHER.
CLINK
CLINK
CLINK
STAY AWAY!
I'M NEVER PLAYING WITH YOU AGAIIIN !!
AAGHH...
CHEER
CHEER

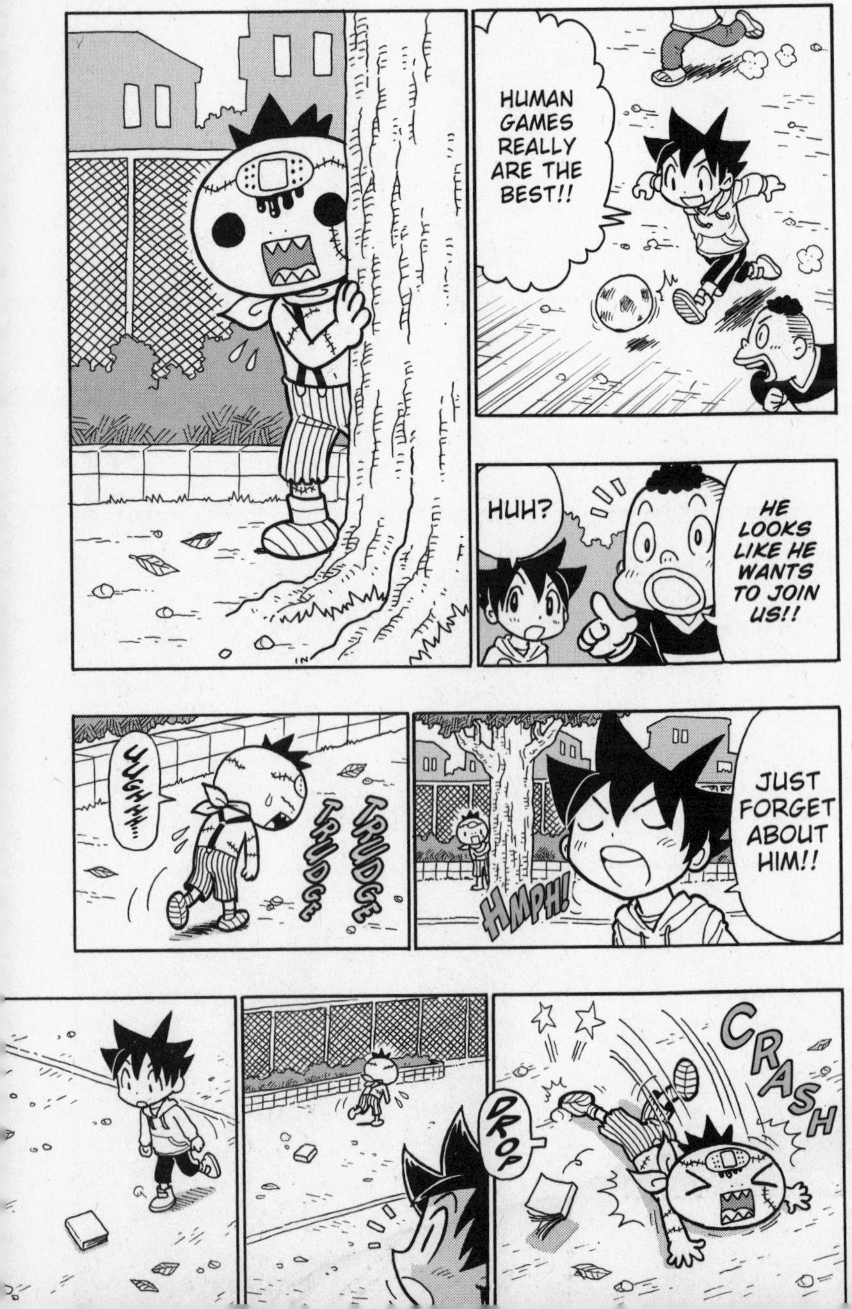
HUMAN GAMES REALLY ARE THE BEST!!
HE LOOKS LIKE HE WANTS TO JOIN US!!
HUH?
JUST FORGET ABOUT HIM!!
HMPH!
TRUDGE TRUDGE
UUGHHH...
CRASH
DROP

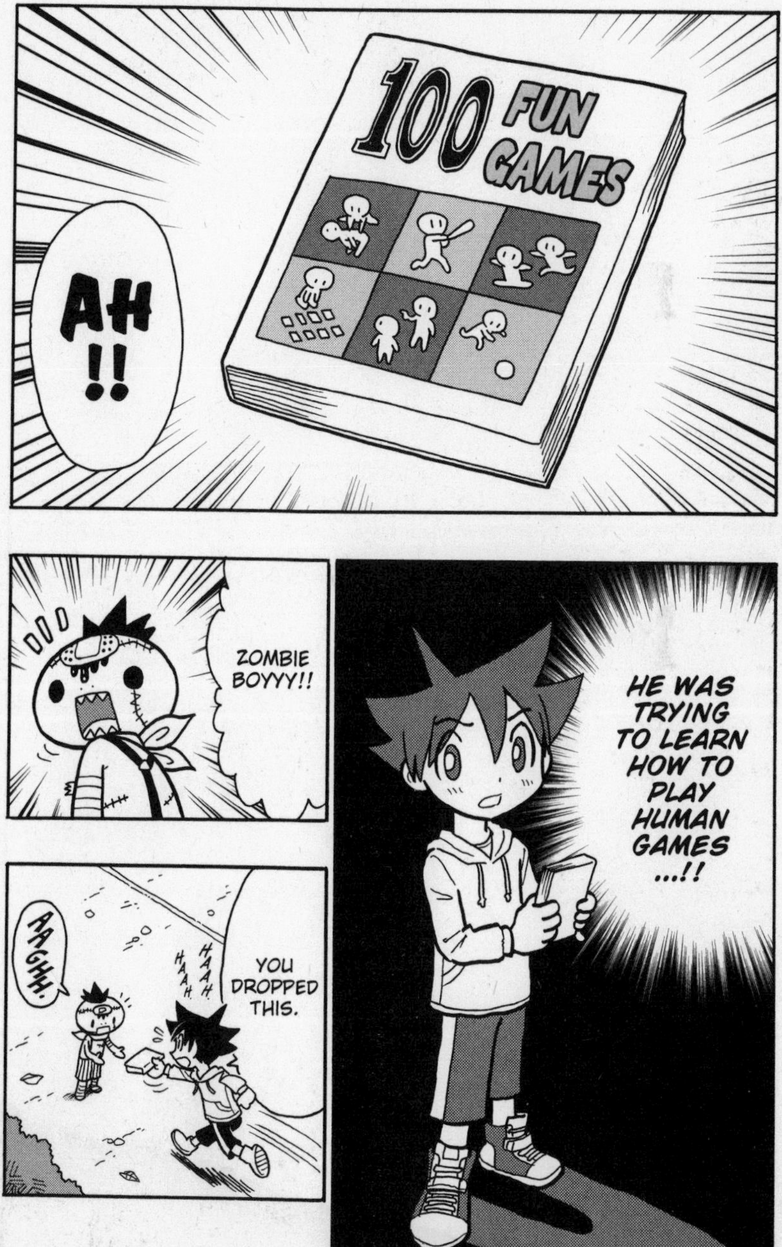
100 FUN GAMES
AH!!
HE WAS TRYING TO LEARN HOW TO PLAY HUMAN GAMES ...!!
ZOMBIE BOYYY!!
YOU DROPPED THIS.
HAAAH HAAAH
AAGHH.

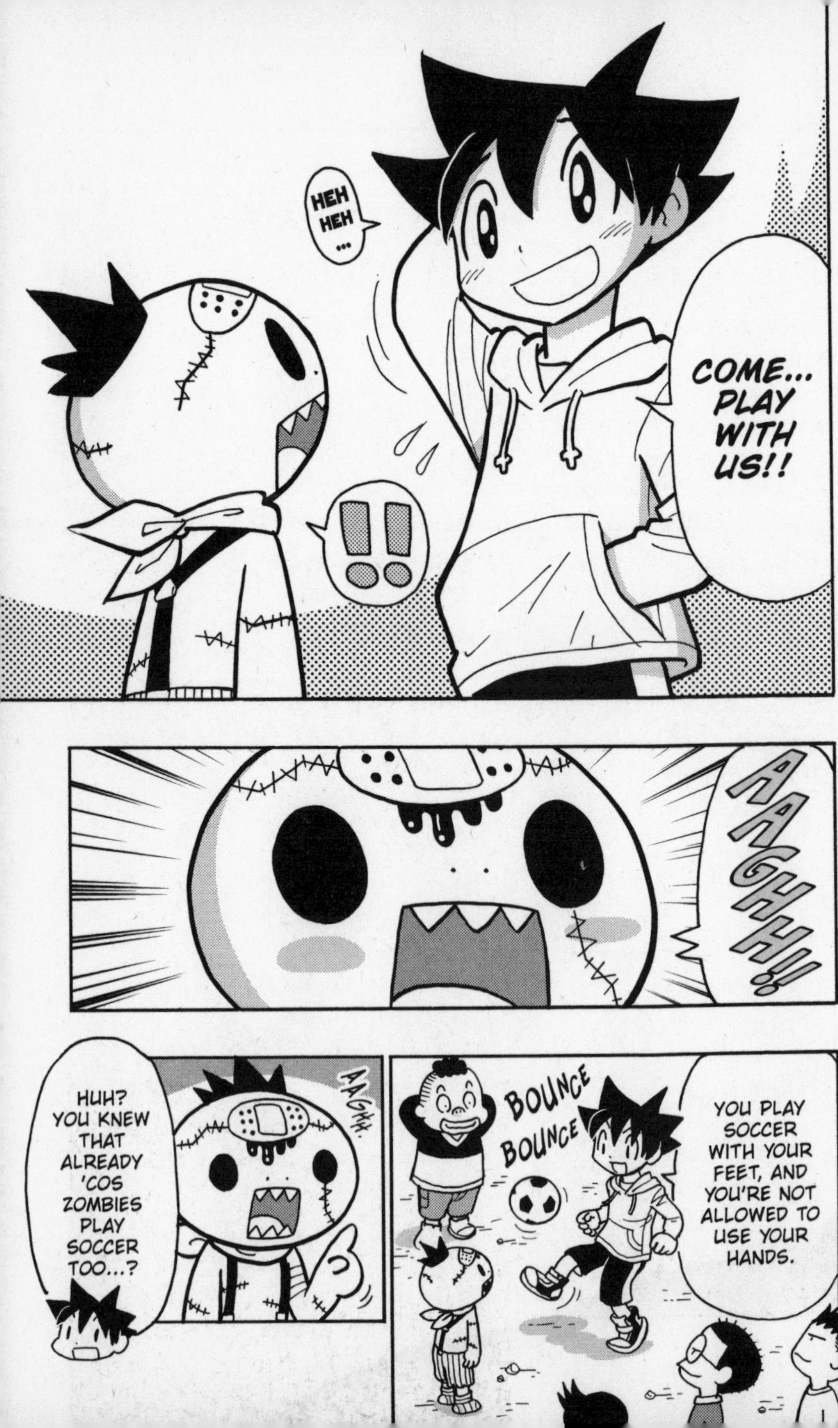
COME... PLAY WITH US!!
HEH HEH...
!!
AAGHH!!!
YOU PLAY SOCCER WITH YOUR FEET, AND YOU'RE NOT ALLOWED TO USE YOUR HANDS.
BOUNCE
BOUNCE
AAGHH.
HUH? YOU KNEW THAT ALREADY 'COS ZOMBIES PLAY SOCCER TOO...?

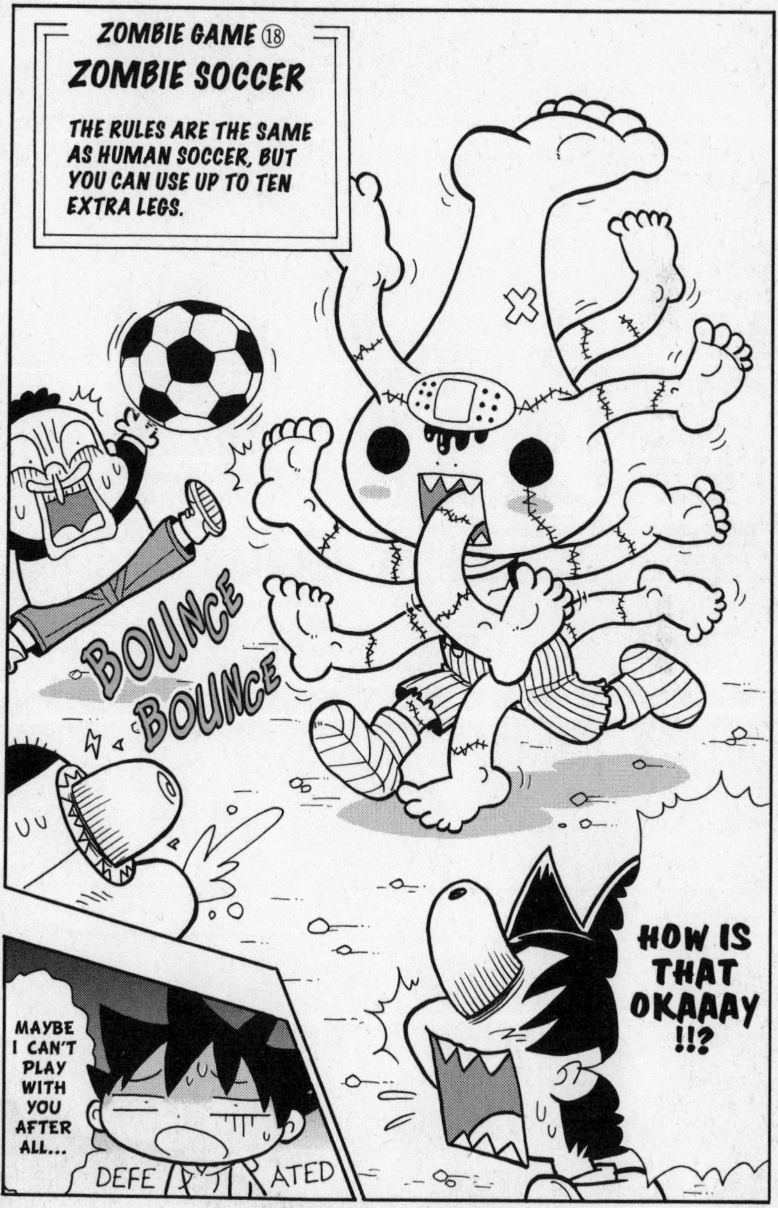
ZOMBIE GAME ⑱
ZOMBIE SOCCER
THE RULES ARE THE SAME AS HUMAN SOCCER, BUT YOU CAN USE UP TO TEN EXTRA LEGS.
BOUNCE
BOUNCE
HOW IS THAT OKAAAY !!?
MAYBE I CAN'T PLAY WITH YOU AFTER ALL...
DEFEATED

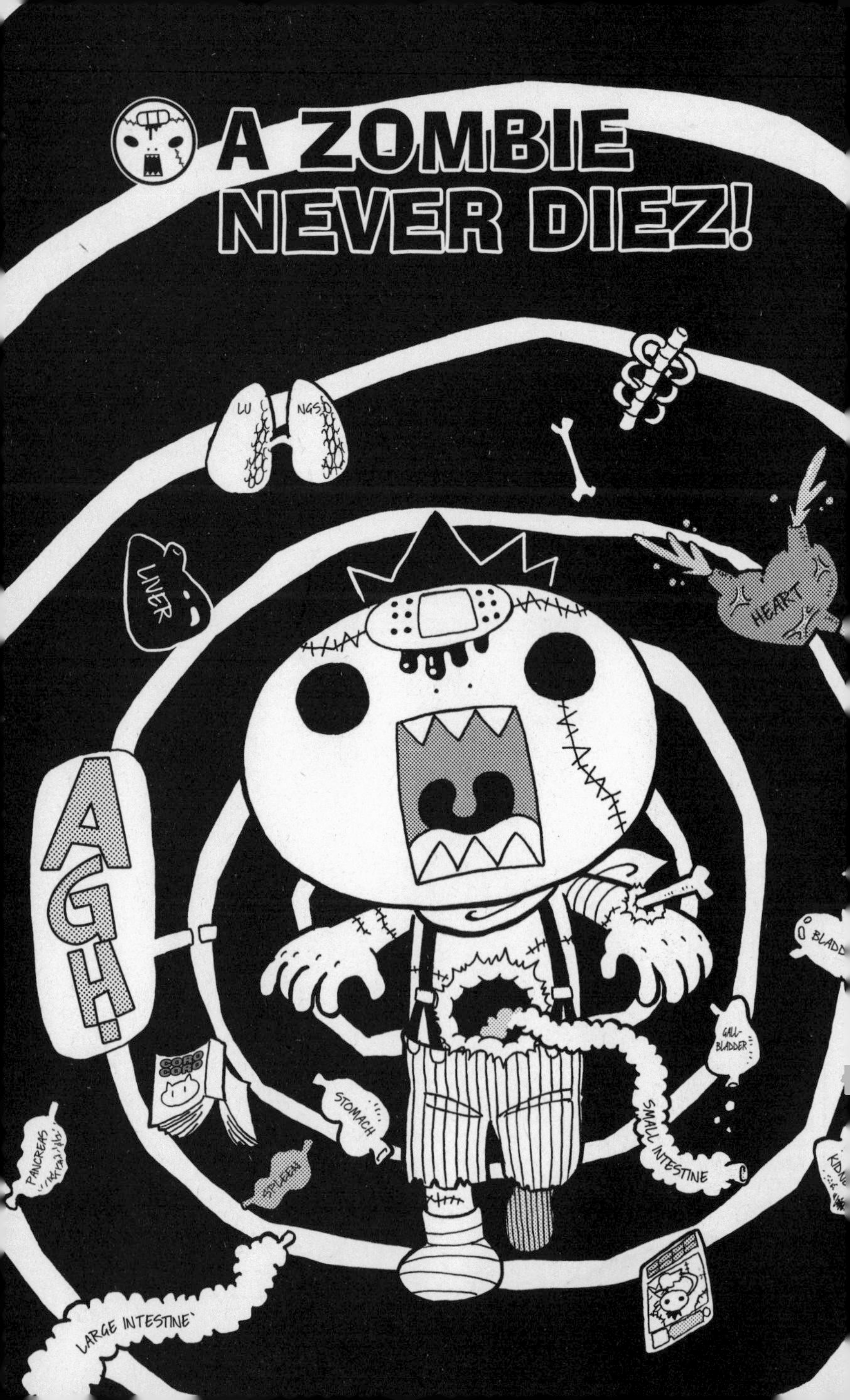
A ZOMBIE NEVER DIEZ!
LUNGS
LIVER
HEART
AGH!
GALL-BLADDER
STOMACH
SMALL INTESTINE
CORO CORO
PANCREAS
SPLEEN
LARGE INTESTINE

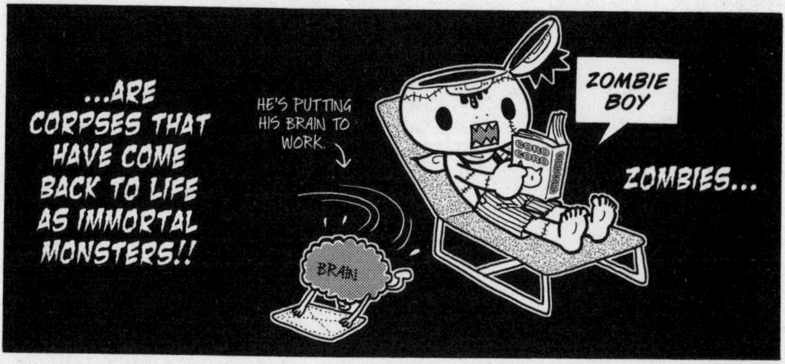
ZOMBIES...
ZOMBIE BOY
CORO CORO
HE'S PUTTING HIS BRAIN TO WORK.
BRAIN
...ARE CORPSES THAT HAVE COME BACK TO LIFE AS IMMORTAL MONSTERS!!

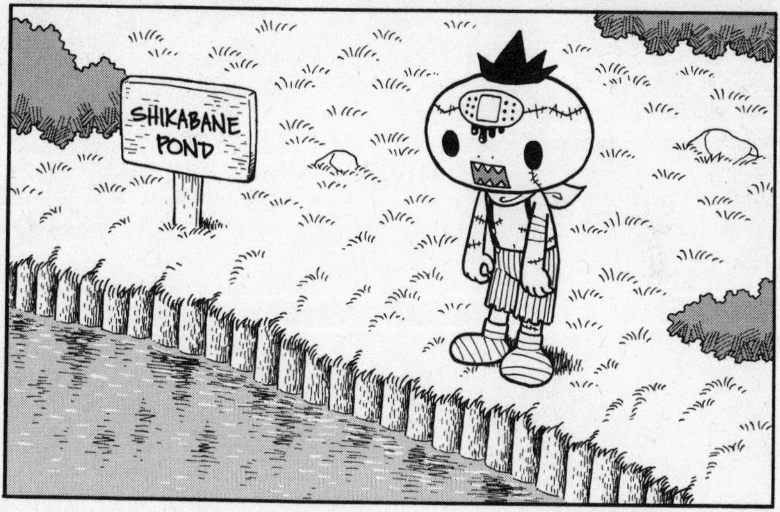
SHIKABANE POND

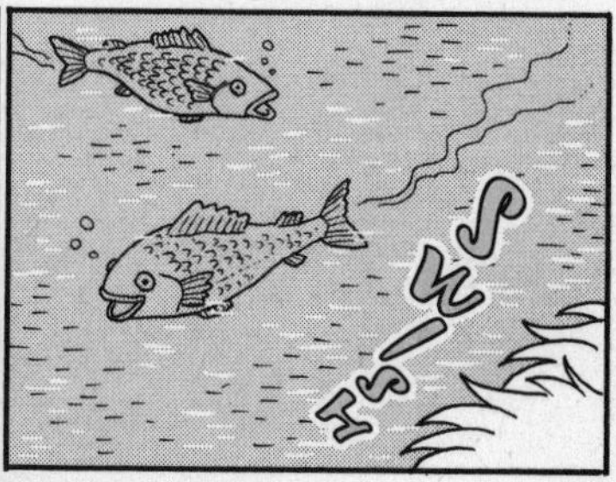
SWISH

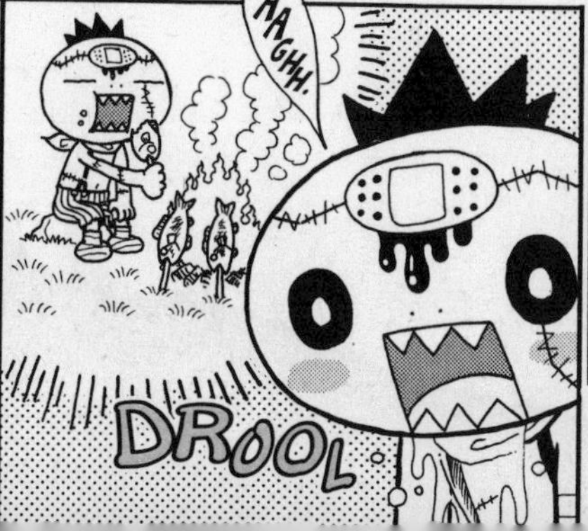
AAGHH.
DROOL

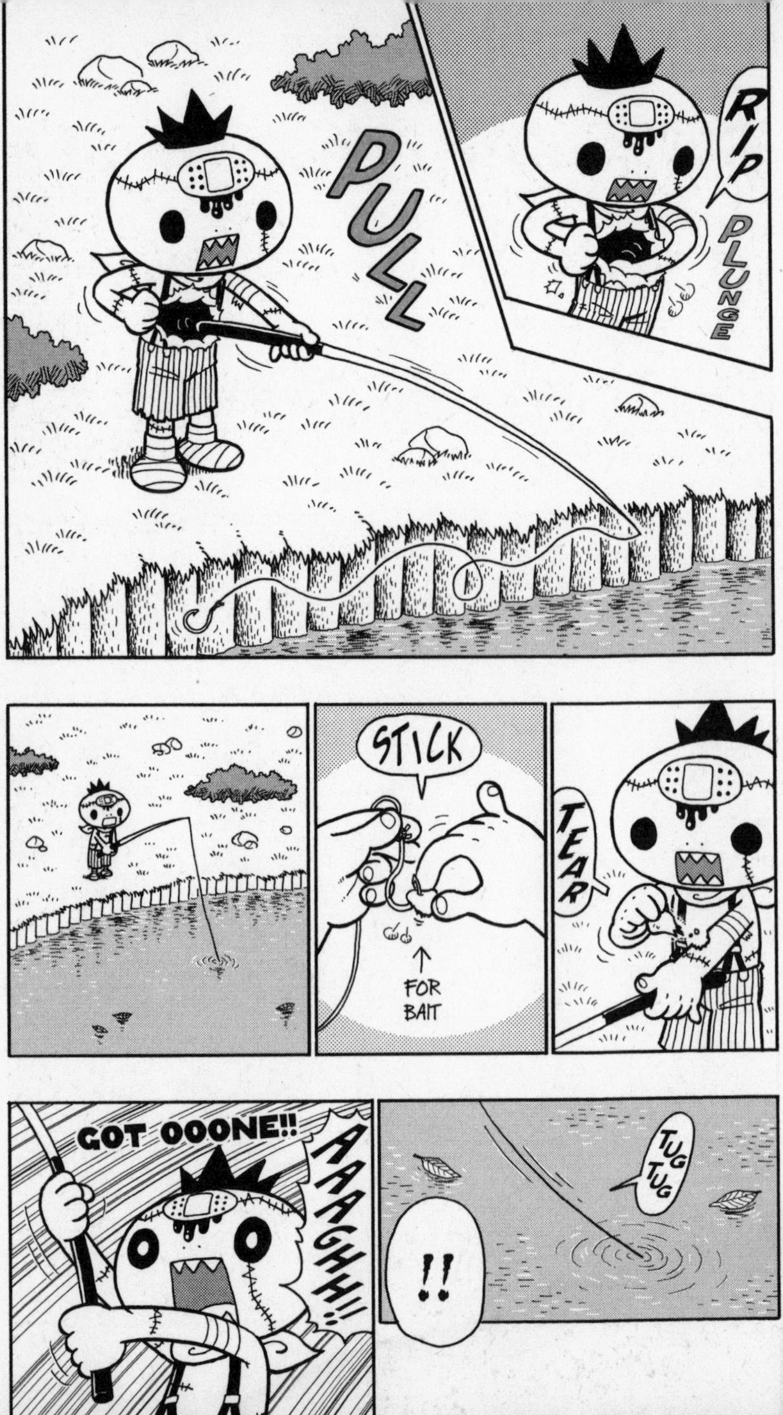
RIP
PLUNGE
PULL
TEAR
STICK
FOR BAIT
TUG TUG
!!
GOT OOONE!!
AAAAGHHH!!!

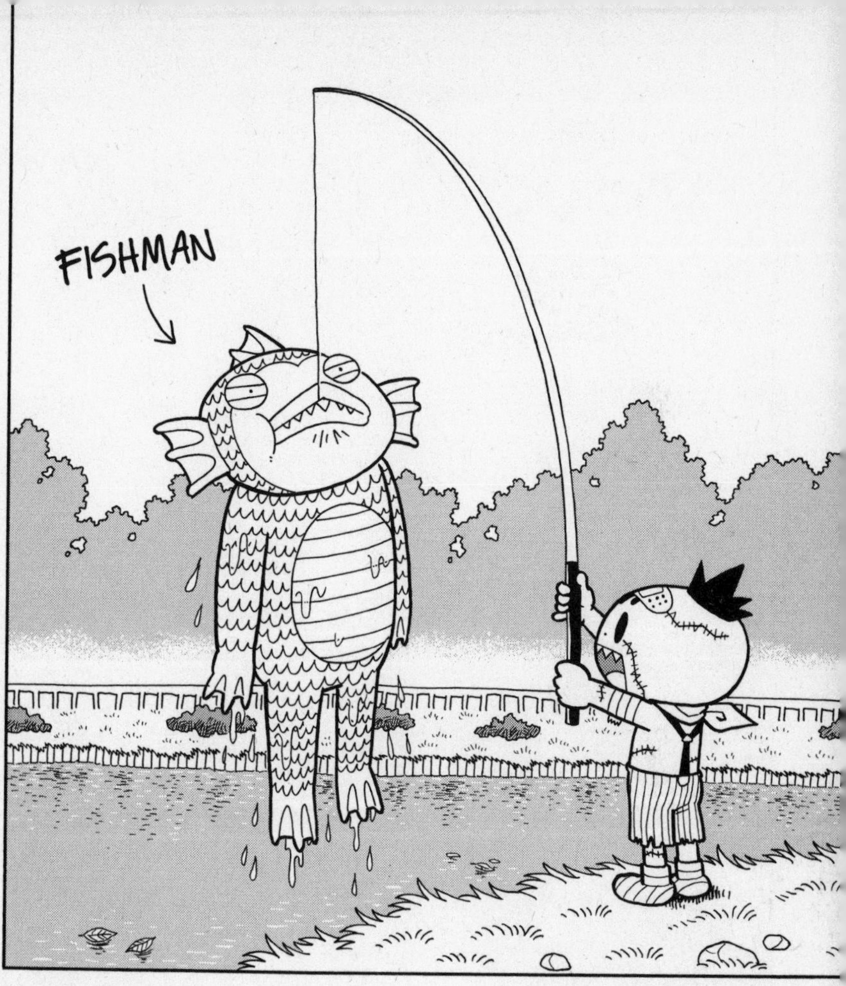
FISHMAN
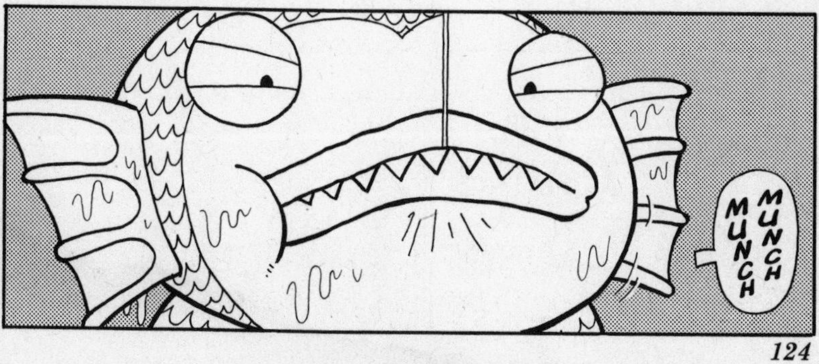
MUNCH MUNCH

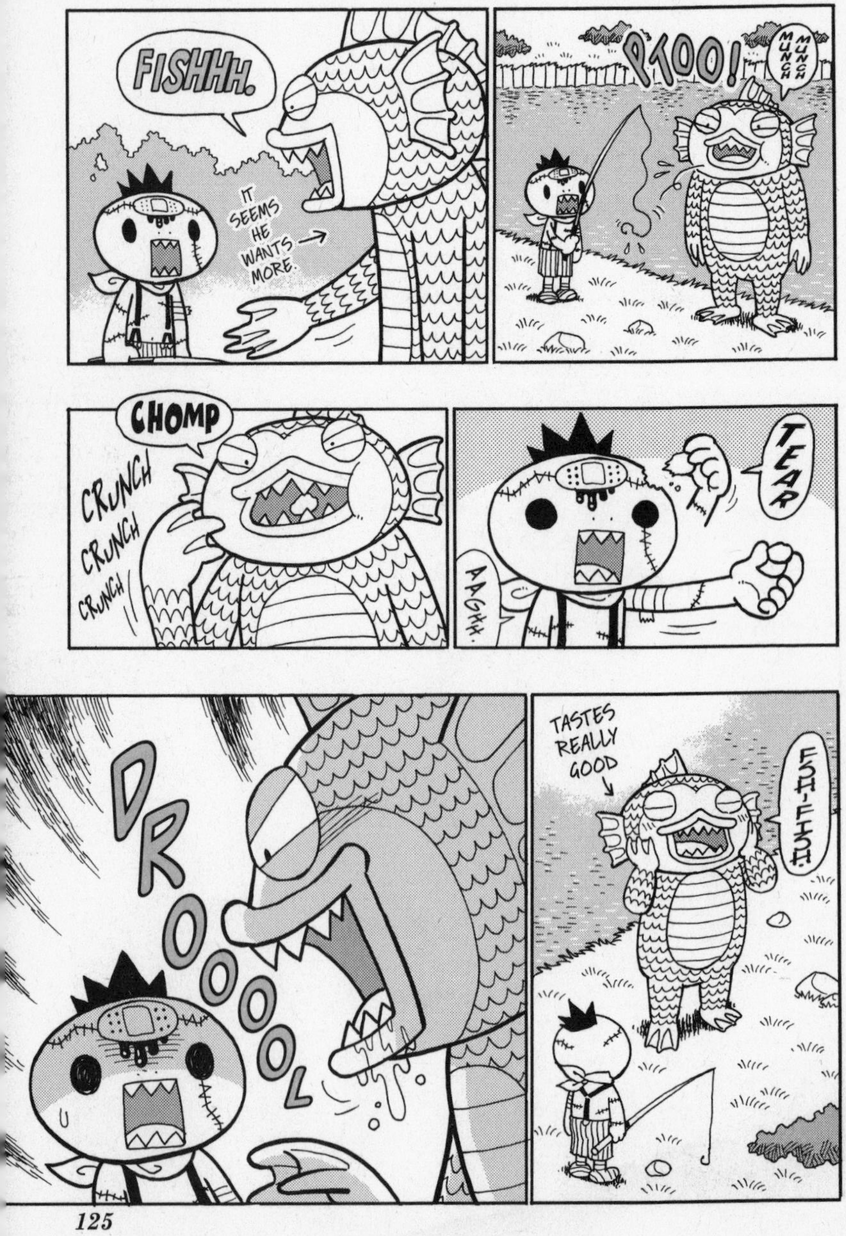
PTOO!
MUNCH MUNCH
FISHHH.
IT SEEMS HE WANTS MORE.
TEAR
AAGHH.
CHOMP
CRUNCH
CRUNCH
CRUNCH
TASTES REALLY GOOD
FSH-FISH.
DROOOOOL

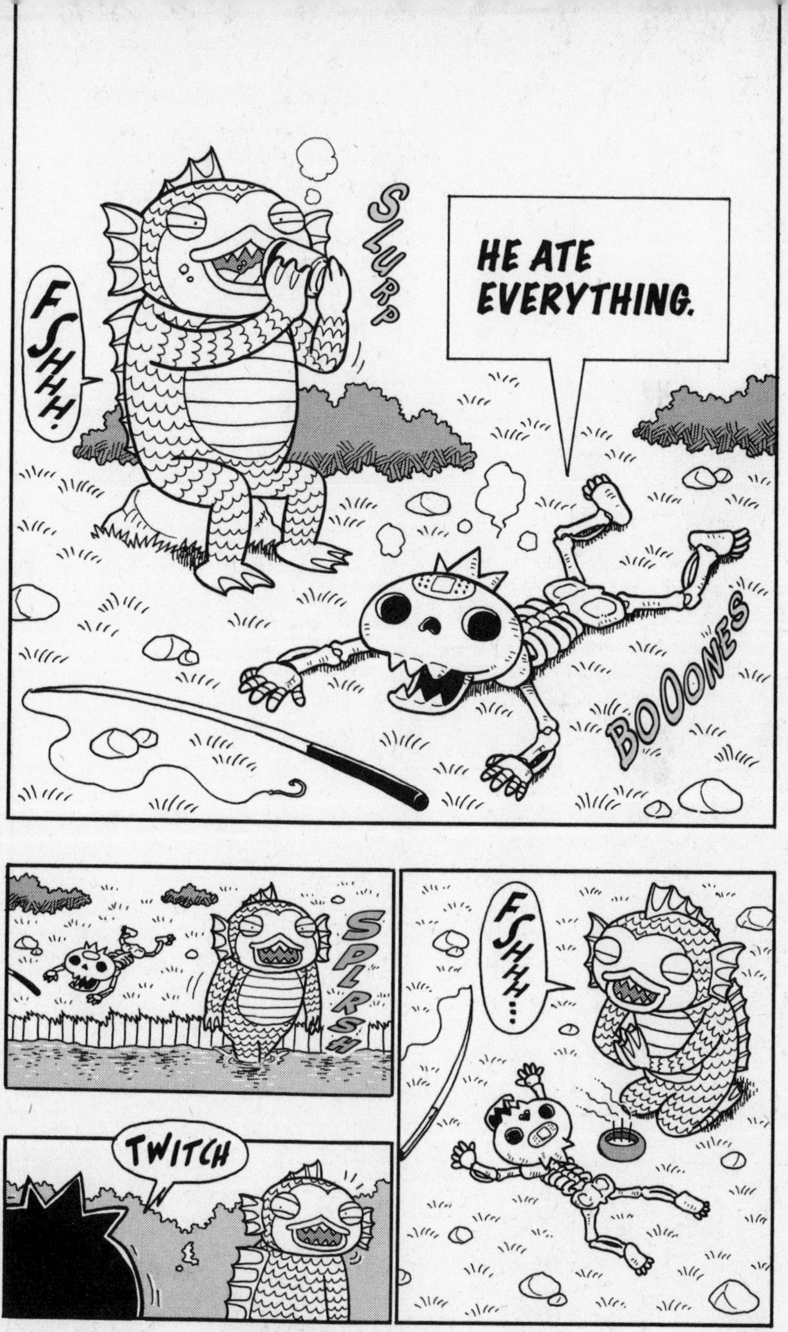
HE ATE EVERYTHING.
SLURP
FSHHH!
BOOONES
FSHHH...
SPLRSH
TWITCH

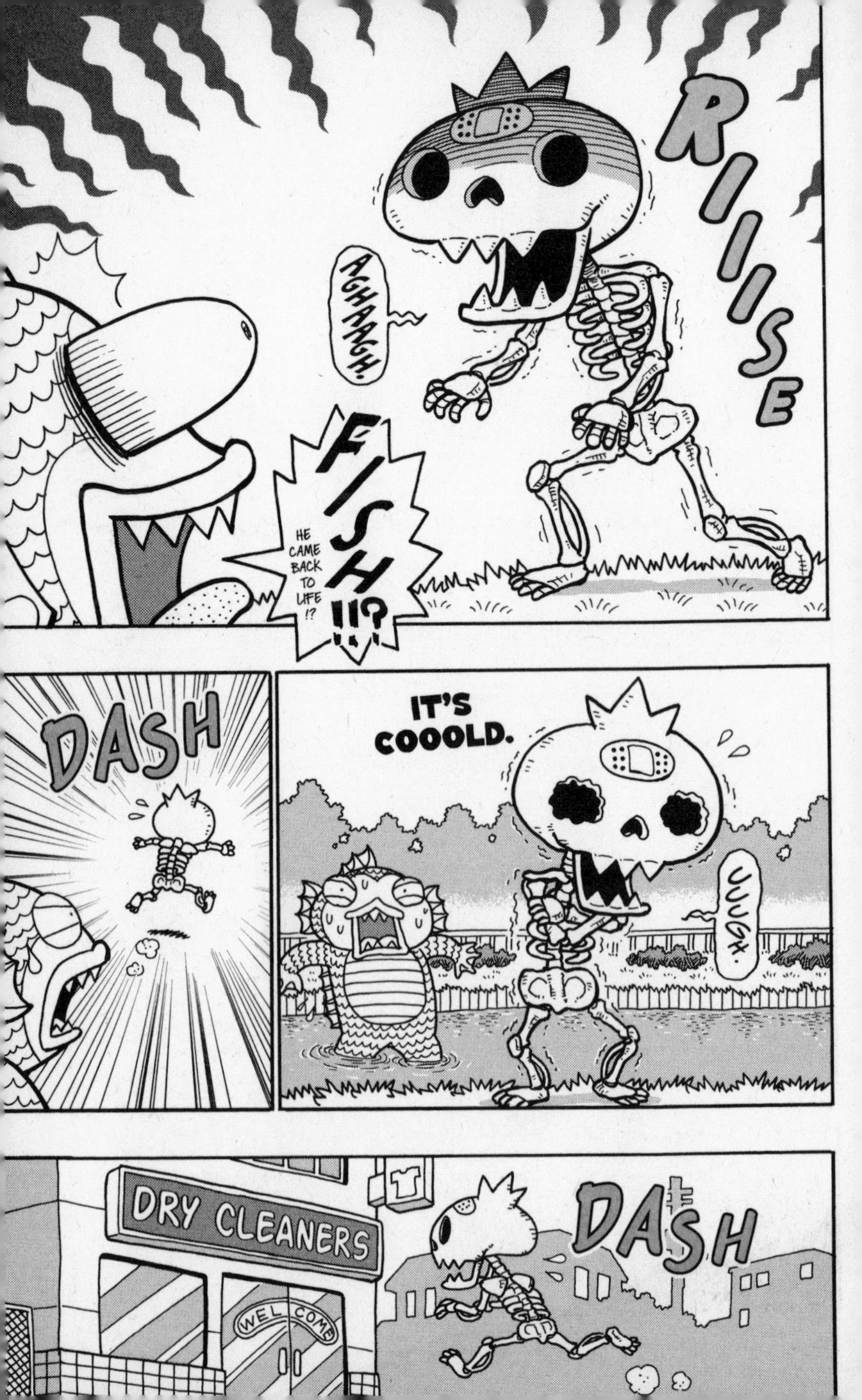
RIIISE
AGHAAAGH.
FISH!!?
HE CAME BACK TO LIFE!?
IT'S COOOLD.
UUUGH.
DASH
DRY CLEANERS
WELCOME
DASH

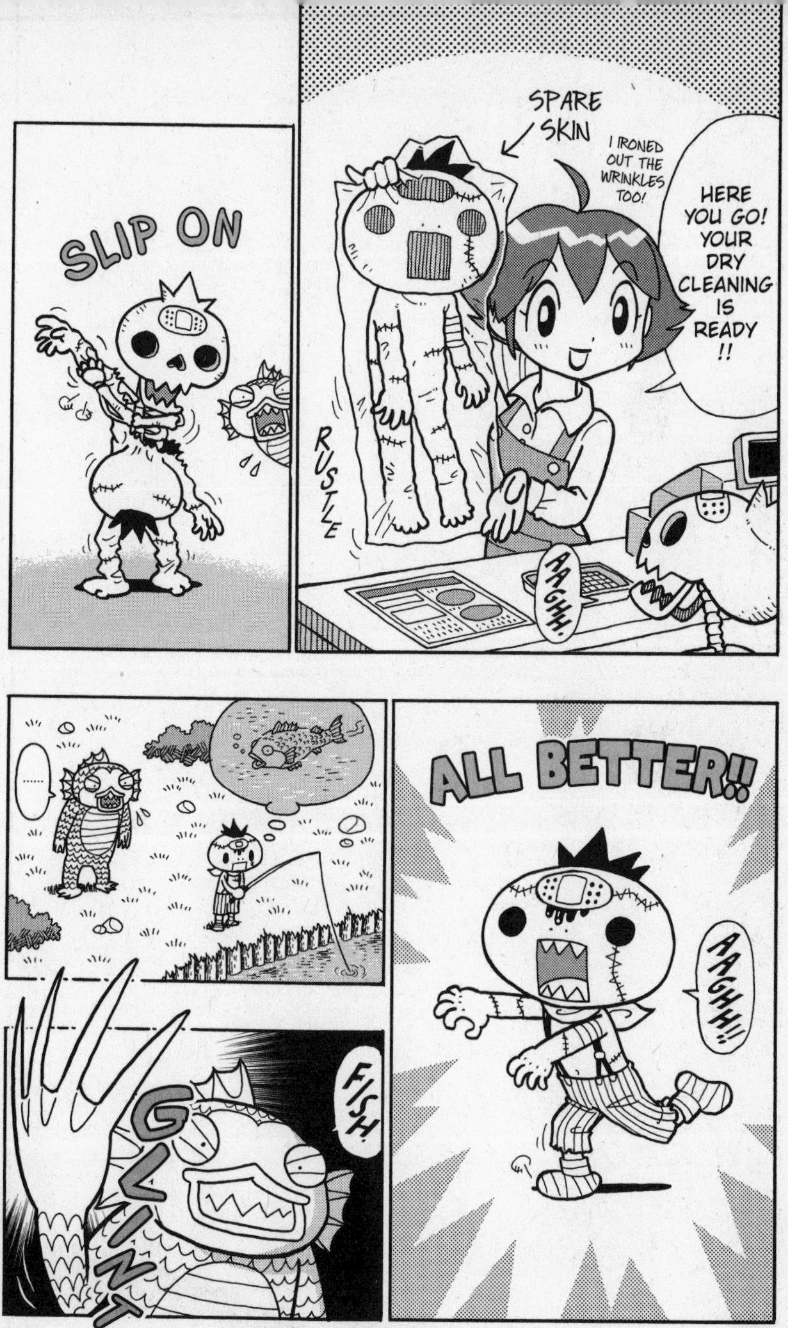
HERE YOU GO! YOUR DRY CLEANING IS READY!!
I IRONED OUT THE WRINKLES TOO!
SPARE SKIN
AAGHH.
RUSTLE
SLIP ON
ALL BETTER!!
AAGHH!!
......
FISH.
GLINT

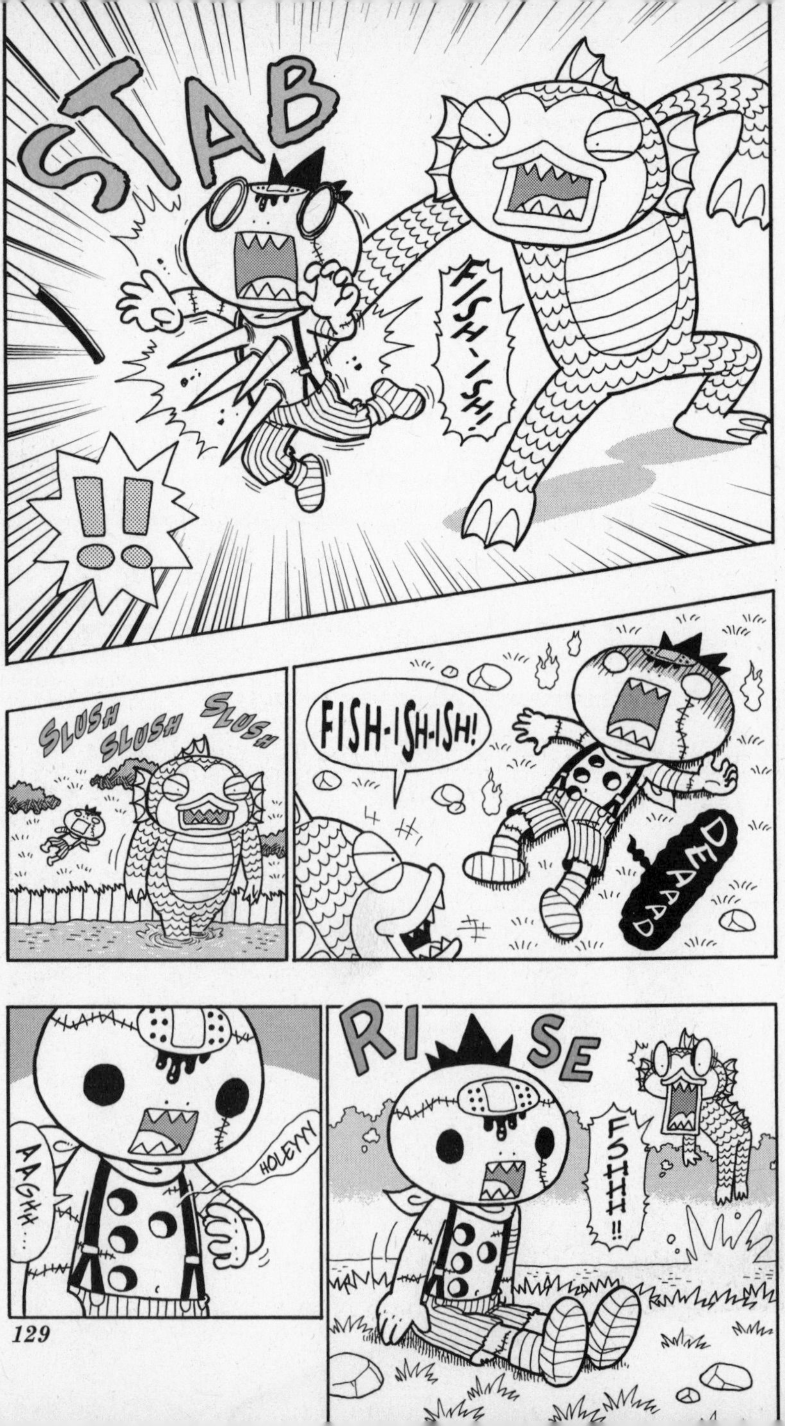
STAB
FISH-ISH!
!!
FISH-ISH-ISH!
DEAAAD
SLUSH
SLUSH
SLUSH
RISE
FSHHH!!
HOLEYYY
AAGHH...

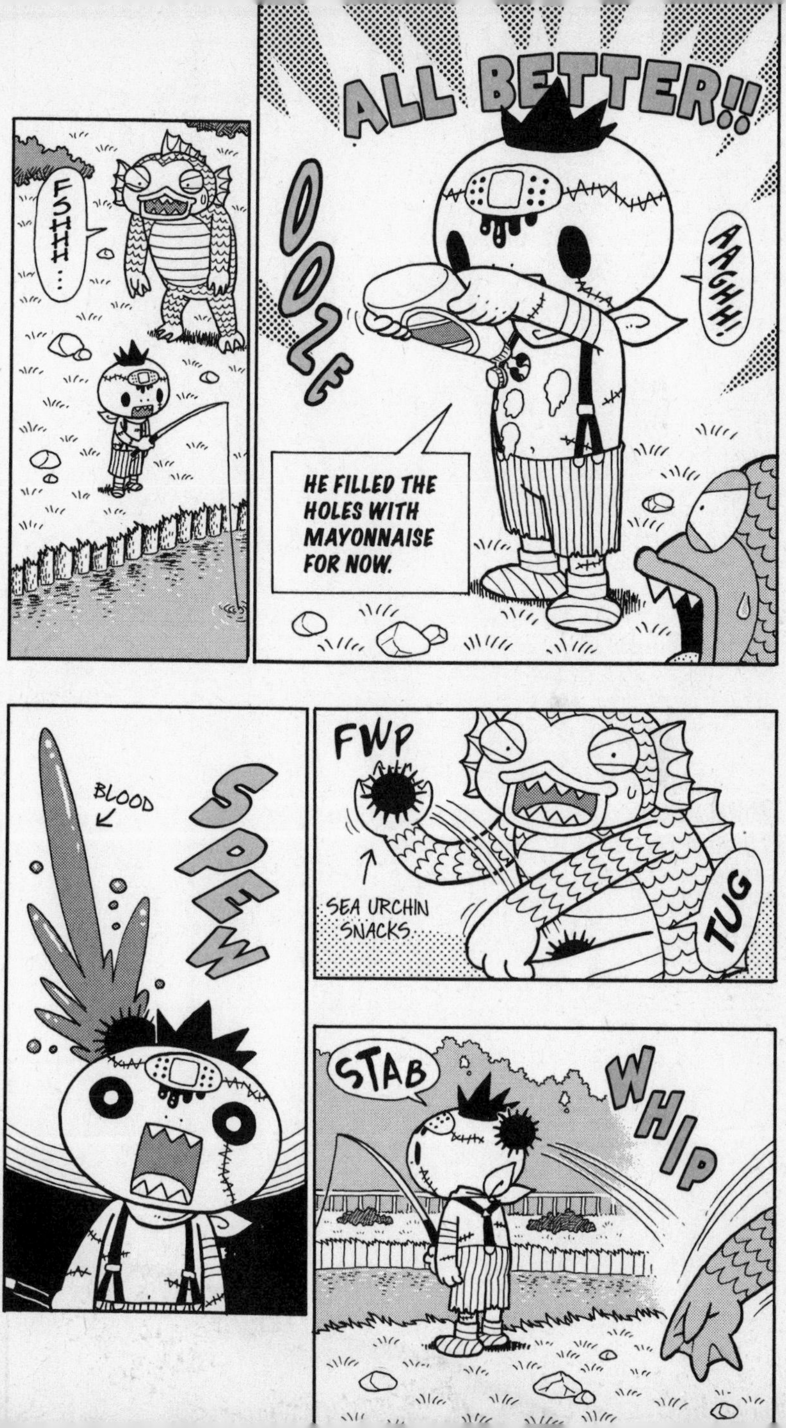
ALL BETTER!!
AAGHH!
OOZE
HE FILLED THE HOLES WITH MAYONNAISE FOR NOW.
FSHHH...
FWP
TUG
SEA URCHIN SNACKS
WHIP
STAB
SPEW
BLOOD

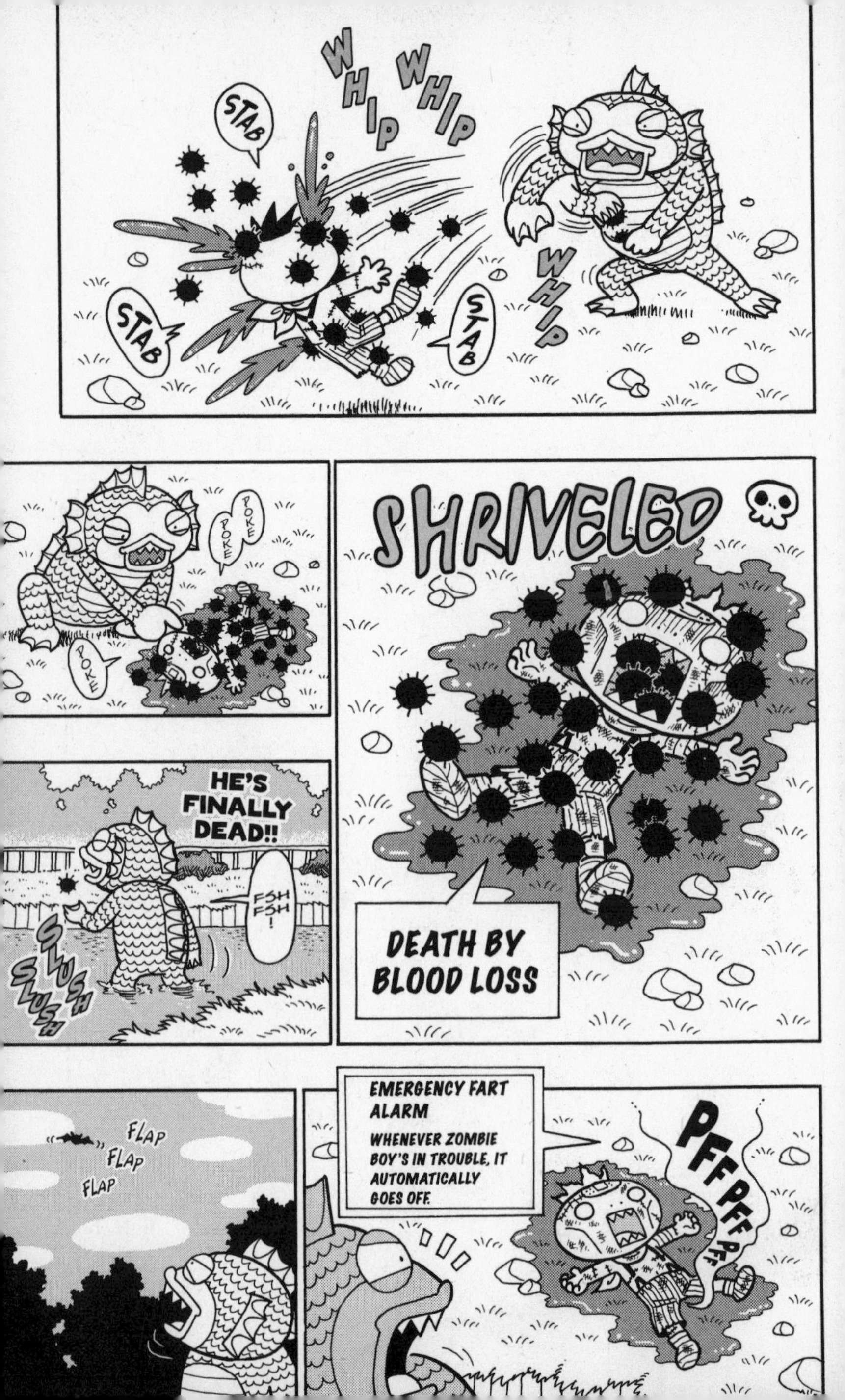
WHIP WHIP
WHIP
STAB
STAB
STAB
SHRIVELED
DEATH BY BLOOD LOSS
POKE POKE
POKE
HE'S FINALLY DEAD!!
FSH FSH!
SLUSH SLUSH
EMERGENCY FART ALARM
WHENEVER ZOMBIE BOY'S IN TROUBLE, IT AUTOMATICALLY GOES OFF.
PFF PFF PFF PFF
FLAP
FLAP
FLAP

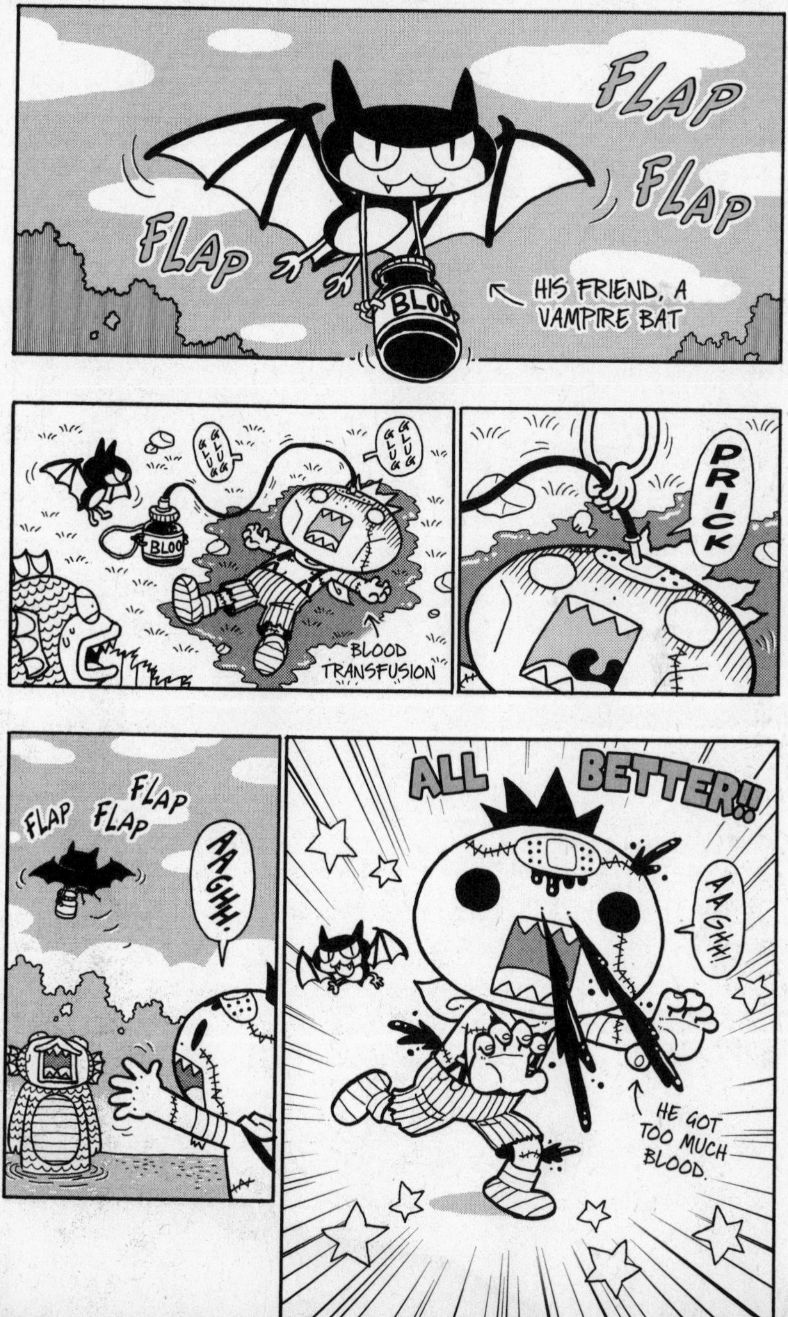
FLAP
FLAP
FLAP
BLOO
HIS FRIEND, A VAMPIRE BAT
PRICK
GLUG GLUG
GLUG GLUG
BLOO
BLOOD TRANSFUSION
ALL BETTER!!
AAGHH!
HE GOT TOO MUCH BLOOD.
FLAP
FLAP
FLAP
AAGHH.

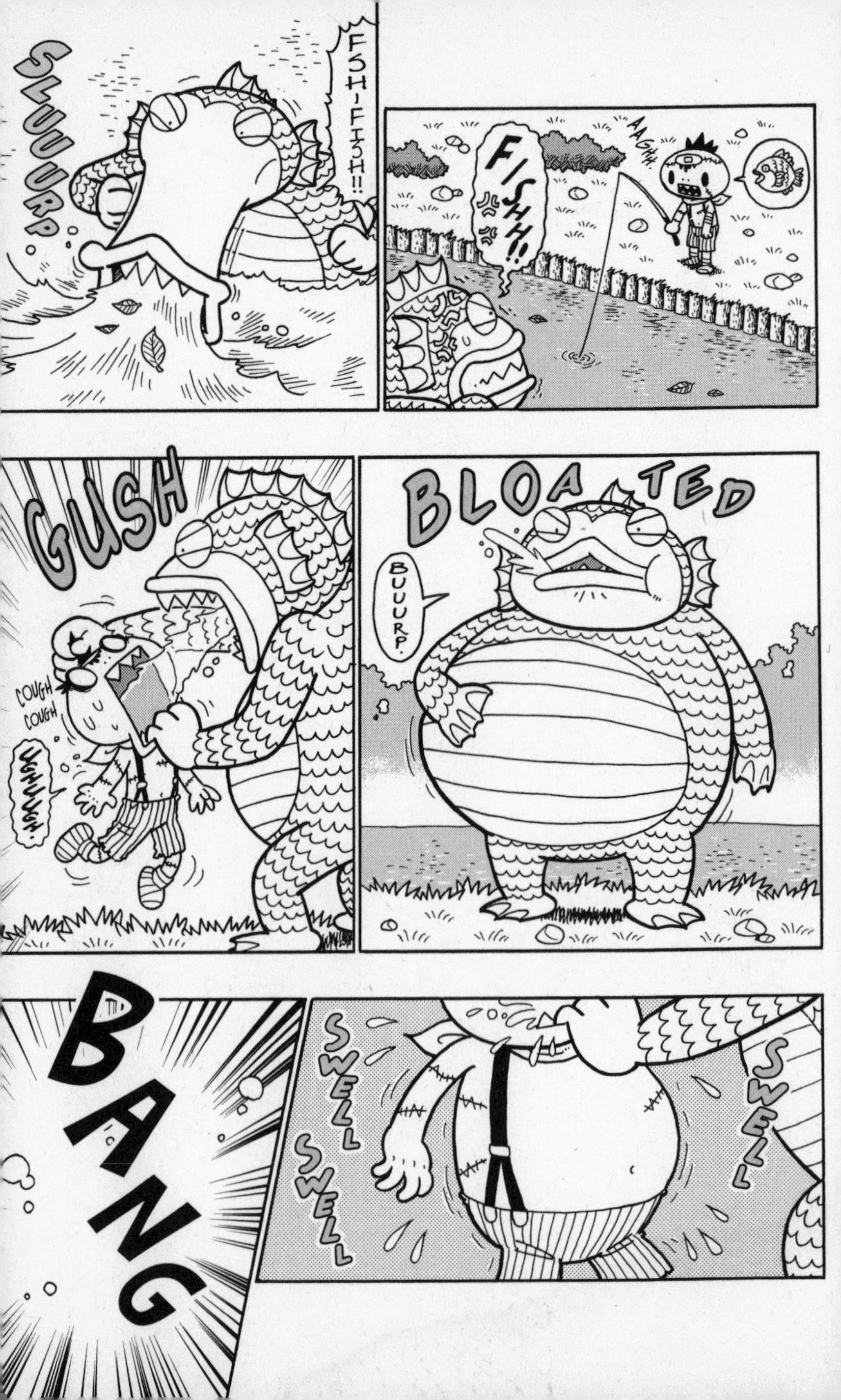
AAGHH.
FISHH!!
FSH-FISH!!
SLUUURP
BLOATED
BUUURP.
GUSH
COUGH COUGH
UGHUUGH.
SWELL
SWELL
SWELL
BANG

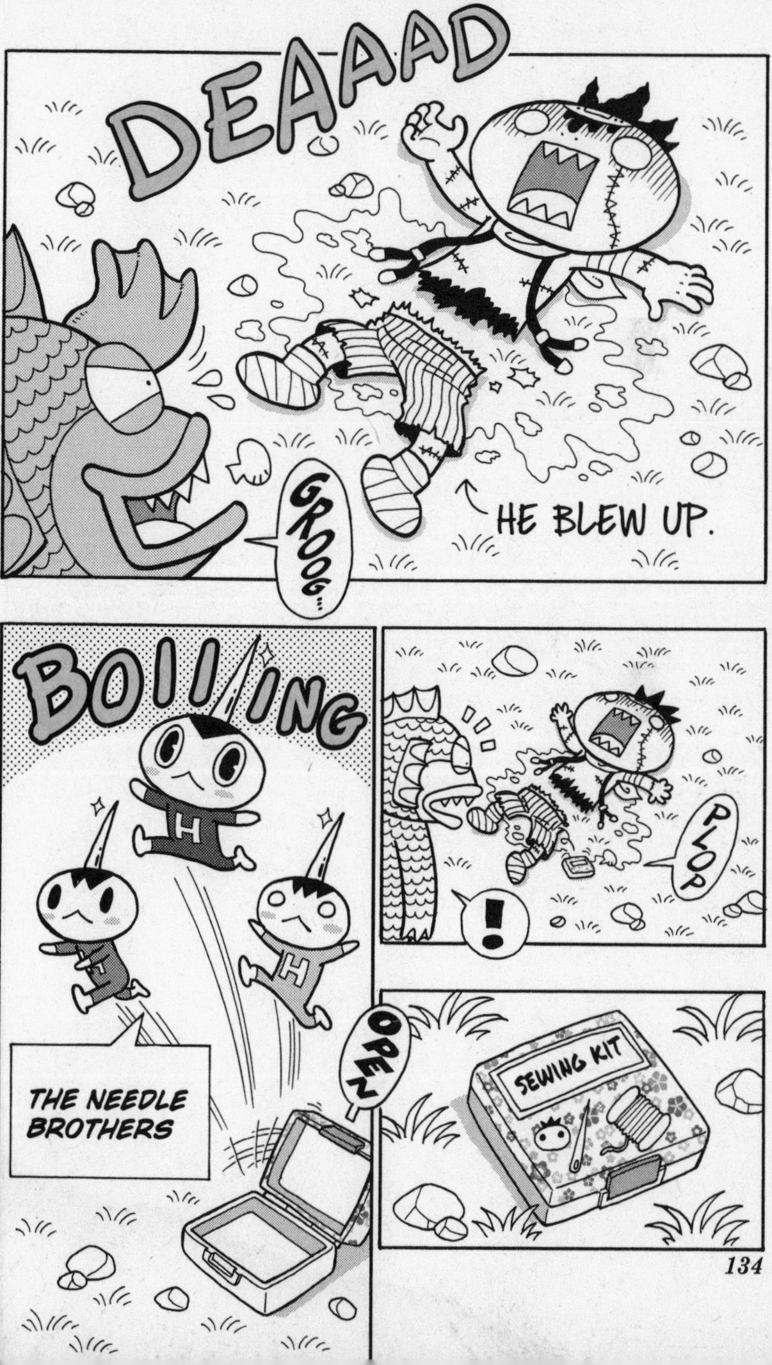
DEAAAD
HE BLEW UP.
GROOG...
PLOP
!
SEWING KIT
BOIIING
THE NEEDLE BROTHERS
OPEN

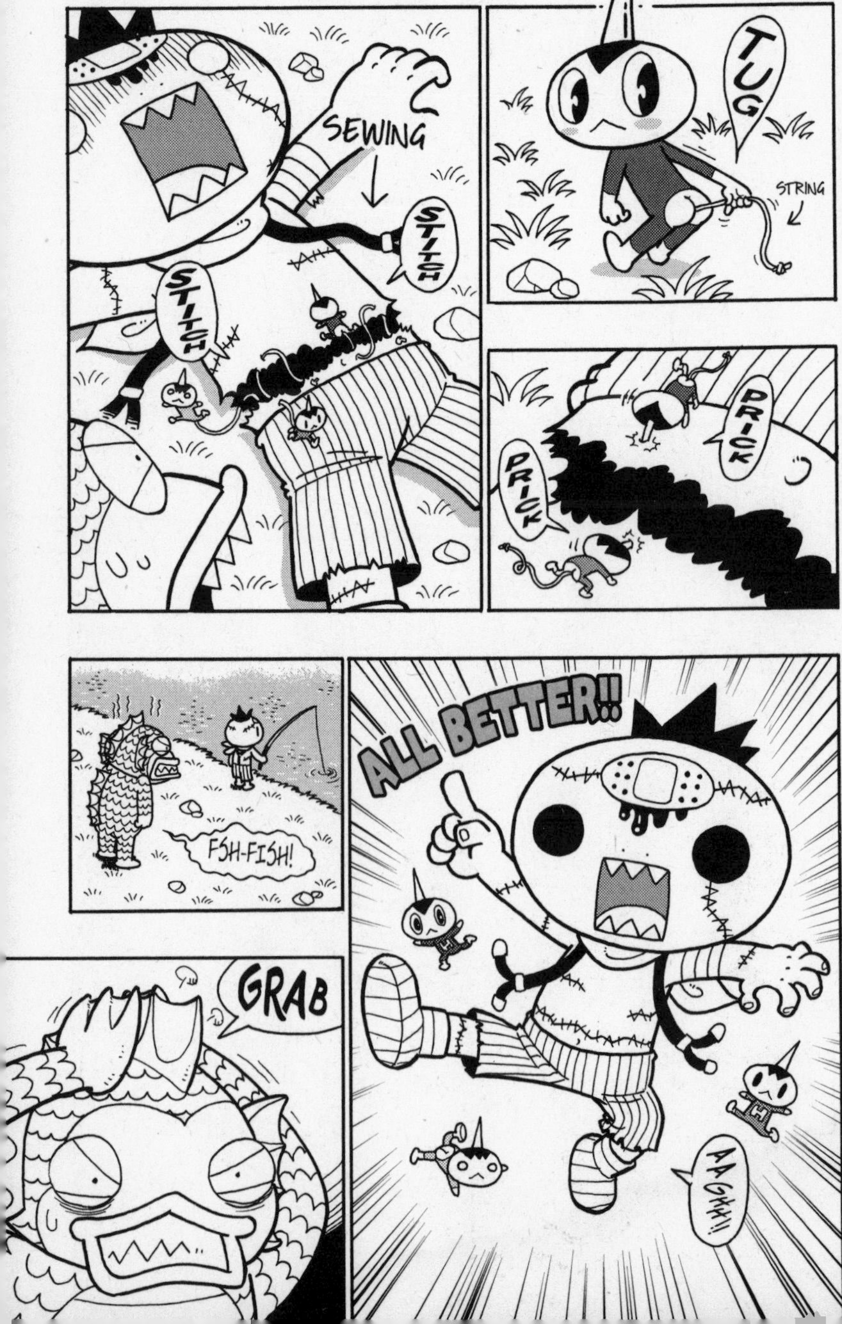
TUG
STRING
PRICK
PRICK
SEWING
STITCH
STITCH
ALL BETTER!!
AAGHH!!
FSH-FISH!
GRAB

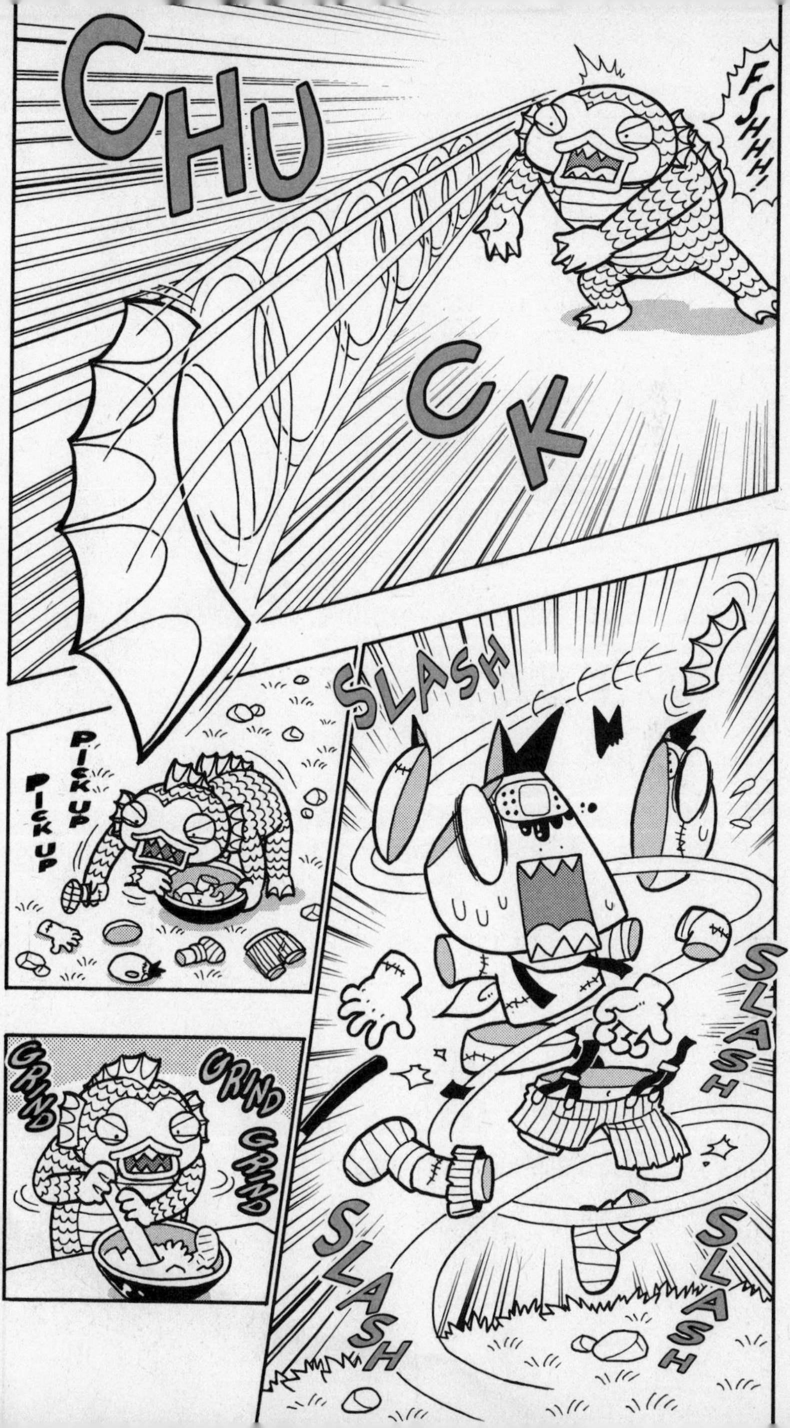
FSHHH!
CHU
CK
SLASH
SLASH
SLASH
SLASH
PICK UP
PICK UP
GRIND
GRIND
GRIND

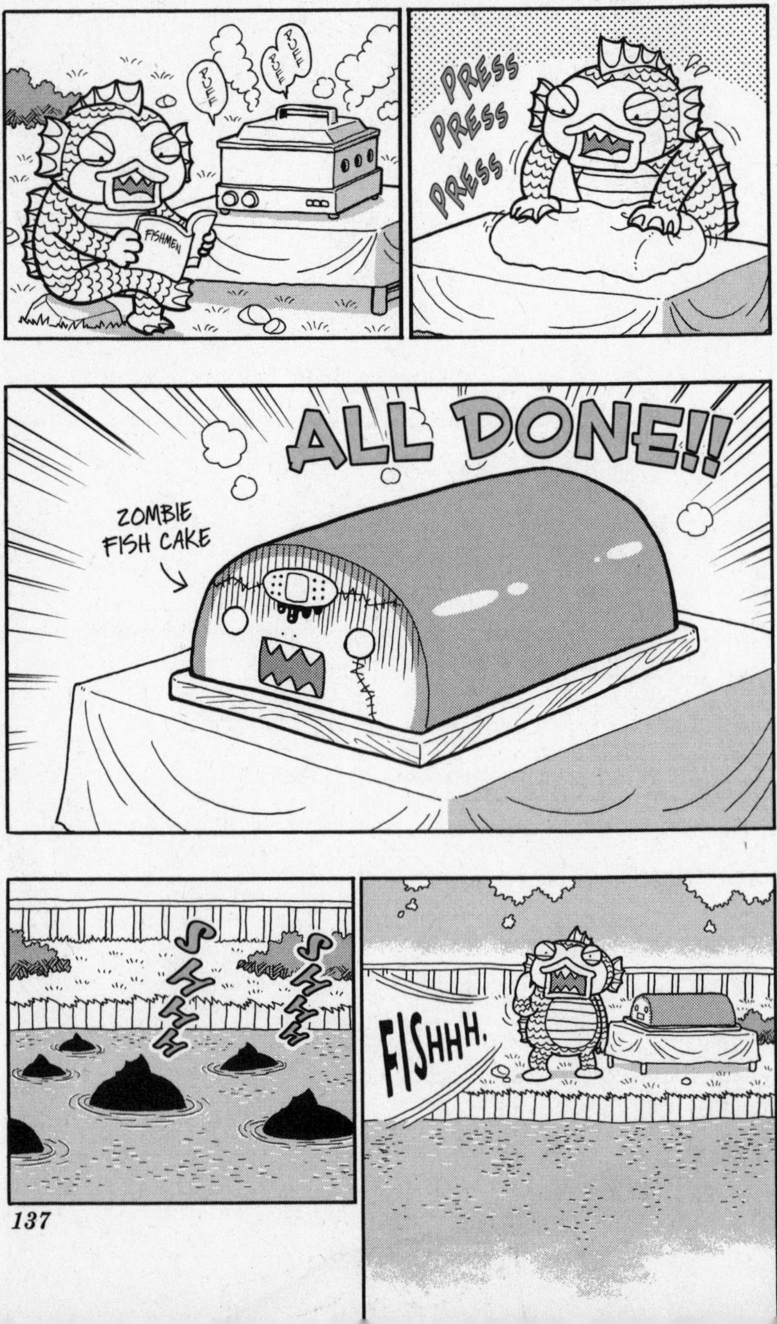
PRESS
PRESS
PRESS
PUFF
PUFF
PUFF
FISHMEN
ALL DONE!!
ZOMBIE FISH CAKE
FISHHH.
SHHHH
SHHHH

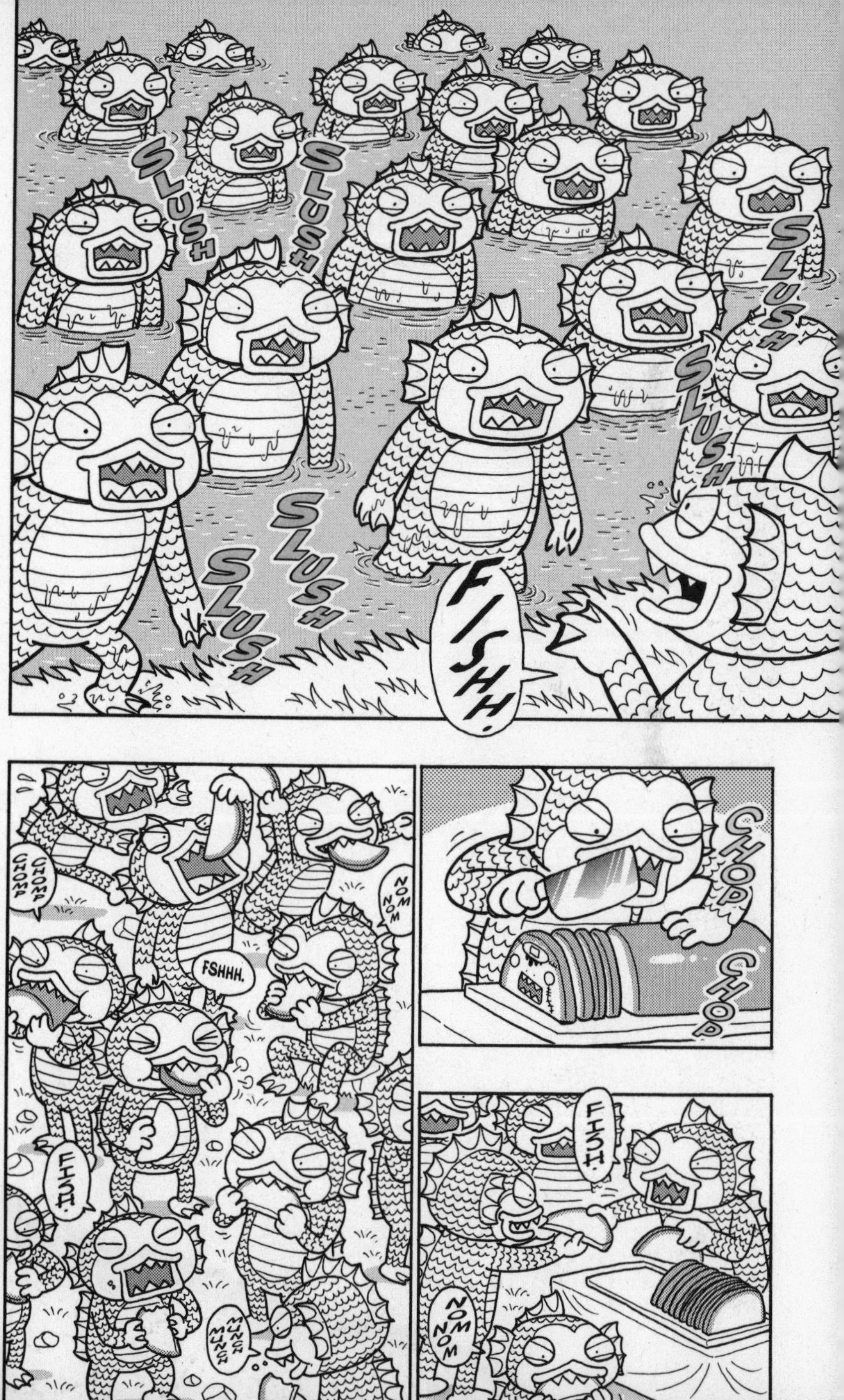
SLUSH
SLUSH
SLUSH
SLUSH
SLUSH
SLUSH
FISHH!
CHOP CHOP
CHOP
FISH.
NOM NOM
NOM NOM
CHOMP CHOMP
FSHHH.
FISH.
MUNCH MUNCH

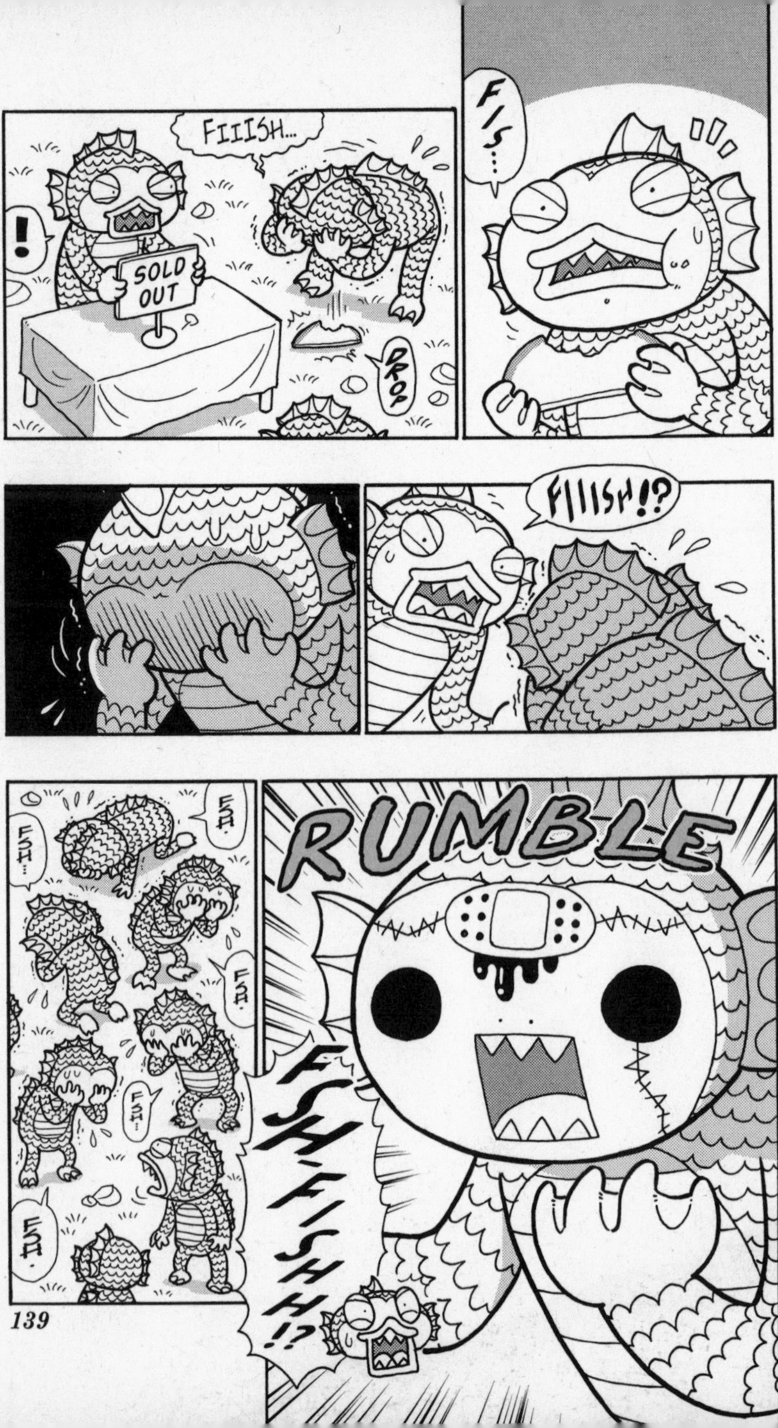
FIS...
FIIISH...
!
SOLD OUT
DROP
FIIISH!?
RUMBLE
FSH-FISHHH!?
FSH.
FSH...
FSH
FSH...
FSH.

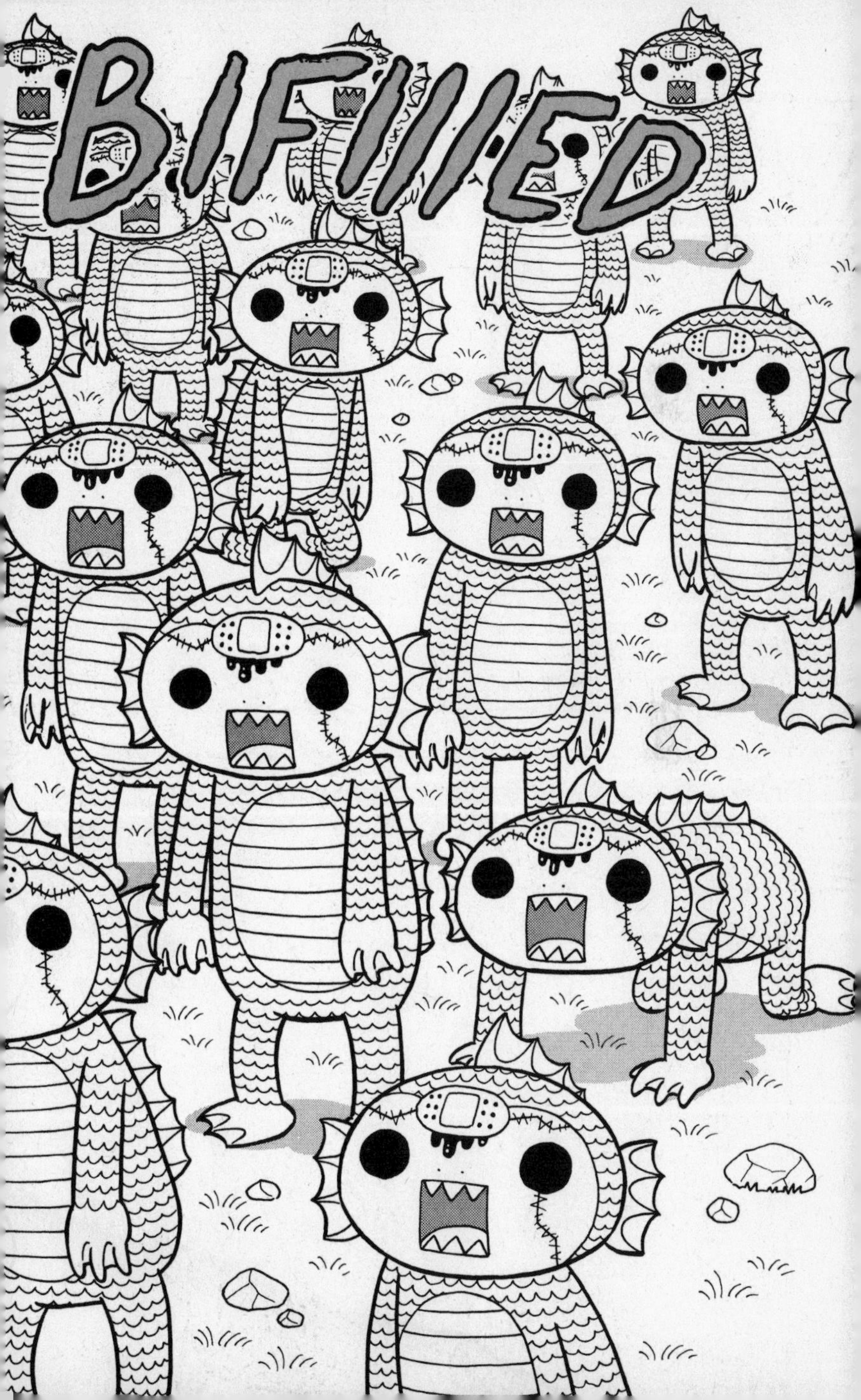
BIFIIIED

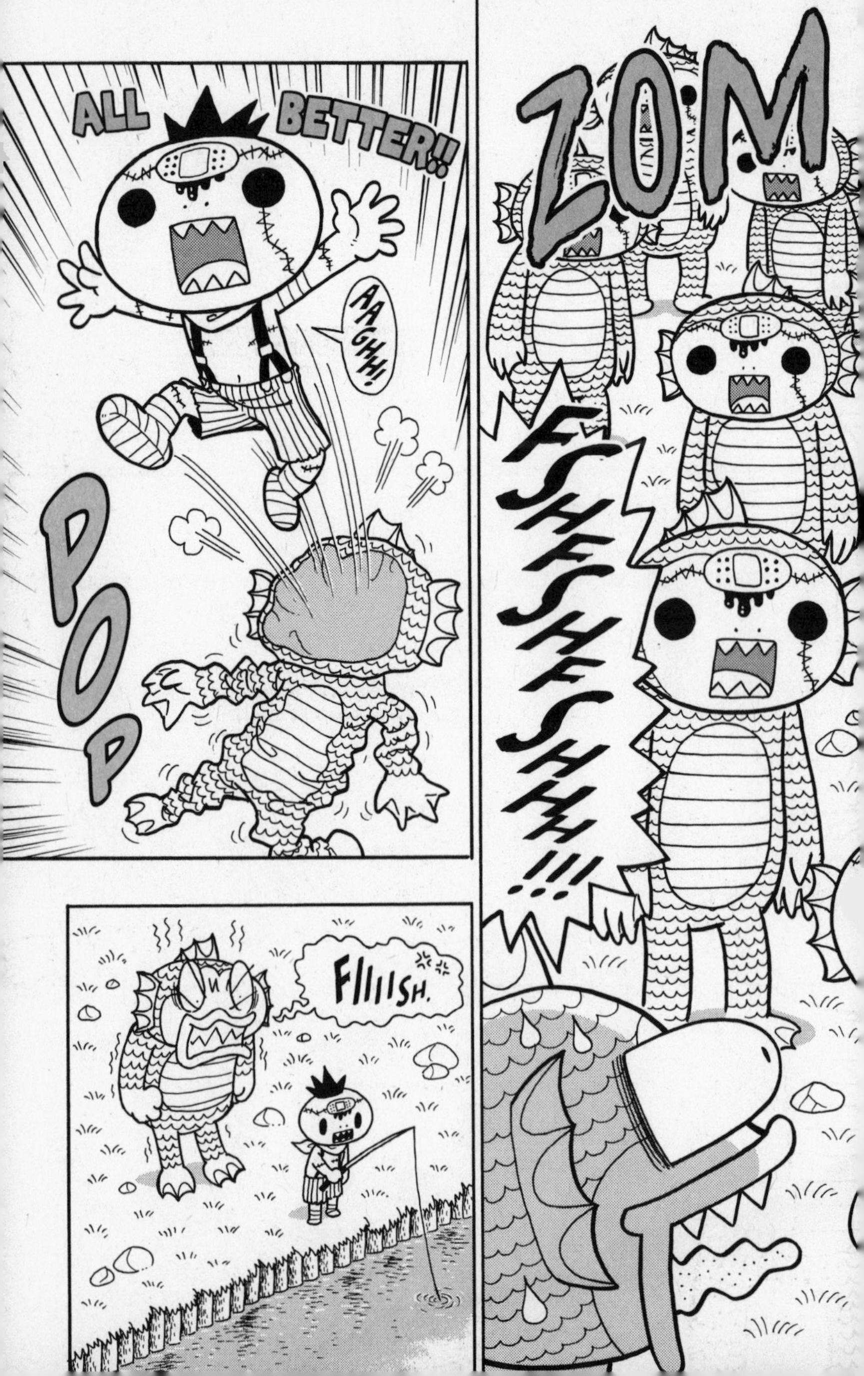
ZOM
FSHFSHFSHHH!!!
ALL BETTER!!
AAGHH!
POP
FIIIISH.

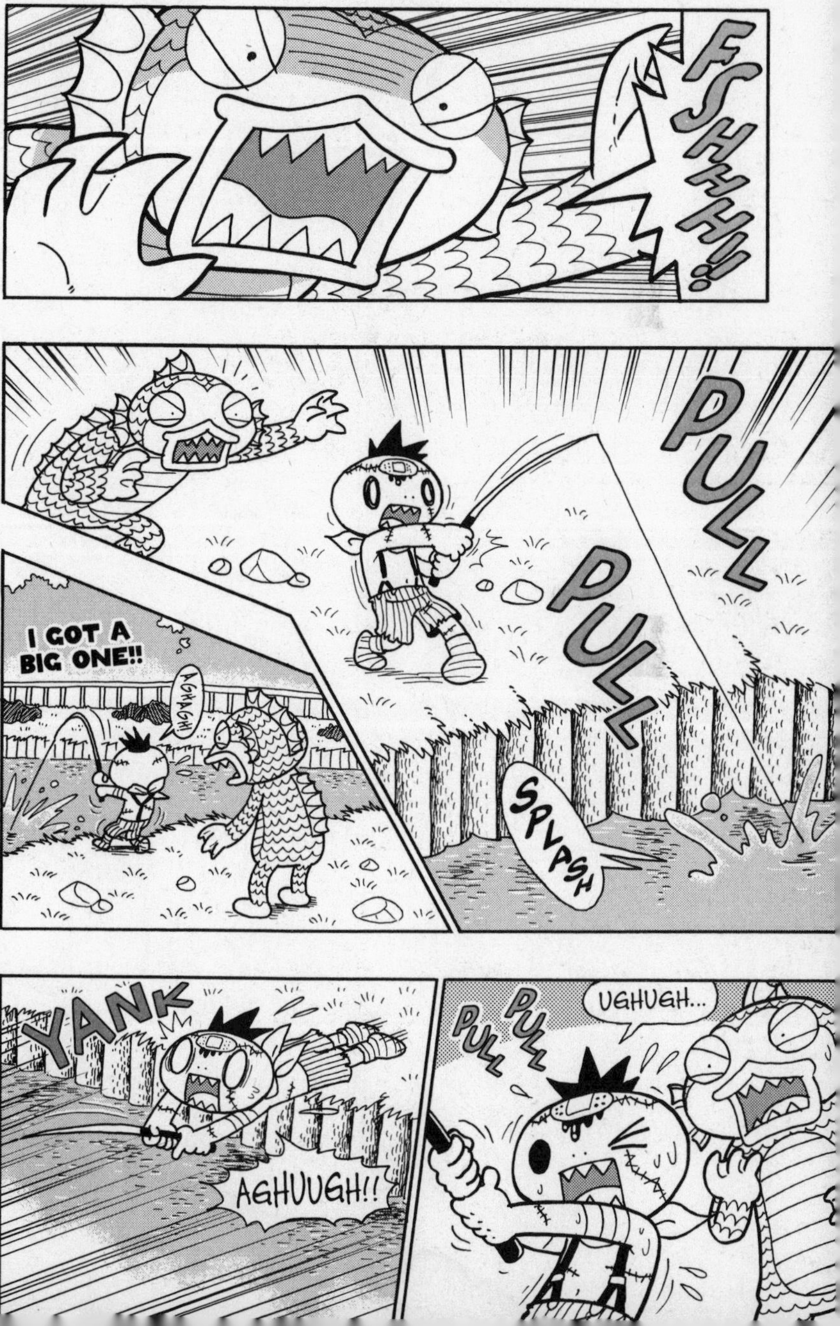
FSHHHH!!
PULL
PULL
SPVPSH
I GOT A BIG ONE!!
AGHAGH!
PULL
PULL
UGHUGH...
YANK
AGHUUGH!!

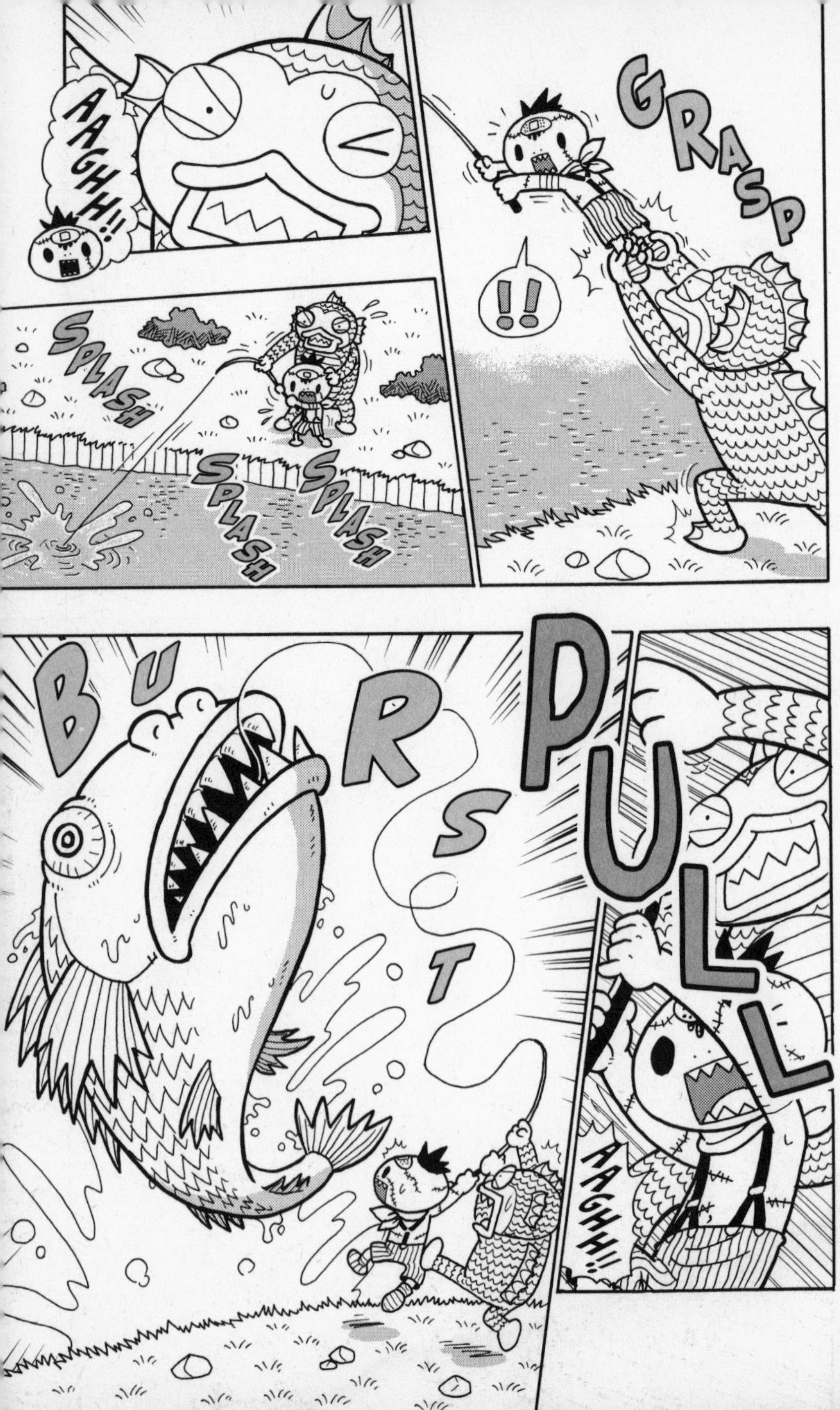
GRASP
!!
AAGHH!!
SPLASH
SPLASH
SPLASH
PULL
AAGHH!!
BURST

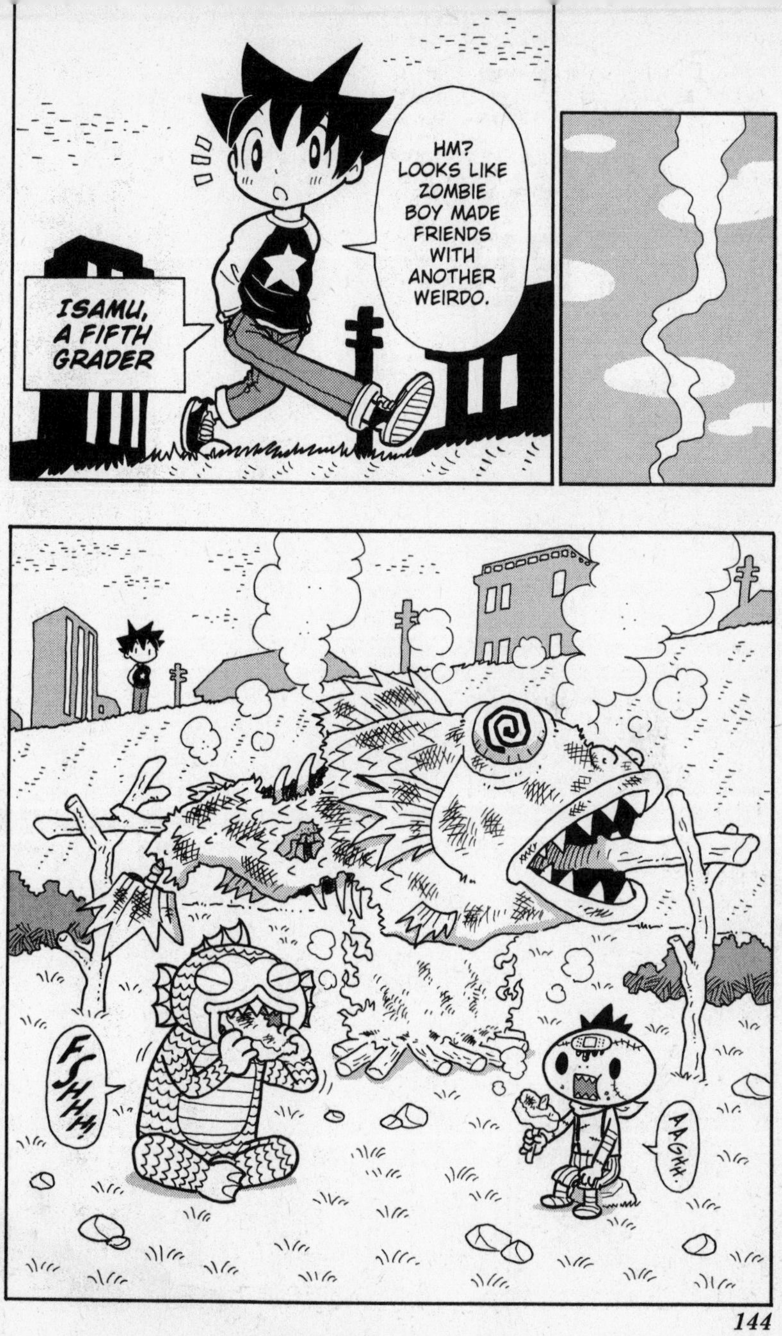
HM? LOOKS LIKE ZOMBIE BOY MADE FRIENDS WITH ANOTHER WEIRDO.
ISAMU, A FIFTH GRADER
AAGHH.
FSHHH.

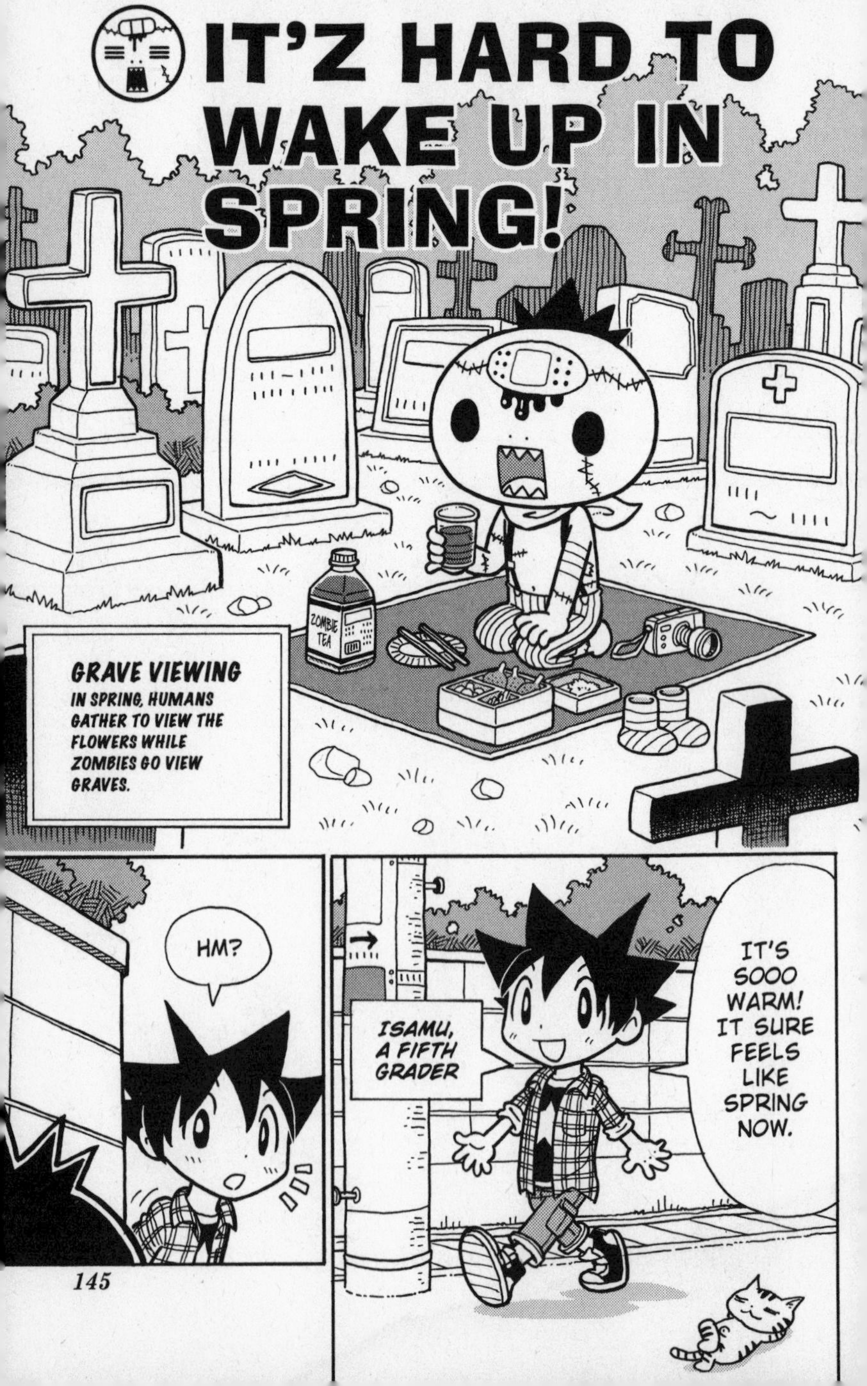
IT'Z HARD TO WAKE UP IN SPRING!
ZOMBIE TEA
GRAVE VIEWING
IN SPRING, HUMANS GATHER TO VIEW THE FLOWERS WHILE ZOMBIES GO VIEW GRAVES.
IT'S SOOO WARM! IT SURE FEELS LIKE SPRING NOW.
ISAMU, A FIFTH GRADER
HM?

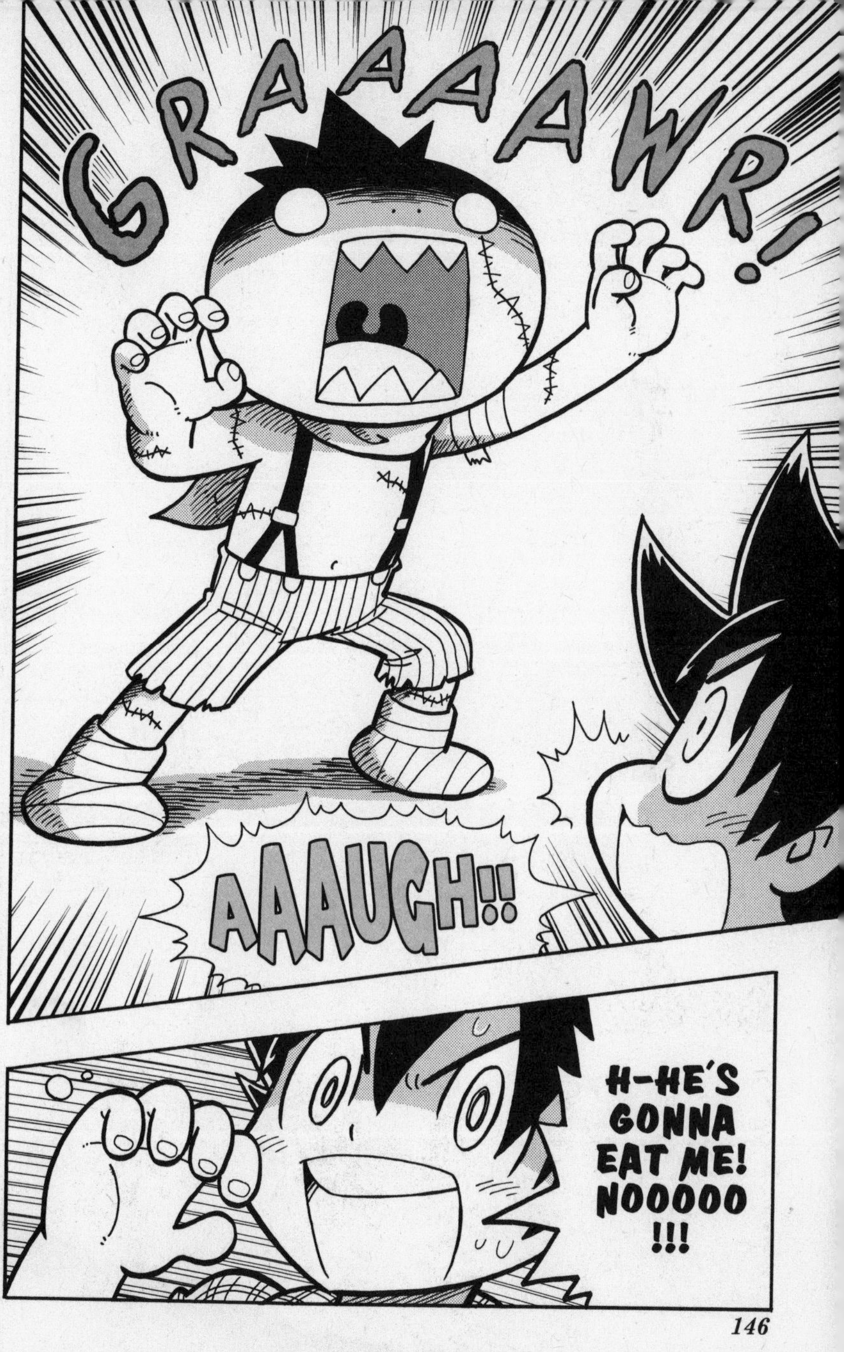
GRAAAAWR!
AAAUGH!!
H-HE'S GONNA EAT ME! NOOOOO !!!

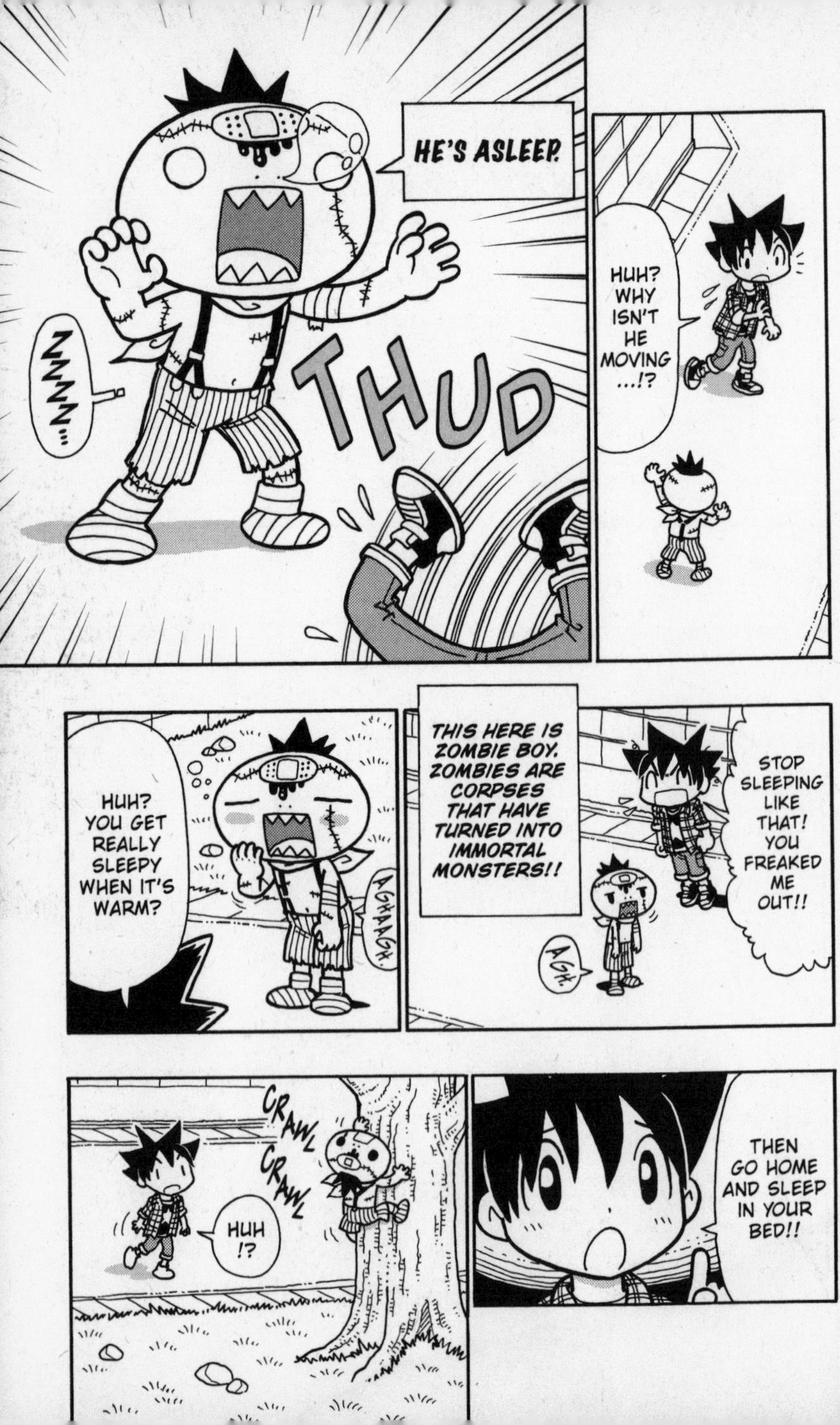
HUH? WHY ISN'T HE MOVING ...!?
HE'S ASLEEP.
THUD
ZZZZ...
THIS HERE IS ZOMBIE BOY. ZOMBIES ARE CORPSES THAT HAVE TURNED INTO IMMORTAL MONSTERS!!
STOP SLEEPING LIKE THAT! YOU FREAKED ME OUT!!
AGH.
AGHAAGH.
HUH? YOU GET REALLY SLEEPY WHEN IT'S WARM?
THEN GO HOME AND SLEEP IN YOUR BED!!
CRAWL
CRAWL
HUH !?

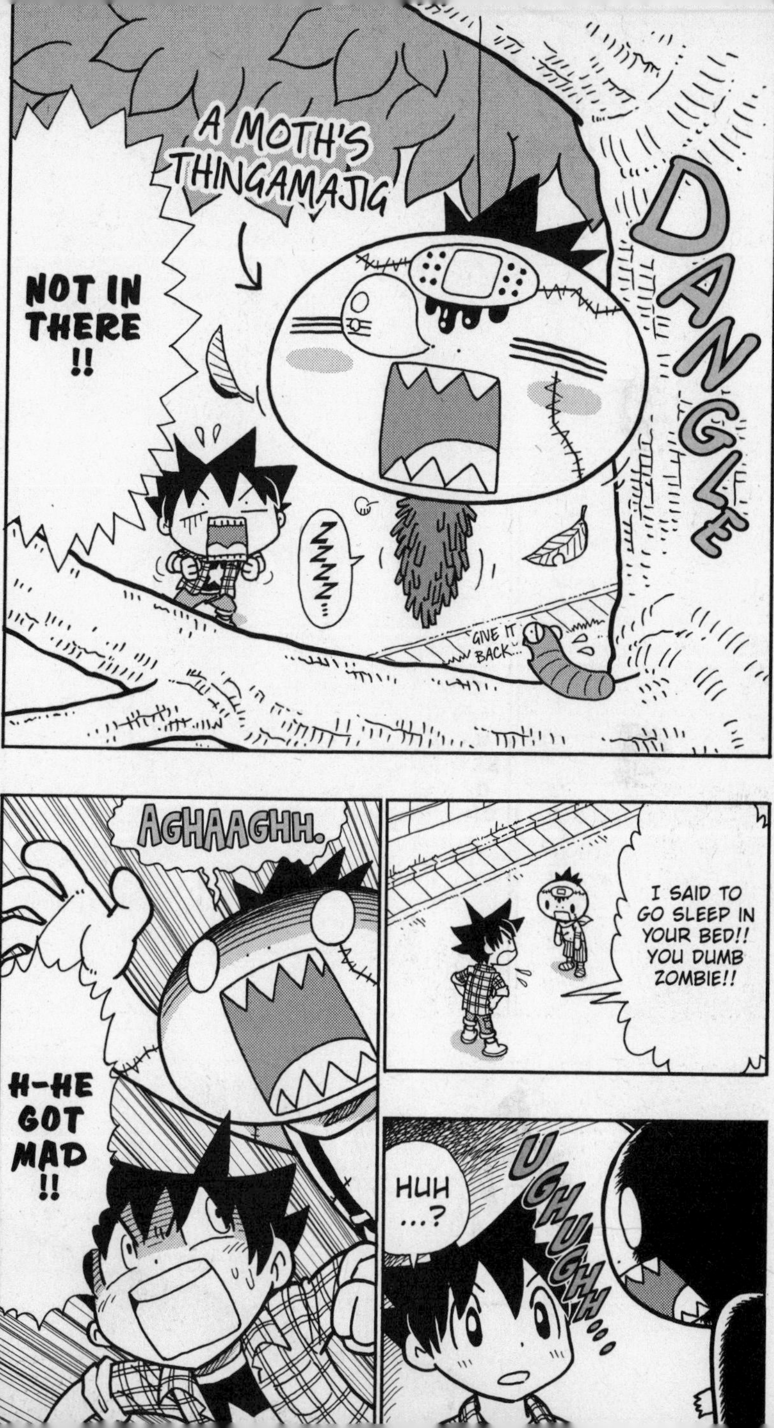
DANGLE
A MOTH'S THINGAMAJIG
NOT IN THERE!!
ZZZZ...
GIVE IT BACK...
I SAID TO GO SLEEP IN YOUR BED!! YOU DUMB ZOMBIE!!
HUH ...?
UGHUGHH...
AGHAAGHH.
H-HE GOT MAD!!

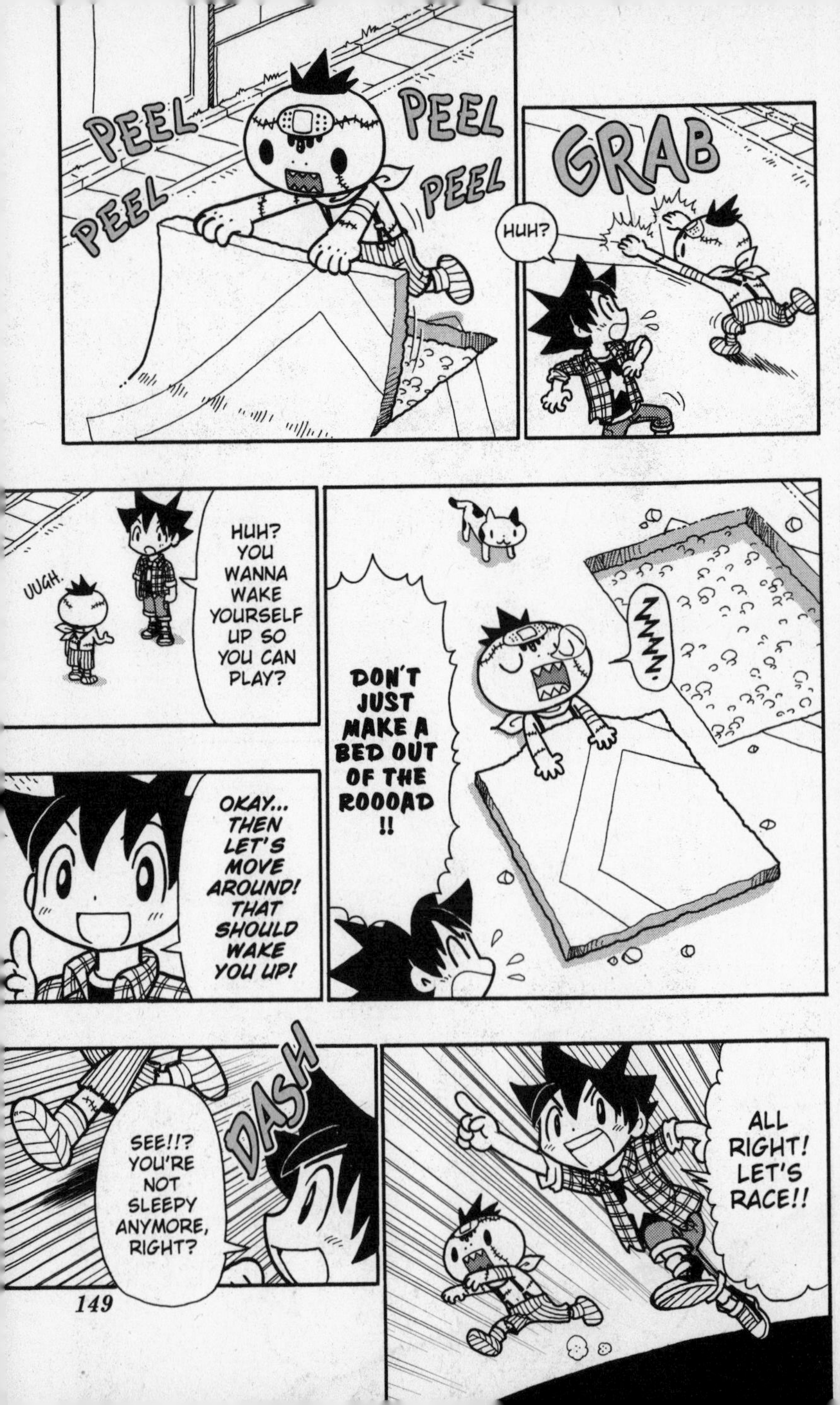
GRAB
HUH?
PEEL
PEEL
PEEL
PEEL
DON'T JUST MAKE A BED OUT OF THE ROOOAD!!
ZZZZ
HUH? YOU WANNA WAKE YOURSELF UP SO YOU CAN PLAY?
UUGH.
OKAY... THEN LET'S MOVE AROUND! THAT SHOULD WAKE YOU UP!
ALL RIGHT! LET'S RACE!!
DASH
SEE!!? YOU'RE NOT SLEEPY ANYMORE, RIGHT?

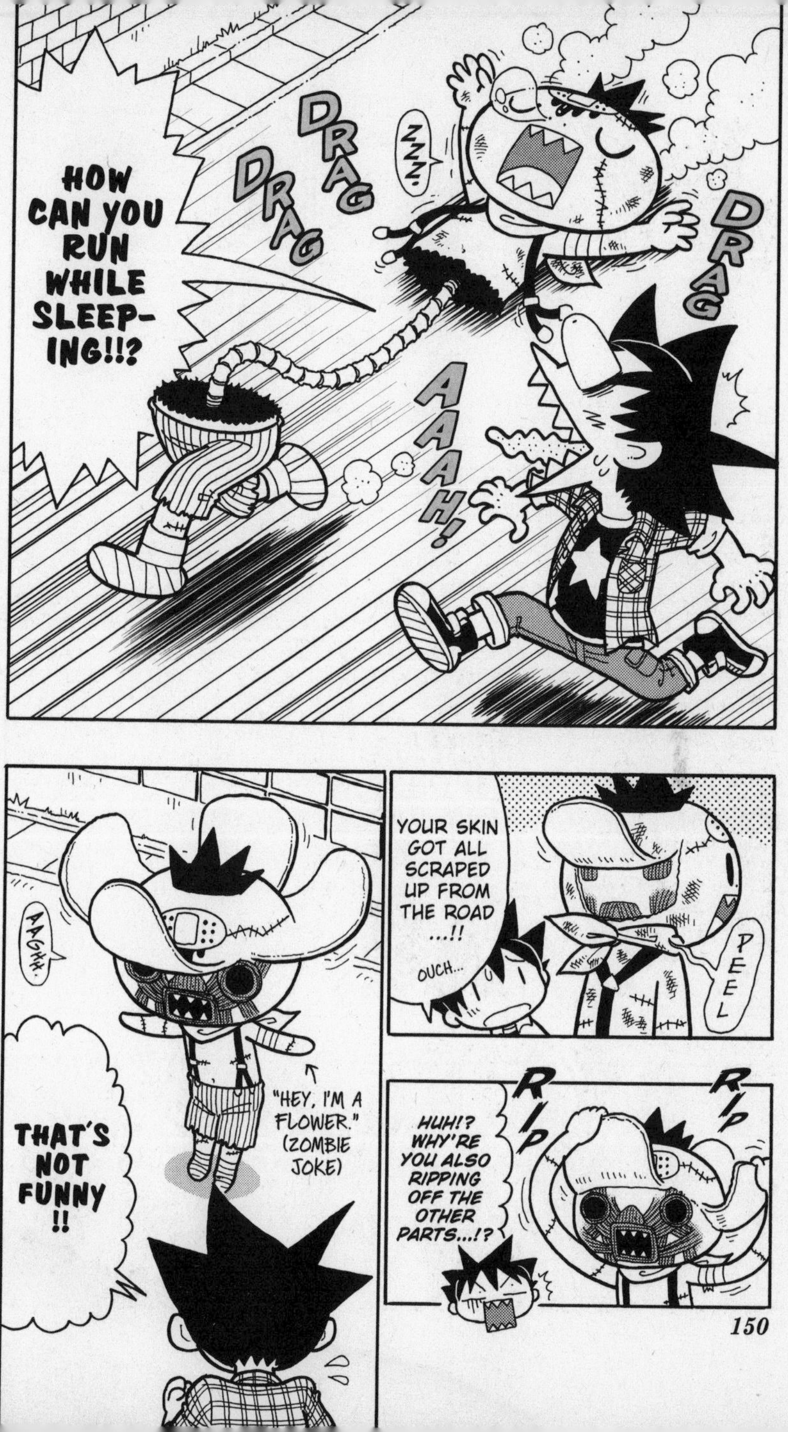
DRAG
ZZZ...
DRAG
DRAG
AAAAH!
HOW CAN YOU RUN WHILE SLEEP-ING!!?
PEEL
YOUR SKIN GOT ALL SCRAPED UP FROM THE ROAD ...!!
OUCH...
RIP
RIP
HUH!? WHY'RE YOU ALSO RIPPING OFF THE OTHER PARTS...!?
AAGHH.
"HEY, I'M A FLOWER." (ZOMBIE JOKE)
THAT'S NOT FUNNY !!

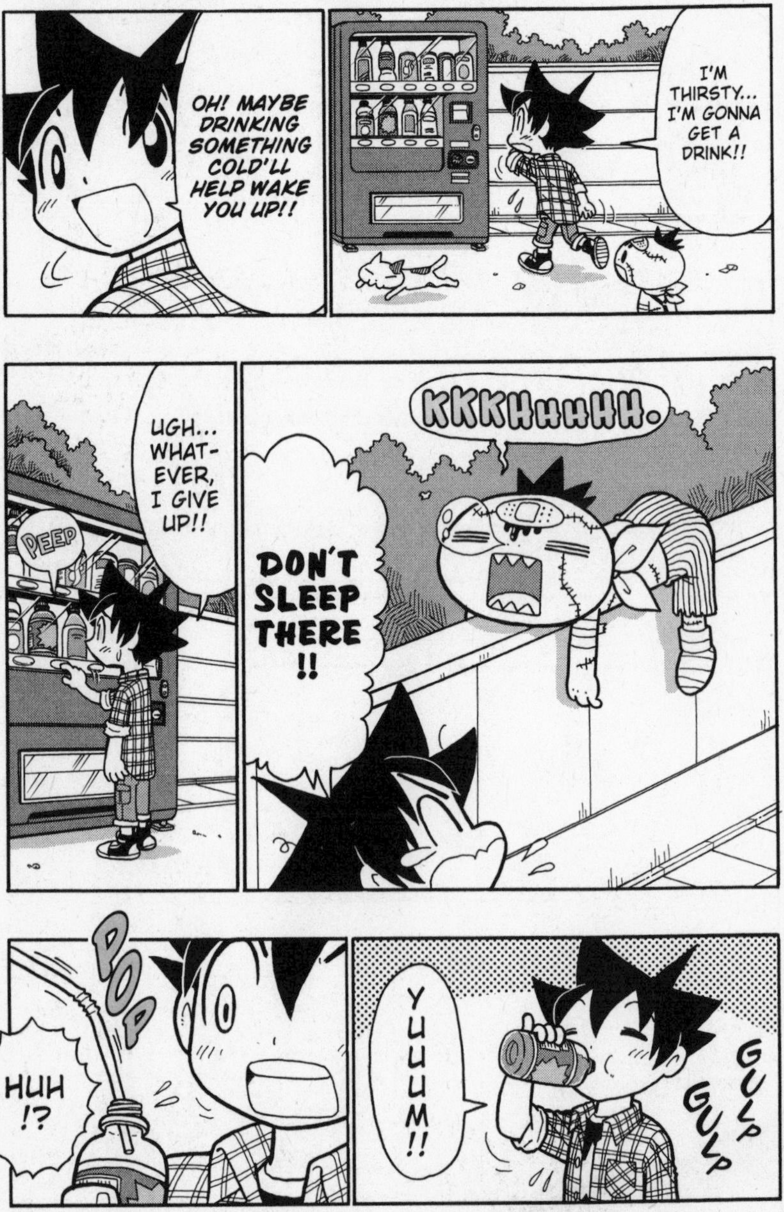
I'M THIRSTY... I'M GONNA GET A DRINK!!
OH! MAYBE DRINKING SOMETHING COLD'LL HELP WAKE YOU UP!!
KKKHHHHHH.
DON'T SLEEP THERE !!
UGH... WHAT-EVER, I GIVE UP!!
PEEP
YUUUM!!
GULP GULP
POP
HUH !?

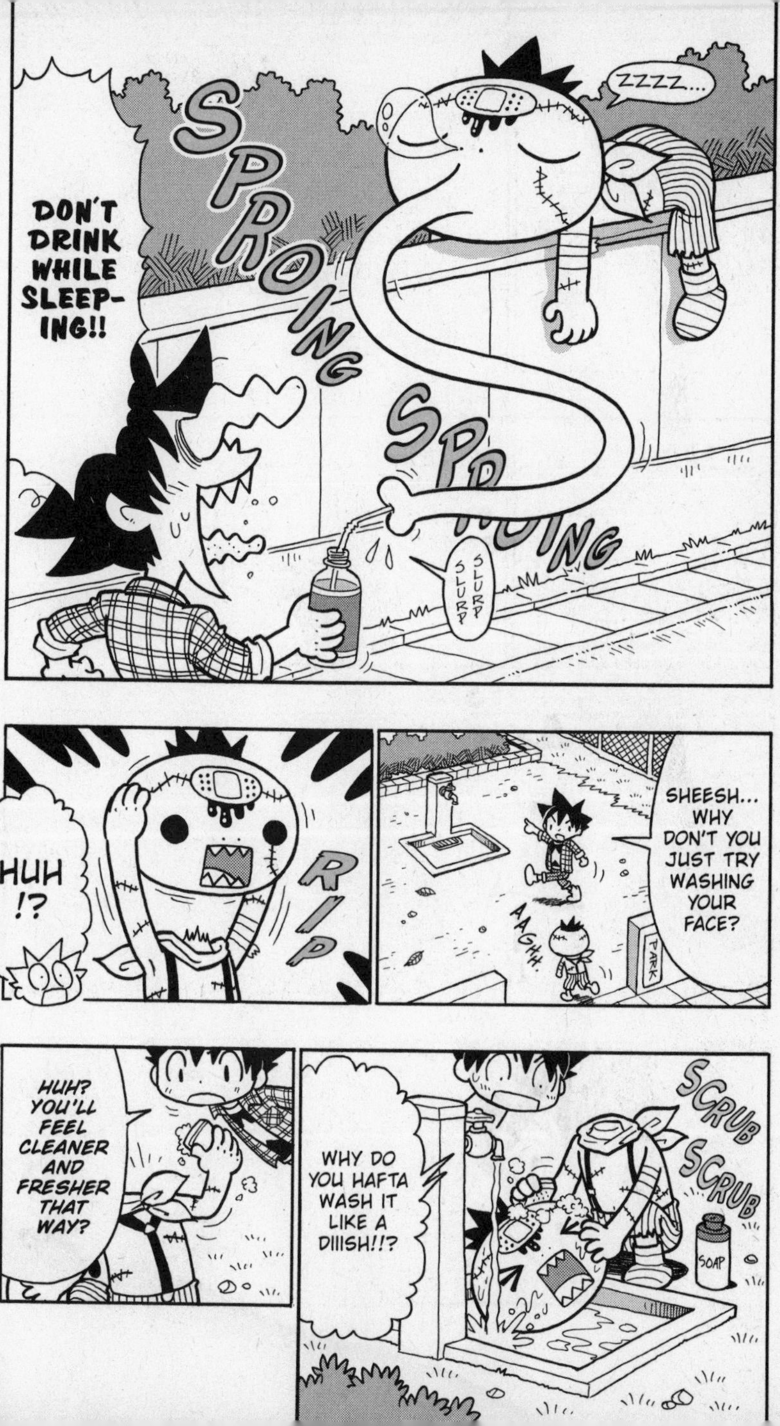
ZZZZ...
SPROING
SPROING
SLURP SLURP
DON'T DRINK WHILE SLEEP-ING!!
SHEESH... WHY DON'T YOU JUST TRY WASHING YOUR FACE?
AAGHH.
PARK
RIP
HUH !?
SCRUB SCRUB
WHY DO YOU HAFTA WASH IT LIKE A DIIISH!!?
SOAP
HUH? YOU'LL FEEL CLEANER AND FRESHER THAT WAY?

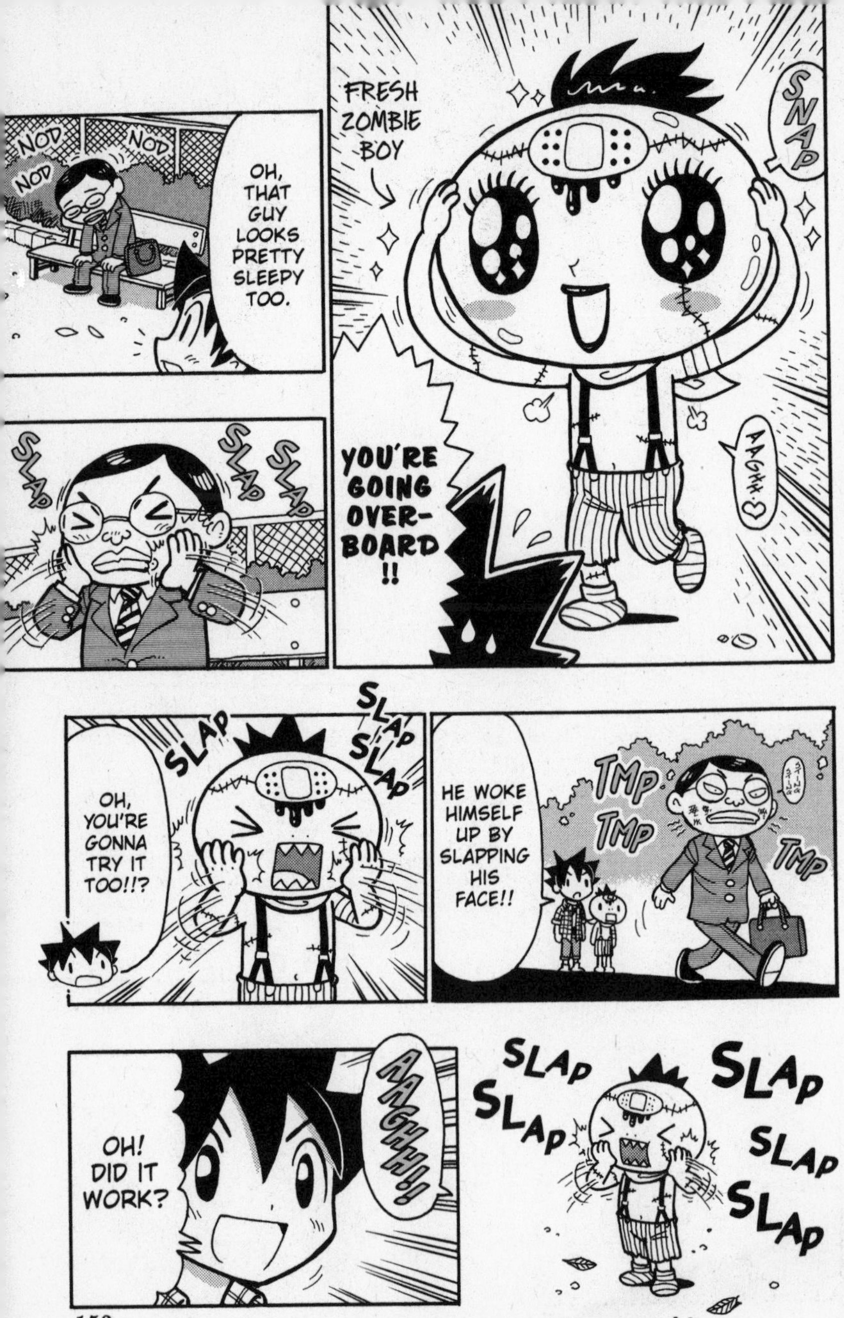
FRESH ZOMBIE BOY
SNAP
AAGHH♡
YOU'RE GOING OVER-BOARD!!
NOD NOD NOD
OH, THAT GUY LOOKS PRETTY SLEEPY TOO.
SLAP SLAP SLAP
TMP TMP TMP
HE WOKE HIMSELF UP BY SLAPPING HIS FACE!!
SLAP SLAP SLAP
OH, YOU'RE GONNA TRY IT TOO!!?
SLAP SLAP SLAP SLAP SLAP SLAP
AAGHH!!
OH! DID IT WORK?

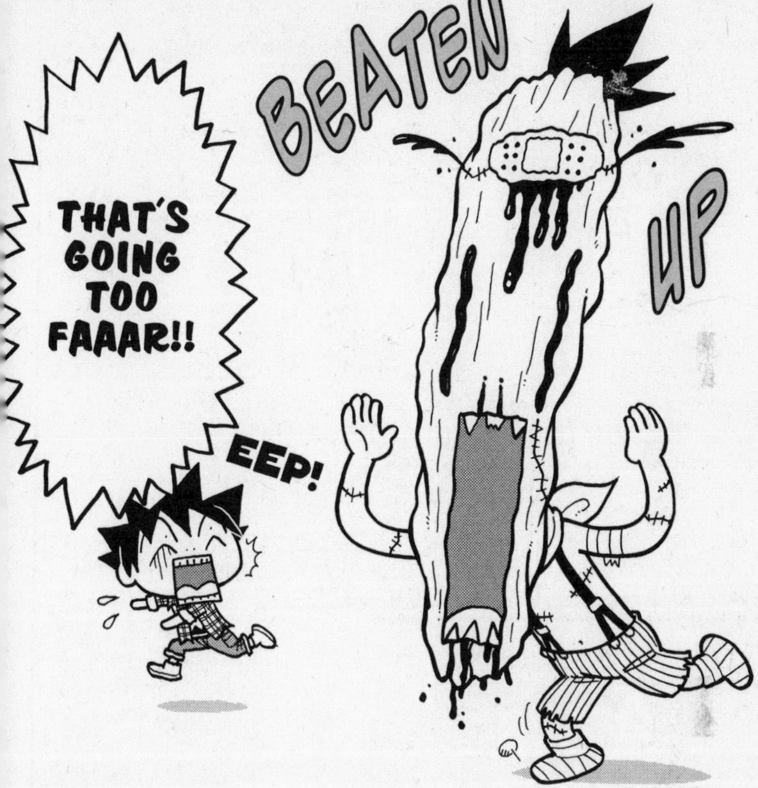
BEATEN UP
THAT'S GOING TOO FAAAR!!
EEP!

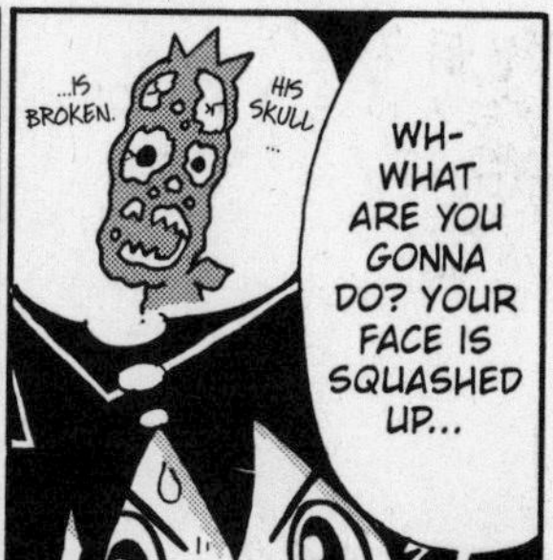
WH- WHAT ARE YOU GONNA DO? YOUR FACE IS SQUASHED UP...
HIS SKULL...
...IS BROKEN.

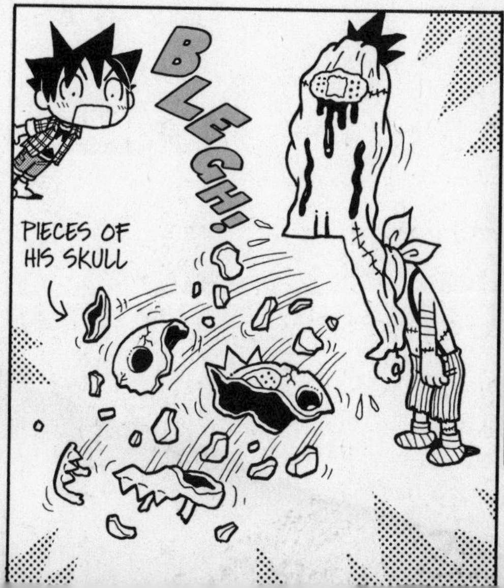
BLECH!
PIECES OF HIS SKULL

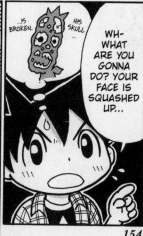

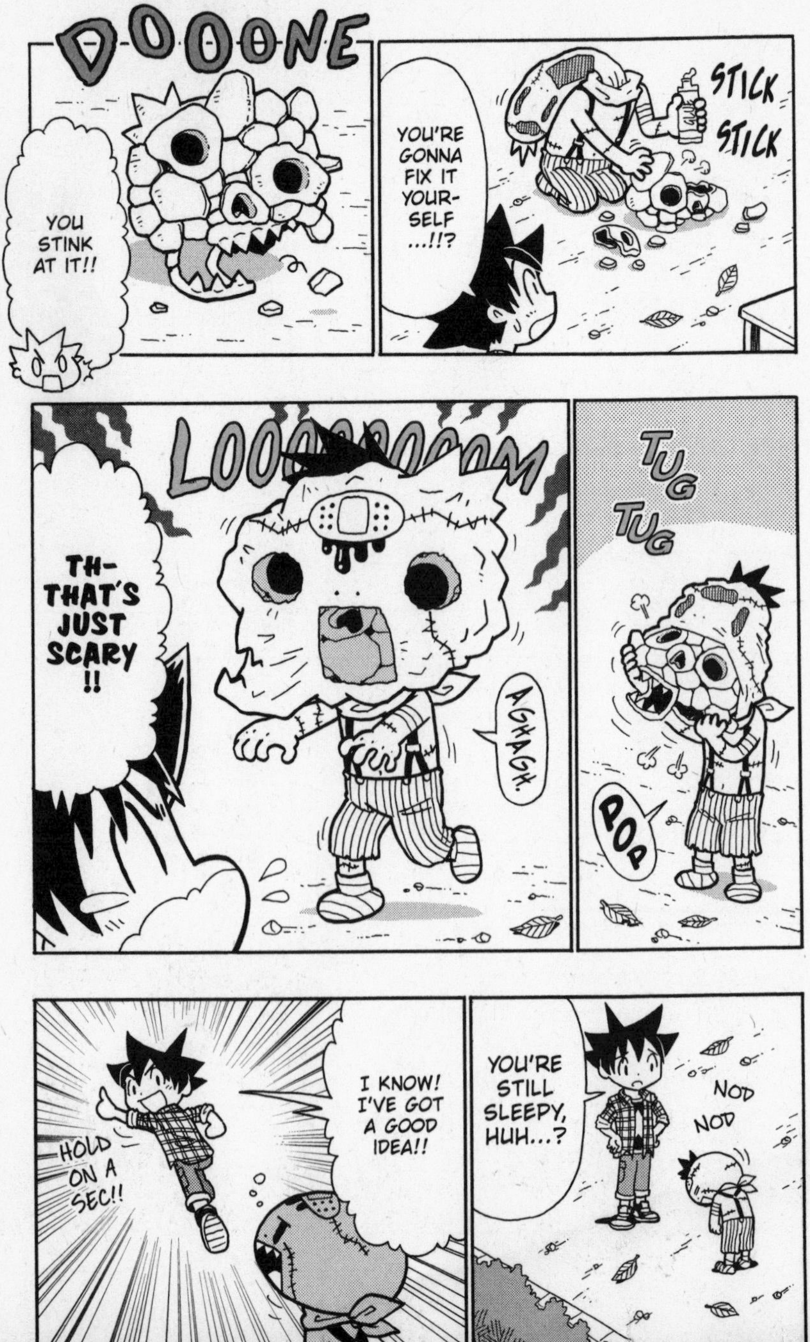
STICK
STICK
YOU'RE GONNA FIX IT YOURSELF ...!!?
DOOONE
YOU STINK AT IT!!
TUG
TUG
POP
LOOOOOOOOM
AGHAGH.
TH-THAT'S JUST SCARY!!
YOU'RE STILL SLEEPY, HUH...?
NOD
NOD
I KNOW! I'VE GOT A GOOD IDEA!!
HOLD ON A SEC!!

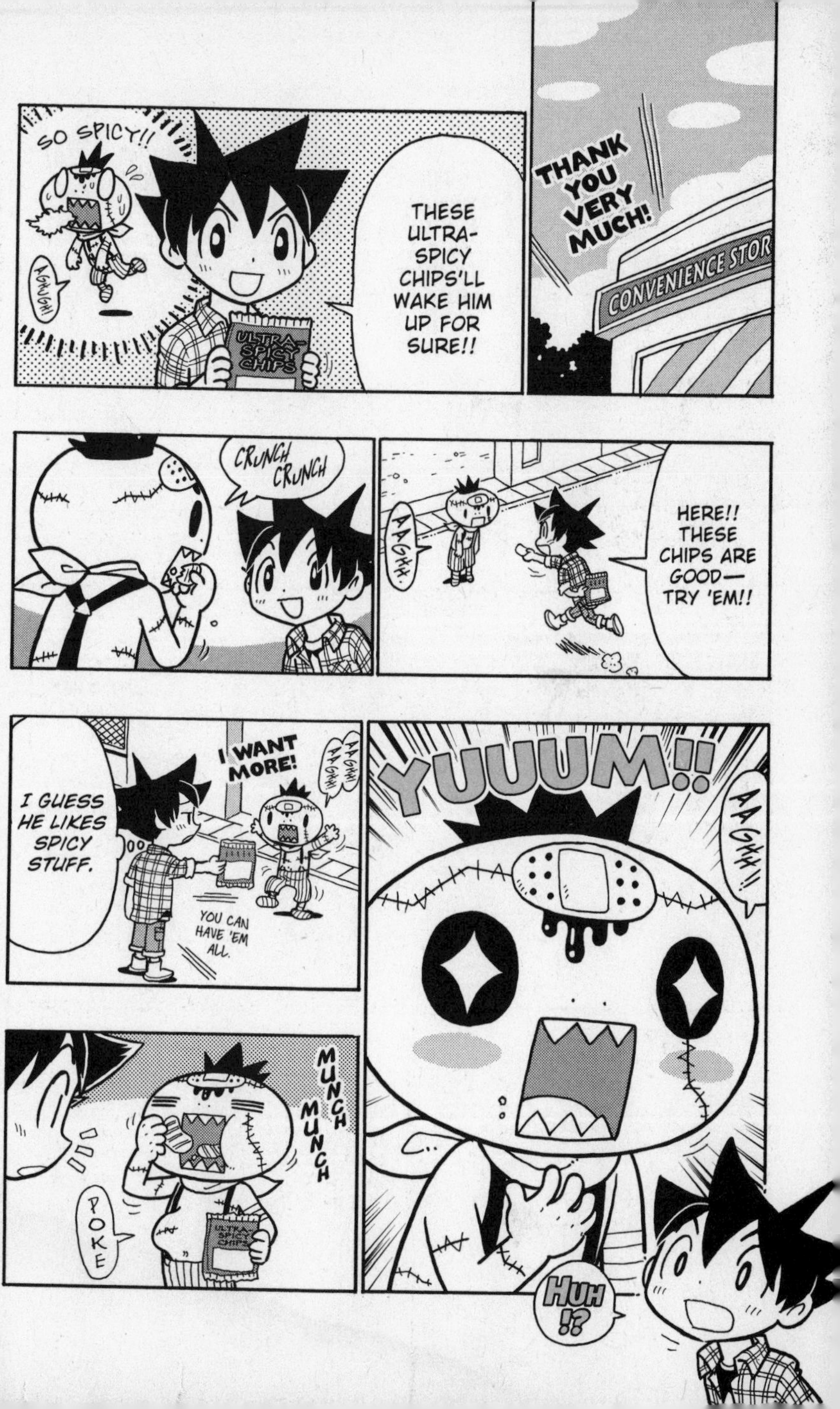
THANK YOU VERY MUCH!
CONVENIENCE STOR
THESE ULTRA-SPICY CHIPS'LL WAKE HIM UP FOR SURE!!
SO SPICY!!
ULTRA-SPICY CHIPS
AGHUGH!
HERE!! THESE CHIPS ARE GOOD—TRY 'EM!!
AAGHH.
CRUNCH CRUNCH
YUUUM!!
AAGHH!!
I WANT MORE!
AAGHH AAGHH
I GUESS HE LIKES SPICY STUFF.
YOU CAN HAVE 'EM ALL.
HUH!?
MUNCH MUNCH
POKE
ULTRA-SPICY CHIPS

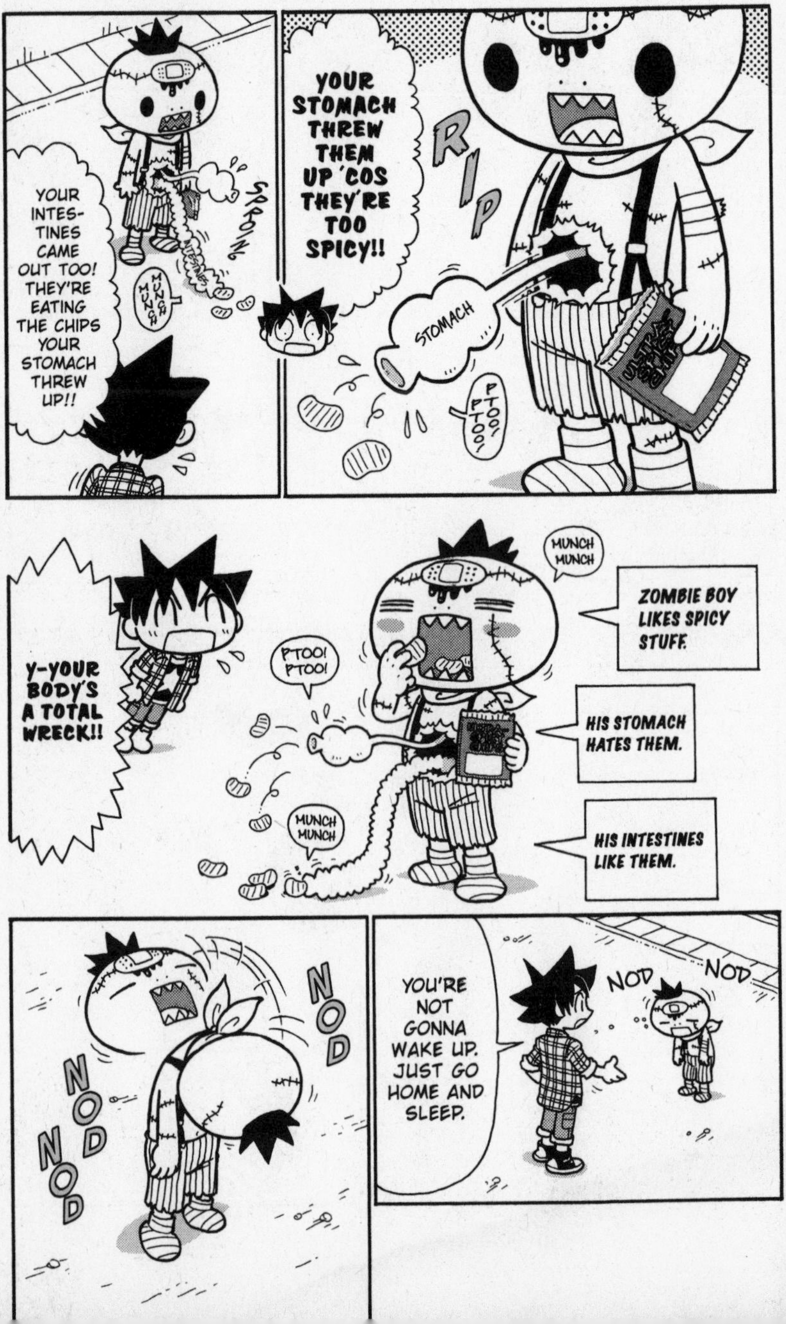
RIP
YOUR STOMACH THREW THEM UP 'COS THEY'RE TOO SPICY!!
STOMACH
PTOO! PTOO!
SPROING
MUNCH MUNCH
YOUR INTES-TINES CAME OUT TOO! THEY'RE EATING THE CHIPS YOUR STOMACH THREW UP!!
MUNCH MUNCH
ZOMBIE BOY LIKES SPICY STUFF.
HIS STOMACH HATES THEM.
HIS INTESTINES LIKE THEM.
PTOO! PTOO!
MUNCH MUNCH
Y-YOUR BODY'S A TOTAL WRECK!!
NOD NOD
YOU'RE NOT GONNA WAKE UP. JUST GO HOME AND SLEEP.
NOD
NOD
NOD
NOD

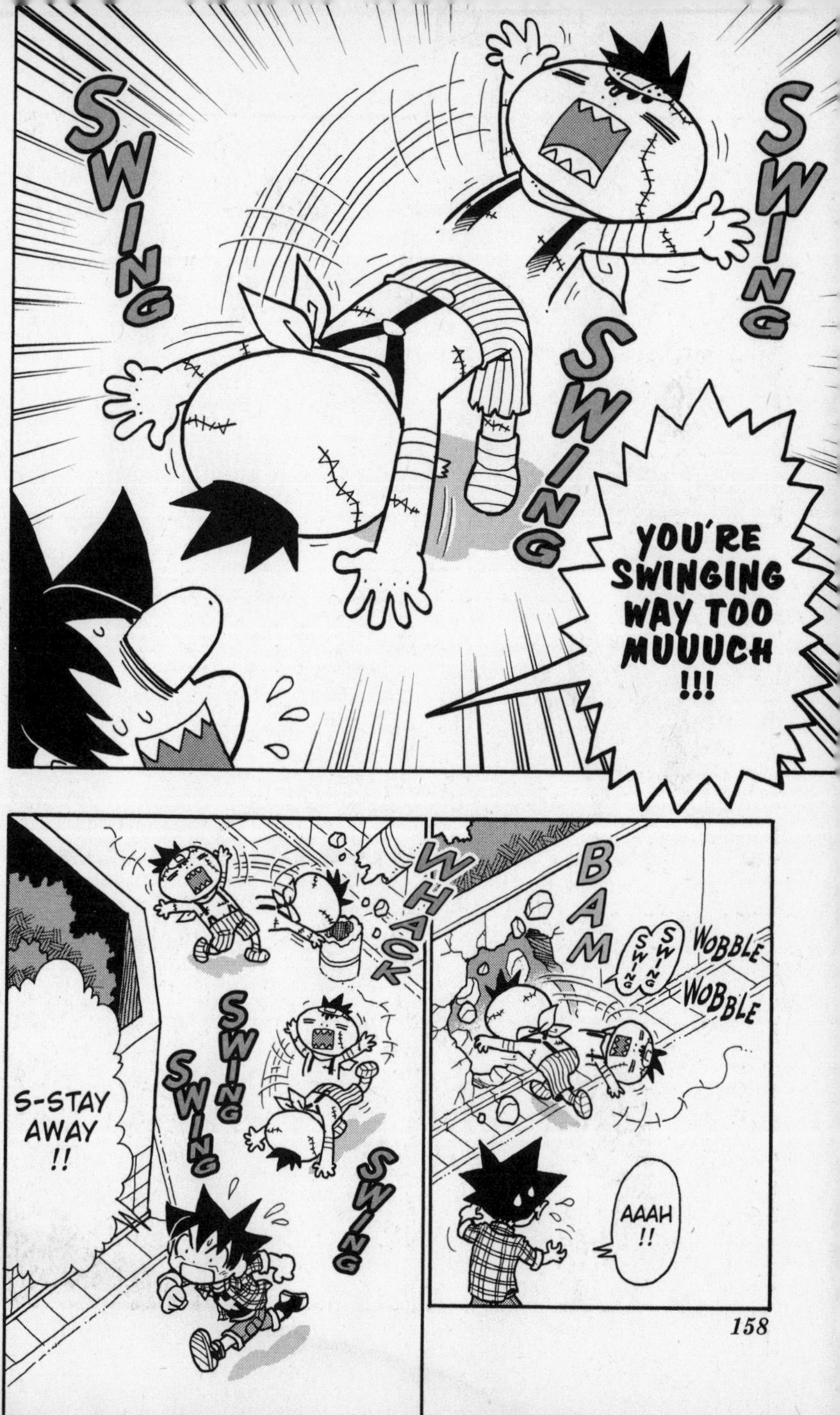
SWING
SWING
SWING
YOU'RE SWINGING WAY TOO MUUUCH !!!
BAM
SWING SWING
WOBBLE WOBBLE
AAAH !!
WHACK
SWING
SWING
SWING
S-STAY AWAY !!

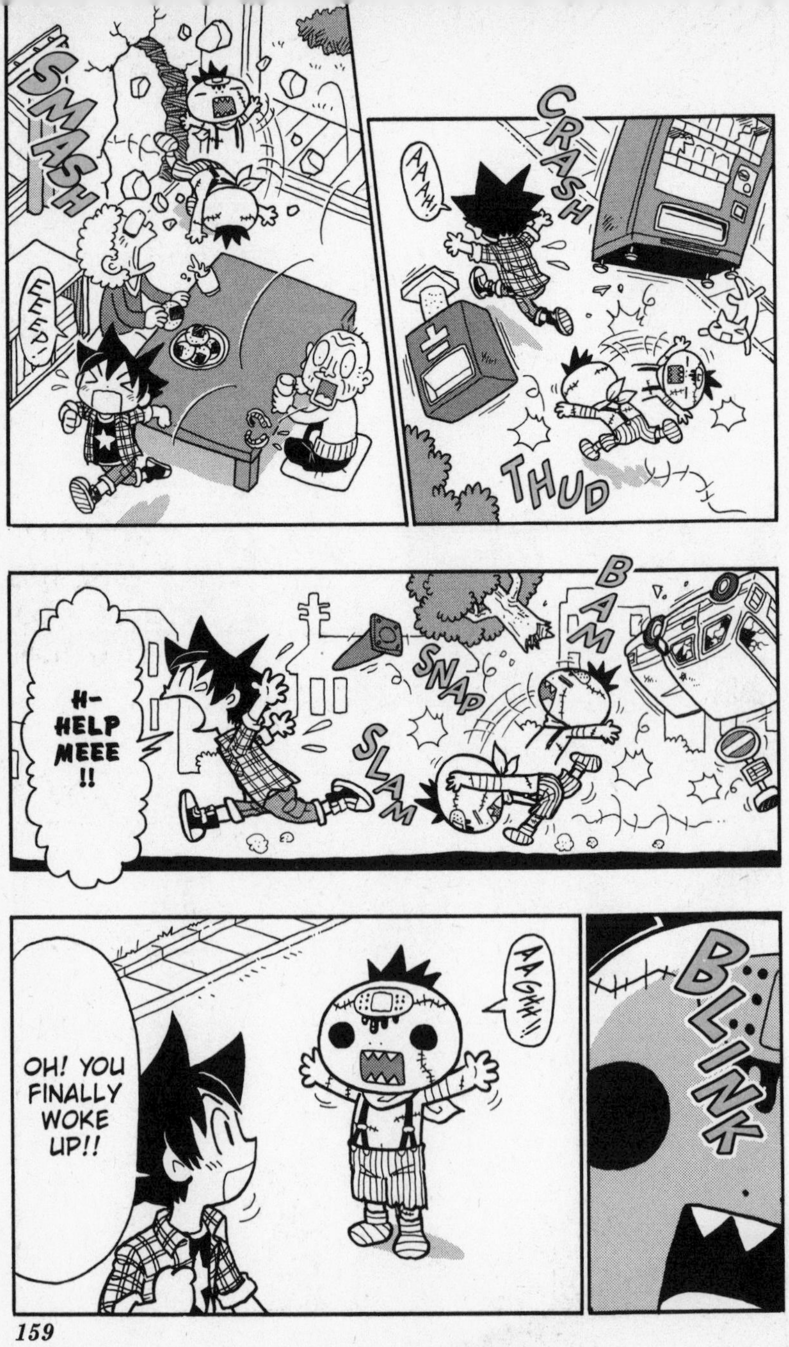
CRASH
AAAH!
THUD
SMASH
EEEP!
BAM
SNAP
SLAM
H-HELP MEEE!!
BLINK
AAGHH!!
OH! YOU FINALLY WOKE UP!!

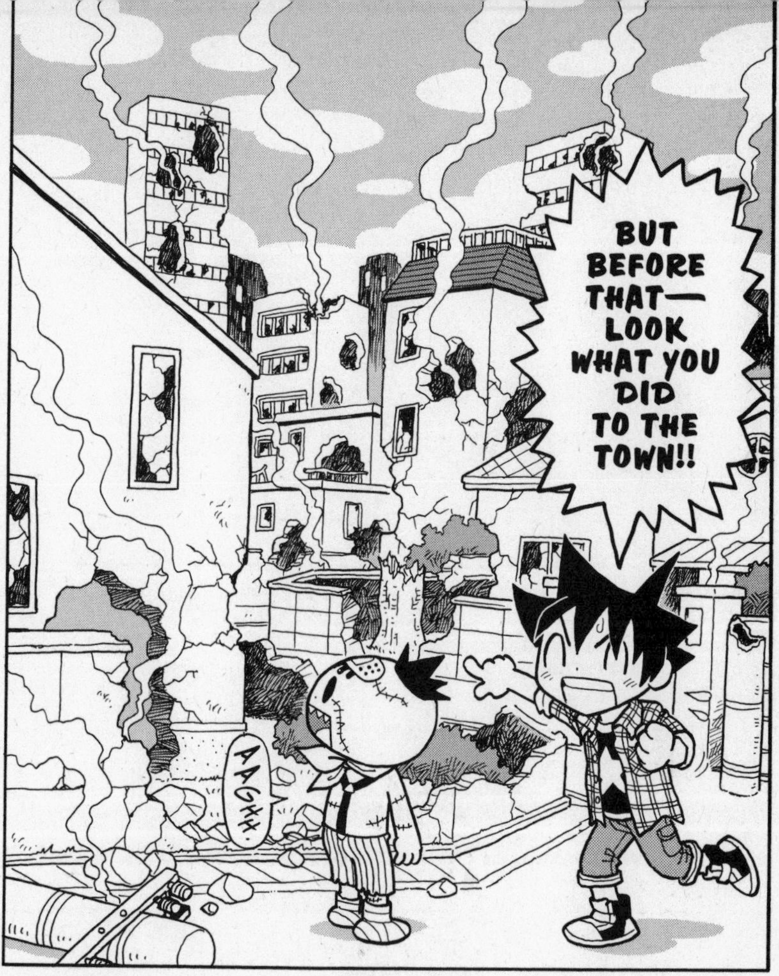
BUT BEFORE THAT— LOOK WHAT YOU DID TO THE TOWN!!
AAGHH.

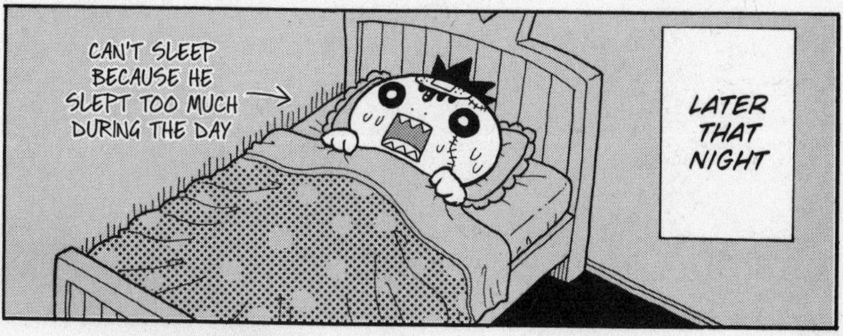
LATER THAT NIGHT
CAN'T SLEEP BECAUSE HE SLEPT TOO MUCH DURING THE DAY

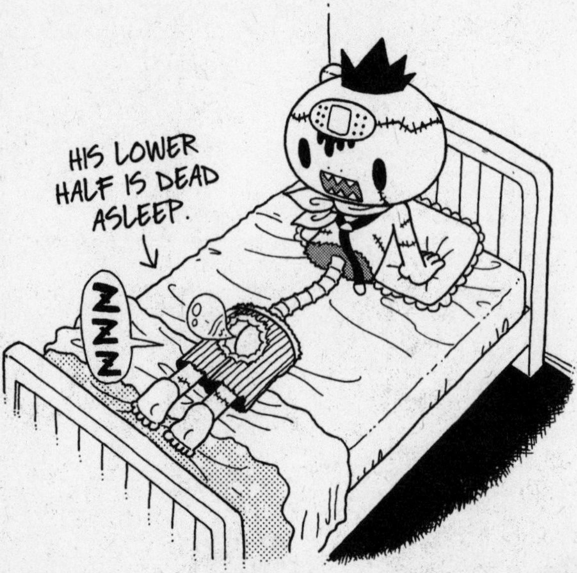
HIS LOWER HALF IS DEAD ASLEEP.
ZZZ

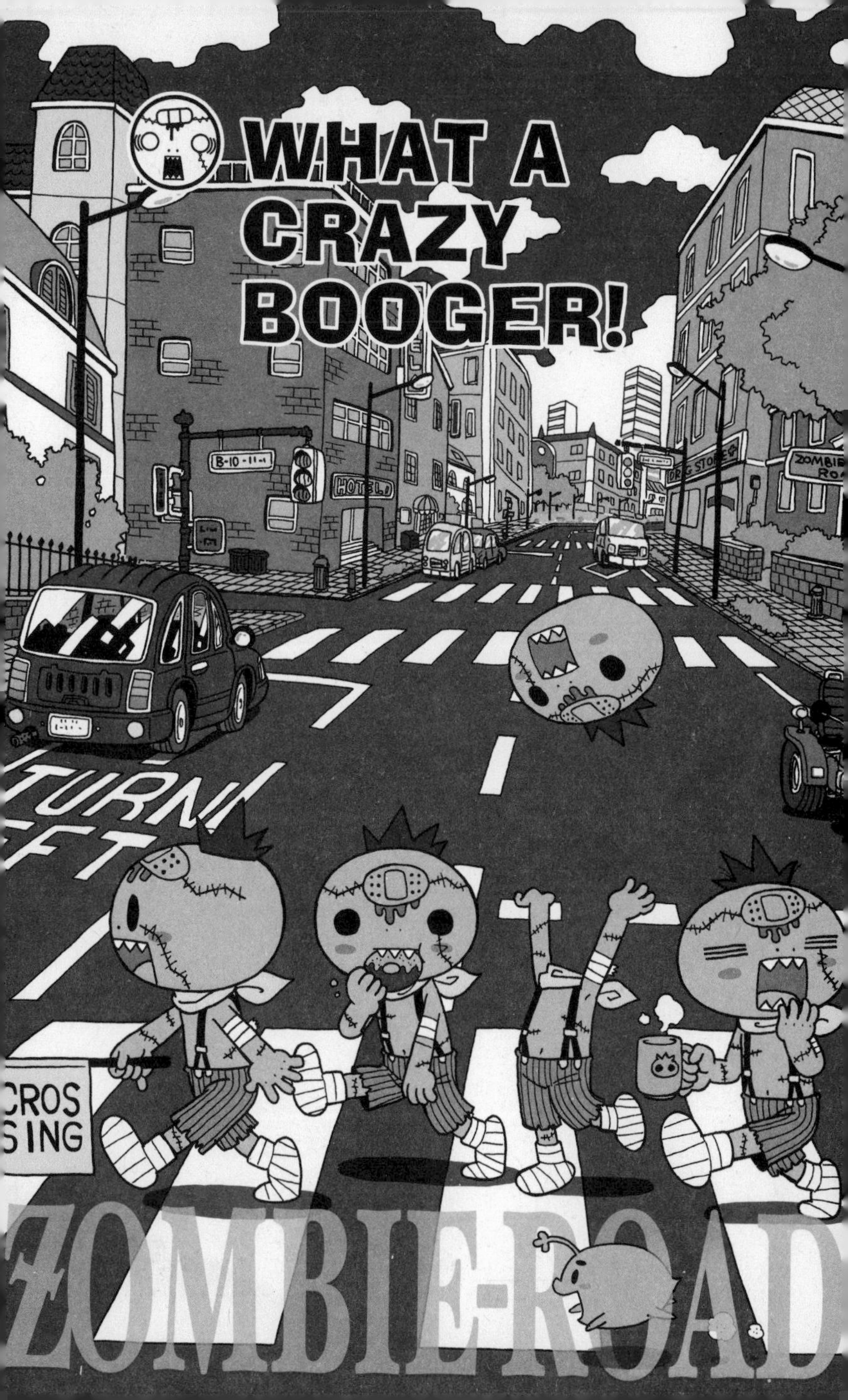
WHAT A CRAZY BOOGER!
HOTEL
ZOMBIE-ROAD

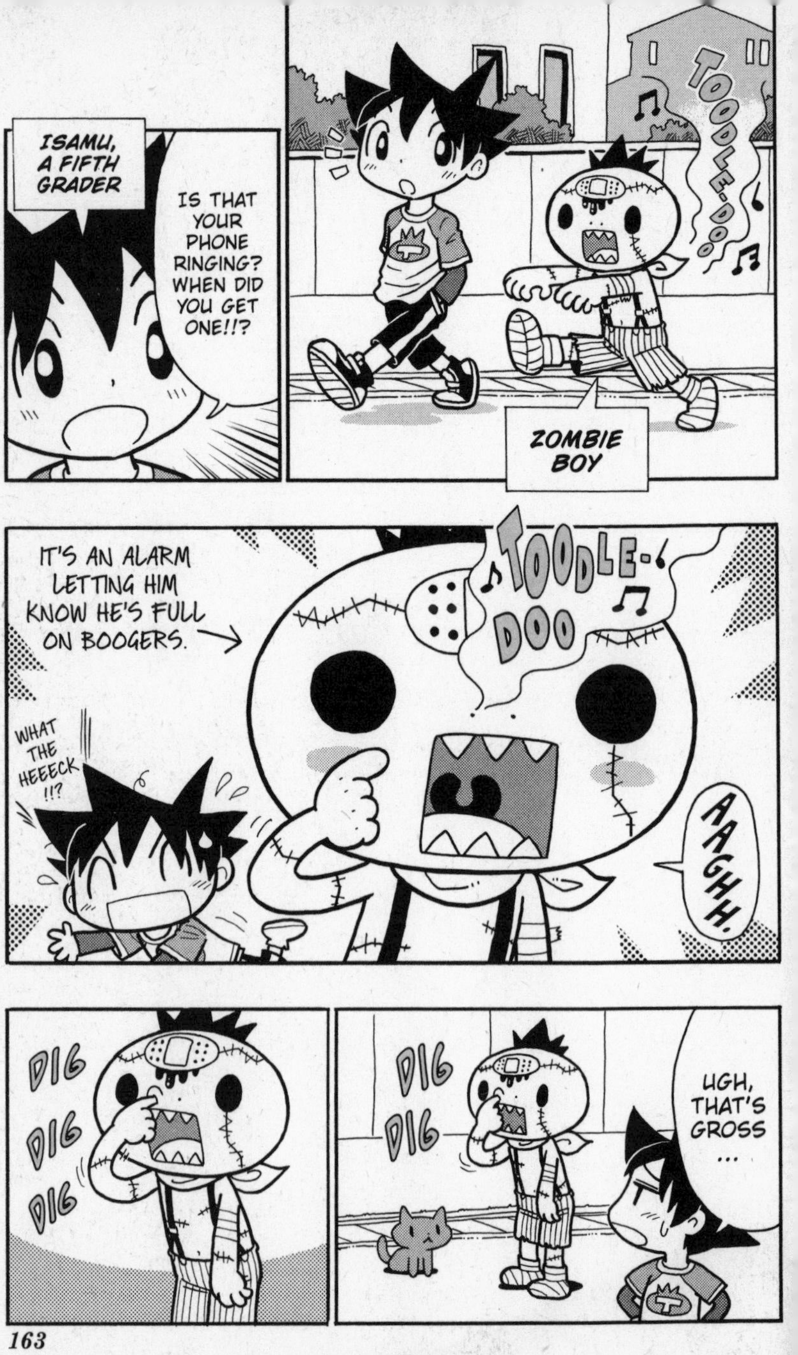
TOODLE-DOO
ZOMBIE BOY
ISAMU, A FIFTH GRADER
IS THAT YOUR PHONE RINGING? WHEN DID YOU GET ONE!!?
TOODLE-DOO
AAGHH.
IT'S AN ALARM LETTING HIM KNOW HE'S FULL ON BOOGERS.
WHAT THE HEEECK!!?
DIG DIG
UGH, THAT'S GROSS ...
DIG DIG DIG

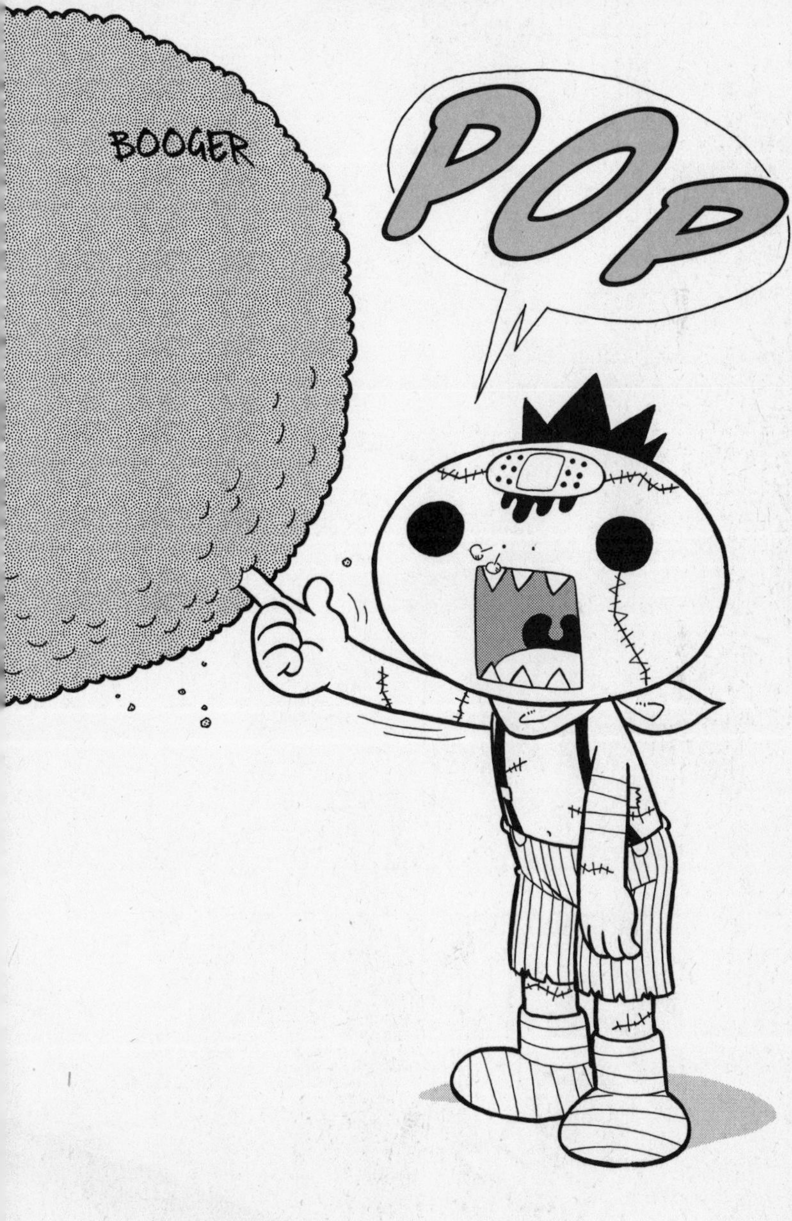
BOOGER
POP

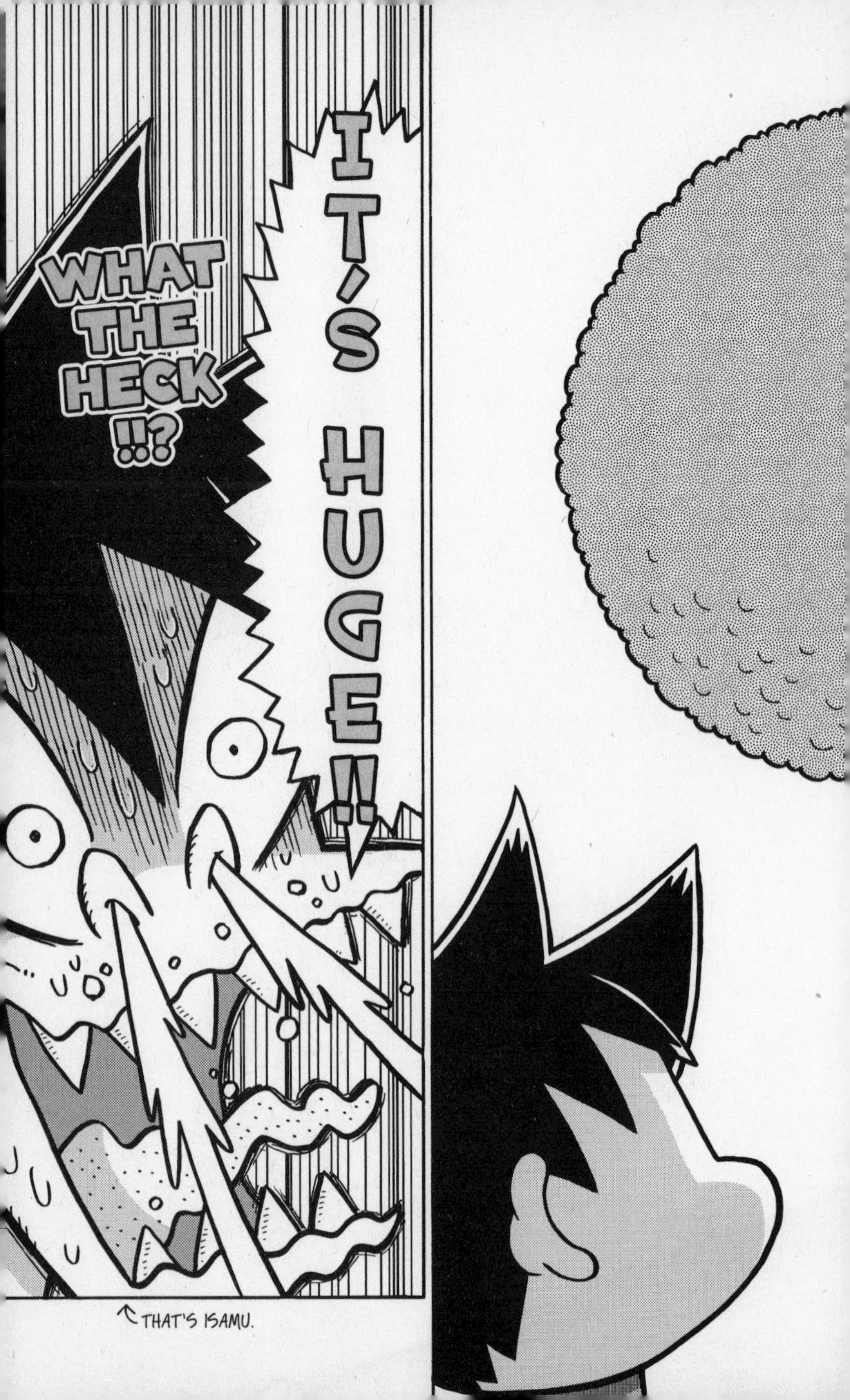
IT'S HUGE!!
WHAT THE HECK!!?
THAT'S ISAMU.

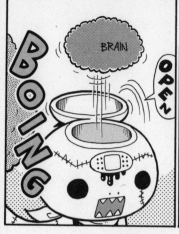

BRAIN

OPEN

BOING

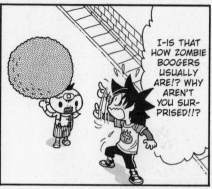

I-IS THAT HOW ZOMBIE BOOGERS USUALLY ARE!? WHY AREN'T YOU SUR-PRISED!!?

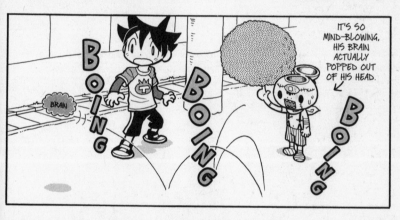

IT'S SO MIND-BLOWING, HIS BRAIN ACTUALLY POPPED OUT OF HIS HEAD.

BOING

BOING

BOING

BRAIN

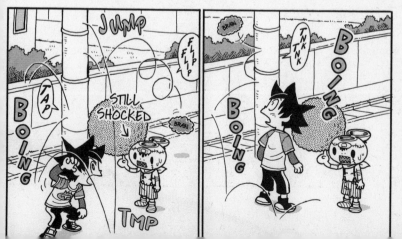

JUMP

FLIP FLIP

STILL SHOCKED

BOING

TAP

BRAIN

TMP

BRAIN

TNK TNK

BOING

BOING

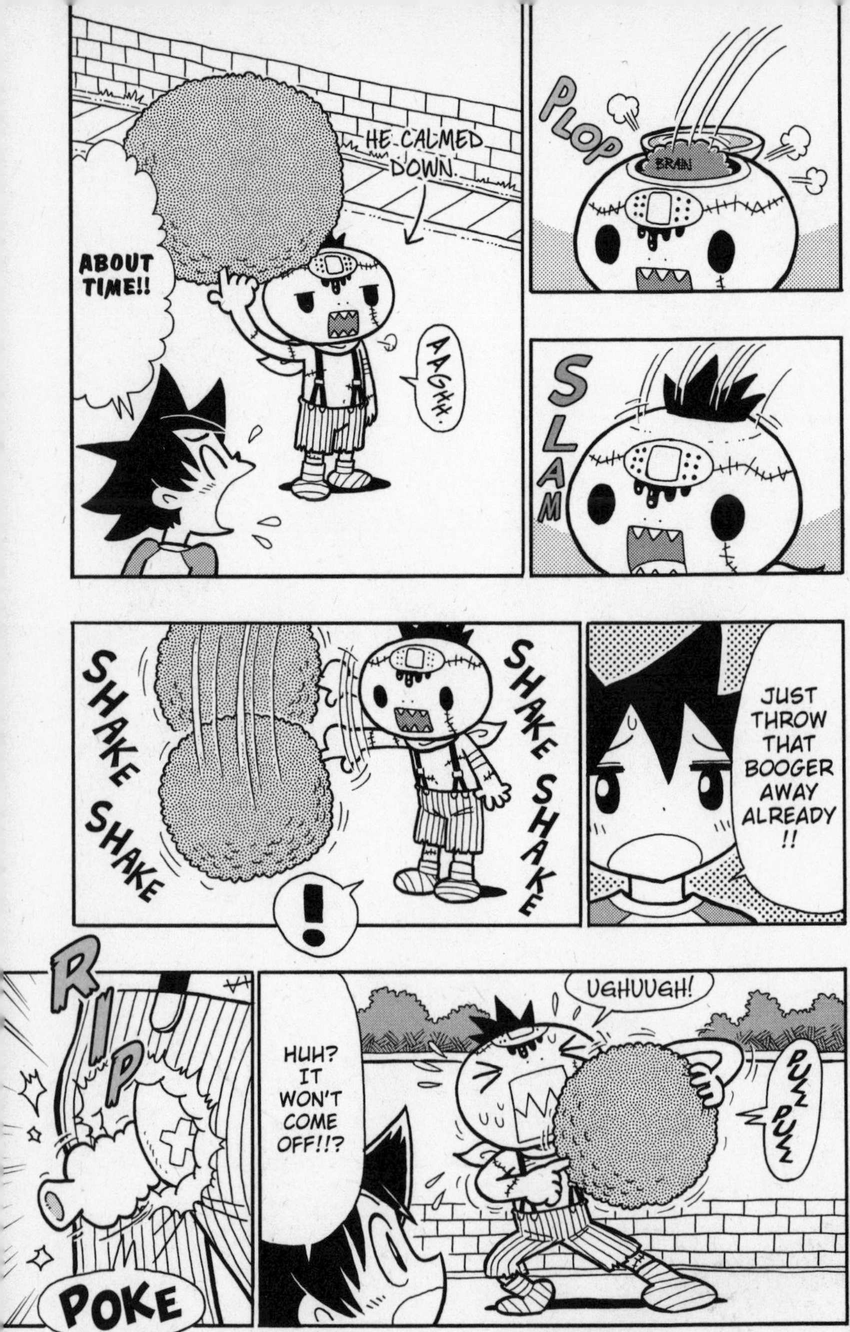
PLOP
BRAIN
SLAM
HE CALMED DOWN.
AAGHH.
ABOUT TIME!!
JUST THROW THAT BOOGER AWAY ALREADY!!
SHAKE SHAKE
SHAKE SHAKE
!
UGHUUGH!
PULL PULL
HUH? IT WON'T COME OFF!!?
RIP
POKE

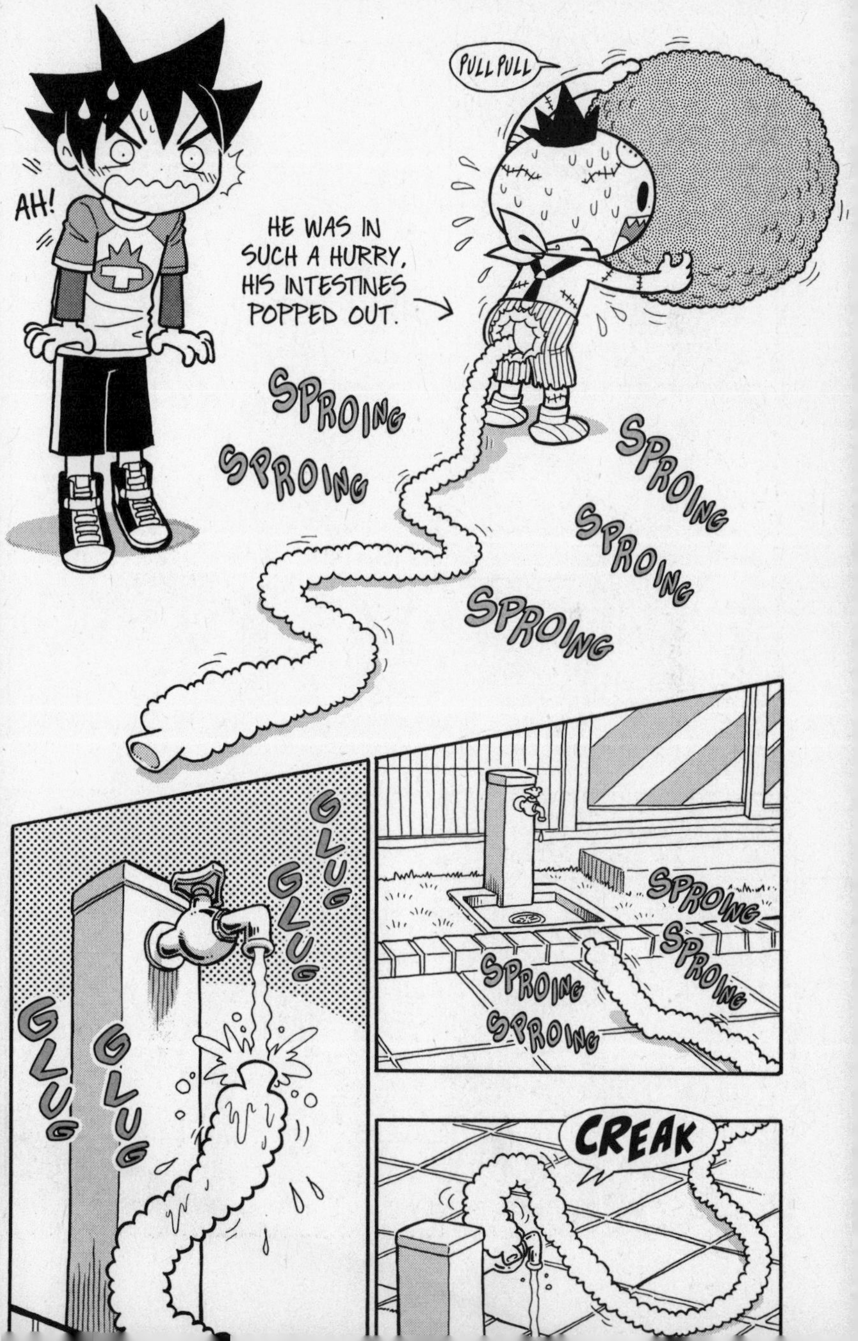
PULL PULL
HE WAS IN SUCH A HURRY, HIS INTESTINES POPPED OUT.
AH!
SPROING
SPROING
SPROING
SPROING
SPROING
SPROING
SPROING
SPROING
SPROING
CREAK
GLUG
GLUG
GLUG
GLUG

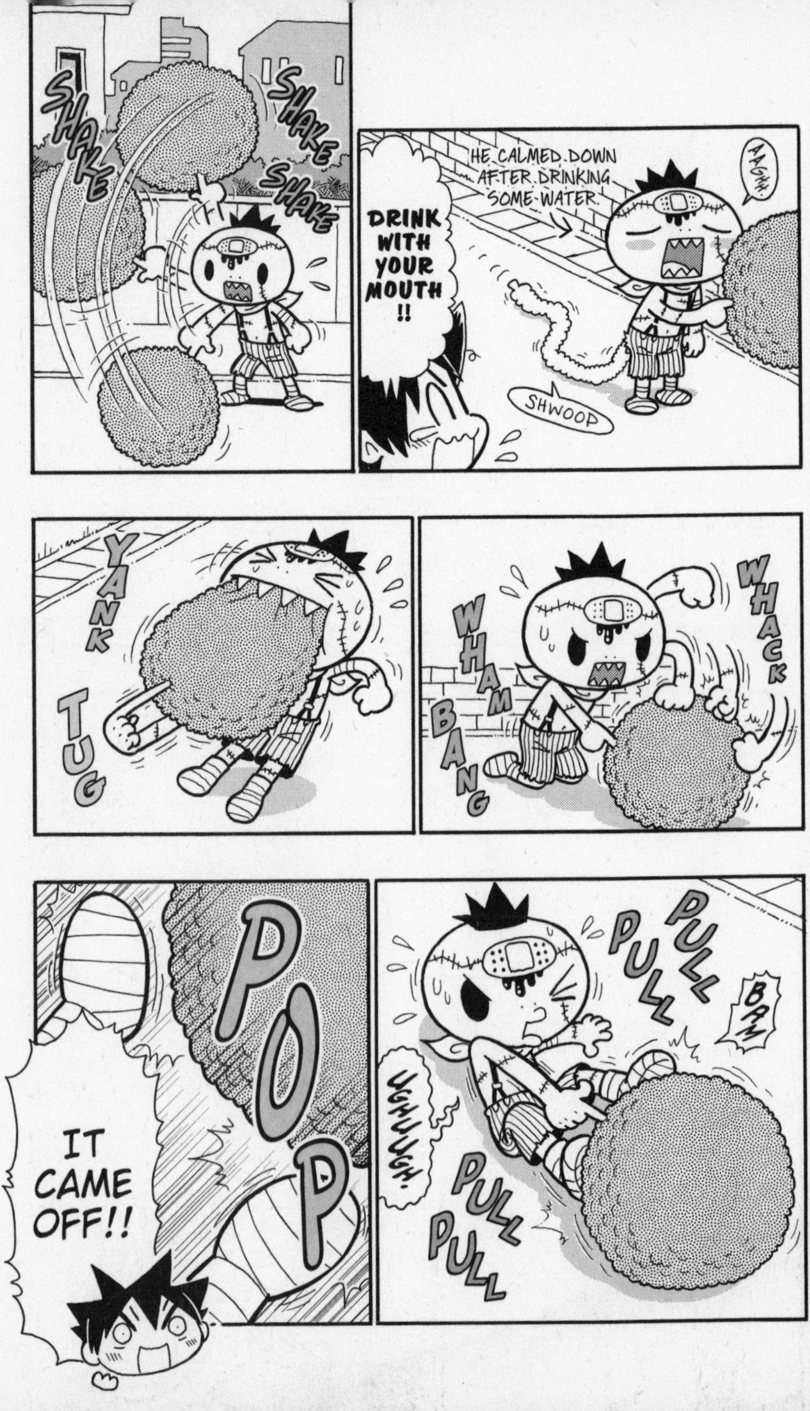
AAGHH.
HE CALMED DOWN AFTER DRINKING SOME WATER.
DRINK WITH YOUR MOUTH!!
SHWOOP
SHAKE
SHAKE
SHAKE
WHACK
WHAM
BANG
YANK
TUG
PULL
PULL
BAM
UGHUUGH.
PULL
PULL
POP
IT CAME OFF!!

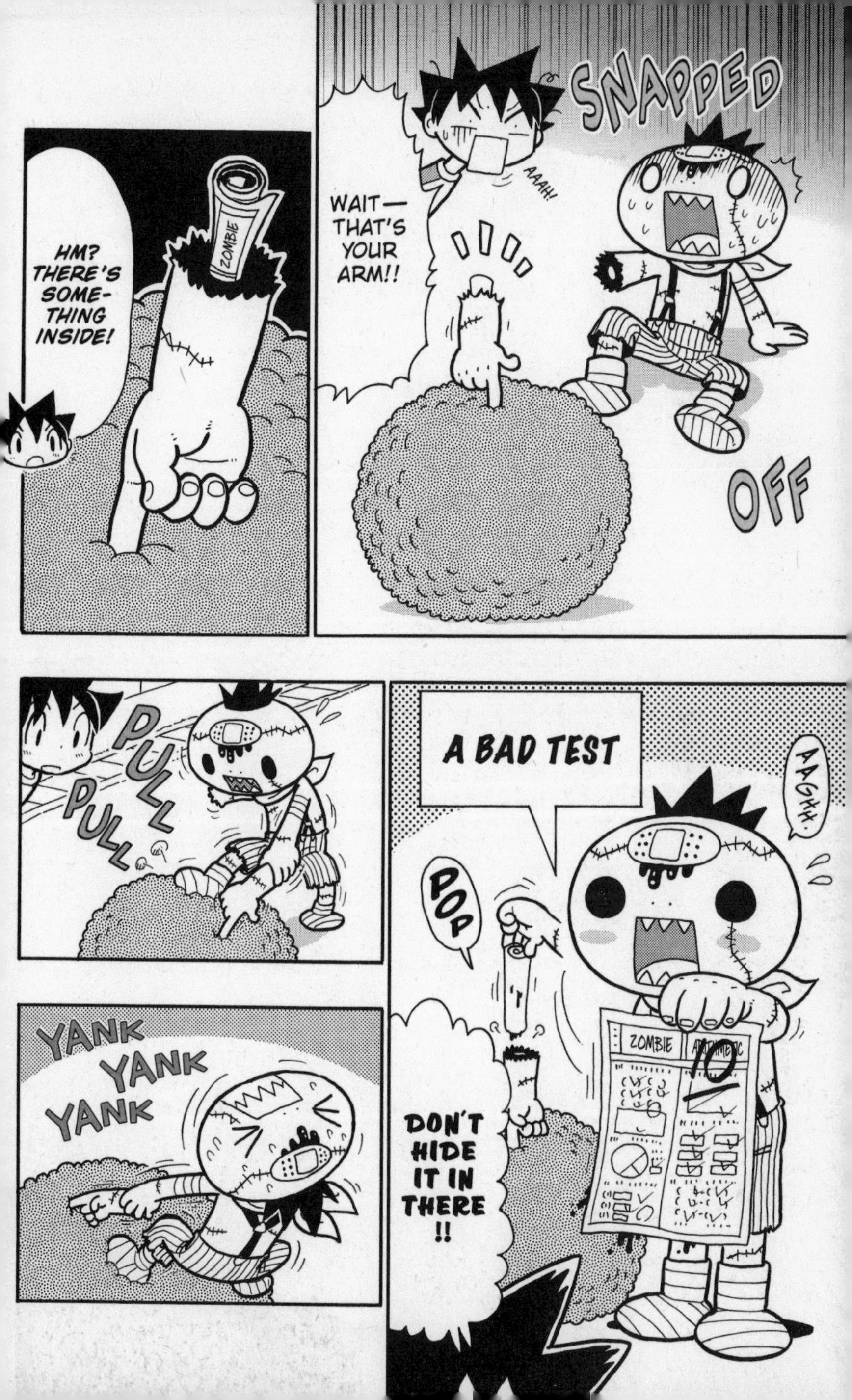
SNAPPED
AAAH!
WAIT— THAT'S YOUR ARM!!
OFF
ZOMBIE
HM? THERE'S SOME-THING INSIDE!
A BAD TEST
AAGHH
POP
ZOMBIE
10
DON'T HIDE IT IN THERE!!
PULL
PULL
YANK
YANK
YANK

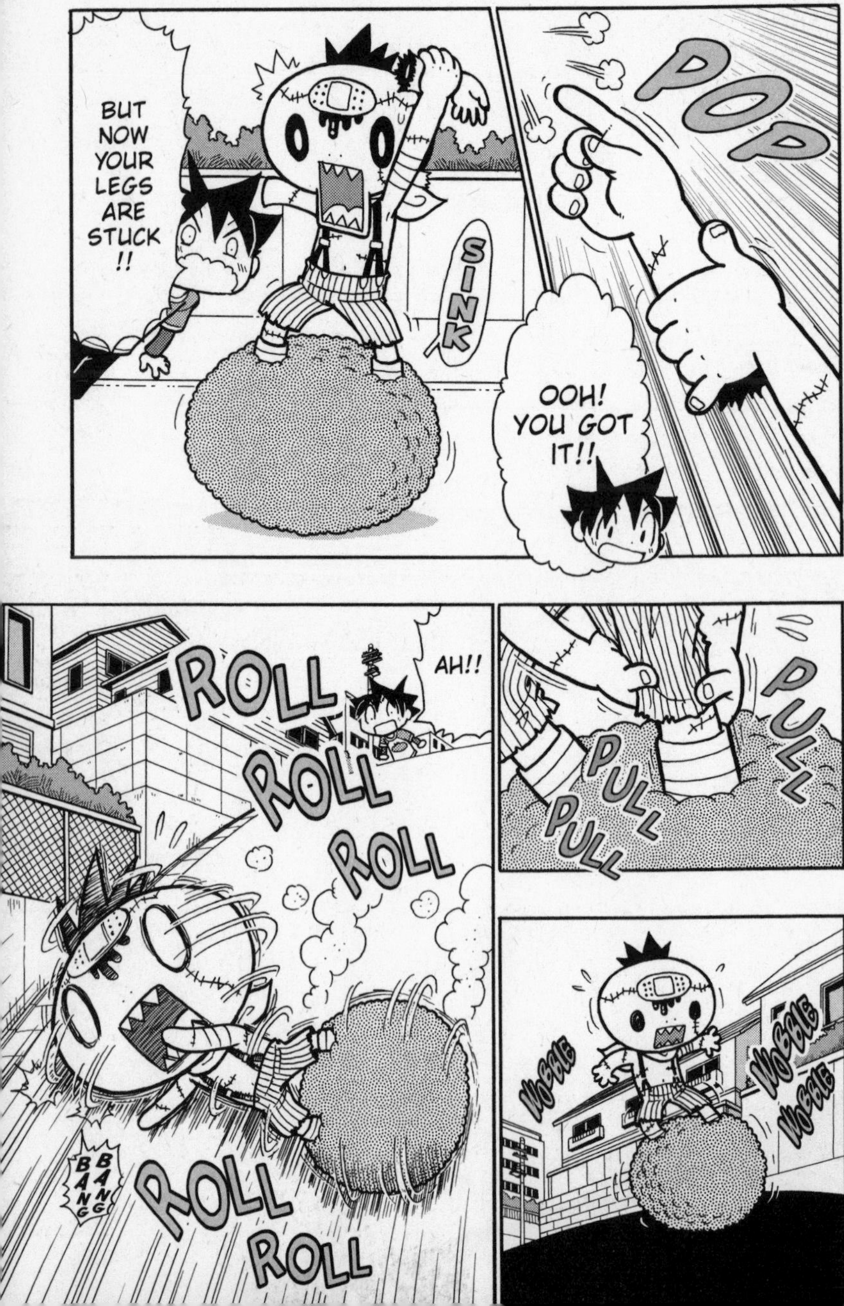
POP
OOH! YOU GOT IT!!
BUT NOW YOUR LEGS ARE STUCK!!
SINK
PULL
PULL
PULL
WOBBLE
WOBBLE
WOBBLE
WOBBLE
AH!!
ROLL
ROLL
ROLL
BANG
BANG
ROLL
ROLL

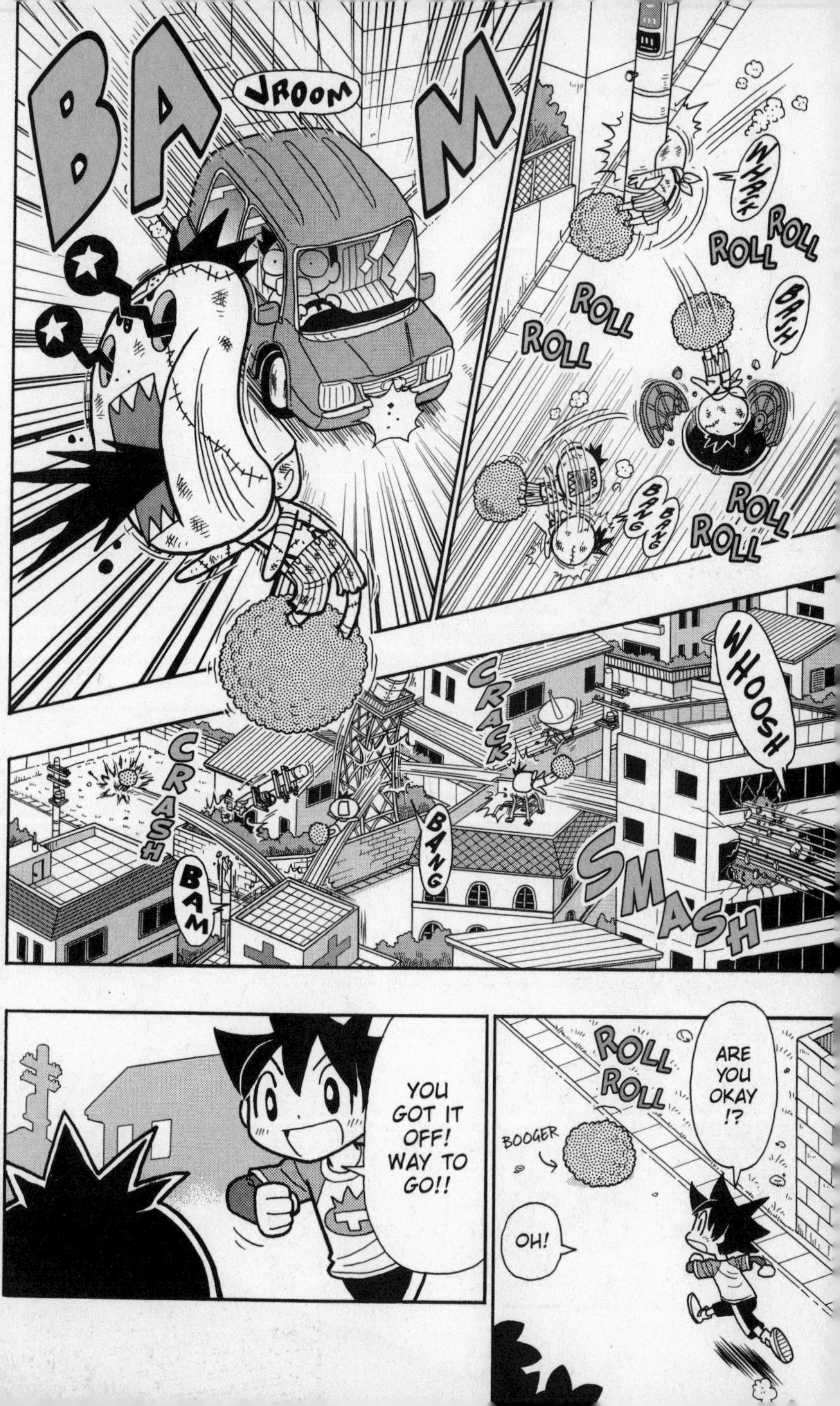
WHACK
ROLL ROLL
BASH
ROLL ROLL
BANG BANG
ROLL ROLL
BAM
VROOM
WHOOSH
CRACK
SMASH
BANG
CRASH
BAM
ROLL ROLL
ARE YOU OKAY !?
BOOGER
OH!
YOU GOT IT OFF! WAY TO GO!!

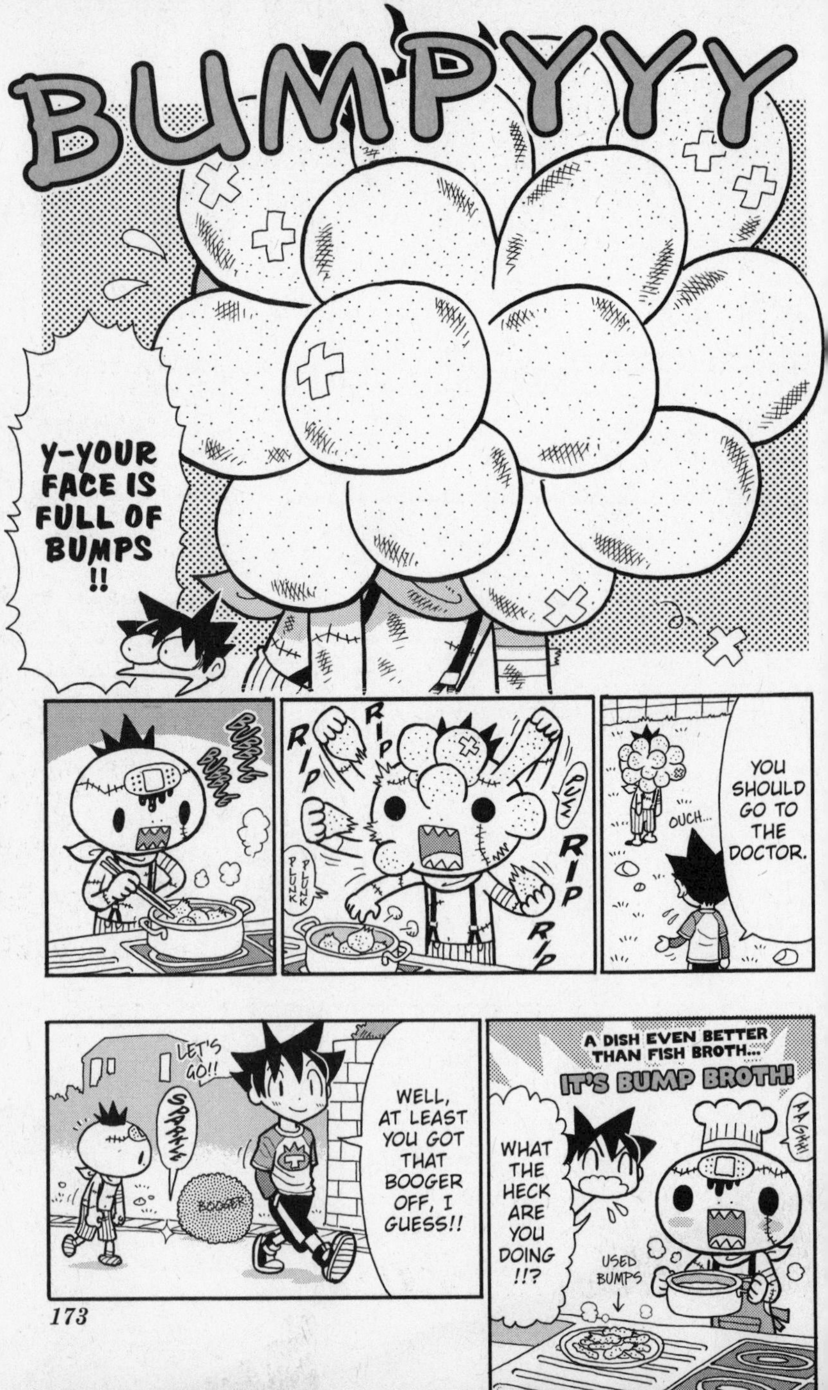
BUMPYYY
Y-YOUR FACE IS FULL OF BUMPS !!
YOU SHOULD GO TO THE DOCTOR.
OUCH...
RIP
RIP
RIP
RIP
PLUNK PLUNK
BUBBLE
BUBBLE
A DISH EVEN BETTER THAN FISH BROTH...
IT'S BUMP BROTH!
WHAT THE HECK ARE YOU DOING !!?
USED BUMPS
WELL, AT LEAST YOU GOT THAT BOOGER OFF, I GUESS!!
LET'S GO!!
BOOGER

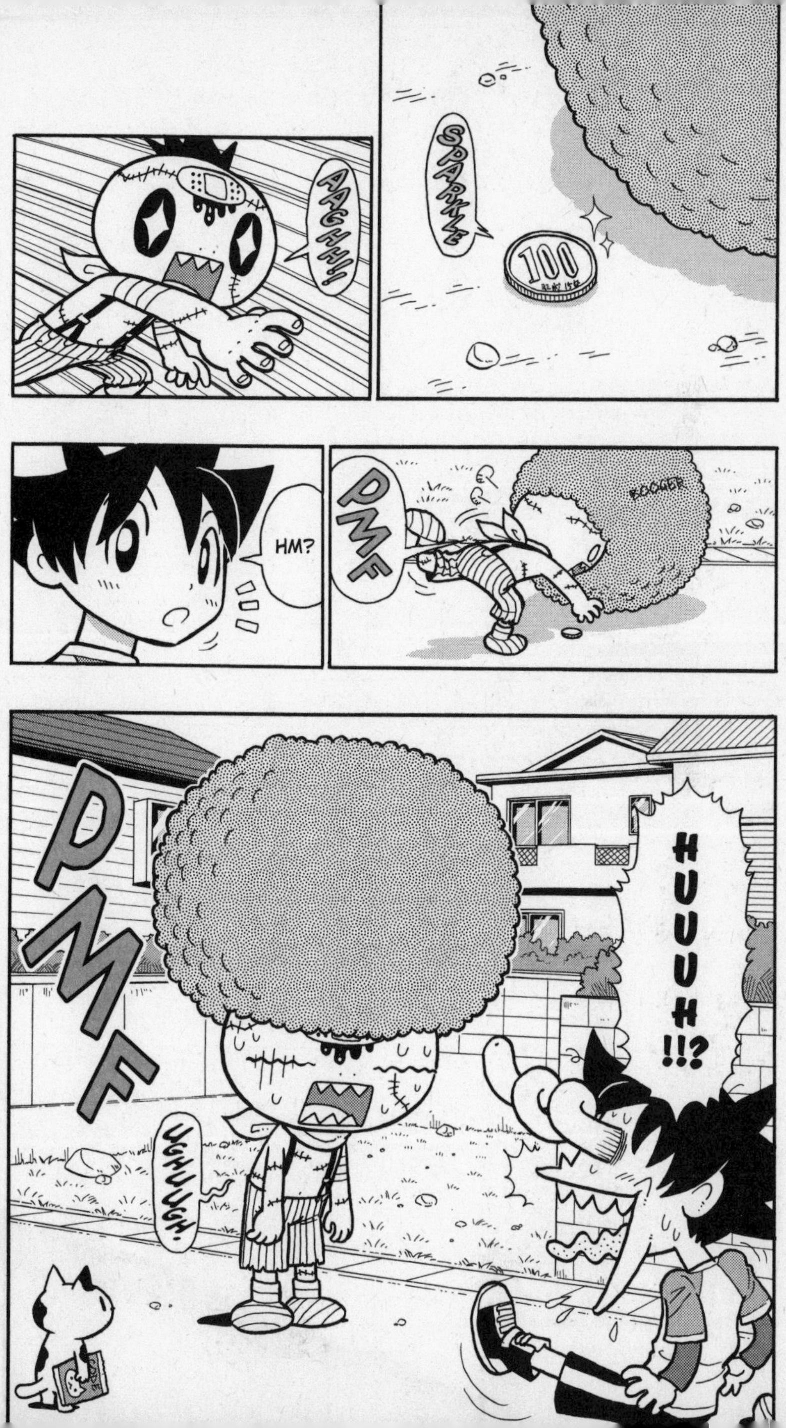
SPARKLE
100
AAGHH!!
PMF
BOOGER
HM?
HUUUUH!!?
PMF
UGHUUGH.

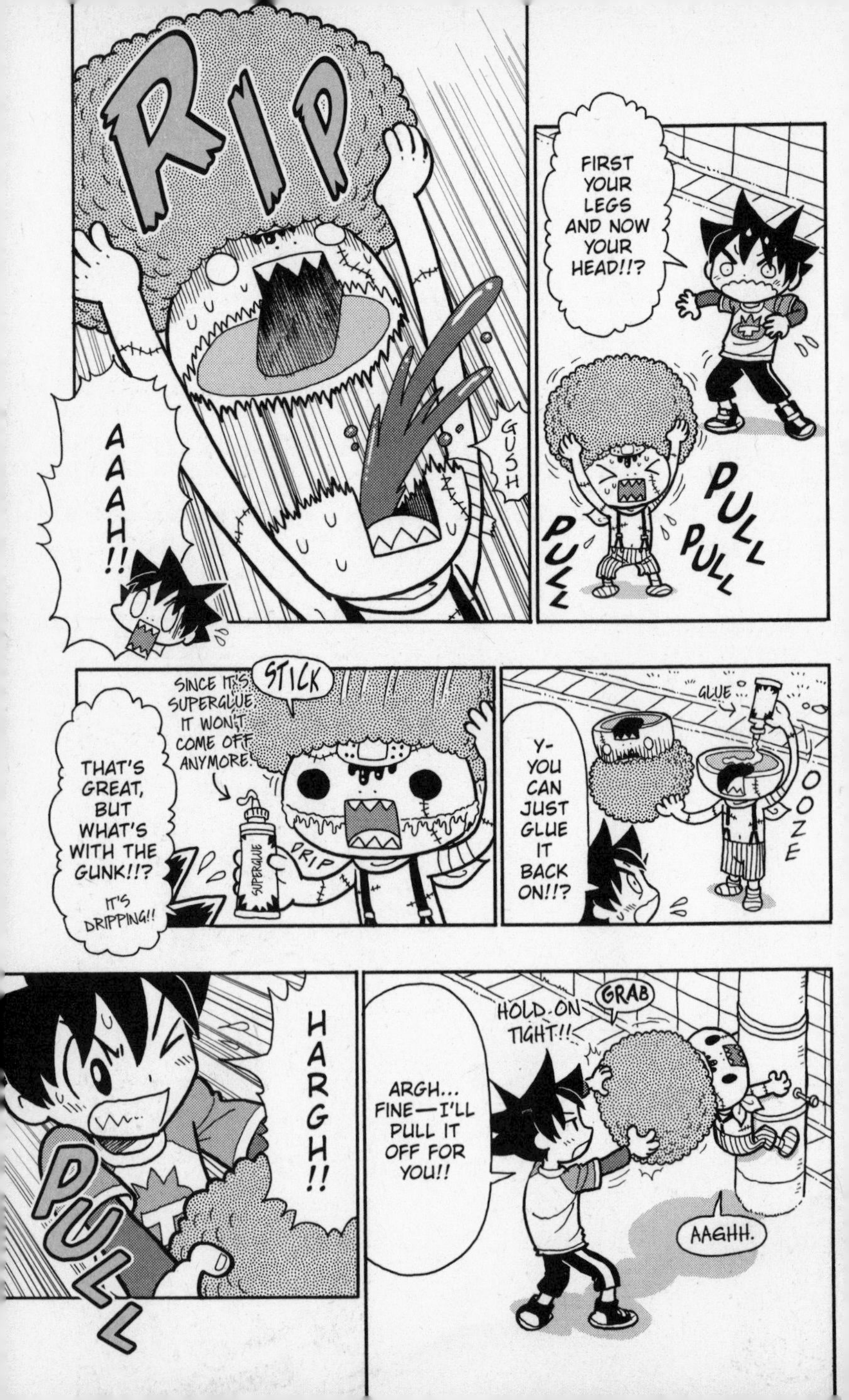

FIRST YOUR LEGS AND NOW YOUR HEAD!!?
PULL
PULL
PULL
RIP
GUSH
AAAAH!!
GLUE
Y-YOU CAN JUST GLUE IT BACK ON!!?
OOZE
STICK
SINCE IT'S SUPERGLUE IT WON'T COME OFF ANYMORE.
SUPERGLUE
DRIP
THAT'S GREAT, BUT WHAT'S WITH THE GUNK!!?
IT'S DRIPPING!!
HOLD ON TIGHT!!
GRAB
ARGH... FINE—I'LL PULL IT OFF FOR YOU!!
AAGHH.
HARGH!!
PULL

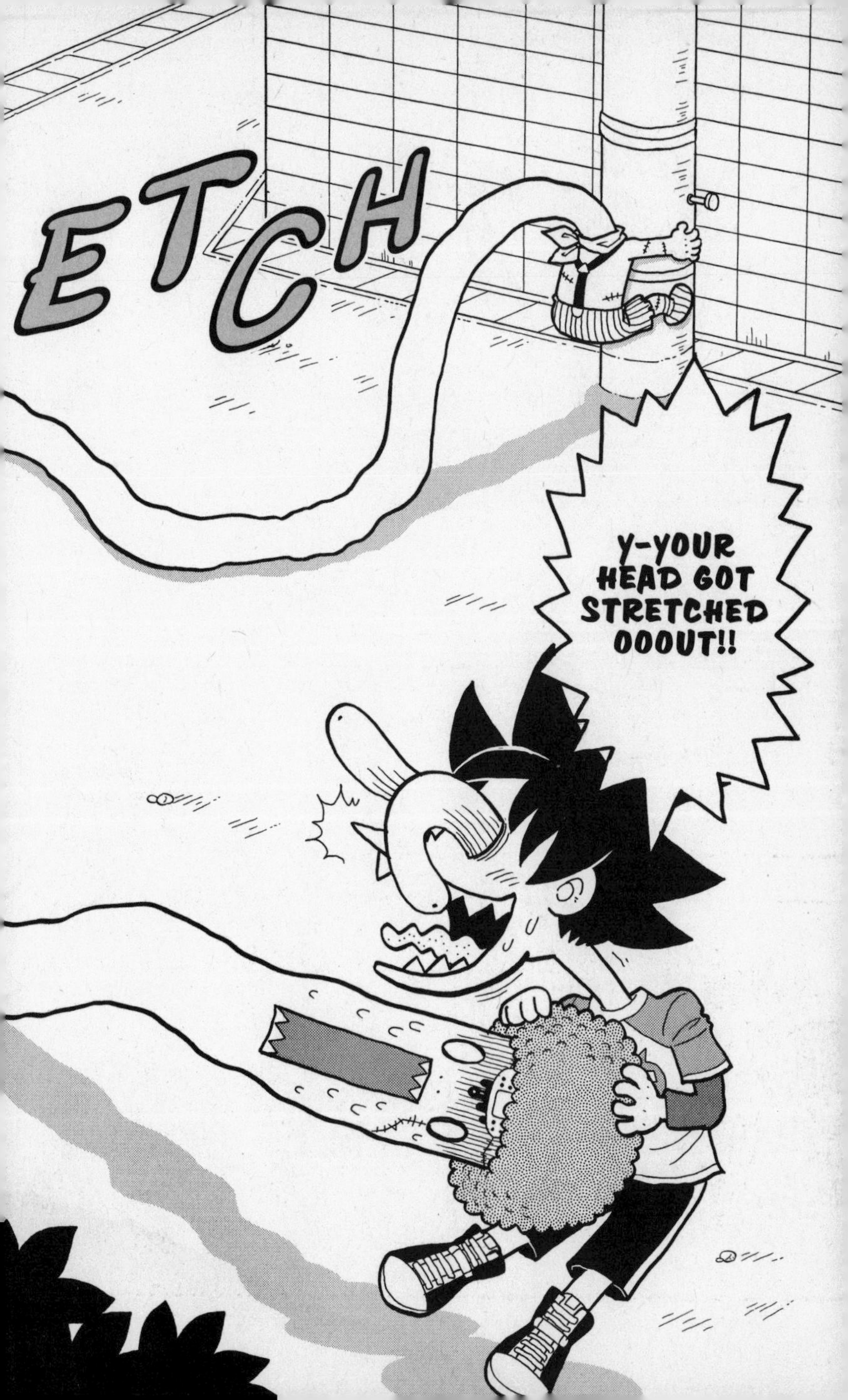
ETCH
Y-YOUR HEAD GOT STRETCHED OOOUT!!

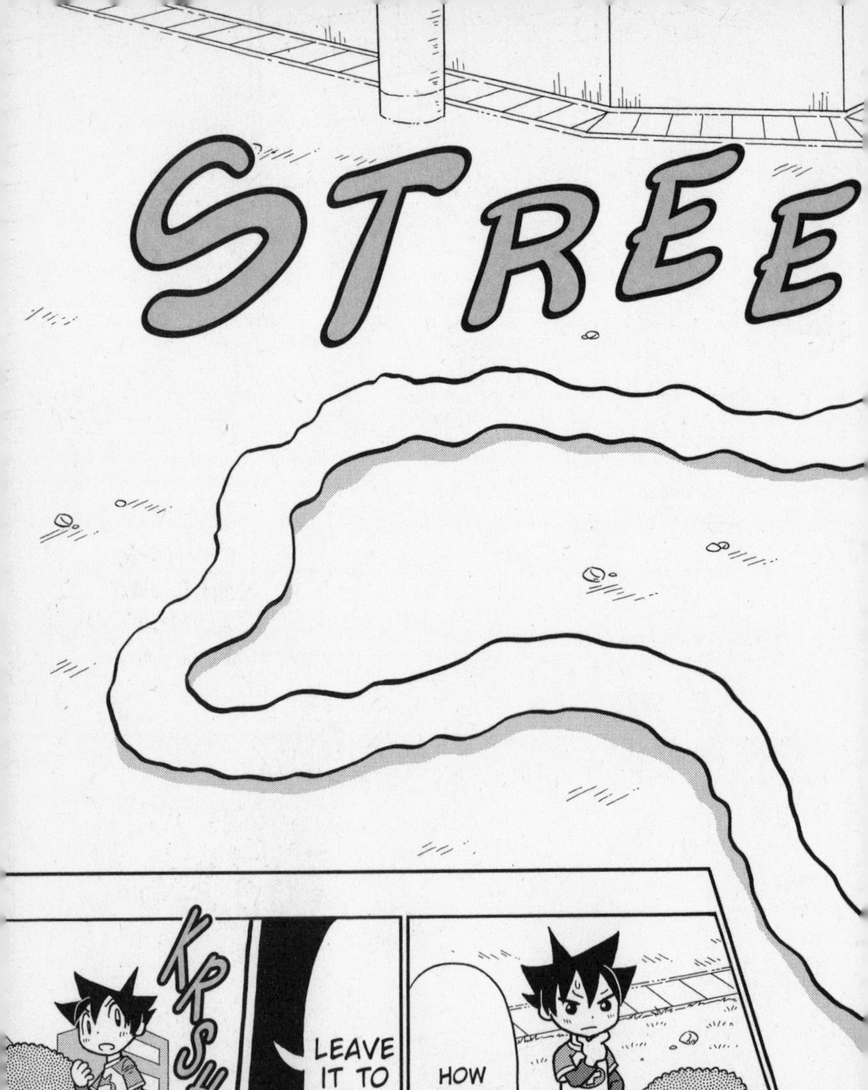
STREE
HOW CAN WE GET IT OFF...?
UUGH...
LEAVE IT TO ME!!
KRSH

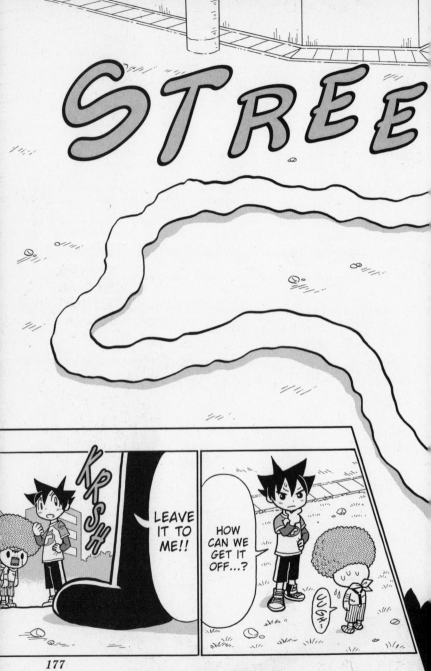

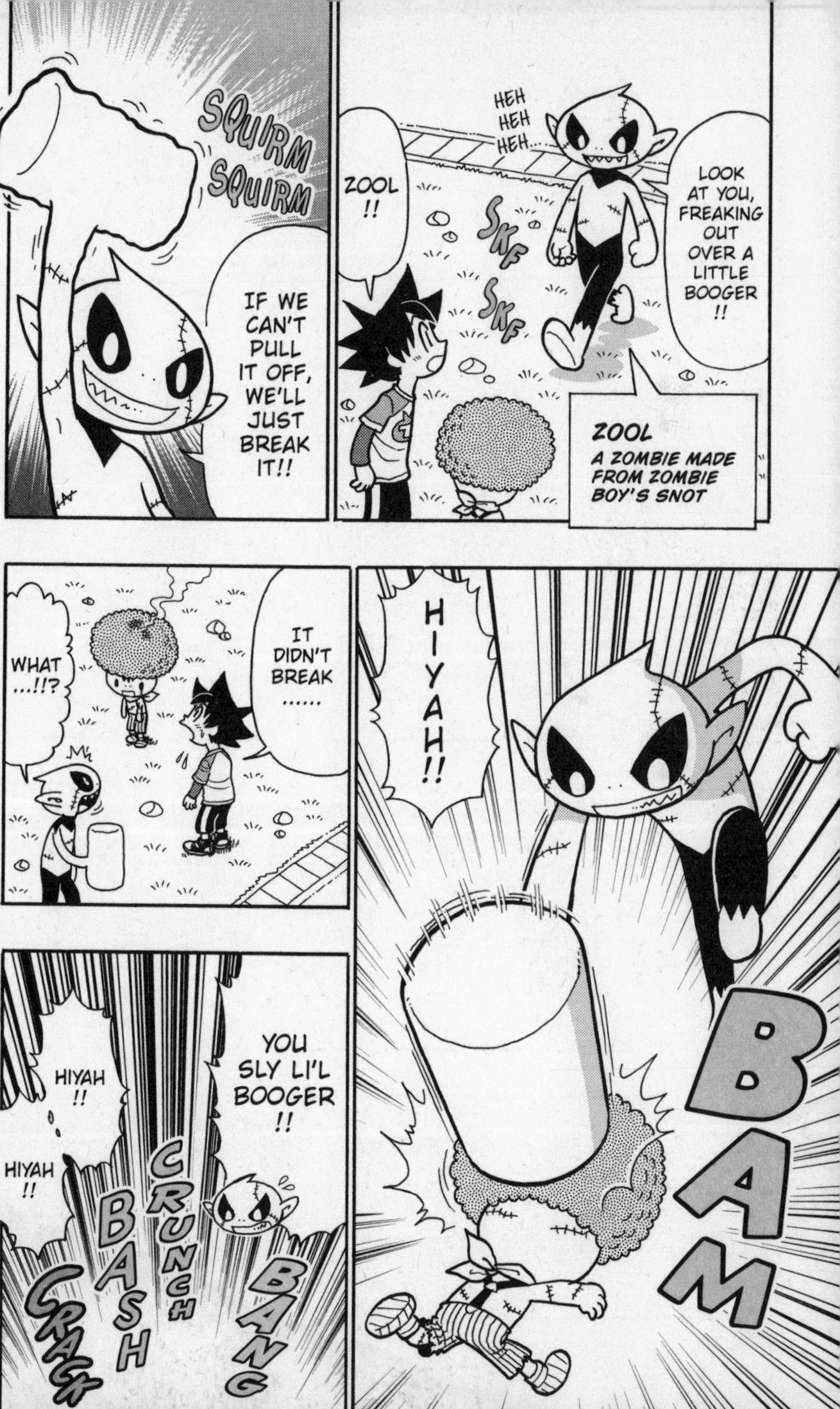
LOOK AT YOU, FREAKING OUT OVER A LITTLE BOOGER!!
HEH HEH HEH...
ZOOL!!
SKF
SKF
ZOOL
A ZOMBIE MADE FROM ZOMBIE BOY'S SNOT
SQUIRM SQUIRM
IF WE CAN'T PULL IT OFF, WE'LL JUST BREAK IT!!
HIYAH!!
BAM
IT DIDN'T BREAK......
WHAT...!!?
YOU SLY LI'L BOOGER!!
HIYAH!!
HIYAH!!
BANG
CRUNCH
BASH
CRACK

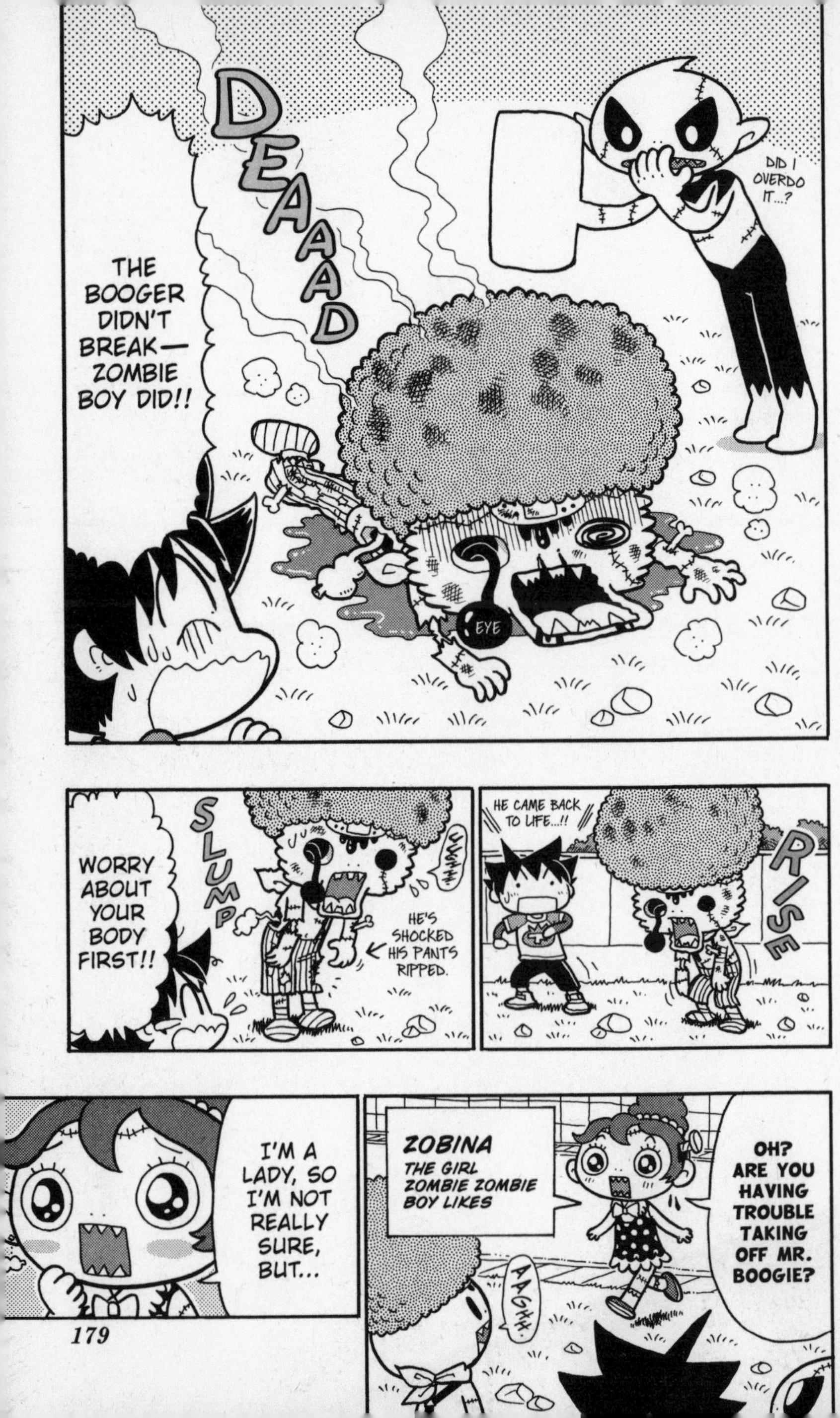
DID I OVERDO IT...?
DEAAAAD
THE BOOGER DIDN'T BREAK—ZOMBIE BOY DID!!
EYE
HE CAME BACK TO LIFE...!!
RISE
UGHHH
SLUMP
HE'S SHOCKED HIS PANTS RIPPED.
WORRY ABOUT YOUR BODY FIRST!!
OH? ARE YOU HAVING TROUBLE TAKING OFF MR. BOOGIE?
ZOBINA
THE GIRL ZOMBIE ZOMBIE BOY LIKES
AAGHH
I'M A LADY, SO I'M NOT REALLY SURE, BUT...

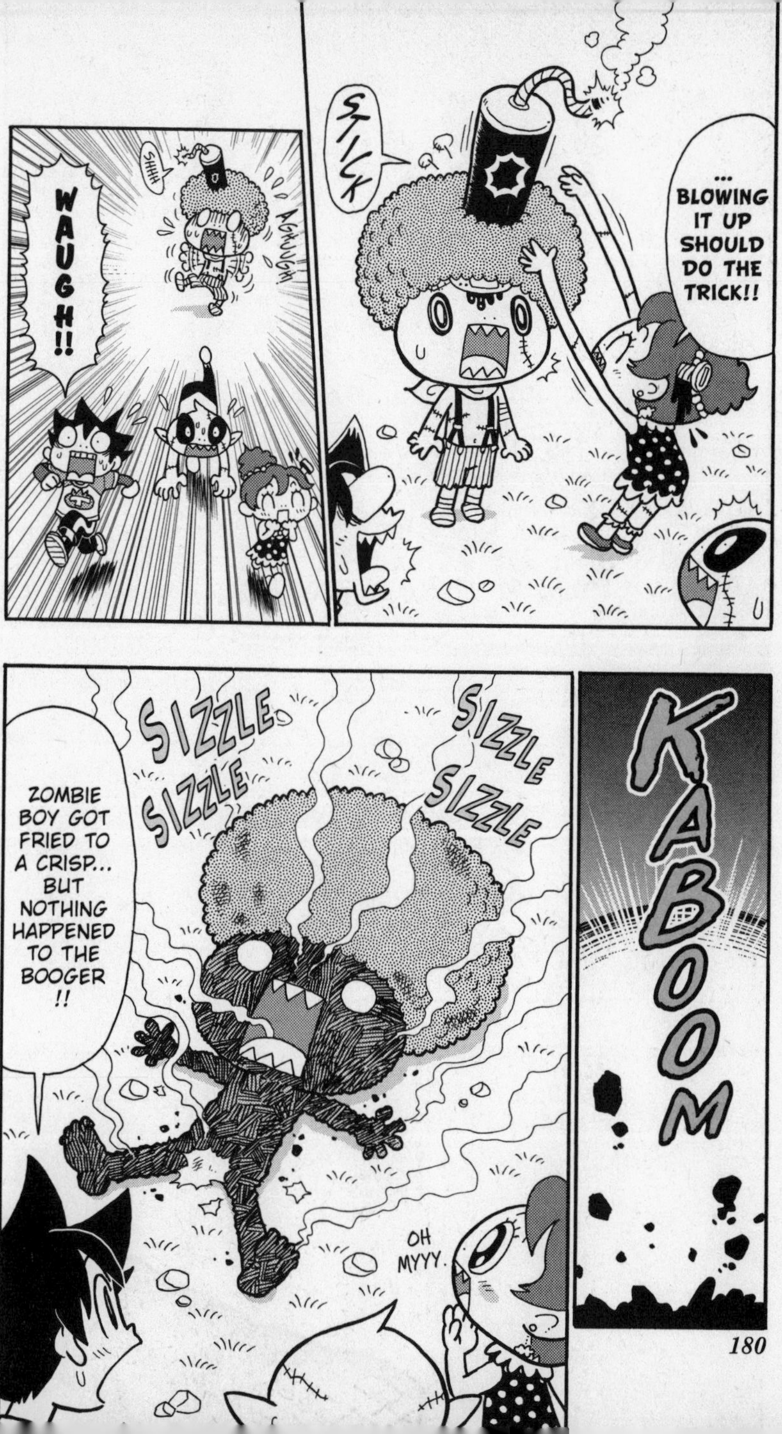

...BLOWING IT UP SHOULD DO THE TRICK!!
STICK
SHHH
AGHUUGH!
WAUGH!!
KABOOM
SIZZLE SIZZLE
SIZZLE SIZZLE
ZOMBIE BOY GOT FRIED TO A CRISP... BUT NOTHING HAPPENED TO THE BOOGER!!
OH MYYY.

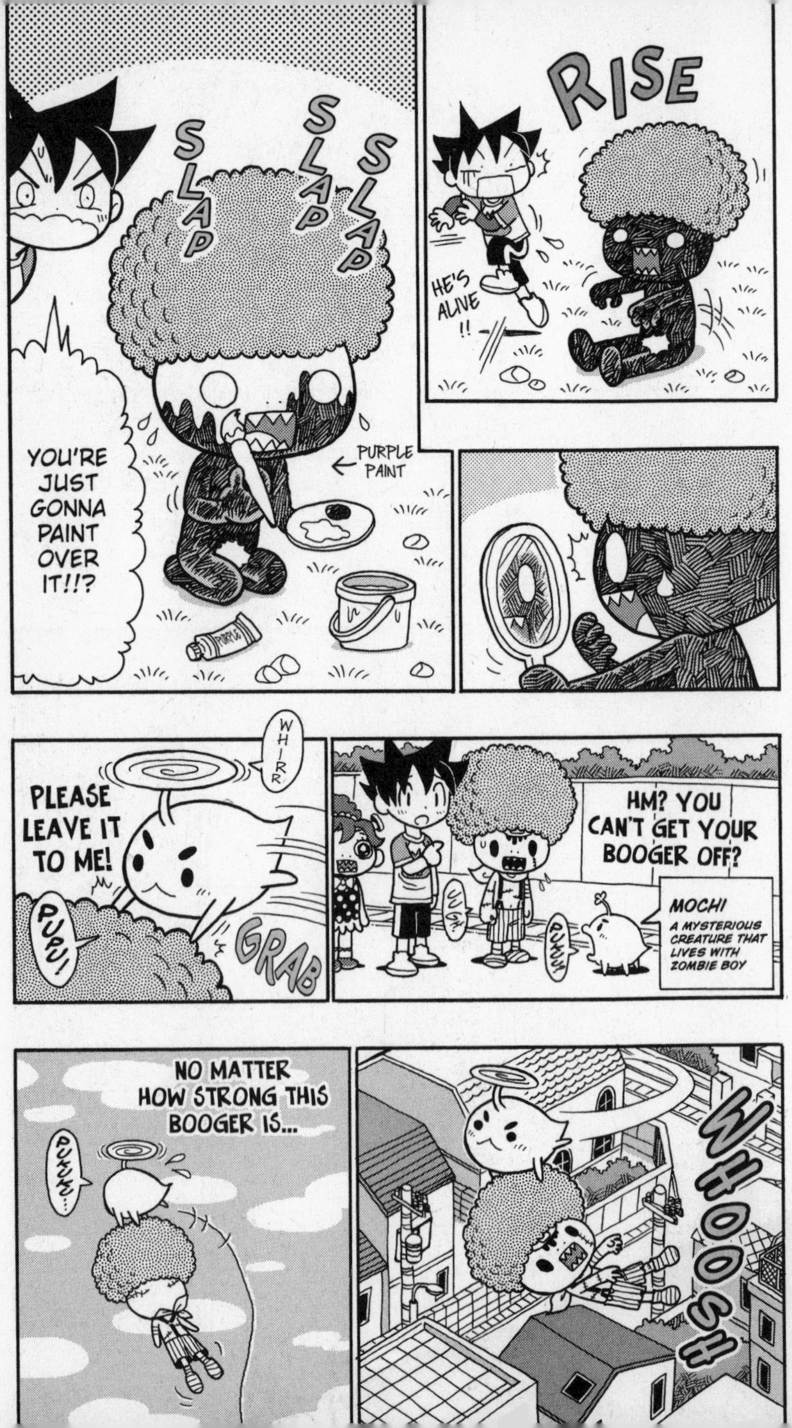
RISE
HE'S ALIVE!!
SLAP SLAP SLAP
YOU'RE JUST GONNA PAINT OVER IT!!?
PURPLE PAINT
PURPLE
HM? YOU CAN'T GET YOUR BOOGER OFF?
UGH?
PUKYU!
MOCHI
A MYSTERIOUS CREATURE THAT LIVES WITH ZOMBIE BOY
WHIRR
PLEASE LEAVE IT TO ME!
PUPU!
GRAB
WHOOSH
NO MATTER HOW STRONG THIS BOOGER IS...
PUKUKU...

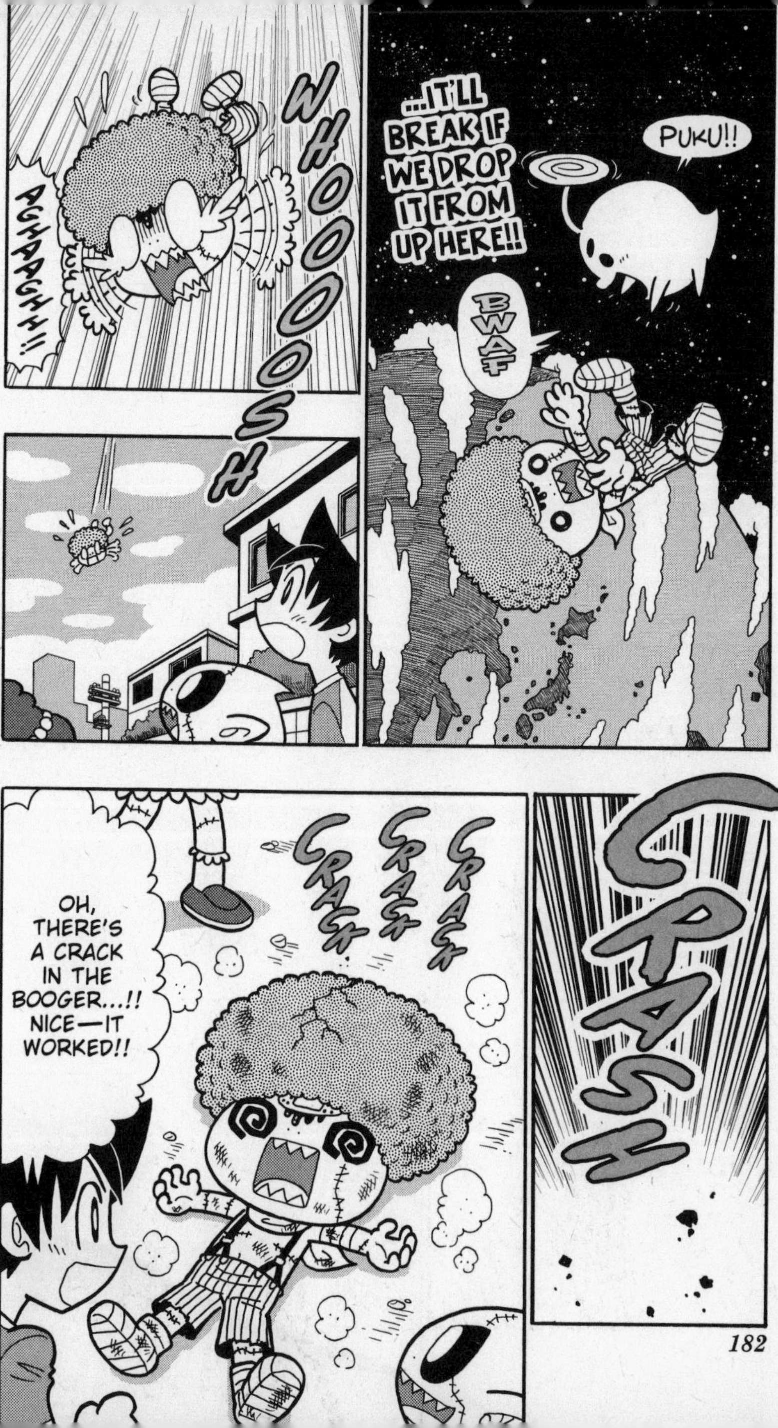
...IT'LL BREAK IF WE DROP IT FROM UP HERE!!
PUKU!!
BWAF
WHOOOOOOSH
AGHAAGHH!!
CRASH
CRACK
CRACK
CRACK
OH, THERE'S A CRACK IN THE BOOGER...!! NICE—IT WORKED!!

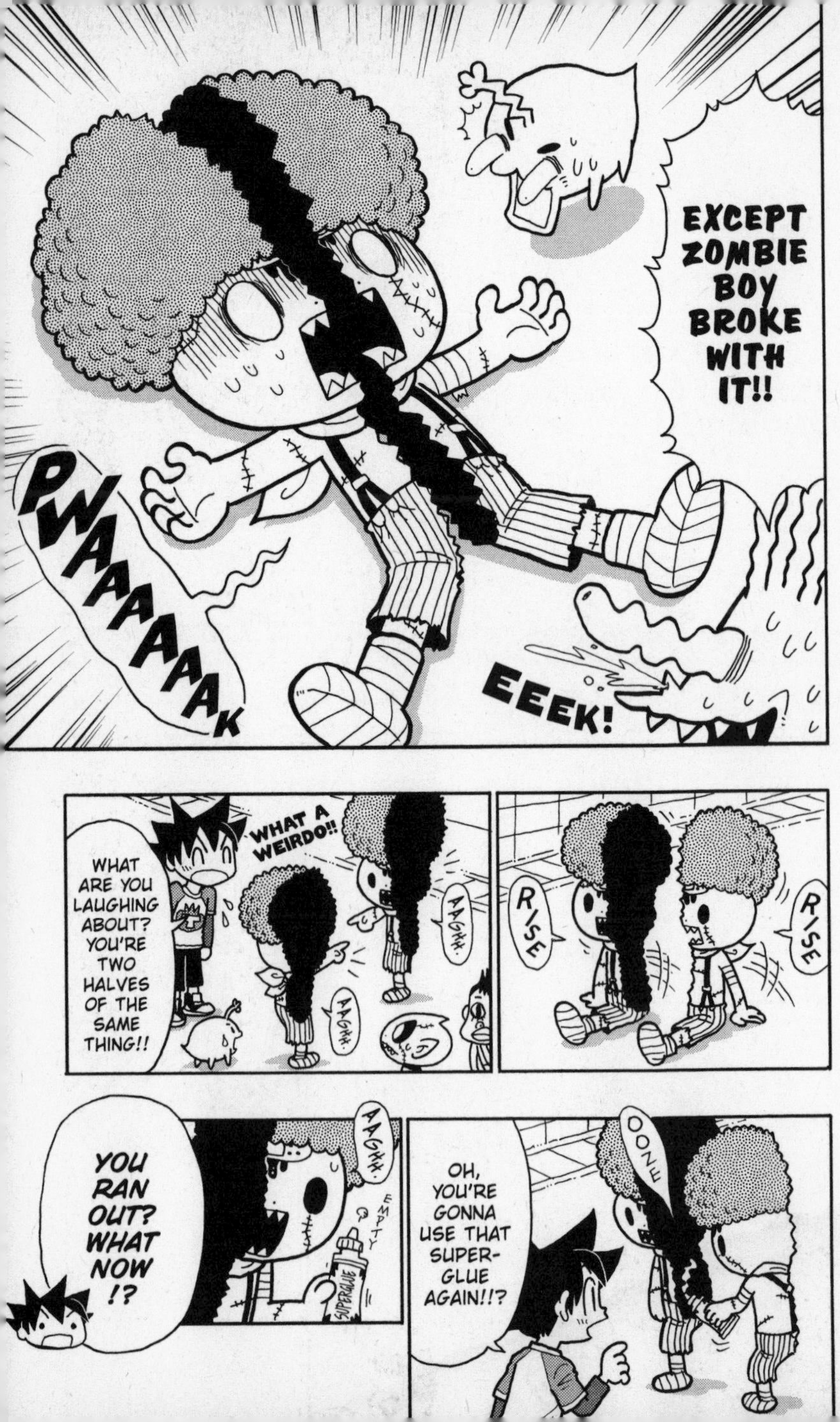
EXCEPT ZOMBIE BOY BROKE WITH IT!!
PWAAAAAAK
EEEK!
RISE
RISE
WHAT A WEIRDO!!
AAGHH.
AAGHH.
WHAT ARE YOU LAUGHING ABOUT? YOU'RE TWO HALVES OF THE SAME THING!!
OOZE
OH, YOU'RE GONNA USE THAT SUPER-GLUE AGAIN!!?
AAGHH.
EMPTY
SUPERGLUE
YOU RAN OUT? WHAT NOW!?

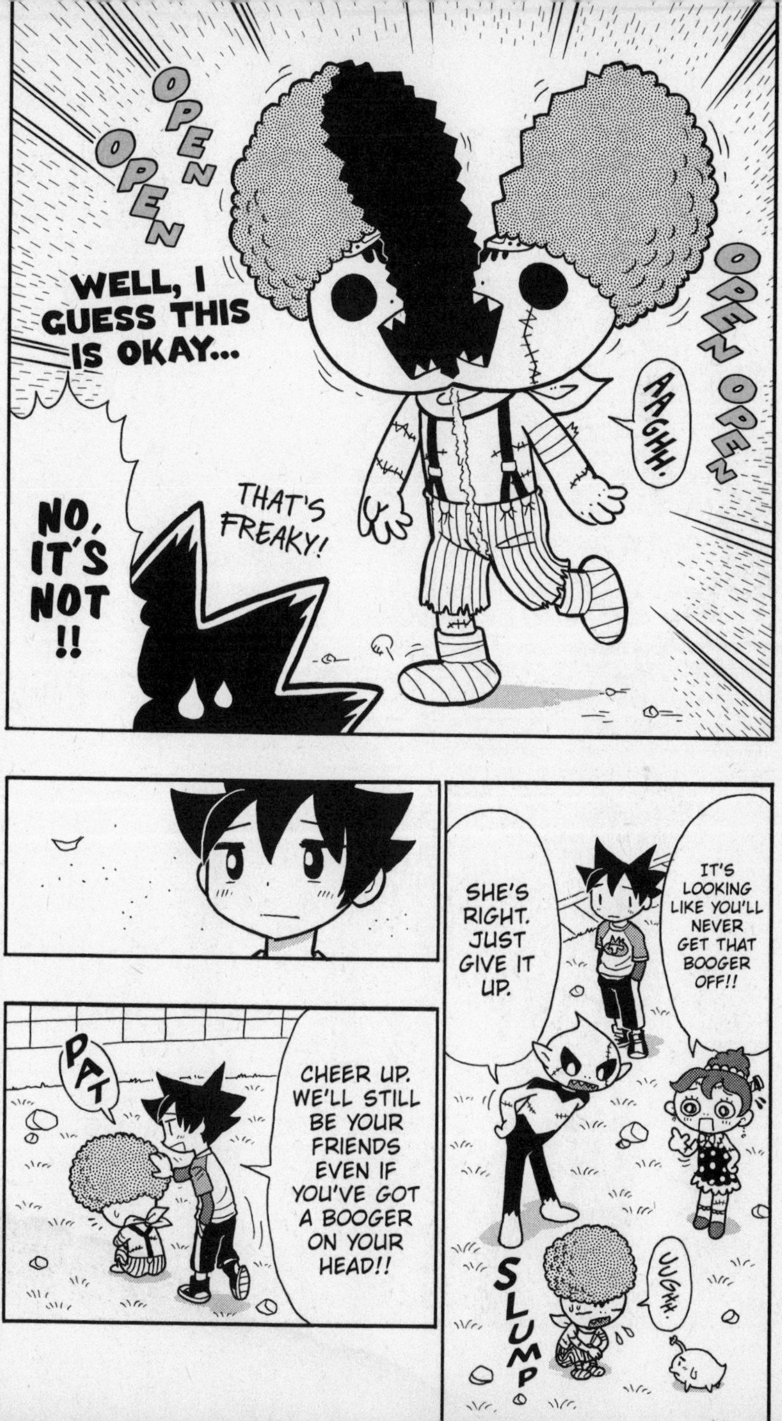
OPEN OPEN
AAGHH.
OPEN OPEN
WELL, I GUESS THIS IS OKAY...
THAT'S FREAKY!
NO, IT'S NOT!!
IT'S LOOKING LIKE YOU'LL NEVER GET THAT BOOGER OFF!!
SHE'S RIGHT. JUST GIVE IT UP.
UUGHH.
SLUMP
CHEER UP. WE'LL STILL BE YOUR FRIENDS EVEN IF YOU'VE GOT A BOOGER ON YOUR HEAD!!
PAT

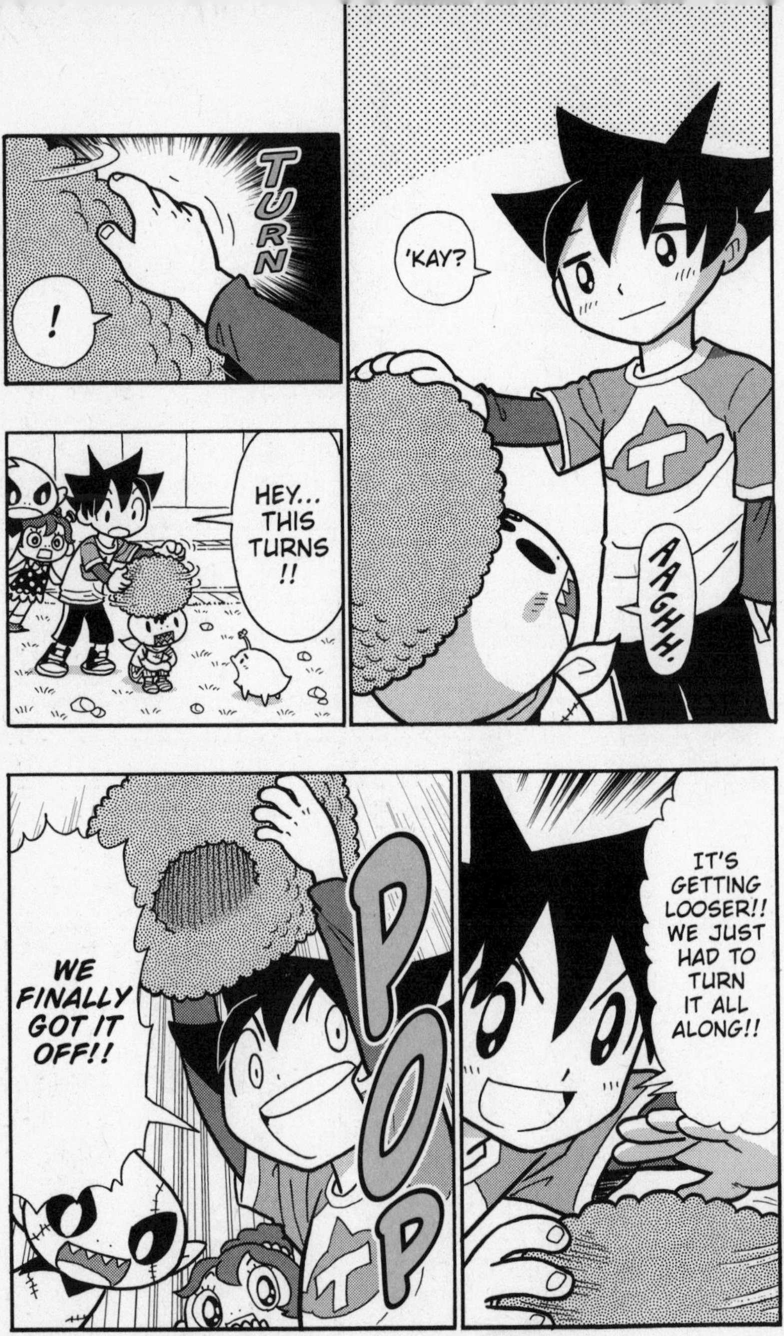
'KAY?
AAGHH.
TURN
!
HEY... THIS TURNS!!
IT'S GETTING LOOSER!! WE JUST HAD TO TURN IT ALL ALONG!!
POP
WE FINALLY GOT IT OFF!!

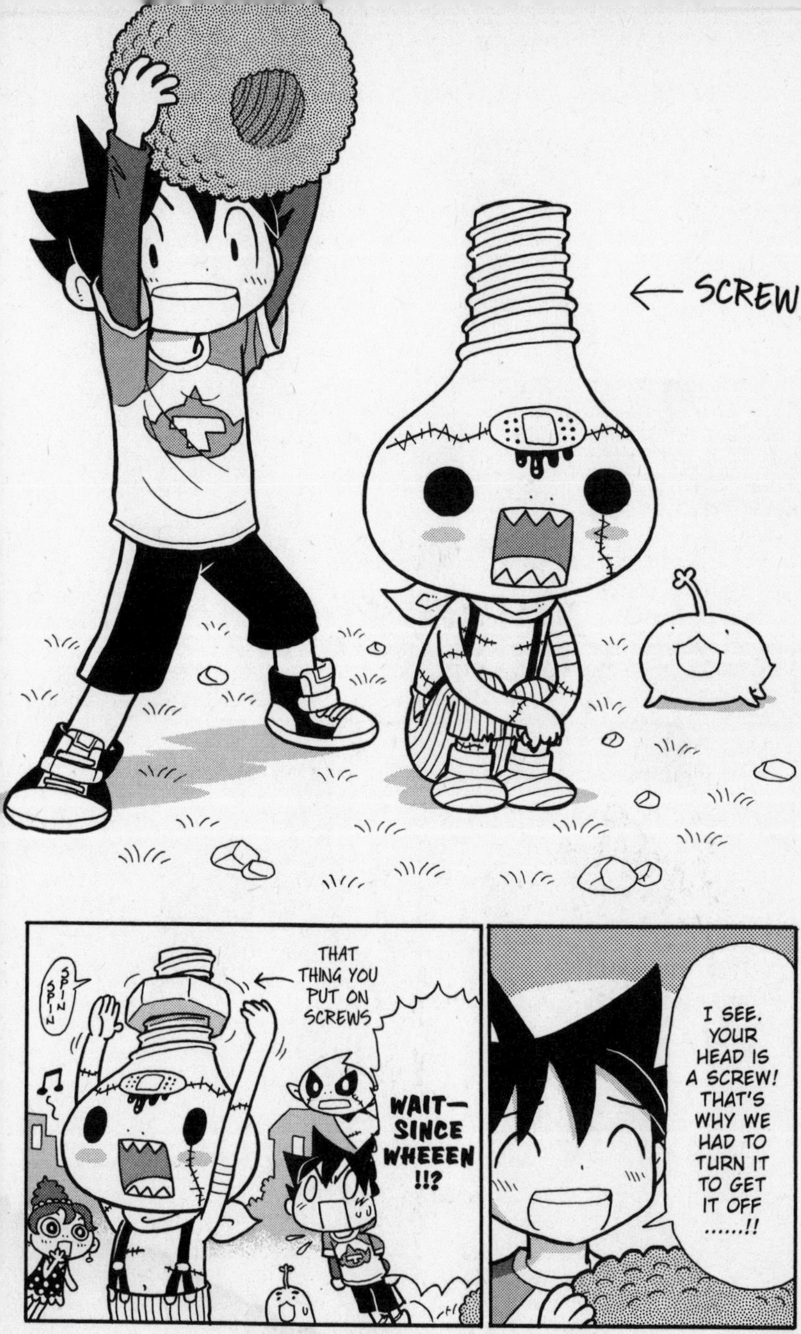
SCREW
I SEE. YOUR HEAD IS A SCREW! THAT'S WHY WE HAD TO TURN IT TO GET IT OFF ......!!
THAT THING YOU PUT ON SCREWS
WAIT—SINCE WHEEEN !!?
SPIN SPIN

SEE YOU AGAIN IN VOLUME 7!!

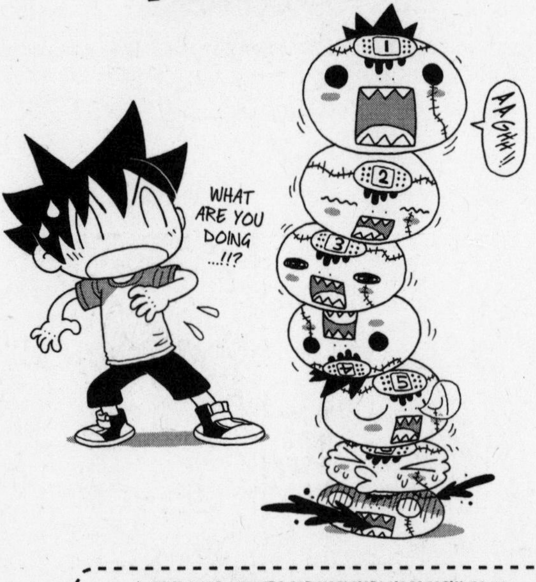

AAGHHH!!
WHAT ARE YOU DOING ...!!?

★ SEND YOUR LETTERS FOR YASUNARI NAGATOSHI TO ▼

JY
150 West 30th Street, 19th Floor, New York, NY 10001

ZO ZO ZOMBIE 6 THE END

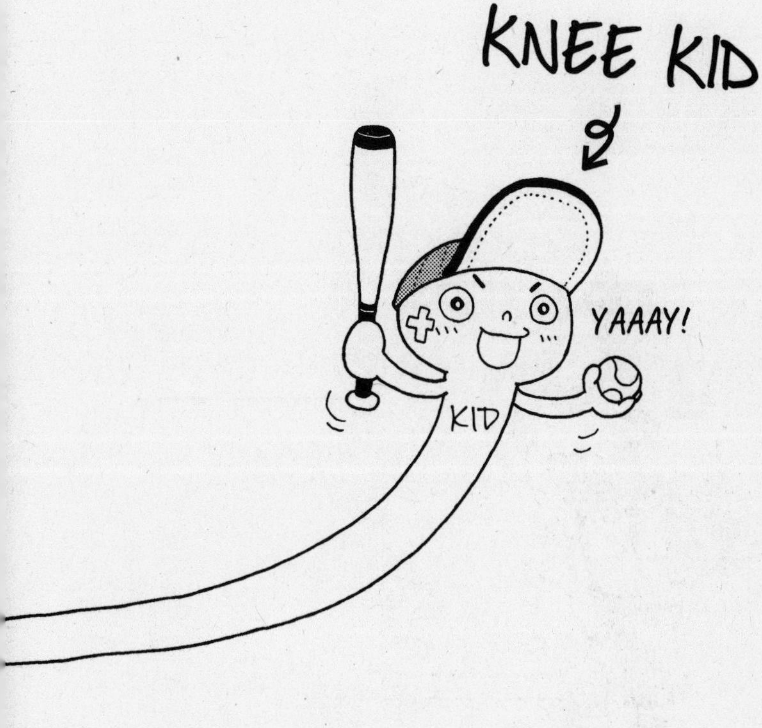
KNEE KID
YAAAY!
KID

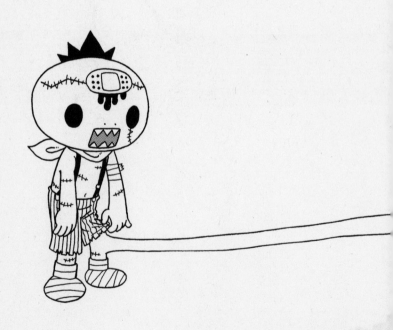

Keep up with all their adventures in this award-winning series!

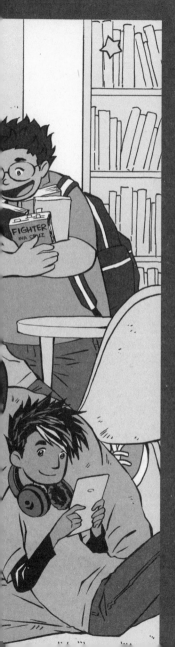

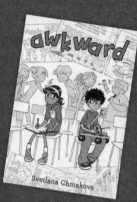

AWKWARD

ISBN: 9780316381307
(Paperback)

ISBN: 9780316381321
(Hardcover)

ISBN: 9780316381314
(Ebook)

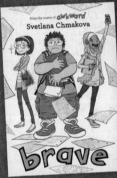

BRAVE

ISBN: 9780316363181
(Paperback)

ISBN: 9780316363174
(Hardcover)

ISBN: 9780316363167
(Ebook)

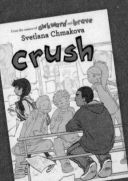

CRUSH

ISBN: 9780316363242
(Paperback)

ISBN: 9780316363235
(Hardcover)

ISBN: 9780316363198
(Ebook)

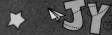

For more information, visit www.jyforkids.com

Have you met the kids from Berrybrook Middle School yet?

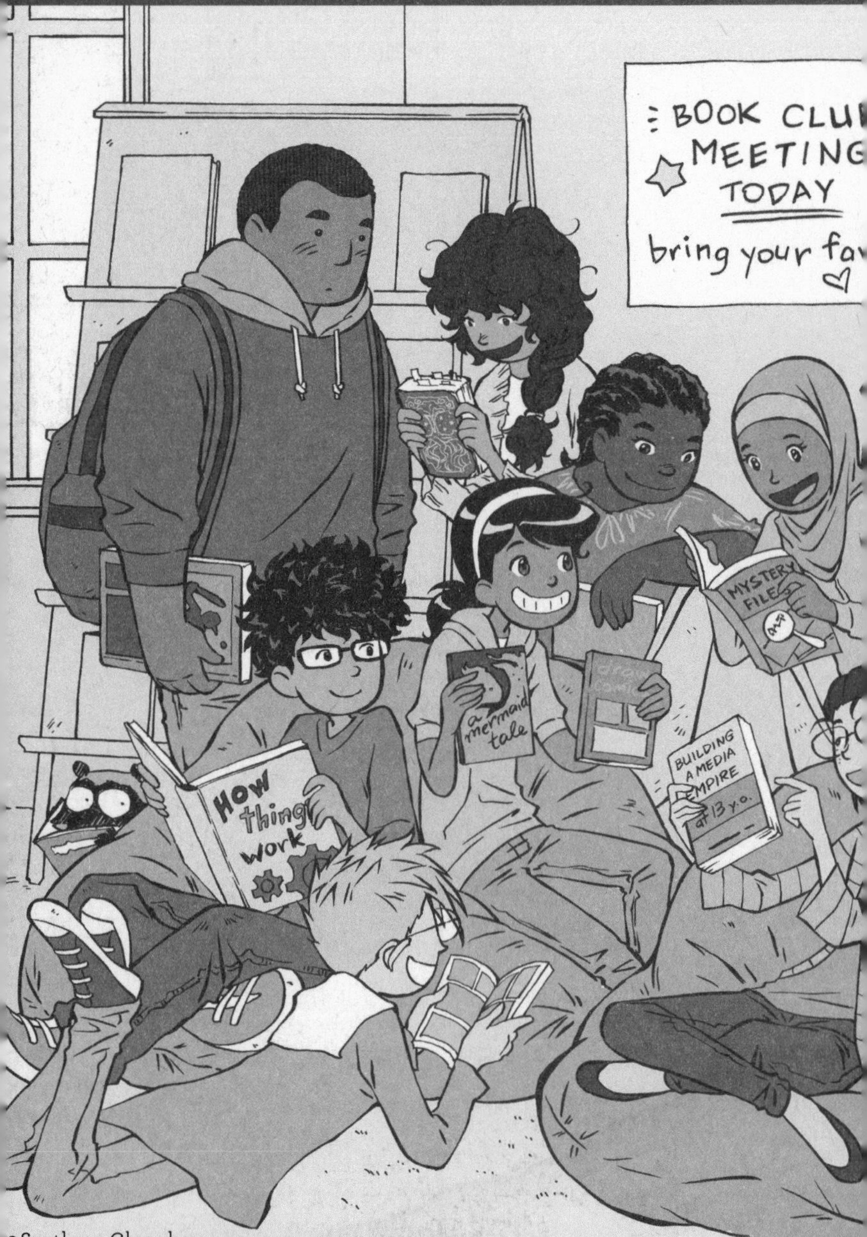
BOOK CLU
MEETING
TODAY
bring your fa
MYSTERY FILES
a mermaid tale
BUILDING A MEDIA EMPIRE at 13 y.o.
HOW thing work

ENJOY EVERYTHING.

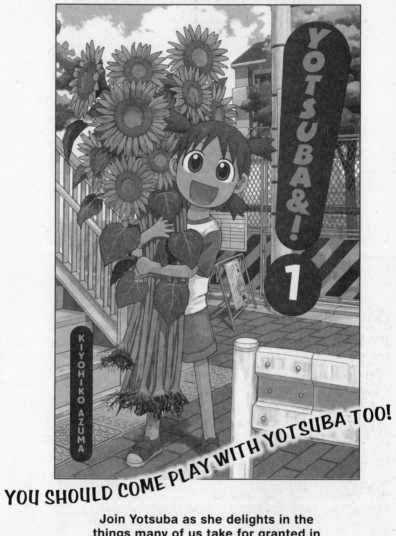

YOU SHOULD COME PLAY WITH YOTSUBA TOO!

Join Yotsuba as she delights in the things many of us take for granted in this Eisner-nominated series.

VOLUMES 1-14 AVAILABLE NOW!

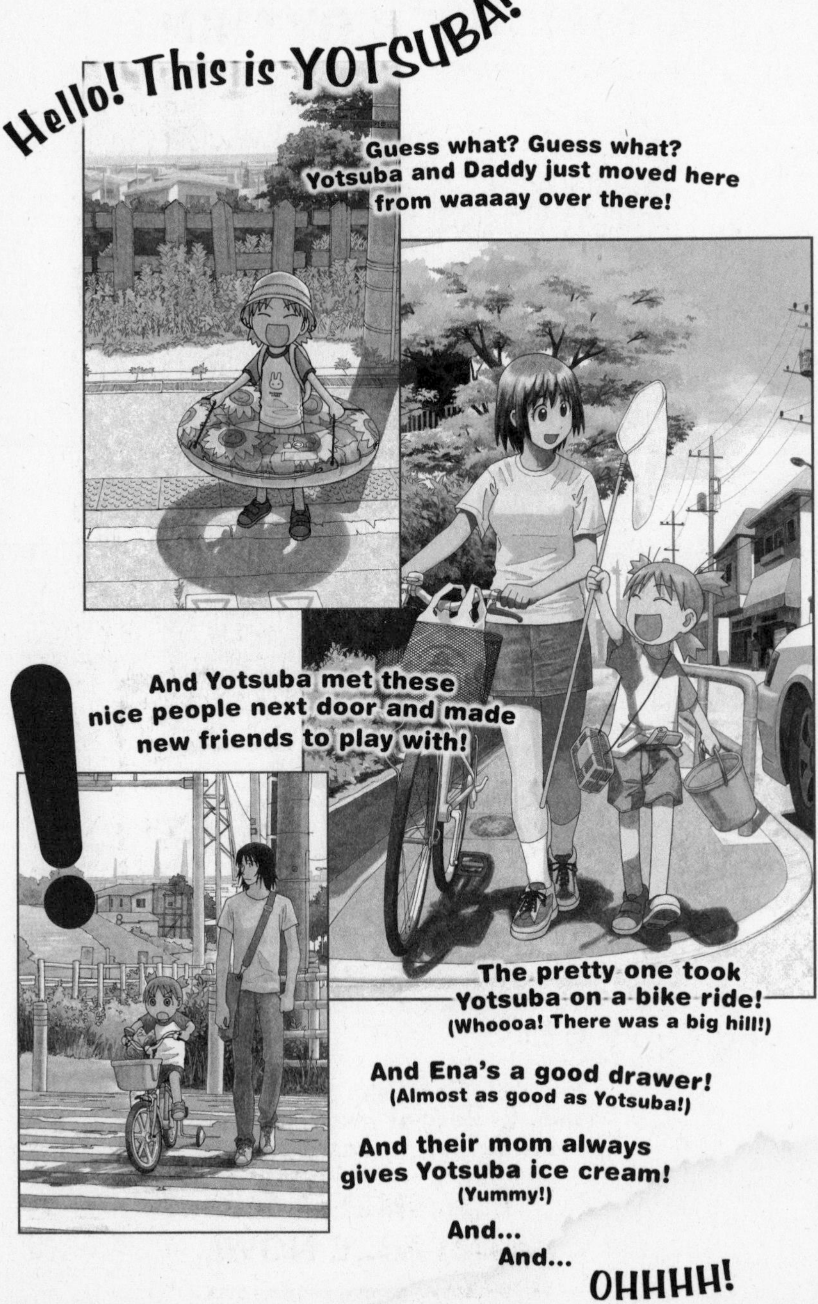
Hello! This is YOTSUBA!
Guess what? Guess what? Yotsuba and Daddy just moved here from waaaay over there!
And Yotsuba met these nice people next door and made new friends to play with!
The pretty one took Yotsuba on a bike ride!
(Whoooa! There was a big hill!)
And Ena's a good drawer!
(Almost as good as Yotsuba!)
And their mom always gives Yotsuba ice cream!
(Yummy!)
And...
And...
OHHHH!

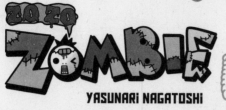

ZOMBIE 6

YASUNARI NAGATOSHI

Translation: ALEXANDRA MCCULLOUGH-GARCIA ♣ Lettering: BIANCA PISTILLO

This book is a work of fiction. Names, characters, places, and incidents are the product of the author's imagination or are used fictitiously. Any resemblance to actual events, locales, or persons, living or dead, is coincidental.

ZOZOZO ZOMBIE-KUN Vol. 6
by Yasunari NAGATOSHI
© 2013 Yasunari NAGATOSHI
All rights reserved.
Original Japanese edition published by SHOGAKUKAN.
English translation rights in the United States of America, Canada, the United Kingdom, Ireland, Australia and New Zealand arranged with SHOGAKUKAN through Tuttle-Mori Agency, Inc.

English translation © 2020 by Yen Press, LLC

Yen Press, LLC supports the right to free expression and the value of co...

The s...
a thef...
mat...

tw...

JY is an imprint of Yen Press, LLC.
The JY name and logo are trademarks of Yen Press, LLC.

The publisher is not responsible for websites (or their content) that are not owned by the publisher.

Library of Congress Control Number: 2018948323

ISBNs: 978-1-9753-5346-9 (paperback)
978-1-9753-8632-0 (ebook)

10 9 8 7 6 5 4 3 2 1

WOR

Printed in the United States of America